CATHERINE COOKSON

THE
Tinker's Girl

CORGI BOOKS

THE TINKER'S GIRL
A CORGI BOOK : 0 552 14827 X

Originally published in Great Britain by Bantam Press,
a division of Transworld Publishers

PRINTING HISTORY
Bantam Press edition published 1994
Corgi edition published 1995
Corgi edition reprinted 1995 (three times)
Corgi edition reprinted 1996
Corgi edition reprinted 1997

This book is set in 10/12pt Monotype Plantin by
Phoenix Typesetting, Ilkley, West Yorkshire

Corgi Books are published by Transworld Publishers,
61–63 Uxbridge Road, London W5 5SA,
a division of The Random House Group Ltd,
in Australia by Random House Australia (Pty) Ltd,
20 Alfred Street, Milsons Point, Sydney, NSW 2061, Australia,
in New Zealand by Random House New Zealand Ltd,
18 Poland Road, Glenfield, Auckland 10, New Zealand
and in South Africa by Random House (Pty) Ltd,
Endulini, 5a Jubilee Road, Parktown 2193, South Africa.

Printed and bound in Great Britain by
Cox & Wyman Ltd, Reading, Berkshire.

Catherine Cookson was born in Tyne Dock, the illegitimate daughter of a poverty-stricken woman, Kate, whom she believed to be her older sister. She began work in service but eventually moved south to Hastings where she met and married Tom Cookson, a local grammar-school master. At the age of forty she began writing about the lives of the working-class people with whom she had grown up, using the place of her birth as the background to many of her novels.

Although originally acclaimed as a regional writer – her novel *The Round Tower* won the Winifred Holtby award for the best regional novel of 1968 – her readership soon began to spread throughout the world. Her novels have been translated into more than a dozen languages and more than 50,000,000 copies of her books have been sold in Corgi alone. Fifteen of her novels have been made into successful television dramas, and more are planned.

Catherine Cookson's many bestselling novels established her as one of the most popular of contemporary women novelists. After receiving an OBE in 1985, Catherine Cookson was created a Dame of the British Empire in 1993. She was appointed an Honorary Fellow of St. Hilda'a College, Oxford in 1997. For many years she lived near Newcastle-upon-Tyne. She died shortly before her ninety-second birthday in June 1998.

'Catherine Cookson's novels are about hardship, the intractability of life and of individuals, the struggle first to survive and next to make sense of one's survival. Humour, toughness, resolution and generosity are Cookson virtues, in a world which she often depicts as cold and violent. Her novels are weighted and driven by her own early experiences of illegitimacy and poverty. This is what gives them power. In the specialised world of women's popular fiction, Cookson has created her own territory'
Helen Dunmore, *The Times*

BOOKS BY CATHERINE COOKSON

NOVELS

Kate Hannigan
The Fifteen Streets
Colour Blind
Maggie Rowan
Rooney
The Menagerie
Slinky Jane
Fanny McBride
Fenwick Houses
Heritage of Folly
The Garment
The Fen Tiger
The Blind Miller
House of Men
Hannah Massey
The Long Corridor
The Unbaited Trap
Katie Mulholland
The Round Tower
The Nice Bloke
The Glass Virgin
The Invitation
The Dwelling Place
Feathers in the Fire
Pure as the Lily
The Mallen Streak
The Mallen Girl
The Mallen Litter
The Invisible Cord
The Gambling Man
The Tide of Life
The Slow Awakening
The Iron Façade
The Girl
The Cinder Path
Miss Martha Mary Crawford
The Man Who Cried
Tilly Trotter
Tilly Trotter Wed

Tilly Trotter Widowed
The Whip
Hamilton
The Black Velvet Gown
Goodbye Hamilton
A Dinner of Herbs
Harold
The Moth
Bill Bailey
The Parson's Daughter
Bill Bailey's Lot
The Cultured Handmaiden
Bill Bailey's Daughter
The Harrogate Secret
The Black Candle
The Wingless Bird
The Gillyvors
My Beloved Son
The Rag Nymph
The House of Women
The Maltese Angel
The Year of the Virgins
The Golden Straw
Justice is a Woman
The Tinker's Girl
A Ruthless Need
The Obsession
The Upstart
The Branded Man
The Bonny Dawn
The Bondage of Love
The Desert Crop
The Lady on My Left
The Solace of Sin
Riley
The Blind Years
The Thursday Friend
A House Divided

THE MARY ANN STORIES

A Grand Man
The Lord and Mary Ann
The Devil and Mary Ann
Love and Mary Ann

Life and Mary Ann
Marriage and Mary Ann
Mary Ann's Angels
Mary Ann and Bill

FOR CHILDREN

Matty Doolin
Joe and the Gladiator
The Nipper
Rory's Fortune
Our John Willie

Mrs Flannagan's Trumpet
Go Tell It To Mrs Golightly
Lanky Jones
Nancy Nutall and the Mongrel
Bill and the Mary Ann Shaughnessy

AUTOBIOGRAPHY

Our Kate
Catherine Cookson Country

Let Me Make Myself Plain
Plainer Still

PART ONE

I

Jinnie Howlett stood at the end of the long table in the sorting room of the workhouse. This particular room was known as the 'dead store', because in its cubby-hole-lined walls it held the remnants of clothing and articles belonging to inmates past and present, mostly past, because clothing worn by new admissions was very often in such a condition that it practically walked unaided to the incinerator.

The room had a peculiar smell, one that Jinnie had always termed a hot gingery smell, for the atmosphere would at times cause her to sneeze.

If there was any part of this workhouse she liked it was this room, not for itself, but because in it she often found herself alone with Miss Caplin.

Miss Caplin was a seamstress, but she had also part-time duties, such as taking in admissions and seeing that they were stripped and bathed, then garbed in the uniform of the workhouse. In these duties, as in the sewing-room, she chose for a helper, as often as possible, young Jinnie Howlett.

Miss Caplin straightened Jinnie's straw hat, then gave a little tug at the collar of the long grey coat that came to the top of the child's boots. And quietly, she said, 'Now, Jinnie, you will remember all I've told you, because I cannot tell you often enough that if you are brought back from this, your second place, you'll be kept in here for years,' and she moved her head from side to

7

side before repeating, 'years. Just think of Phoebe now, won't you?'

'Oh, yes, Miss Caplin. Oh yes, I'll think of Phoebe, poor Phoebe. But it was the truth I told you about that other place, Miss Caplin. I swear to God it was. He . . . he crawled into my cupboard under the stairs and I screamed and . . .'

'Yes, yes, I believe you, every word you said. But as I've warned you, should that happen again, leave your mark on him, tear at his face and scream your hardest. Now, as I've told you, I know of the farm you are bound for. I say I know of it, although I haven't seen it. But being up in the hills as it is, it will likely be a very raw place, in many ways. You have glimpsed the farmer. He looked a very odd man to me. But then you cannot go by outward appearances. I imagined he was rather stupid; not so his son; but they are men and you must always be aware of men. You understand that, Jinnie?'

'Oh yes, Miss Caplin, I do.'

'And you know why you are going: the wife at the farm is sickly and cannot see to meals and household chores. Well,' – she now gave a little smile – 'you'll be very good at household chores, but as for meals, I think it will be a matter of learning as you go along.'

'Well, at that other place I made breakfast, Miss Caplin, and I cooked bacon and made porridge.' Then after a pause Jinnie shook her head, and added, 'I'll never understand why she lied so, when she was so kind at first and showed me how to do things, such as cook, then to say that I had . . .'

'Yes. Yes.' Miss Caplin again straightened the young girl's hat, saying, 'Put it at the back of your mind. What you must remember now is what I have told you about my aunts. You will come across their cottage some way after you have passed through Whitfield. Max will point it out to you, as it lies in a tree-covered hollow and cannot be seen from the road. But, as I've told you, if anything untoward should happen again and you fear they are going to send you back—' she now wagged her finger as she emphasised, 'but not unless, mind, you must do your best to get away and make for the cottage, and my aunts will look after you until I come. But, of course, as you know, I can only visit them on my leave day, once a month. So you might have to bide there, in hiding, for some time. Last week when I told them of the position you are taking up in the Shaleman farm' – she omitted to say that they had held their hands up in horror – 'they said they hoped you would be strong enough to tackle some farm work. Still, I understand it is a small farm, mostly sheep.'

In the ensuing silence Jinnie sniffed and said, 'Oh, I'm goin' to miss you, Miss Caplin. Nobody's been good to me like you have.' And Jane Caplin had the urge to thrust out her arms and draw the slim figure into a tight embrace, for there were times when she saw this child as the daughter she had been deprived of through the machinations of a loving father.

What she did now was to cup the thin face in her hands and say softly, 'I'm going to miss you, too, Jinnie. But we'll keep in touch through my aunts. As I've told you before though, don't mention their name to your new master. It is better that you pretend you know no-one.'

Jinnie was nodding her head and was about to speak again when the door was thrust open. A tall, bony woman stood there, and in a tone that matched her expression, she said, 'Matron's waiting for the tinker's girl.'

Jinnie did not immediately move towards the labour mistress, but she stared at her for a moment before

9

turning again to Miss Caplin and saying, 'Goodbye, Miss Caplin. Goodbye.'

'Goodbye, Jinnie.'

'Put a move on, girl!'

Jinnie forced herself to cast her eyes downwards as she passed the woman, for if she hated anybody in this workhouse, it was the labour mistress who had, from the day she first entered the place at the age of seven, always referred to her as the tinker's girl. She still held a vivid memory of this woman ordering two inmates to carry her father from the cart, and into what was called the hospital block. And when she wouldn't let her follow them, she had screamed and fought her, only to be silenced by repeated slaps across the face. And although the guardians had sold the cart, the old horse and what remained of the merchandise, instead of giving her father a decent funeral, he was buried as a pauper. She had been told that what money had come from the sale of his belongings would be needed to support her until she was able to work for herself. And, two years before she had been sent out to work for herself, only to be returned in disgrace.

Followed by the labour mistress, she walked across the yard and into the main hall and approached the matron, who was standing behind a table on which was an assortment of clothes. When she neared it she dipped her knee and waited. But the matron did not speak until the labour mistress was by her side. And it was to her she turned and said, 'Count them out,' while pointing towards the articles of clothing on the table.

'Two calico nightgowns, one shift, one petticoat; one print dress, one pair of calico bloomers, two white aprons, one coarse; one habit shirt; one pair of stockings, one pair of working clogs, six body pads.' On touching the last item, the labour mistress spread out the six pieces of calico to the ends of which were attached lengths of tape. And lastly she reached out and brought forward a small Bible.

Now the matron spoke to her, saying, 'You're very lucky to be given a second chance, you know that?'

'Yes, ma'am,' Jinnie replied immediately.

'And if you are brought back again, well, you know what to expect, don't you?'

'Yes, ma'am.' The reply came sharper this time, and it caused the labour mistress and the matron to exchange a quick glance, as if astonished at the attitude of this troublesome girl, who should really be on her knees thanking the matron for her clemency.

Jinnie now watched the labour mistress thrust one article after the other into a small hessian sack. And it was when she came to the pieces of linen that she spoke, saying, 'Mind you wash these out every month . . . boil 'em.'

Jinnie did not reply. To her, those pieces of linen still evoked a terrifying experience, for it was something that happened to older girls, but . . . but never happened to her. It was Miss Caplin who had reassured her that nothing bad or sinister was happening to her; only that nature was beginning its long and tiresome process towards procreation.

Again the matron was speaking to her. 'You may be a long way off, but don't forget I'll have my eye on you.'

Jinnie had an immediate picture of one of the matron's bulbous eyes stretching into a long way off. And as her imagination often did, it made her want to smile or even giggle.

The hessian bag was now thrust at her and she was swung round by the labour mistress's heavy hand and pushed towards the double door at the end of the room.

At their approach a female inmate pulled the doors

open, and Jinnie almost did smile when she caught sight of the farm cart with Max standing by the horse's head.

The matron, too, had come to the door and here admonished her, saying, 'You're very lucky you haven't got to shank it all the way. If he' – she now nodded towards Max – 'if he hadn't been already detailed to fetch a beast from The Hall at Whitfield, you would have had a trail before you. Anyway, beyond Whitfield, you will be met. He knows all about it.' She again nodded towards Max. And now she added, 'Well, get away! Get away!'

The very big man approached Jinnie and, taking her bundle from her, threw it on to the high seat; then putting his hands under her oxters, he hoisted her after it and, without a word to either of the women who stood watching him, swung himself up into the seat with an agility that defied his height and bulk. He made a sound in his throat, and the horse jerked the high-backed cart forward. And so he drove Jinnie Howlett out of the main gates of the workhouse.

Jinnie did not speak to the man at her side for some time, but she looked about her. She was out in the open, the real open. She was free again! 'And oh, dearest Lord,' she actually prayed, 'don't let me ever go back. Please! Please!'

The man at her side looked down at her and a smile spread over his great, flat-featured face. The eyes were spaced widely apart and now seemed to be of an indeterminate colour, whereas at other times, when she was to see him in a temper, they would appear to be almost black. His nose was large and the nostrils were wide. Only his mouth appeared normal; it was full-lipped. But the words he spoke were uttered in a manner that was in keeping with his main features, for his language was disjointed, his words tending towards a stammer. Yet, whatever he uttered always had a reasonable meaning. And now he said, 'Good!' The word came from deep in his broad chest and had a ring to it.

To this Jinnie answered quickly, 'Oh yes, Max. Good, good. D'you know where I'm goin', Max?' She did not have to space her words in order to make him comprehend, and he nodded, saying, 'In hills, High . . . High Farm.' And then, taking one hand from the reins he put his thumb and first finger about an inch apart, which gesture indicated the size of the farm. And at this she said, 'Small.'

His head bobbed.

She looked ahead now and more to herself than to him, she said, 'I hope I like it, and . . . and I hope they like me, and . . . I don't have any trouble.'

At this his hand came out again and he patted her shoulder, saying, 'Somethin' f-f-for you. Somethin' saved.' And then he swept his hand forward as if shooing flies from the horse, as he said, 'Later.'

At this Jinnie said quickly, 'You'll tell me later?'

'Aye.'

There were times when Jinnie felt she could read Max's mind; at least, the meaning of his stilted speech always seemed clear to her.

Max was the only man she had ever been allowed to speak to. He was the only man to be allowed anywhere near the women's quarters. Likely it was because he was considered harmless. He had been born in the workhouse, and she knew of his strange history from old Aggie McMahon, who had brought him into the world.

It would appear that thirty years ago a woman had been brought in raving, so much so, she had to be put into a strait-jacket before being flung into the quiet room. The very thought of the quiet room made Jinnie shudder, for she herself had once been sent there. That was the day after her father was buried. However, they had soon had to haul this woman out because she was about to give birth to a child. As Aggie said, Max was a huge baby. He could have been six months old when he was born, so big was he. And that was why he had grown into this huge man. When the time came to have him christened, Aggie had told her, the woman had returned to some kind of normality. Yet, she must still have been odd, for she had insisted that his name was Maximilian and that he was a descendant of a Roman emperor. Aggie said there had been nothing on the woman to say who she was or where she had come from, but that her clothes were highly respectable and that she wore bloomers, a garment rather like knickerbockers, only made of soft material. Anyway, she died when her child was ten days old and she was buried, like many another, in a pauper's grave. Max, as he became known, grew rapidly and was thought to be mentally deficient. But from when he was put on the farm at five years old, it was discovered that he could count. This emerged when he implied that the hens weren't laying so well, and he counted out the discrepancy on his fingers. The farmer, who was also the labour master, told the parson, whose weekly visits were mainly intended to instil the fear of God into his wretched congregation, about the ungainly child he had under his control, one who must have a bright spot somewhere because he could count, and that no-one, to his knowledge, had shown him how to do it. It was from then that the parson had taken an interest in the child. After reading a Bible story to the Sunday school he would point out the letters to Max, whose ability to remember them was eventually accepted as proof that he couldn't be entirely mental. That he wasn't at all mental, Miss Caplin had herself already discovered some time before. As for Jinnie, she had never thought of him other than as a normal man who was unfortunately handicapped in his speech. And she had known for a long time that if she really loved anybody other than Miss Caplin in that dismal, work-wearying place, it was this man. He had, in a way, taken the place of the father she had lost; even seeming to possess the same warm disposition. Yet she had heard of an incident in which he had developed a deep rage which had quickly turned to violence. A dog on the farm had attached itself to him, and when, one day, Max found an inmate, who was decidedly mentally ill, ferociously kicking it, he had almost throttled the man, and had, so she understood, then lifted him bodily and thrown him against the wall. For this he was put into the quiet room for a time, and his mental state was again questioned. It was only the fact that he stood in good stead with the labour master-cum-farmer that he wasn't transferred to menial tasks, such as stone-breaking, or midden cleaning.

After about two hours the cart passed through Haydon Bridge and turned into the road that led through Langley and past the old smelting mills. It was as they came to a green sward opposite the dam that Max pulled the horse to a halt, saying, 'Rest . . . eh?'

'Oh yes, Max. It's lovely here, isn't it?' She pointed to the water shimmering in the sunshine. 'I've never seen anything like that, it's beautiful.'

As the horse began to munch the fresh grass at the side of the road, she flopped down from the cart and, rubbing her hands over the ground on each side of her, she said, 'Oh, 'tis lovely, lovely.'

Max too stood gazing across the water; then letting himself slowly down on to the grass at her side, he said, 'Something f-f-for . . .' And now he wagged his forefinger at her before bringing out the word, 'you.'

15

'Something for me?'

He bowed his head deeply; then putting his hand into the inside of his three-quarter-length coat, he drew out a small case about seven inches long and two inches wide, and as he began to mulch it between his hands, he said, 'Leather . . . st-stiff long time.'

'You've had it a long time? What is it, Max?'

'I've . . . I've had it a . . . long time. N-not mine . . . yours,' he explained and thrust the case at her.

'What is it?' she said, feeling the leather pouch.

Now, his hand over hers, he slowly withdrew from the pouch a knife and fork and spoon. They were bone-handled, but they were discoloured and the knife was somewhat rusty.

'Y-your father.'

'My father's?'

His head bobbed slowly.

'But how? Why?'

'Clothes b-burnt, belt an' all. That—' his forefinger was wagging again towards the pouch, and he demonstrated as he said, 'Deep . . . in . . . lining.'

Slowly she turned her head away from him and the pouch and looked across the water, and just as if he were sitting in the middle of it, she envisaged her father, his face smiling as he wiped the knife and fork that he had been using and the spoon which she had used. She could see him rubbing them and rubbing them until they shone, then slipping them back into the pouch.

In a quick movement she swung herself round on her knees and, putting her hand out to Max, she said, in a broken voice, 'I . . . I remember, Max, eating with these. Dada using a knife and fork and me the spoon . . . Oh yes, yes. But I had completely forgotten about them.' She paused before asking him: 'Does anyone know you kept them?'

He shook his head quickly, and then, pouting his lips, he blew out his cheeks and said, 'No . . . no. Hide. Got . . . hole in the . . . boiler-house.'

'Oh, you hid them in the boiler-house, in the bricks?'

He was grinning at her now as he repeated, 'In the . . . bricks. Loose.' And he demonstrated the pulling out of a brick.

She answered his grin with a wide smile. 'Not supposed to have knives. They would have taken it.' And she now tenderly replaced the knife and fork and spoon in the pouch, then pressed it against her breast for a moment before she said, 'Thank you, Max. Oh, thank you. Now I have something of Dada it makes me feel better, not so . . . lost. You know what I mean?'

'I . . . know. Yes. I . . . know.'

'You are very like my father, Max.'

At this the big man put his head back and laughed out loud, then said, 'Like . . . nobody . . . me. Nobody.'

'No? Perhaps you're right.' Her face was solemn as she nodded at him. 'There are very few people as kind as you. I couldn't remember even having a barley sugar until you gave me one. I don't know how I would have fared back there if it hadn't been for you and Miss Caplin.'

'Miss Cap . . . lin good lady . . . very.'

'Yes, she is a very good lady. She told me we'll pass the cottage where she comes to on her leave days. Her aunts live there.'

'Yes; I . . . know. Dyke . . . Cottage. Duckworth ladies.'

'Yes, her aunts. Have you been up to this farm where I'm going, Max?'

He shook his head. 'No . . . not that . . . f-far. Well up . . . hills. Windy.'

'I like the wind. I like it to blow through my hair.'

She patted the top of her hat and he said, 'Bonny hair.'

Her face straight again, she said. 'They were going to cut it off; but Miss Caplin came to the rescue. You know what she said?'

He shook his head.

'She told the labour mistress that if she let it grow for another year or two my plaits could be sold, and you could get money for hair like mine. I was very sick about it, because it was only . . . well . . . well . . .'

She was stumped for words when he said, 'Re . . . prieve?'

'Oh yes.' Her face brightened. 'You are clever, you know, Max. Reprieve, yes. Like they get when they're going to be hung.'

They were both laughing now. Then, jumping to his feet, he said, 'Me get . . . hung . . . get . . . back if I . . . don't hurry,' and he pulled the horse reluctantly from its feeding, before helping her up and back on to the high seat of the cart. And when he was again seated beside her, they smiled at each other broadly . . .

Presently the road sloped and twisted downwards until it crossed the river and then divided. Max did not turn the horse towards Whitfield but took the road that would climb towards Alston. After a few minutes they passed a narrow lane, and Max, pointing back to it, said, 'D-Dyke Cottage.'

'It's as Miss Caplin said, you can't see it from the road.'

'No. No. Hidden . . . not much . . . further now, J-Jinnie.'

'You say I'll be met?'

'Yes. They said n-next to the . . . turning . . . stile.'

'Oh, there's a stile?' She was now sitting on the edge of her seat straining her eyes forward and upwards to the rising land all about her. Even from this partly wooded road it looked bare and lonely, and of a sudden she swung round and gripped Max's arm with both hands, saying, 'You . . . you won't forget me, Max, will you?'

For a moment she thought he was about to pull the horse to a stop, but then, transferring the reins to one hand again, he took hold of hers as he said fervently, 'Never! N-never forget. Some time I . . . I ask holi . . . day.'

'And you would come and see me?'

His head bobbed again.

'Oh, thank you, Max.'

'I . . . I write you.'

'A letter? You'd write me a letter?'

'Ah-ha . . . ah-ha.' He seemed both amused and pleased by her surprise.

'Oh, I'd love a letter. I *can* read a bit.'

He tugged on the reins again. Then the next minute they were round the corner and there was the stile, with a man seated upon it.

On their approach he slid to the ground. And when Max drew the horse to a stop in the narrow road, the man stood staring up at them. He did not speak, nor did Max, but he, jumping down, held out his arms to Jinnie. And when she was standing on the rough road she was able to look closely at this man who, she supposed, would be her master, or at least one of them. She vaguely remembered him, for she had only seen him and his father for the matter of a minute. And the minute had been mostly spent in their listening to the matron, who was detailing her character to a very small man and his tallish son.

The man spoke for the first time. 'Well, you've got here,' he said, 'and almost on time.' He looked from her to Max and gave a nod of approval. And Max, smiling at him said, 'Quicker . . . th-than train.'

At this the young man answered his smile with a laugh, saying, 'Well, if you say so.' Then turning to Jinnie, he said, 'Have you got a bundle?'

Even as he was speaking, Max's hand was reaching behind the seat and pulling the hessian bag forward, and when he handed it to her the man asked, 'Is that her lot?' and Jinnie answered, 'Yes, that's my lot.'

There followed a moment's silence; then the man said, 'Well, we'd better be making a move.' And at this she turned to Max and, impulsively stretching up her arms, she drew his head downwards and placed a kiss on his cheek. Then, grabbing up the bundle, she moved towards the grass verge, leaving the two men looking at each other.

Max's voice came deeper than ever when he said, 'She be . . . all right . . . treated?'

The young man seemed to hesitate before he said, 'Oh yes. Yes, she'll be all right. Don't worry. You a relation?'

'Re-lation? No.'

'Well, she seems very fond of you . . . So long. You picking something up in Whitfield?'

'Calf . . . bull calf.'

'Oh, a bull calf. Well, well! From Maddison's I suppose?'

Max thought a moment before he replied, 'Aye, Madd . . . ison's.'

The young man now pointed up the road: 'It widens out a few yards further on,' he said. 'You could turn comfortably there.'

Max looked towards where the man was pointing, then at Jinnie and said quietly, 'So l-long.'

'So long, Max.'

She stood for a moment on the grass verge before walking towards the stile. The man was now on the other side of it, and as she went to climb it, he said, 'Give your bundle here.'

This she did. Then, dropping down on to the narrow path, she walked behind the man who was now a step or so in front of her. That was until she heard the horse neigh. At this, she turned swiftly to where the cart was passing the stile. Max was looking in her direction and when she waved to him, he waved back. She stood watching until the cart moving away disappeared around the bend in the road, when the man's voice brought her attention round to him again: 'You fond of him?'

She blinked the moisture from her eyes two or three times before she answered briefly, 'Yes.'

'He an inmate in the workhouse?'

'Yes.'

'Big fella. Can't say I've seen bigger; giant size.' He smiled at her now as he added, 'Wouldn't like to come against him in an argument, like.'

'No.' She jerked her chin upwards and repeated, 'No, you wouldn't. But . . . but he doesn't fight.' She paused, thinking of the dog incident, then added, 'If he got angry at someone doing something bad, he might.'

The man turned and looked at her closely, and she returned his look for a moment. Then she watched him look ahead as he asked, 'You worked on a farm before?'

'No. But Max has. He helps the house farmer a lot. He's very good with animals.'

Ignoring this last remark, the man, still looking ahead, said, 'Then you have no idea of work on a farm? Any kind of a farm?'

Again she said, 'No,' but more definitely this time, then added, 'I understood I'm just for cooking and looking after a sick lady.'

He turned his head sharply towards her and his tone

flat, he said, 'It's my mother you'll have to tend. And she's no lady, she's a working woman; or she was. And the farm: well, the house is very small.' Then his voice rising, he said, 'You've got to understand that life is rough up here.' His hand jerked past the peak of his cap as if he were indicating the sky and not the hills ahead.

Her voice was low and almost a mutter as she said, 'I'm used to hard work.'

'There's hard work and hard work. It all depends where it's placed, and who you're working for.' But then his tone changed and, looking at her again, he said, 'I don't suppose things were easy in the workhouse.'

'No, they were not. I did me share of scrubbing stone corridors after the sewing day was over.'

'They said you could cook; can you? Were you in the kitchen?'

It was a moment or so before she replied, 'No, not there.'

'Then where did you learn to cook?'

'Out . . . outside, in service.'

'Oh!' His step altered. 'You've been out afore?'

'Yes.'

There was another pause before he said, 'They didn't say. Why did you come back?'

When she didn't answer, he said, 'Like that, is it?' Then he was actually surprised when she rounded on him and cried in no small voice, 'No! it wasn't like that, or whatever you're meaning, mister. I had a reason for coming back, and it was a good one.'

There was a half smile on his face now as he said, 'Oh aye? Well, whatever it was, if it can stir you like that, it must have been a good one, as you said.'

They were walking up a steep incline now and when she began to gasp for breath, he said, 'You'll get used to them. There's three like this, short; but after that it'll be easy going.'

As he said, there were three short steep hills before them. And when she reached the top of the third she stood gasping for breath, while at the same time being surprised at the scene before her, for it stretched away gently into the far distance, where she espied a huddle of small buildings. But to each side of her there rose hills, dotted here and there with sheep. The man, too, was standing still and, pointing, first to one side then to the other, he was saying, 'Our land stretches away on both sides, but this is where it begins.' He now lifted a foot and stamped his heel into the hard ground.

Looking up at him now, she said, ' 'Tis bonny; round about, I mean. 'Tis bonny.' Then she asked, 'How far is your farmhouse,' indicating the huddle of buildings ahead, 'from the road?'

'A mile.' He shrugged his shoulders. 'A little more, perhaps.' And now he smiled at her, as he said, 'Distances are deceiving. You think you've come a long way now, but although it looks plain sailing to the house, that's a longer stretch than you've already travelled.'

She looked back down the hills, then into the distance again, and she exclaimed, 'Really!'

'Aye, really. Flattish plains are deceiving. Aye, well, come on. If we intend to cross it we'd better keep goin', hadn't we?' He was smiling at her in a kindly fashion, and she smiled back as she thought, I'll get to like him, that's if . . . She didn't allow her thoughts to pinpoint the main reason why, on the other hand, she might get to dislike him.

They had walked some distance when she realised that his head was bent all the time as if he were picking out a path that wasn't there. She realised he was in

23

deep thought, and so her voice was muted as she said, 'Mister.'

'Yes?' His head was erect again.

'Are there many in your family?'

'No, not many. Just my parents and my brother and me. And you don't have to call me "mister". Keep that for me da. My name is Bruce.'

'Just the four of you?'

'That's all.' Then he added, 'Mainly three. My brother works in the lead mine.' He threw his head back as if indicating the mine. 'And he's not home every night; mostly at week-ends.'

She wanted to ask, 'Is your mother very sick?' but told herself she must be if she were unable to look after her man and her son. Anyway, she would soon know. But one thing seemed certain, there wasn't a squad of them and them not being gentry, like them in the place she had been in, using six pieces of cutlery each to eat a meal and expecting them to be polished before you put them away, especially the forks, in case a tiny speck of food had got stuck in them. Besides which, having to iron even the lady's shifts and polish the boots. But there wouldn't be much need for boot polishing up here, she thought. The ground might seem firm, but she had already squelched in one or two soggy patches.

As they came within viewing distance of the buildings her step slowed, and this brought his eyes down to her, although he made no comment.

Jinnie's open mouth could not fully convey her surprise, for the huddle of buildings she was seeing and which she had imagined to be the outhouses, were mainly the farm cottage itself. Her impression of a large building must have been created by the hill that seemingly loomed immediately behind.

Her steps seemed to be dragging now as she neared

the cottage, which was brought about not only by her legs being tired from the long, uphill trek, but also from the feeling of trepidation that was now creeping up through her whole body. The place was so small . . . and poor-small. The workhouse had been big, every part of it, day rooms, dormitories, sewing room, laundry, all big . . . and clean. Oh yes, clean. A scrubbing brush, blue mottle soap and aching arms saw to that.

'Come in. Come along in.' He was beckoning her from the doorway, for she had stopped some feet away. After taking in a short breath that sounded in her own ears like a gasp, she walked towards him, then past him and into the room. And there she stood, her expression one of amazement at what confronted her.

The room was larger than it had appeared from the outside. In the middle of it stood a table covered with oilcloth on which were piled pans and dirty dishes. A fire was smouldering on a low-barred hearth, above which dangled a black kale-pot suspended from a chain attached to a cross-bar just below the chimney opening. To one side of the fire was what could be an oven and to the other a hob on which stood a kettle. Further along one wall was a rack of open shelves, although what they held she could not make out, for they were lost in the dimness of that end of the room.

Flat against the wall at the other side of the fire-place stood a long wooden settle.

Out of the corner of her eye she glimpsed a door leading from the wall to the left of her. But what reluctantly drew her gaze to the wall opposite was the sight of a woman, who appeared to be lying in the wall, although the light from the square window to the side of the door was not enough to allow her to be seen clearly.

'Come and say hello to my ma.' The man's hand was on her arm and he drew her around an armchair; then with his foot he thrust a single chair under the table. And then, there she was, standing almost face to face with the woman, whose eyes were set in deep sockets, provided by the cheekbones. Her nose was thin and pinched and the lips of her large mouth were formless. The skin was tightly drawn over her whole face, giving the effect of its having been moulded in parchment. It was a frightening face, until the lips moved and the woman spoke.

'You've got here, then, hinny. But you're much younger than I thought maybe.'

Jinnie drew in a sigh of relief, for the woman's voice, although much rougher, common like, sounded kind, like her son's.

'The house is in a mess, lass. The men are no good with crocks. Anyhow, there's no time, with Bruce there' – she nodded towards her son – 'and his da out with the sheep most times. And Hal only putting his neb in the door when it suits him. He's my other son,' she added by way of explanation . . . 'Can you cook, hinny?'

'Yes, missis. Well, a little bit. I can make bread and do fries; and,' she added, 'I have made a stew with dumplings.'

Jinnie now watched the wide mouth open further to disclose a set of broken yellow teeth, and her new mistress said, 'Oh, that'll be fine. Oh, you'll do well enough. The last one couldn't boil water, could she, Bruce?'

Her son smiled and said, 'Well, she could boil water, Ma. But it all tasted the same to me, the stuff that was in it, whether tea, meat or taties.'

Jinnie watched the woman lie back on her pillow now and as her chest began to heave she pressed her hands on it as if to still some emotion, perhaps laughter in this instance. Then in a thick muttered tone, she said, 'Show her the ropes, Bruce, show her the ropes.'

Pointing to a chest of drawers in the dim corner of the wall in which the bed was inserted, he said, 'That holds linen and such. All rough but hard wearing. There's a lot of it ready to wash outside.' He thumbed towards the door on the opposite wall. Then again pointing, he added, 'That ladder leads up to our sleeping quarters, those of me brother and me.'

She seemed to detect something of relief in his tone as he added, 'But I have it mostly to meself.' Then, he pulled open one of the two drawers in the side of the table, saying, 'Knives and forks and such you'll find in here.'

'Yes. Yes.'

At the door leading to the other room he turned and pointed towards the kale-pot that was showing bubbling water, and he explained, 'We keep that going for washing-up and such. But in here' – he pushed the door open – 'other things necessary for all you'll want. It's a big scullery.'

Facing her was a mangle, and a poss-tub, together with a poss-stick. From where she stood, half of the poss-stick shank was visible, which meant it was resting on soaking clothes. One wall was taken up with shelves, empty except for a large black pan, and a brown earthenware cooking bowl. On the floor was a grease-filled frying pan and a griddle plate. Below the window was a shallow brown stone trough with a hole in its centre, from which a pipe led into a bucket beneath. To the side of the trough was a pump and she watched him now put his hand on the handle and press it downwards, so that a spurt of water fell into the trough. She had been wondering about how they would have to get water in when he, voicing her thoughts, said, 'This saves a lot of lugging from the pond. We had it fixed up a few years back.' He again pressed the handle and looked at the contraption as if he was proud of it. Then turning to her, he said, 'This is the part that I never like to explain: up there . . . up them steps, is your billet . . . where you sleep. It's very low; no use trying to stand up, even in the middle. There's a straw pallet and you can change the straw every week if you like. It's up to you.' Then in an aside he added, 'Some would leave it until it crawled out by itself.'

She looked towards the stone steps, one side of them bordered by the far wall, the other without a rail of any kind. She saw they were shallow steps with no width, and she thought it was just as well there were not too many of them else she could fall off. She didn't like heights, not close heights anyway, the kind that you felt you were going to topple over. Only once had she experienced such a height and she had a bad memory of it far, far back, when she had a father and he took her on jaunts; that is if, of course, they had been settled in a kindly farmer's field where their belongings were safe.

She was surprised when Bruce touched her arm, saying, 'Don't look so scared, it's quite comfortable. And after all, you lie down when you're sleepin', don't you?' He was smiling at her again. She hadn't known she had looked scared.

When a loud grunt interrupted what he was about to point out next, he looked towards another door which apparently led outside; and for explanation, he said, 'Sow; she's nearing her time. We're expecting a good litter.'

'Oh.' She returned his smile for she had seen a sow and her litter on the workhouse farm, and, unlike most people, she liked pigs.

'Come and see her.'

Outside, and passing what she recognized by the smell

was the swill-house, he said, 'That's the boiling-up house,' and coming to the pigsty, he looked down on a very heavily laden sow and said, 'Still hanging on, are you?' and when Jinnie put her hand over the sty wall and scratched the pig's ear, he exclaimed, 'You're not frightened of her?'

'No. I . . . I think I like pigs.'

'Good! Good! That'll be a help anyway. Come on, round here.'

The end of the building presented a surprise. She had imagined the hill to go straight up, almost, as she thought, forming a wall. But there was about a hundred feet of level ground before it rose, and then abruptly. In this area was a long hen run and quite a large, but low barn, and a stable beyond. This was empty, although the floor showed evidence of a horse, and she asked eagerly, 'You've got a horse?'

'Aye, horse and cart. Me da's got them to market. It's store day once a month; store day.' His face looked blank now and the tone of his voice was one she hadn't heard before: there was bitterness in it as he had added, 'Store day.'

'Over there,' he went on, 'is an outdoor closet, if you want to use it. And along there' – he was indicating beyond the hen runs – 'at the far end is a midden.' Then he added quickly, 'We . . . we empty our own slops; but you'll have to see to Ma's.'

'Aye, yes. Yes, sir. I mean . . . mister.'

He stopped and, looking down at her, and in his ordinary tone, he said, 'You could call me Bruce.'

Her delay in answering was as if she was considering this personal invitation; then she said, 'Thank you, but it should be "mister";' and she added, 'Miss Caplin would say it should be "mister".'

'Who's Miss Caplin?'

'She's an officer in the house, and she was kind to me; very.'

'Oh, well then, it'll be "mister".'

His chin now slowly drooping towards his chest, he surveyed her for some seconds before he said, 'You're a funny lass, aren't you? But I hope you'll stick it out here, because me ma needs somebody like you. She wasn't always sickly like this, you know. At one time she was spritely and, believe it or not, bonny. That was until this thing got a hold of her. But she's fought it. She's very plucky, is me ma. It'll win in the end, though, but until then she'll need help.'

A great wave of pity flooded her. Strangely, not only for the woman in the bed in the wall, but for her son here, her caring son; for that's what he had already shown himself to be.

She answered quickly, saying, 'I'll do me best, mister. I promise you, I'll do me best. And I'll clean the place up and brighten it. And I'll cook as best I can, and I'll see to her. I'm used to old people, you know, although she doesn't look all that old. But there were a lot of old people in the house. And I was on the wet ward once for months and . . .' She ended simply by nodding, and he did not enquire what she meant by wet ward. But he said, 'I'm sure you will. I have a feeling that you will. Well, come on; I'll lift the kale-pot off and it'll give you hot water to start on that lot on the table.'

They were in the room again, and seeing her pulling off her hat and coat, he said, 'I'd take your bundle' – he lifted it from a chair and thrust it towards her – 'and go up where I showed you, and get into something rough. You have another frock, I suppose?'

'Yes. Yes, a working one.'

'Well, do that.'

After she had actually run from the room he stood

looking towards the open door, before turning to the bed and saying, 'She'll do all right, I think, Ma.'

'I . . . I hope so, lad.' Her voice was low. 'It's a pity it's market day though.'

'Aye. Aye, it is. Well, I've shown her the ropes, and now I'll leave her to get on with it.'

'Couldn't you give her a hand with that lot off the table first?'

'Ma, I should have been in the top field an hour ago. You know what he'll say when he gets in. And if any of them have got over the hump, God above, we'll go through the same pattern again. Not that he'll see to any of them himself. Oh no! There's going to be a showdown here, Ma, before long.'

'All right. But now get yourself away. I'll sit on the edge and tell her what to do.'

'You'll do nothing of the sort. You can tell her what to do just from where you are.' He leant over her and thrust another bare tick pillow behind her back, saying, 'Now you can see enough from where you are, and you've still got a voice on you.' His own voice had softened and when she answered, 'That's about the only thing that's left,' he said swiftly, 'Now, now! I've told you.'

'All right, all right.' Her voice had risen. 'Get yourself away. Go on, because one thing is certain, you mustn't be in the house when he gets back. But that's a point . . . if he comes straight back.'

'I wouldn't bank on that, Ma. Anyway, now I'm off.' He leaned towards her and touched her cheek gently with his fingers; then, from a nail in the back of the door he pulled off an old coat and cap, replacing them with those he had been wearing; then again he glanced towards his mother before hurrying from the room . . .

* * *

She had cleared the table. The crockery had been washed first, the mugs needing to be scoured to remove the old tea stains. As for the pans, she had taken them outside, and, kneeling by the side of an open drain at the end of the building, had scraped off the encrusted soot. Then, after scouring them inside, she had arranged them on the shelf in the scullery room, and the mugs and plates on the rack in the kitchen.

During her comings and goings the woman hadn't said a word, but had watched her every move. It wasn't until Jinnie said, 'Can I get you something to drink, missis?' that she said, 'Yes, lass; and get yourself one an' all,' for which suggestion Jinnie was thankful.

'But how do I get the kettle on the fire, missis, with a kale- pot there? I carried it back when it was empty and filled it; but I couldn't lift it off now.'

'Oh.' The woman pulled herself slowly upwards; then twisting round in the bed to look towards the fire, she said, 'Two of the bars come down and act as a hob. There's a small rake at the side, so just lift them down and they'll hold the kettle.'

'Oh yes. Yes, thank you.'

After some trial and error she managed to lift the bars from their sockets to form a flat stand, and on this she placed the kettle and pressed it towards the glowing embers.

The kettle wasn't all that large, and so by the time she had taken outside the heavy clippie mat that fronted the hearth and shaken it, before turning it upside down and jumping on it to loosen the grit from the hessian backing, as she had been made to do back in the house, the kettle was bubbling.

She lifted it hastily to the side before going to the bed again and saying, 'What'll I make you? Have you tea?'

'Yes, lass; in the caddy on the mantelpiece, the left-hand one. The teapot's under the rack over there. Put in two spoonfuls. That won't make it too strong, 'cos there's no milk. Bruce brings that over the night. He picks a can up from the wall where one of the farm lads will have left it. It saves him a long trek at the end of a hard day.'

She mashed the tea, let it draw for a while, then poured out a mug and took it to the woman, who held it between both hands as if warming them before she said, 'Thank you, Jinnie. You did say your name was Jinnie, didn't you?'

She couldn't remember having said what her name was, and when she didn't answer, the woman said, 'Bruce must have heard it.'

When she asked her what she would get for a meal, her mistress again lay back on her pillow as if having to search her mind. Then she pointed up to the ceiling where, attached to a beam were a number of large hooks, from which hung what Jinnie could see were pieces of meat.

The woman now said, 'There are two hams up there and a shoulder and a leg of lamb. Them two could be a bit high, but the hams are just right. But then it's no use, you couldn't reach them. You'll have to wait until . . .'

'I could, missis, if I stood on the table.'

There was again a semblance of a smile on the woman's face and she said, 'Yes, lass, you're right. You could if you stood on the table, but you'd have to keep your head bent or you'd go through the roof. Anyway, get yourself up and unhook this end one.'

Still propped up on her elbows, she watched the frail-looking girl climb on to the table and, with shoulders hunched, stretch out her arms and unhook the ham. But

33

the weight of it brought her double and she dropped it on the table.

On the floor once more, Jinnie laughed and said, 'It's much heavier than it looks, missis.'

'Fetch it here.'

She took it to the bed and the woman now pressed her long bony thumb into the top of it, saying, 'That's all right; it'll be nice for frying.' Then she added, 'About six o'clock—' She now inclined her head towards the mantelpiece on which stood a Staffordshire pottery figure of two people holding a round-faced clock in their entwined arms, and she said, 'Around six o'clock, Bruce should be back. He'll lift the kale-pot off and you'll have a big pan ready full of taties. You'll get them out of a sack in the barn. You know, round the corner. You'll put the peelings next door where the boiler is for the pig food. It hasn't been on for a day or two . . . the boiler, and she's had to have them raw. But she likes the hot mash, and at this time she needs it. I'll get Bruce to show you how to light the boiler and make her mash. But in the meantime, when you're waitin' for the taties to boil, you'll cut six slices of ham off that end' – she pointed to the ham – 'the first four thick, about so—' She now demonstrated the thickness of the required slices, then added, 'The next two not so thick, one for you and one for me. You understand?'

'Yes, missis.'

'Well, take it out and put it in yonder cupboard until it's needed.' She was pointing over her shoulder now.

Jinnie took the ham and made her way to the end of the room, slightly mystified because she couldn't see any cupboard, until she espied what looked like a hatch in the corner next to the chest of drawers.

Lifting this up she saw a shelf that went deeply into the recess of the wall, and after placing the ham on it,

34

she returned to the bed and, smiling at her mistress, she said, 'It took a little finding; it's a hidey-hole all right.'

The woman nodded at her, saying, 'Aye, this side of the house is very thick, all of three feet, or perhaps a bit more. Then, of course, they had to build on to there.' She was now indicating the wall behind where she lay. 'They had to do it in order to get a double tick in. Me man's grandfather did it when they built the place.' She now dropped back heavily on to her pillows and sighed. It was an audible sound and had the effect of saddening Jinnie and making her enquire, 'Is there anything I can get you, missis? I mean, a wash, like?'

'No, lass. As for the wash, I had the flannel round me face this mornin'. Bruce sees to that. But if you'd bring me the po, it's under that bit curtain there' – she indicated the bottom of the bed – 'where the curtain drops to the floor.'

Following these directions, Jinnie saw a piece of ragged curtain hanging from a frame attached to the wall beyond the bed and, lifting it, she saw another shelf, on which was a china chamber-pot. The smell that wafted over her was almost a stench. She closed her eyes for a moment and bit on her lip in order not to show her repugnance.

After handing it to the woman, she was surprised to hear her say, 'I know it smells, lass; I haven't been able to scald it for months; but come the better weather I might be able to get on me feet again and . . . and go to the closet.'

'Oh, it's all right. It's all right, missis,' Jinnie was quick to reassure her; but the woman paused before thrusting the pot underneath the bedclothes and, looking into Jinnie's face, she said, 'You've got the makings

35

of a good lass. I only hope you'll be able to stick it.'

'Oh, missis, I'm sure I will. I won't mind looking after you.'

'Oh,' the woman said, and closed her eyes tightly for a moment: 'there's more to put up with than me. But anyway, let's wait and see.'

A few minutes later, Jinnie said, 'Where do I empty it, missis?'

'There's a bucket outside the door. Put it in there until it's full, and then you take that to the middens. It's round beyond the hen crees. But you won't have to do that often, as Bruce sees to it, except when they're lambing and times like that when he's up all night, or . . .' She stopped abruptly.

It was some time later when she was washing the grime off the window that her mistress said to her, 'You hungry, lass?' and she answered quickly, 'Yes, I am a bit, missis.'

'Well, it'll be some time afore they're in. So, look in the cupboard in the scullery. You'll find pig's fat there and the remains of a loaf, so Bruce says. But you'll find it as hard as flint; the other one couldn't bake.'

On Jinnie's enquiring look, she said, 'It was the lass . . . No, she was no lass, she was a woman, but she was as lazy as she was long. Used to public-house work behind a bar, I think, most of her life. And why she put in for this job, God knows; or, at least, I've got an idea. But she found nothing doing in that quarter.' And there being no following up of this enigmatic statement, Jinnie went into the scullery, and there in the pantry found a jar of pig fat. She spread some on a slice of the dry bread and sprinkled it with salt. It tasted good; and as she cut a second slice she told herself it would make a lovely meal if the bread was toasted . . .

It was about two hours later when the woman, pulling herself well up in the bed, said, 'Go to the door and see if you can hear a cart coming.'

After doing what she was bid, Jinnie came back to the bed and said, 'No, missis, I could hear nothing. It's quiet out there, and there's no wind either.'

The woman's hands were gripped together tightly against her chest as she said, 'Well, lass, when my man comes in, I'd ask you not to take any notice of what he says, 'cos he'll likely be . . . well, you'll find out sooner or later. He'll be in the drink. Of course, that's nothing unusual, but he . . . well, he always seems to go for it in a big way on market day.'

During those five weeks she had been in service in Newcastle she'd also had some experience of a man in drink. More than once the master of the house had come in very cheery, and twice he had talked to her and joked with her in the kitchen. But on each occasion the mistress was out. He had questioned her a lot about the workhouse and herself, and she had liked him until the night he crawled into the cupboard and got on top of her. She had been sound asleep and she had screamed. So yes, she knew what men were like when in drink.

She had set the table for three with the rough cutlery and, having found a well-washed tray cloth in the chest of drawers, she had put it on the tin tray set ready for her mistress's meal. And whilst waiting for the men's home-coming, she re-filled the coal scuttle, bringing the coal in a shovel at a time, because she could hardly lift the brass container when empty, let alone when it was full of coal. Then she banked up the fire and blew it into a blaze with the bellows, so that the flickering light from it gave a softness to the room.

They both started when the door was suddenly thrust open and Bruce entered. His entrance was like that of somebody about to fight, at least verbally. But then, his manner changing abruptly, he looked from Jinnie, who was standing near the table, to his mother in the bed. And it was to his mother he spoke as he walked up the room, saying with surprise, 'Not back yet?'

'No, lad; not back yet.'

'It's close on seven o'clock.'

'Yes. Yes, I know.' Then she put in quietly, 'Perhaps he's goin' to follow Hal's pattern and stay down there all night.'

'Let's hope to God he does. But no such luck.'

'No, as you say, lad, no such luck . . . Been busy?'

'Yes.' He turned away from her now, pulling off his cap and coat. However, instead of moving immediately to hang them on the door he looked towards the table, then around the room, and after a moment he said, 'Somebody's been busy.'

'Yes, the lass is goin' to be all right. She's a good lass, willing, and a worker.'

'Good,' he said, and turned to smile at Jinnie standing at the far side of the table, the while saying, 'That's a reference for you. And you've not been in the house five minutes.'

After hanging up his coat and cap, he turned to her again and enquired, 'How's it been?'

'All right, thank you. I've . . . I've got the dinner ready. I've mashed the taties; they're on the hob. But I've got to fry the ham. If you'll take the kale-pot off for me, please.'

Without further ado, he lifted the kale-pot on to the hearth, and immediately she put the frying pan on the glowing embers, and the sound of sizzling filled the kitchen.

'D'you like it done well or light?'

He paused for a moment as if thinking, then said, 'Just as it comes, Jinnie. Just as it comes.'

Ten minutes later she dished up the ham and the mashed potatoes, and she placed one plate on the tray and another at the far end of the table. The plate with the thinnest slice of all she placed to one side.

During the frying of the ham, he had been in the scullery, and now he came in rubbing his hair with a coarse towel. His shirt collar was turned in and his face was still wet. He went on rubbing as he watched her take the tray to the bed and place it before his mother, then push a pillow into her back as if to give her support.

After hanging the towel on the rod that was fitted below the low mantelshelf, he sat down at the table and he stared at his plate of heaped-up potatoes and the thick slice of browned ham. Then, after a further look around, he attacked the meal. At least he had taken a number of mouthfuls before he looked up to where Jinnie was now screwing the kettle on to the fire. 'Leave that and come and eat your food,' he said.

When she was seated at the table, she did not immediately tackle her dinner, although she was feeling very hungry, but, looking at him, she asked, 'Is it all right?'

'I'll tell you by the time I finish. If I take a long time over it, it's no good. If I gollop it, it'll be fine.' He was smiling at her now; then once more he was eating, and rapidly.

He had come to the last mouthful on his plate when his head came up as he heard the neighing of a horse and the grinding of wheels outside. But he didn't rise from the table, nor did he take up the last bite on his plate. Instead, looking at Jinnie who had also stopped eating, he said, 'Carry on. Take no notice; just carry on eating.'

It was as if the door had been kicked open, and an undersized man entered the room. Jinnie put the name to him straightaway. His small stature was as noticeable as was the size of Max.

He looked towards the table, not at Jinnie, but at his son, and he growled, 'Huh! Huh. It's comin' to somethin'. I'm out of me house five minutes and me place at the table is taken, is it? Get the hell out of that seat!'

When Bruce didn't move the man seemed to take a jump from within the doorway to the side of the table, on which he thumped so hard that the crockery bounced as he cried, 'You heard me, paleface! You heard me!'

'Shut up!' The words were quietly spoken, but with emphasis.

'What did you say? Bugger me! we've come to somethin' else now. Not only me place is taken, but me mouth closed.'

'Sit down, Pug, or go into the barn and sleep it off.' It was the woman who had spoken, and quietly.

The man looked towards the bed and, his voice changing, but still loud, he said, 'Me missis at me now. Always a warm homecoming. No, "Sit down, Pug, and have a bite," but, "Get into the barn, that's your place."'

'There's a bite for you in the oven. The girl's kept it.'

'Oh, aye. Oh, aye, the girl.' Now he was looking across the table into Jinnie's startled face. And after a moment of surveying her, he said, 'The workhouse skivvy. The best they could turn up: not as thick as two spelks, and a shilling a week. Begod! a shilling a week for that.' His voice had risen into a bawl. 'If you're here to work, fetch me plate, and round here to the side of the table and not to the head. Oh no! no! Leave the house for five minutes and your place is taken.'

Jinnie rose hastily and went to the oven to fetch the plate of dinner. Pug Shaleman pulled a stool from beneath the table and had just seated himself on it when Jinnie, by his side, tentatively leaned forward to place the plate before him.

What happened next came upon them all so suddenly it even brought the invalid up in the bed, her legs hanging over the side, for as Pug Shaleman's hand grabbed Jinnie's buttock, she let out a high scream, before, as if remembering Miss Caplin's advice on how to deal with men who would handle her, her forearm came up in a hard swipe and caught him fully across the face, overbalancing his already rocking body. The next minute he was lying on his back, one leg in the air and supported against the fallen stool.

Bruce had already sprung to his feet, and now he was pulling Jinnie away from the vicinity of his father, who was endeavouring to haul himself up from the floor by grasping the table leg.

'Did you see that?' he was yelling to his wife.

'You must have done somethin' to deserve it.'

'Oh aye, I deserved it all right; I nipped her arse. She could have blinded me, swipin' me right across my eyes. By God!' He now turned to where Jinnie was standing near the door, and he yelled at her, 'You'll have more than your arse nipped before you leave here, me lass. Let me . . .' His voice was cut off, as were all of them silenced by the young girl's yelling at him defiantly, 'You were going to say, "Let me tell you". Well, let me tell *you*, mister, you'll not handle me, drunk or sober, 'cos I'll not stay here to be handled. I'm here to work, and that's what I'll do. I'll look after your missis, but you touch me again and it won't only be me arm you'll get.'

She could hardly herself believe what she was saying; but she knew that at the end of her tirade, her mind was reminding her that she had a knife in her dada's dinner

41

set. Yet she was also asking herself: what had come over her?

The man was standing utterly silent now, swaying slightly, but blinking at her as if he were seeing something he couldn't really believe was real; an oddity.

His wife had drawn her legs back under the cover and was lying down, her head turned away from the room, her face buried in the pillow. Whether she was laughing or crying, could not be determined, but the heavy quilt that covered her was in motion, more so than from her usual tortured breathing.

Taking hold of Jinnie's arm Bruce propelled her through the doorway, saying, 'There's work to do out here.' But when they were outside she moved away from him and stood biting on her thumb-nail as she looked across the open land and into the gathering twilight. Up to then, everything had been nice, because she liked her mistress and she liked the son, and she had promised herself that tomorrow morning the mistress wouldn't just have a flannel around her face, she'd get that tin dish on to a stool near the bed and she'd give her a wash down. In the workhouse there had been a time when she had had to assist in seeing to admissions, when they all had to be bathed and their heads inspected for dickies and nits. And she had planned that she would comb her mistress's hair and tie it up on top of her head. That's if she had any hairpins. She hoped she would have some, because she hadn't enough to keep her own hair up, the plaits were so heavy. She had considered asking her mistress if she could wear her plaits hanging down. But all these plans would be for nothing now because of that awful little man in the house. She already knew that she disliked him; she had known even before she had struck out at him. And he was lying when he said he had nipped her . . . backside.

He had grabbed a whole handful of it, and so hard she had nearly capsized herself before toppling him.

'Look, forget about it.' Bruce broke into her thoughts. 'You'll find he's a different man in the morning. He always plays the big fellow when he's drunk and carrying more than usual. Anyway, come along and help me clear the cart.'

The cart was similar to the one at the house farm, the one Max had driven. As for the horse, it looked much older than the animal the workhouse owned.

He was pointing things out now. 'The taties, they go in the barn, you know. That sack's flour; you keep that in the scullery; it's cooler there. Oh' – he pulled a piece of hessian towards him – 'he's managed to get some yeast. It's gone a bit dry, but it'll be all right tomorrow. And there'll be tea and sugar in that parcel there. Here! You take them; and the yeast and the flour. I'll see to the rest,' and he indicated some bales of hay and some further sacks. Then he turned towards her and in a low voice he said, 'Take it in the side door, and then get up to bed. 'Tis early, I know, but you've had a long day.'

'What . . . what about the dishes?'

'I'll see to the dishes; and if I don't, they'll still be there in the morning for you. And, I promise you, things will be much quieter tomorrow.'

She made no reply.

As he piled the things into her arms, she asked tentatively, 'Can . . . can anyone get into me?'

'No; and nobody would want to. Anyway, put the bolt in the door leading out here, then anybody who wants to get . . . at you, would have to come through the kitchen, wouldn't they? And, I can assure you right now, I have no intention of . . . getting at you, even going as far as to nip your backside. Does that surprise you?'

43

Yes, it did, really. She peered at him through the fading light. He was different. That little man back there and that sickly woman were his parents, but he was like neither of them; somehow he was different. She couldn't say he was a gentleman, not like those in the town who wore collars and ties and had walking sticks and high hats, or the workhouse guardians who were supposed to be gentlemen. But as Miss Caplin had once said, gentlemen is as gentlemen does. No, this man was certainly not any kind of a gentleman; but he was different. And what was more surprising, she felt she could believe what he said . . . whatever he said, which, in a way, was more surprising still when she had known him only a matter of hours.

'Good night, Jinnie. Sleep well.'

'Good night, mister.'

Before she had reached the scullery door he was at her side again, saying softly, 'There's a candle in a stick in the cupboard to the side of the trough. Light it to see your way up. But, for God's sake, put it out as soon as you get your things off. Whatever you do, don't go to sleep with it on. We nearly had one disaster that way not long ago. You understand?'

'Yes. Yes. I'll put it out as soon as possible.'

'Good. Good.'

After dropping the parcels on to the table, she found the tin candle-stick and some matches.

The glow from the tallow candle illuminated the rough working room and gave to it a homely touch; it could do nothing for the staircase but emphasise the fact that there was no rail at the open side. When she had taken her bundle up earlier on to change her clothes, it had been something of an achievement, both the mounting of the steps and the changing, for it was impossible to stand up under the roof unless you bent your back double.

44

She had found it easier to kneel. The roof space was as wide as the room below but much longer and she guessed that it must also cover one of those outhouses at the back. Her bed was a straw-filled tick, and the pillow was the same. And when she lay down on it she thought back to the workhouse and the flock-filled pillows which were a luxury compared with this one, for the straw here and there was pricking her face, as was the straw from the tick piercing even her calico nightdress. And she wondered why, until she realised the straw had been chopped into chaff, presumably to make it more comfortable for sleeping. But she wasn't finding it so.

She had been staring into the deep blackness of the roof space when, drugged with tiredness and almost on the point of sleep, she heard her mistress's voice almost yelling in her ear, as it were. During the few hours she had been in this house she had imagined that her mistress was not strong enough to shout; but she was shouting all right now. She had, earlier, been aware of a murmur of voices rising and falling; but now, quite clearly the words came, 'You'll . . . you'll not get in this bed tonight, Pug Shaleman. I've told you till I'm sick and tired, I suffer you when you're sober, and I repeat, suffer you. But I've warned you time and again not to come near me when you've got a skinful and act like a frustrated ram. I haven't much strength left, but I warn you, you attempt to lay your hands on me this night and I'll gather enough in me to tear you to shreds. So, you have your choice, as usual: it's the mat in front of the fire or the barn.'

She was sitting up on the tick now, her head almost touching the rafters, and once more she was biting on her thumb. Her mind was telling her that all this was to do with what Miss Caplin had been talking to her about. It wasn't absolutely clear, but in some way

45

2

The next morning she was woken, not by the sound of the cock, for it must have been crowing for some time, but by the grating sound of the pump being used. At the far end of the roof, streaks of light showed that it was daylight. And now, bending forward, she leant over the hatch and looked down into the scullery, there to see Bruce, his body naked to the waist, sluicing his head and shoulders under the pump. For a moment she watched his one hand blindly pumping, the other rubbing at his thick fair hair. When he straightened up she quickly withdrew her head, only to make contact with a beam, which made her eyes water. Then she was kneeling on the pallet, pulling off her nightdress and scrambling into her cold shift and the rest of her clothes, which were equally chilled, whilst telling herself that tonight she'd pack her underclothes all round her. She wondered why she hadn't thought of it before.

She waited until he had left the scullery before she descended the stairs, keeping tight against the wall as she did so. Then she, too, was sluicing herself under the pump, though not her head.

She had no real idea of the time, and wondered whether she might have slept in and felt she must ask at what time she had to rise in the morning.

She opened the door into the kitchen very quietly and, to her surprise, saw the table laid out roughly for breakfast, with Bruce standing at the fire and staring at

47

the pot that was bubbling on the hob. He turned and smiled at her, saying, 'Sleep well?'

'Yes. Yes, thank you.'

'Good. Porridge'll be ready in a minute.'

She looked towards the bed. There was a stool close to the side of it and on it was the big tin dish from the scullery which, yesterday, she had used for washing up the dishes. The woman was bending over and washing her arms up to her elbows, and she looked towards Jinnie as she picked up a towel from the coverlet to dry herself, and she asked, 'Had a good night, lass?'

'Yes, thank you, missis. But I don't know what time I should get up.'

'Oh, a little afore this, but not all that much. It's half-six now. Anyway, sit down and have your porridge and eat your fill because that's all you'll get till noon, except for a drink. And I'll tell you now, sometimes we have our main meal in the middle of the day. But other times not until the night. It all depends on the work that's got to be done. You understand?'

'Yes. Yes, missis, and . . . and I'll get up earlier tomorrow.'

Bruce turned from the fire, saying, 'You haven't got a clock. Well, I'll be your clock: I'll hammer on the bit of ceiling below you. That should make you jump. The only thing is, don't jump too quickly and come down the steps in your shift.'

When he laughed and her mistress joined in, she was forced to smile, but was slightly surprised. She hadn't expected him to say a thing like that; it didn't seem the kind of remark he would make. And yet, what did she know of him? Again she had to tell herself, this time yesterday morning she hadn't known he was alive, nor his mother, nor anyone else in this strange house, which wasn't like a house at all when she came to think of it.

'Sit down. Sit down.' He was pointing to the table. 'And don't look so bewildered. The sun's shining, it's warm and there's no wind. And although it isn't a good day for running, it's a good day for the ordinary human being.'

'Oh, Bruce' – this came from his mother – 'you and your running.'

'D'you like to run?'

Jinnie shook her head before she said, 'I've never run, well, not really; just when somebody's shouted for me.'

'Oh, that isn't running, that's obedience. Some afternoon when things are slack and there's nothing to do, you want to lift up your petticoats and take to your heels and run across the hills. Try the one behind the house first.' His head was bobbing backwards now. Then quickly he said, 'Oh no, you'd better not, for you were out of puff coming up the little inclines, weren't you? And that was just walking at a steady pace. You'll have to break yourself in. Try running back to where you stood and said you thought the view was bonny.'

'Tollet's Ridge?'

He looked towards the bed now as he nodded, saying, 'Yes, Ma. Tollet's Ridge.'

The woman's voice sounded faint now, because she was once more leaning back among her pillows. But the words that came to Jinnie's ears had a sad note, for she was saying, 'The first time I stood on top of the Ridge. Oh yes' – she nodded her head – 'the first time I stood on top of the Ridge. But as they say there's a first time for everything and an end to a beginning.' Her next words were quiet: 'Take a bowlful along for him, will you, lad?'

There was no answer to this at first, then Bruce said, 'I will on my way out. Doubt if he'll be awake yet. Anyway, with the head he will have on him this morning, he'll be wishing for more than porridge.'

A few minutes later she had finished her breakfast, an outsize bowl of porridge which tasted slightly salty, but which had the advantage of being stiff enough to hold to the spoon, not like the skilly that would run off it, back in the workhouse. What was more, it had been covered with a good dollop of milk.

Bruce, she saw, was ready to go. He had on his old working coat and a pair of breeches, different from the ones he wore yesterday, for these looked to be made of strong corduroy and were laced at the sides. They reached below his knees and their ends met the top of a pair of high, strong boots. He looked, as she put it to herself, ready for tramping those hills.

His mother was saying to him, 'Are you bringing any down?' And he replied, 'Oh, no, not if the weather stays like this. The grass is lush in parts up there. But that's the trouble, the more lush patches they find the further afield they go, and I know I'll have to go well beyond the boundary of Philip's farm today. I hope they haven't strayed into the woodlands of the big house.'

'Oh, they would never get that far.'

'Have you forgotten last year, Ma, and Mr Gregory coming over those hills as quick as a bullet shot from a gun?'

'Oh, yes. Yes, I forgot.' Then she said, 'Master Richard should soon be home now from his holiday. He went the beginning of June, didn't he?'

'Yes, he did. But once Miss May and him get abroad in France, they forget to come back.'

'It's the first time they've gone away so early. D'you miss him running with you?'

'Yes. Yes, I suppose so. It's good to have companionship. But running is running, after all, and you run for running's sake. Anyway, I must run now, Ma, if I'm to see how they're faring.'

There was a crackle in her laughter, and as he reached the door, she said, 'Have you got a good pack with you? It'll be cold up there, you know, no matter what it is down here.'

'Shoulder of lamb and three pig's feet,' he said, laughing. Then he beckoned to Jinnie from the door of the scullery and, there, he said quickly, 'If you hear her groan, she'll be having a pain. In the left-hand side of the chest of drawers you'll find a bottle of pills. Give her one; then take her a mug of hot water. It helps to melt the tablet quickly. Understand?'

'Yes. Yes. Is . . . is she often bad?'

'You never know; now and then. She keeps a lot to herself. But listen out for that moan. Oh,' he jerked his chin; 'you'll hear it all right. Now I don't know what time I'll be back; but it'll be late evening. Anyway, do what you can inside. Make some bread and that, my dad'll be seeing to the outside. And take that look off your face; there's nothin' goin' to happen to you. You'll find him different altogether this mornin'. Not very polite, perhaps, but you needn't be afraid of any repeat of last night. Understand?'

'Yes.'

'So long.'

'So long.' . . .

At about ten o'clock she was making her way to the hen run when, for the first time that day, she encountered the man who was her master. He seemed to be even smaller than he had appeared to be last night. And what she noticed right away, and hadn't taken in before, was that he limped. The thought came to her that likely this was the reason he did not go out with his son to see to the sheep. She waited until he was half-way up a short ladder before she said, 'Mister, missis says I've got to try my hand at a bacon and egg pie, and I have no eggs.'

'Well, you know where to find them, don't you?'

She was standing near the side of the ladder, and for a moment he looked down into her face, and she up into his. And she knew now why his wife had called him Pug, for his nose was definitely flat. Yet the rest of his face could have been pleasant, she decided, if his eyes hadn't been bleary. She was thinking of the event of last night when she knocked him on to his back with her forearm, and she was wondering if he too was recalling it. And she would have been surprised to know that he could indeed recall the whole event, for the amazement he felt had somewhat sobered him. Yet, looking at her now, he couldn't imagine she had the strength to knock him over.

'Missis says there's tea on the hob.'

When he didn't answer but went to step up on to another rung, she said, 'Could I bring you a can out?' And at this he turned on her sharply, saying, 'No you won't bring me a can out; if I want tea, I know where to get it.'

She stepped back from the ladder, her chin jerking now, then made her way towards the hen crees. She collected nine eggs from the boxes and when she returned to the kitchen, she said to her mistress, 'There were only nine. Some of the hens looked to me as if they are moulting. I used to feed the chickens at one time, in the house, and they never laid when they were moulting.'

'Nine?' Rose Shaleman smiled and repeated, 'Nine? If you had been there a little earlier you might have found thirteen, or even fourteen. Raw eggs straight from the shell go a long way towards relieving a headache, especially after the sort of load he had on last night.'

It seemed natural to Jinnie that her mistress should refer to her husband as 'he'.

The rest of the morning passed pleasantly, with questions and answers, such as, how much pig's fat you should put in the flour to make the pastry? And was it to be thick or thin on the bottom plate?

Having covered three large plates with her pastry, she was then instructed to cut from the ham twelve large thin slices, and to divide them with the eggs, among the three plates, and to cover each with pastry.

As the oven would hold only two plates at any one time, the third had to wait its turn.

Following this, her mistress guided her through the making of bread . . . a different way altogether from that which the lady of the town had shown her.

It was three o'clock in the afternoon before she took the last loaf and a number of bread buns out of the oven, and as she stood looking at the array of her efforts on the table, she smiled widely, and her smile was picked up by the woman in the bed. 'Well done, lass,' she said; 'I couldn't have done better meself. Now do something else for me. Split open three of those bread buns and lather them with fat. Then cut a generous shive from one of your plates and put it on a platter and brew up a can of tea and take the lot out to himself. Will you do that?'

'Yes, missis. Yes.'

Although she had quickly agreed to the suggestion, she felt more than a little nervous as, the can in one hand and a large plate covered by a piece of clean white linen in the other, she approached the man who was now in the barn. And the sight of him brought a feeling of pity to her. He was sitting on a box and was sewing the side of a sack with string, using a large curved needle.

Again they were looking at each other face to face, for now, seated, his head was almost on a level with hers.

'Missis says, will you kindly taste these?' Jinnie said.

He put out a hand and raised the cloth; then, dropping the cloth and picking up the can, he surprised her by saying, 'You gonna stay?'

There was a long pause before she answered, 'If I can.'

'You get on all right with the missis?'

'Oh yes. Yes. Yes, we get on all right.'

Again he was staring into her face. Now he asked, 'How old are you, really?'

'Fourteen, coming up fifteen in three weeks' time; July twenty-first.'

'You don't look it; not fourteen.'

He again took the cloth off the plate and this time handed it to her. Then picking up the slice of bacon and egg pie, he bit into it. And she stood and watched him, waiting for a word of approval on her achievement. But what he said was, 'Come winter, it won't be as easy as now. Think on that. Everything's plummy in this weather, but come winter it'll change and you'll feel it an' all.' Again, he bit into the pie, and as she went to turn away, she said, 'Well, I hope I'm here to feel it, mister. Yes, yes, I do.' And on this she walked from the barn.

She still felt sorry for him, but she didn't know why. And he hadn't said if he liked the pie or not. But then he wasn't Bruce, so he wouldn't say, would he? She realised she was looking forward to Bruce's return and to hearing his opinion of her day's work.

But before Bruce came home they had another visitor.

As she rounded the end of the building she was brought to a stop by the sight of a man dismounting from a large horse standing opposite the cottage door. She remained still while she watched him look around.

On seeing her, he said, 'Oh . . . Good-afternoon. Is . . . Is Bruce anywhere about?'

She went quickly forward now, saying, 'He's . . . he's gone to see to the sheep, sir. But his father's in the stable,' and she thumbed over her right shoulder; then she added, 'But his mother's in the kitchen. She's . . . well, she's not . . .'

'Yes, I know.'

She now hurried forward and pushed open the cottage door then stepped aside to allow him to enter. But he came no further than the step, and from there he said, 'Good afternoon, Mrs Shaleman.'

'Oh, good afternoon to you, Master Richard. You're back then.'

'Yes, I'm back.'

'Have you enjoyed your holiday?'

'Indeed, yes. It was a lovely time.'

'Bruce'll be glad to know you're back, sir. He'll be up beyond the peak today.'

'Oh, well, I'll ride that way. How are you feeling?'

'Oh, not too bad, sir, not too bad.'

He paused for some seconds before his eyes seemed to flicker about the room, and then he asked, 'Would you like some fruit sent up?'

'Oh, it's very kind of you, sir, but that would be putting The House to a lot of trouble.'

'No trouble at all. From what I could see in the gardens yesterday, much of the soft fruit is going bad for want of picking. Well, goodbye, Mrs Shaleman. If I shouldn't happen to come across Bruce, tell him I called and I'm ready for a run, will you?'

'Oh, sir, surely you wouldn't want to be running in weather like this, unless you really had to.'

'There's always the dawn, Mrs Shaleman. There's no sensation like running in the dawn, as your son only too well knows. Goodbye now. I'll be seeing you again.'

'Goodbye, Master Richard. Goodbye, sir.'

As he stepped into the road and walked towards his horse, Jinnie, closing the door behind her, stood looking after him. She had never seen anyone so thin. Bruce was thin, but this young man was thinner still. He had a lovely skin. His face was deeply tanned and the colour merged with his eyes, which were a darker brown still. She was thinking that his liking for running must have taken all the fat off his bones, when he turned about and said, 'You're new here?'

'Yes, mister . . . sir.'

He was about to put his foot into the stirrup when he hesitated and, as if the thought had just struck him, asked, 'You are a relation?'

'Oh, no, sir.' She shook her head quickly. 'No, not me. I'm no relation, I'm . . .' She could not say, I'm from the house. It was too deprecating, too lowering, as she put it; you were always known as a pauper if you came from the house. She'd heard that often enough, and she was determined that she wasn't ever going to be a pauper, because that meant not having enough money to look after yourself and keep away from the house. And wasn't that another funny thing? It must have been this gentleman's home to which the missis was referring when she mentioned The House. She hadn't said Manor House or Hall, just The House.

He had mounted his horse before he spoke again, and then it was a statement. 'You are engaged here to work, then?'

'Yes, sir, to work, cook, like, and clean and look after Mrs Shaleman.'

It looked as if he were about to shake his head, but he smiled at her and said, 'Well, see that you work hard;' then he pressed his heel into the horse's flank and it moved off. And she moved from the door to stand in the middle of the rough stone path, watching him until he disappeared round the curve of a hill, her thoughts tumbling over each other. Fancy him coming to look up Mr Bruce! As nice as Mr Bruce was, she had told herself before that he was no gentleman, not in that sense. But the rider just gone, he was a gentleman all right. Yet he was so thin. It was a good job he wasn't over-tall, else he would look like a lamp post. Fancy him actually calling here, though, for it was a poor enough place, inside and out. Everything in that room was made of wood, one way or another, except for the iron stove, of course. And it must be some long time since the rough brick walls had been lime-washed. As for the outside, as far as she could see nothing could be done to alter its appearance as something little more than a hovel set in a plain of rugged, sparse grassland. Why any man should want to build on a piece of land like this, she could not understand. Shale they called it. And that's where his family got its name from, she supposed: Shaleman. Miss Caplin once said that all names sprang from places and things.

'Jinnie.'

She turned quickly about and opened the kitchen door and rushed in, saying, 'Yes, missis? Yes, missis?'

'Why were you standing there like a stook? I could see you through the window. Were you so surprised at the gentry deigning to call on the likes of us?'

'No, missis. No. Only, he is so thin.'

'Thin?'

'Yes; that's what struck me about him; he is very thin.' She laughed softly now. 'It made me think. In the Bible it says that a rich man hasn't any chance of getting into heaven, no more than a camel getting through the eye of a needle.'

'Oh, you tell that one to Bruce and he'll explain to you all about that eye of a needle. They were, I think, referring to the eye of a farm needle that pins down the cover on the huge haystacks. It was the size of a man himself.'

'Really? No funnin'?'

'No funnin', really.'

The woman in the bed was laughing now, but the sound she was making ceased suddenly and her face became straight. 'Come here, lass,' she said holding out her hand.

When Jinnie stood by the bedside the woman took her hand and, looking into her face, said, 'Tell me truly, was it only yesterday you came into this house?'

Jinnie was smiling softly now as she answered, 'Yes, missis, it was only yesterday. But to me I seem to have been here a long time.'

'Yes, lass, yes, a long time, because I'll tell you something: you brought something to it. I don't know what it is, but you brought something to it.'

'Well, missis, it won't be bad, 'cos I never wish anyone bad.' Her head drooped now. 'Oh yes, I did,' she now confessed, 'and I still do in a way.'

'Who d'you wish bad on, lass?'

The voice was a murmur as she said, 'Me last mistress.'

The hand was dropped, and now the fingers came under her chin and jerked her head upwards and Rose Shaleman asked in surprise, 'You hated your last mistress? What for?'

''Cos . . . 'cos she lied about her man. Her man tried to handle me and I went at him like . . . like I did last night.' The head was inclined to droop again but the fingers kept it up. 'But she swore, the mistress, and said it was me who made what she called advances to her husband when he was having a nap. She even came to the house,' and as if to differentiate between

58

the two houses she added, 'the workhouse, and told the matron and the only people who didn't believe her were Miss Caplin and Max.'

'Max?'

'Yes, he's the man who brought me on the cart. He's a good man. Very, very big. He's always been on my side. He looked after me when he could.'

'Is he an old man?'

'Oh no, no. I don't know. He's aged, I should think, about thirty.'

Aged . . . about thirty. The woman was smiling now, saying, 'Well, lass, I'm going to tell you something. Here's another one that believes you. Did you leave a mark on him? Because you nearly left a mark on my man last night.'

'Yes, I did. I dug my fingers in his neck, because he just had a night-shirt on. But then he wore high stiff collars during the day.'

Rose Shaleman lay back on her pillows now, and again the eiderdown was moving up and down quickly as she said, 'Well, lass, the next one that lays a hand on you in that way . . . the wrong way, you know, you leave the mark where it can be seen. Eh?'

'Yes, I will, missis, I will.' The laughter now trailed off from her voice as she muttered, 'I don't like to be touched, I mean, handled. Max never handled me. I . . . I never knew you could be handled until I went to that place.'

The woman was nodding her head now, and her face was solemn as she said, 'Well, prepare yourself, lass, 'cos I can promise you this; you'll be handled a lot in your lifetime whether you like it or not. I think you've got something about you that'll make men want to handle you in one way or another. But let's pray that the majority of the handling will come in a good way, eh?'

Jinnie was some time in agreeing with this and then, with a puzzled expression on her face, she said, 'Aye, missis. Aye.'

'Well now—' changing the conversation abruptly, Mrs Shaleman said, 'there'll be somebody glad to know Mister Richard's back. And that'll be our Bruce. He's missed him; he always does.'

'Is *he* the one he goes running with?' There was surprise in Jinnie's tone, and some pride in her mistress's as she answered, 'Go running with him? Yes, he does, and has done for many a year, ever since he got back on his legs. Oh—' And now the woman closed her eyes and jerked her head before she explained, 'Well, you see, it was like this. I know it must seem strange to you, a fella like our Bruce, and mind' – the finger was digging at her now – 'there's not a better or straighter fella than my son. Yet, I'm sensible enough to know there's gulfs all over the world. There's a lot of them in this neck of the woods, and they separate people. And it's surprised more than you that my lad goes running with the son of The House. But they owe my lad more than they can pay. You see, it should happen that the young lad, home from his boarding school, was lost one night. The horse goes home, but there's no Master Richard on it. They searched until they were forced to stop and to wait for daylight. But not so my Bruce; he went on because there's nobody knows holes and corners like he does, and he knows them as well in the dark as in the light. Once, when he was four years old he was lost in the hills for hours before he came toddling in and, as cool as you like, said he was hungry. Anyway, to cut a long story much shorter, as far as I can gather Master Richard must have ridden well up before being thrown by his horse, and this was into a gully, a deceiving gully full of nooks and crannies. And it was here my Bruce found him on the

60

freezing ground. Well, Bet wasn't with Bruce this time; that was Flossie's mother; she had worn her legs off with running all day and was lying up, although I bet she was wide awake, as she always was for him till the day she died. Anyway, what did he do? As he said himself, he hugged Master Richard to try to make him melt and to bring him round, and then he pulled him up and on to his back and, crawling and slithering and stumbling in the dark, he brought him home. If he hadn't known the path so well they both would have died. When they reached the courtyard he collapsed an' all, and he lay in The House for four days before we could bring him back here. His hands and knees had been torn, but I am telling you he was very lucky to get off with his life that time; but Master Richard, he developed rheumatic fever and he was in bed for nearly a year.'

'Nearly a year?'

'Yes, lass, nearly a year; and they thought he would never walk again. His legs were like spindles and his body not much thicker, but our Bruce told him he'd soon be running. You see, the young lad had demanded to see—' here she paused before, her tone full of bitterness, she went on, 'Pug Shaleman's son. You see, Pug weren't thought much of in those days, 'cos this place was a pigsty all right, then. Pug's people were bone lazy, both of them, and I was brought into this house because I had nowhere else to go.' She now turned her face fully on Jinnie and said, 'I got drunk one day at the fair, like the rest. When I was let out for my full day off, half-year time, I always went mad. I'd worked in the kitchen ʃm when I was eight in that very house, the very house in which my son was later to be openly welcomed by their son, but at that time, lass, I was considered something lower than you'd find under a stone. Oh yes, lower than that. On that fair day, I was just on sixteen and I met one Pug Shaleman, and when I came to my senses some months later and found myself going to have a bairn, me own people from near Bardon Mill pointed the way, and not with a finger but with me dad's boot, and its direction was to the workhouse. But there was Pug waiting, 'cos he had guessed what would happen; and him the size he was and not presentable in many ways, he saw that my predicament was going to stand him in good stead: he'd have a wife and someone who would skivvy for him and his people. And that's how it happened; that's how I came into this pigsty. And it must look like that to you now, but imagine what it looked like to me in those days, almost twenty-seven years ago.' She paused and pressed her head back into the pillow, and Jinnie stood staring at her.

She could find nothing to say; it was such a strange story. Everybody's life had a story, that's what Miss Caplin had said, but this was a strange, sad story, and she felt further saddened when her mistress spoke again, saying, 'My elder son Hal is twenty-six. He's like his father in many ways, but not in looks and size, and I tell you, girl, before you meet him, you won't like him. He's a rough character. He's a heavy drinker and woman chaser. I say this to put you on your guard; and yet I have no fear for you in that direction.' She turned her head on the pillow now and smiled at Jinnie as she added, 'No; no fear for you, for I can see you dying before you'd let the wrong man lay hands on you.'

Jinnie felt a great heat sweep over her, like a sweat she used to experience during a day of stone-flagged corridor scrubbing back in the workhouse. Then her own words surprised her when she said, 'Bruce is not like that, missis; he's different . . . Why? How?'

'You ask why, girl . . . you ask how . . .' and Rose Shaleman looked away again from Jinnie, saying, 'Yes, he is different, and thank God for it. Oh yes, thank God for it. I've got little to thank God for in this life but I do for my Bruce, and you know why I called him Bruce?' She turned her head again to look at Jinnie, whose own head was shaking.

'Because I'd once heard a parson preaching. You see, we were taken to church every Sunday on the wagon, so I learned something about the Bible. Anyway, I don't suppose this fella belonged to the Bible, but they called him Bruce. He was a king, I think, and was running away from his enemies and he had little chance of escaping. But then he saw a spider and as he watched it, twice it failed to stick its silken thread to the wall, but off it went for a third time, and this time the thread stuck. I think that's where the saying comes from: if at first you don't succeed, try, try, try again. Have you heard that one?'

'No, missis.'

'Oh well, that's what Cook used to say in the kitchen down there when she would take the rolling-pin and bring it across my knuckles for not being able to swivel a big pie dish on one hand and trim the pastry edges with a knife on the other. I always made a mess of it, and she always made a mess of me afterwards. I suppose I wasn't such a quick learner as you are, girl. You're a very quick learner. You know that?'

'Thank you, missis.'

'Well now, don't you think we've gossiped enough for one day? The mister will come in for his meal all right tonight, so we'll have it no later than seven. Bruce's will keep, as it's a stew, and dumplings don't rot. But let me tell you first that tomorrow you must get your hand into real work and get down to the washing. It's always a heavy day, the washing here, but you might be lucky; the weather might hold and a wind might come up. That's what I used to pray for every week; the sun and the wind together, to bring the clothes-line alive.'

The sun and the wind to bring the clothes-line alive. A strange saying, thought Jinnie; but nice.

She was about to turn away when a thought struck her, and she gave voice to it by asking, 'Does the gentleman still run with Mister Bruce?'

'Oh yes, whenever he's home. They've run together for years; but . . .' and now she turned her head completely away and looked towards the rough wall to the right side of her, and muttered, 'People change; they forget what they owe you. The lad doesn't, I'm sure. He's one of them that doesn't see the gulf as his people do. That's why the baskets haven't come regular since he went away on his holidays. No. You'll see, they'll start again. Oh yes, they'll start again.'

She didn't go on to explain about the baskets, so Jinnie, thinking ahead as she was wont to do, went into the scullery and sorted out the heap of dirty washing that spoke to her of immense neglect and proffered an explanation for the chest of drawers being practically empty. She sorted the clothing into heaps: rough sheets and towels; an assortment of men's shirts and small clothes; and the woman's undergarments, badly stained and just as rough. And when the sorting was finished she stood looking down at the piles of washing and sighed as she, too, hoped for sun and wind on the morrow. Every article here was like its surroundings, rough and coarse. If it hadn't already been discoloured or stiff when it was bought, it had gained this characteristic with wear and tear over the years.

No; there was no refinement here.

Her mind sprang back to the workhouse. In comparison, in a way, that place had been sort of genteel, for there had always been the voice and mannerisms of Miss Caplin that spoke of an air of refinement, of another world from that in which she worked; that which emanated from her made everything in her vicinity appear pleasant. And then there was Max.

Could she use the word 'refinement' when thinking of Max? She had questioned the word 'gentleman' in connection with him some time back, yet now, in some way, she knew he was a gentleman; and yes, there was something different about him. He was big and ugly and gangly, yet at the same time these three things merged into love and kindness, and surely love and kindness should be coupled with refinement. Oh, she wished she had someone to talk to and to explain things to her.

Suddenly she pulled open the door leading from the scullery to outside, and stood looking up into the sky; and there came over her a longing to see Miss Caplin and Max again. She could hear herself talking to them and telling them all about the strangeness, the mixture, and the lowliness of this place. Yet this lowliness had been touched by the presence of the gentry.

3

She had been here for ten days; yet it could have been ten weeks, ten months, even ten years, for the pattern of the evenings had stayed the same. At times she couldn't recall how she had spent the evenings in the workhouse. Except for that particular evening when the sow had littered, here the routine was unvaried: the last meal of the day was usually around seven o'clock. If Bruce was late getting back from the hills, she kept his meal warm in the oven, but should he sit down with his father and her, after they had eaten, the table would be cleared and she would wash the crocks. Afterwards she would clean the oilcloth with a damp rag, then dry it off; the mister would then go to the chest of drawers, take out a pack of cards and proceed to spread half of them in decreasing rows on the table. Bruce had told her it was a game that required patience and that was why it was called Patience, but that there were many variations of it. Yet his father had always played this particular form. Some evenings he would sit for two hours and play his cards but not open his mouth, the while his wife and son would carry on a desultory conversation about the happenings of the day or the titbits he had picked up from Peter Locke the drover. She herself never attempted to join in the conversation. She would sit by the fire, but was never idle. There were sheets to patch and stockings to darn. She was quite a good sewer but not so proficient at darning, and the stockings she found she was expected to darn had soles on them almost as tough as leather.

But this particular evening the routine changed. In fact, the whole day had been different. It had started at breakfast time when Bruce said to his father, 'You'll have to see to those lower fields, I can't be in three places at once, and until those walls are mended on the high bank there's no way of stopping the sheep straying, and you know that, and you know where they'll stray to.'

At this his father had replied, 'Well, you would have them marked, wouldn't you?' and Bruce had answered, 'Aye, yes; and that works both ways. I'd rather be ordered to come and retrieve our scum from The House grounds than have Stevens swear black was white that they were his: Look there! with his mark on them. Well, it's our mark that's on them. And by the way, when you next see Arthur Stead you'd better see what he wants for that young collie; Flossie's getting on; she's not as fast as she was.'

'You're telling your granny how to suck eggs.'

'I wouldn't have to tell you how to suck eggs if there wasn't such a thing as market day and you were wanting to show off,' and at this Bruce had turned and stalked out.

But this evening all was peaceful in the kitchen. The mistress was sitting up in bed looking at the illustrations in an old magazine that Bruce had brought in. It was the kind of magazine that he would never have bought and she guessed its source. She looked a different woman to the one Jinnie had first seen lying in that bed: now she was wearing a clean nightie, her hair had been brushed and combed, and what is more, only that morning Jinnie had washed her down, after having explained to her that she used to help bath the newcomers into the workhouse, in some cases introducing their bodies to water for the first time. Moreover, she had found a patchwork quilt in the corner of the bedroom loft above the kitchen, and had washed this and replaced the soiled one on the wall bed.

The silence that had settled on the room for some minutes was broken by Pug Shaleman saying, as if to no-one in particular, 'I'd prepare for a bedmate if I was you the night, well, if not the night, soon then.'

It was almost thirty seconds before his son said, 'How did you come by that?'

'Oh, from Peter Locke. He was passing up the stile road and he hailed me in the top field. He'd just come back from Newcastle; been on the road the last couple of days. Happened to mention *The Admiral* was due in last night, in fact he said it was just stuck outside Shields waiting for the high tide. There's still sandbanks there after all that dredging. I'll go down to Shields and have a look round one of these days. Yes . . . yes, I will.' And he picked a card up from one end of the pile on the table and placed it at the other end.

'What time did you see Peter?'

'What?' Pug Shaleman raised his head with a jerk as if he hadn't heard what his son had said, and repeated, 'What?'

Bruce's reply was slow-worded: 'I asked you what time you saw Peter.'

'Oh. Oh, well, it was early on, nineish, I should say. Yes, that's what I said, nineish.'

Bruce was on his feet now and standing at the other side of the table and looking down on his father's bent head: 'You never thought, I suppose, of getting word to Hal at the mine?' he said.

'Why should I think about getting word to Hal at the mine?'

Jinnie almost jumped in her chair at the sound of

Bruce's voice. It vibrated round the room in something between a shout and a scream as he yelled, 'Because you bloody well might have stopped your son from being murdered. Sammy Valasquey would be quite capable of it if he found him in the house; and God knows what would happen if he found them together.'

'My God! Listen to who's talking.' The small man had pushed back the chair now and was standing supporting himself by his two clenched fists pressing on the table. 'You'd think, to hear you, you were bosom pals, best friends, when you hate the bloody sight of him; and what he thinks about you would get another man hung. Yet you go for me for not getting word to him to look out for his whore's man popping in. But let me tell you that Valasquey will get him one day, in the daylight or dark, and for my part, I hope he does. He's spent more money on his whoring than would have kept the wolf from this door many a time. He only comes here when there's not a bed open to him in one village or the other, or when things get too hot for him, and a lot of the beds will have cooled to him while Valasquey's been away.'

'He's always tipped up at the weekends he's come back,' Bruce reminded his father. 'And don't forget there were years before he went rowdy that he tipped up his wages every week to Ma, there, and, if you remember, you slept it off more often in the barn in those days. Anyway, when he turns up why don't you tell him to get the hell out of it, to go and find lodgings somewhere, or to pick up with one of his other bed-warmers? There are a few widows about down there who'd welcome him with open arms, I know that, so why does he come back here? You wouldn't know, would you? But I'll tell you why he comes back, because you, who's never given a thought to anybody in your life but yourself, happen to be his father, and that woman on the bed from which she's hardly been able to move for the past three years, is his mother, and me, as much as he hates the sight of me, I happen to be his brother, and this mean, uncomfortable stone spot, stuck out here in the wilds, is what is called his home, and it's the word "home" that has the pull. Well, that's my version of why he comes back here; but you, until the day you die, will never understand a word of what I'm saying – you never have – because if you dislike anybody more than you do him, it's me. But let me tell you, I only stay here because of her,' and he stabbed his finger towards the bed. 'If she wasn't here you could go to hell, or to where that child has recently come from, the workhouse, because you've never in your life worked to keep yourself and you never will.'

'You finished?' The small man was again on his feet, and his voice was ominously quiet now as he said, 'I'll remember all you've said, lad, and I won't forget this night. Oh aye, I'll remember this night; and there'll come another night when I'll tell *you* something.' He now turned and looked towards the bed and said, 'It'll keep.' And with this, he went slowly from the room, leaving Bruce with his head bent deeply on his chest and his hands gripping the back of a chair.

'You shouldn't have said all that, lad.' His mother's voice was just above a whisper. 'He knows what he is without it being rammed home.'

At this Bruce swung round to her and hissed, 'What if Valasquey had found him there? There would've been murder done, and he could've prevented it. He's walked the three miles to the mine many a time before when looking to crib a sub, the times when he was craving for a drink. He could've got to him today but he wants him bashed up, as he does me too. He can't do it himself but he'd enjoy seeing somebody else having a go.'

'Life must be galling for him.'

'Ma, after what he's put you through all the years I can look back upon, it amazes me that you can lie there and take his part.'

'I'm not taking his part, lad, I never have. I've got me own thoughts about him, and only God knows what they are, and I hope I may be forgiven for them some day, but that doesn't stop me from understanding how he feels.' Her voice rose now as she added, 'Just look at you both. You are as different from him as chalk from cheese in all ways. Yes, yes; and thank God for that,' she now muttered. Then nodding her head, she went on, 'And look at Hal, the size of him, the breadth of him, he hates Hal more than he hates you. And that's strange. Oh yes, that's strange. It's because he knows that Hal is like himself inside, so they know each other for what they are.'

'And me?' The question was asked quietly, and after a moment she answered it: 'You're a different kettle of fish.'

He made a strange rasping sound in his throat before he said, 'Yes, I thought I might be.' Then almost startling the wits out of Jinnie, he turned and yelled at her, 'What are you standing there gaping for?'

As if she had been lifted bodily from the room, Jinnie found herself standing in the dark scullery, her back against the door, gasping as if she had actually been flung out of the kitchen.

There must be a nasty streak in Bruce, too; look how he had gone for his father. She didn't like his father, yet she had felt sorry for him; but just in a way, because he wasn't a nice man. But why should Bruce bawl at her? She had done nothing and she wasn't gaping.

71

Again she had a longing to hear Miss Caplin's voice or to look on Max. There had always been something soothing about Max. You always felt calm when you were with him; inside, that is. He seemed to know about things, and he straightened them out in his hesitant fashion. Oh, at this moment how she wished she was back in the workhouse.

Then the thought of what that would mean took her from the door and up the steep steps, and once under the roof she lay on her pallet just as she was.

At the end of every day she was so tired she would be asleep almost before her head touched the pillow, and tonight was no exception. Dressed as she was, she fell into a deep sleep.

How long she had been asleep she didn't know, but she awoke, realising first, that she was fully dressed, and secondly, that there were people talking, and quite close by. She raised herself up on her elbow and looked towards the open hatch. Were they down there?

But no – she swung round on to her knees now – the voices were coming from just beyond her head, at least, one voice was, and immediately she realised that it wasn't Bruce's. This voice was thickly guttural, yet there was a touch of laughter in it. 'The old bugger meant me to be caught. If it hadn't been for Peter coming out of his way to tip me the wink and knowing he wouldn't lose by it, Sammy would likely have done for me by now. I can hold me own, you know, like the best of 'em, but Sammy's Sammy. I have known some fathers but ours is a stinker all right and I wouldn't have realised he knew anything about Sammy's coming if the old boy hadn't remarked that he had seen me da earlier on. Well, you know, all day after that, Bruce lad, I kept waiting, but not a hair of him did I see. By God! one of these days!' The voice had risen and then again, 'By God!

one of these days!' And now she recognized Bruce's voice saying, 'Quiet, man! Keep it down.'

'Oh, they can't hear over this range, they never have.'

'No, they never have, but there's a lass next door.'

'Oh!' The voice came very low to her now. 'A lass? That's why this midden seemed to be different tonight. And I wondered about the new bread. What's she like?'

'She's just a child.'

'A child? Huh! Some child, I should imagine, to make an impression on this place.'

'Be quiet! will you.'

There was silence now and gradually she drew off her clothes and put on a cold nightgown. She was just about to lay her head down on the pillow again when the gruff voice said, 'How d'you stand it here, Bruce, day after day? Oh, I know there's Ma, but there's women in the village who'd be glad to take over and look after her.'

The reply was a hiss: 'There are no women in the village who would be glad to take over looking after her. We tried three of them before the lass came.'

'Well, well!' There was another pause; then, 'And she's from the workhouse?'

'Yes, she's from the workhouse.'

'Well, all I can say, lad, having been brought up in this hovel, there's many worse places than the workhouse.'

'Ma can't help being sickly.'

'No, she can't, but it's gone on for a long time, hasn't it, and even when she wasn't sickly she didn't like work.'

'All right, all right. Get yourself off to sleep.'

Jinnie lay staring into the blackness. That other one was suggesting that his mother wasn't all that sick, and had never been overclean. It was a funny house. She wished . . . oh, yes she wished . . . She didn't know what she wished . . . She was so tired. Once again she fell asleep . . .

The next morning she was in the kitchen when Hal Shaleman made his appearance. He stood in the doorway scratching his head while looking at his brother, who was sitting at the table fully dressed for going out and finishing his breakfast. Then he looked towards the bed where the two figures lay. Lastly, at the girl with the porridge pan in her hand. They stared at each other for a moment, before he said, 'No skilly for me. Give us a mug of tea.'

As Jinnie went to lift the teapot from the side hob there was movement in the bed, and she turned swiftly and saw the mister clambering over his wife, and at this, she put the teapot quickly back on the hob and hurried from the room.

'Look!' Hal was shouting after her, 'I want . . .'

'Pour it out yourself,' Bruce said harshly.

'What the hell!'

'She always disappears when he gets out of bed: he's no pretty sight for anybody to watch.'

'Oh, dear! dear! Aren't we getting finicky now! You say she's only a child, but child or no child, she's paid to work, isn't she?'

'Yes; and she earns her pay, but that doesn't include waiting on you. The teapot's there; your mug's on the table; all you've got to do is to introduce one to the other.'

'Oh, now we're coming out with our fancy phrases, aren't we? But I'll do it, brother, I'll do it.'

Jinnie would always busy herself in the scullery until she heard the mister go out of the house and towards the midden; then she would return to the kitchen. However, this morning she did not follow this pattern. Instead, after sorting the dirty clothes, she half-filled the poss tub with water and was putting the sheets in to soak when the door opened and Hal, in a high-falutin' tone,

74

said, 'Will it be in order, miss, that I come in and wash my face at your sink?'

She made no reply; but when she went to pass him and he put his hand out towards her back, she leaped forward, then turned on him, yelling, 'Don't you touch me, mister!'

'God in heaven! What have we here? I wasn't going to touch you.'

'Oh yes you were. Like your father, you were going to nip me. Oh yes, you were.' She stood glaring at him as, leaning back against the trough, he rocked with laughter. Then this suddenly ceasing, and his voice normal sounding, he cried at her, 'They should've put you in a bloody nunnery, not sent you out to skivvy. Get out!'

He was further amazed when she did not instantly move at his bidding, but defiantly walked back to the poss tub, picked up the poss stick, then pounced it three times until the clothes were under the water. After finishing the job she had started, she passed him again, this time keeping her eyes fixed on him, only to be greeted, as she entered the kitchen, with a burst of laughter. Different laughter this. Bruce was looking towards her and shaking his head; then, taking his cap from the back of the door, he thrust it on his head and, still grinning, nodded towards her and said, 'You'll do.'

She didn't know exactly what that meant, but on looking towards his mother, it was to find the missis staring straight ahead. Whether she too had been laughing, she didn't know, but the woman was giving nothing away.

Jinnie went to the stove, picked up the pan and scraped the remainder of the porridge into a bowl. There wasn't a great deal left, but that was her fault: she knew she should have put more oats in, but last night, as usual, she had measured out just enough for three; the mister never ate porridge but the new addition had helped himself apparently.

The missis did not speak to her elder son until he was about to leave the house, when she called to him, 'Should we expect to see you the night?'

He stepped back from the doorway and answered, 'You should, Ma, you should, but I may not be as sober as I was last night. That was an exception, don't you think?' And then he, too, was gone.

And so the day had begun, and it ended in much the same way as the day before! Hal came home sober but although Jinnie tried to keep awake and listen, she did not hear him talk to his brother in the bed beyond her head.

Only once during the following week did she hear, through the wall, an exchange between them, and then the voices were muffled and she couldn't make out what either of them was saying on that particular night . . .

In later years she was to wonder if the warning voice she seemed to be aware of in the night was that of her father talking to her, or of Miss Caplin, or of Max, but since Hal had taken to coming home every night she had taken the precaution of extracting the dinner knife from her father's pouch.

On this particular night Hal had not returned home before she went to bed, and when eleven o'clock came Bruce had said, 'The boat must have sailed,' and his mother had added, 'Aye; so get yourself to bed. You can leave the door on the latch; he still may come staggering in if he's had a skinful, and in that case he won't make the ladder, he'll sleep on the mat.'

So they settled down for the night.

Jinnie had been dreaming: She was sitting in the workhouse cart, with Miss Caplin on one side of her and Max on the other and they were jogging along a

76

country road; but there was no sign of a horse pulling the cart, and they all knew this and were laughing about it; then a strange thing happened. They were in an old shed and Max picked her up by the collar of her dress and hung her from the bough of a tree, and said to her, 'You are the apple of my eye,' and they all laughed again. Then her hair began to fall out and her two plaits dropped on to Max's shoulders. Next, two hands came from behind the tree and gripped her neck before moving down to her legs and the gripping pain brought her awake, wide awake.

A real hand now was gripping her thigh and another was groping at her face, aiming to smother her screaming. At the same time as, with one hand, she endeavoured to free her mouth, the other grabbed her dada's knife from under the pillow, and as she blindly drove it home her whole body was lifted from the bed by the scream that rang through the roof top, followed by a yelling and curses as someone tumbled down the stone steps.

She lay gasping, one hand on her throat, the other still clutching the knife. She was aware of a commotion in the roof-space behind her, then curses and the yelling voice of the missis.

There was a flicker of candlelight coming through the hatch, and she leaned forward and looked down to where Hal was lying in a huddle at the foot of the steps. He was gripping his wrist, and there was blood pouring over his hands.

'In the name of God! what is it?' It was the missis's voice coming from the other room; and when no answer was forthcoming, she yelled, 'What's happened? Is it the girl?'

Then Bruce was answering her: 'No, it's not the girl, but the result of her handiwork on your son; to my mind, getting what he asked for.'

77

'You shut your bloody mouth and get me up! I've twisted me foot; and look, I'll bleed to death.'

As Bruce helped his brother to his feet, he imagined his words might indeed come true, for there was so much blood spilling from the joined hands. He now helped him into the kitchen and lowered him on to a chair placed so that he could put his hands on the table.

'Light the lamp.'

'I haven't got two pairs of hands, Ma; I've got to try to stop this,' and he indicated the blood that was spreading on to the table.

Rose Shaleman's voice now almost rocked the house as she screamed, 'You! girl. You! girl. Come down here!'

The sound seemed to release the stiffness of Jinnie's body as, gasping, she bent over and dragged her coat across the floorboards towards her and after pushing her arms into it and buttoning the neck, she pulled her boots on to her bare feet and descended the steps.

At the kitchen door, she stiffened again, but the missis simply yelled at her: 'Light the lamp, girl, and get the fire going.'

Like a bewildered rat, she scurried to the table and lit the lamp after first having almost upset it. Then, her mind in a whirl, she blew the embers of the fire into a blaze and thrust the kettle on.

'Get that piece of calico from the top drawer and tear it up,' the missis was ordering now.

Meanwhile Bruce was trying to ascertain exactly from where the blood was coming, all the time having a job to keep his brother's hands apart, the while shouting at him, 'Look! if you want me to try to stop this bleeding, then let me get at it.' And he wiped the wrist almost clean with the quick swipe of a wet rag over the hand; then he exclaimed, 'Well, there it is! Now we can do

78

something.' And on this he pressed his thumb on the half-inch cut; and presently the bleeding slowed, and in a much quieter voice he said, 'It's all right. I've got it; I can hang on to it;' and then added by way of consolation, 'It hasn't gone through anything big because it's easing off.'

'What did she do it with?'

Before Bruce had time to answer his mother, his brother answered, 'With a knife, a bloody knife, of course.'

'Well, you weren't at the bottom of the steps when she did it, were you?' Bruce's tone was no longer conciliatory. 'You were trying your hand, weren't you? Well, she had warned you.'

'Shut your bloody mouth and get on with it. But I'll make her bloody well pay for this, you'll see if I don't.'

'Oh no, you won't.'

'Who's gonna stop me?'

'We'll see. You got what you deserved; and she's only a bairn, anyway.'

'A bairn! She's a bloody bitch and a knowing bloody bitch at that; one who carries a knife.'

'Yes. Yes. But where did she get the knife?' It was the mother speaking again. 'I shouldn't think it can be one of ours, they're too big to hide.'

They were talking as if she weren't there, yet all the while she had been standing in the dim corner of the room tearing a piece of calico into strips as she had been bidden, and the muted scream of the linen as it was being torn apart should have made them aware of her existence; but apparently it hadn't, until her voice did when she yelled, 'It's me own knife. It was me dada's from his pouch – he ate with it – and I'll use it again. I will! I will! I'm not sorry and I'm going back

79

the day down to the workhouse. It's better than here. Yes, it is, 'cos I won't be handled. I told you so, and I'll tell them I stabbed him; and I wasn't lying on the floor in a cupboard this time but up in the loft, and there was steps to be climbed. Yes, there were. And I'll tell them. They'll believe me. Yes they will. And I'll have Miss Caplin up, and Max. Max'll sort him out. Yes, he will; he'll sort him out. And I hope the knife has gone right through, I do.'

When her tirade had ceased, the only sound in the kitchen came from yon side of the bed. It could have been the mister was snoring gently or it could have been he was coughing in his throat, or it could have been he was chuckling. And it wasn't until the sound stopped that Bruce said, 'It'll have to be seen to, sewn up, or burned.'

'No! by God, you're not gonna put any poker on me!' Hal tugged his hand away from his brother's only to see the blood starting to run again, and as he gripped his wrist his mother, speaking to Jinnie now, demanded, 'Was your knife clean, girl?'

'It's . . . it's in a case, missis, leather. It's hard now.'

'Is it rusty? Is the blade rusty?'

Jinnie had to think before she said, 'Where it joins the bone handle, it is a bit.'

'That's it then.' Rose Shaleman was speaking to her son again. 'You heard, didn't you; part of it is rusty. If it was rusty at the top it's likely rusty at the end, and if you don't want blood poisoning and to be left with one hand, then you've got to let Bruce do something.'

A silence followed and it was Hal who broke it, saying, 'I can't stand it without a drink.'

'Well, that's what we haven't got here. The next best thing is one of my pills, they'll kill the pain. Take a couple now and wait a few minutes,' and turning to Jinnie she shouted, 'Get the box, girl, out of the top drawer, and take two out and put them on the table.'

Scurrying again, Jinnie got the pills and gave them to Bruce, who said quietly to her, 'Stick the poker into the centre of the fire. Go on; do as you're bid.'

About five minutes later, when everything was apparently ready, Bruce said grimly, 'Da, get out of that bed where you've had your ears cocked all the time and come and hold his wrist. I can't do it all meself and it's unlikely that he'll remain still.'

When there was no movement from the bed, Rose Shaleman's voice growled, 'Get yourself up!'

A few minutes later Pug, small, a grotesque figure in linings and vest, stood to one side of the table gripping his son's wrist, while Bruce sponged the blood away from around the oozing wound. Then without turning to Jinnie, Bruce said, 'Bring me the poker and a wet dish-cloth.'

Jinnie looked dazedly about her before dashing to the scullery to bring back the wet dish-cloth. Then she pulled out the poker from the fire, and dashed to the table, almost thrusting it at Bruce, and the action brought from Hal the exclamation, 'By God! I know where I'd like to stick that iron at this moment.'

'Shut up! Shut your dirty mouth or I know where I'll put this iron instead of on to your hand. Now, I'm warning you!' Then lowering his tone, Bruce said quietly, 'This should take only a minute if you keep still. As Ma said, the pills will dull the pain. It's either this, mind, or losing your hand for, whether the knife was rusty or not, the cut's gone deep, and it's near the thumb. Hold it still, Da!'

Jinnie could see the red hot point slipping over the raw flesh and as a groaning screech from Hal split her head open she fell into a huddle on the floor . . .

'Come on. Come on; you're all right.'

She gasped. She was swallowing water; she must be drowning. 'Come on! Come on, sit up.'

There was an arm around her shoulder pulling her upwards, and slowly she opened her eyes and, looking at Bruce, whimpered, 'I . . . I want to go home.'

'You *are* home.'

'No, no.'

'All right. All right. You'll feel better tomorrow. It wasn't your fault, so don't worry. Ma isn't vexed with you; and, strangely enough, neither is Da.'

'He'll . . . he'll get me.'

'Oh no, he won't; oh no. Don't you worry about that. He won't get you; I'll see to that. Look' – he pulled her round to face him – 'trust me, Jinnie; I'll see that you're never hurt. I wouldn't have you hurt, not for the world, because you're a good girl. I know that and I'll see that he never hurts you. Anyway, he mightn't be here much longer' – his voice dropped – 'he's thinking about going back to sea. He's fed up with the mine; the lead's getting at him.'

She made no reply and he then said, 'Now we get on all right, don't we, me and you and Ma? and even the old man, 'cos he knows where he stands; he's wise.'

She was on the verge of tears now and she whimpered, 'I . . . I won't be handled.'

'No, no, of course you won't.' He did not add, not yet, anyway; not for a long while. She was so young in some ways but so mature in others. She worked as though she were sixteen or seventeen, yet her thoughts were still those of a very young girl; which was strange, she having been brought up in the workhouse.

He now lifted one heavy plait from the front of her shoulder and put it behind her back; then did the same

82

with the other; and in a soothing tone now he said, 'You've got bonny hair, Jinnie. How do you wash it and get it dry when it's so thick?'

She didn't want to talk about her hair, she wanted to lie down and moan, because there was a strange feeling inside her that was demanding expression; but she knew he was only trying to be comforting, and also to reassure her in order to keep her here. Oh, she knew that.

'On a hot day you want to go and wash it in the pool and let it dry in the sun.'

'The pool?'

'Yes; I showed you where the water comes down from the hills and through the rock and makes that pool. That's where we get our water from,' and he thumbed over his shoulder.

'But it would make the pool soapy.'

'Well, that wouldn't matter; there's an outlet and it seeps away quite fast.'

He waited a few seconds, then said, 'D'you think you can manage the steps?'

As he helped her to her feet, she said, 'What happened to me?'

'You passed out. It was his screaming and likely the smell, as nothing smells worse than burnt flesh.'

'I'm not sorry.'

'No, I wouldn't expect you to be, lass.'

He watched her now stumble up the steps, and not until she had disappeared from his view through the hatch did he let out a long-drawn sigh; and then went into the kitchen.

There was no sign of Hal, and his father was back in his place in the bed, but his mother was sitting upright, and she beckoned Bruce; and when he stood by her side she whispered, 'Do you think she'll stay?'

'I hope so. For your sake, I hope so.' But she quickly came back at him, saying, 'Not only for my sake; you're used to your bellies being filled as well.'

'Yes, that's in it, too.'

'What did you say to her?'

'Oh, I led her off the beaten track, talked about her lovely hair.'

'Her hair!'

'Yes; haven't you noticed she's got lovely hair? Well, I told her she should go and wash it up at the pool. You know, Ma, we're very like animals: you frighten a young lamb and it needs a lot of patting, besides sucking on a teat bag, to bring it round.'

She said nothing, only her heart spoke as she thanked God for him.

The next morning, white-faced and weary-eyed, she entered the kitchen to prepare the breakfast; and after Bruce had come down from the loft, she waited in trepidation for Hal's appearance.

When, presently, Bruce said, 'Put your own out, he's gone,' her body slumped with relief.

Bruce did not inform her how his brother had been inveigled into leaving nor did she enquire.

It was half-past six in the morning and he had gone! With that hand, how could he? And so, on a nervous mutter, she said, 'You . . . you . . . haven't done . . . done . . . anything to him?'

'No, Jinnie; I haven't done me brother in, if that's what you mean. That's what you meant to say, isn't it?'

She did not answer but continued to stare at him.

'To ease your mind I'll put you in the picture. I've been up since four o'clock. I took him down on the cart, reluctantly I must say. Oh yes, reluctantly. But he has a number of friends both in the village and in the town. I left him to make his way to one of his own choice. Now take that look off your face and get your porridge. Then see to Ma. She's very tired this morning and I think I'd get her out on to a chair later and change that bed from top to bottom. Turn the tick if you can. If you find you can't, go out to me da and tell him to come and give you a hand. Will you do that?'

She motioned with her head but did not speak . . .

It would appear that life had dropped back into the familiar pattern it had taken before the elder son had put in an appearance. From snatches of conversation between Bruce and his mother she gleaned that *The Admiral* was in dock being thoroughly overhauled and that Sammy, whoever he was, would be still at home and so as long as he stayed there, Adelaide Morgan would now be getting her share. A share of what, she couldn't fathom, but whatever it was the missis implied that her son wouldn't be charged a lot for lodgings. And now being back at work, he'd be well in pocket.

Then came the morning when, at ten o'clock, Bruce unexpectedly came in. He was holding a letter, but instead of making for the bed, he looked over the table to where Jinnie was sitting back on her hunkers from scrubbing the stone flags, and he smiled down at her as he said, 'Well, get to your feet! Here's a surprise: a letter for you.'

When the voice said, 'A letter for her?' he turned to his mother and said, 'Yes, Ma, for her.'

'Do we ever get letters? Can you remember us ever getting a letter? Who's it from?'

'I don't know; and she won't know until she opens it. Can you read?'

She was drying her hands on her coarse apron, and she said, 'A bit, if the print's big. Yes; words.'

'Well, what else would you read but words, girl? It's a silly answer.'

'No, it isn't, Ma. No, it isn't. Anyway, there's your letter, lass. Open it and see who it's from.'

Jinnie had never before received a letter. She looked first at the front of the envelope, and then at the back; then looked about for something with which to open it. The kitchen drawer in the table suggested a knife, so quickly she pulled one out and inserted it into the envelope, and then took from it a folded sheet of paper.

'Well, what does it say? Who's it from?'

She pressed the piece of paper to her breast with both hands and looked from one to the other before she said, 'Miss Caplin.'

'Miss Caplin? She's the one you liked, isn't she?'

She looked at Bruce and nodded, saying, 'Yes. Yes.'

'Well, what does she want to write you a letter about?'

She turned to look at the missis and said, 'She's visiting her aunts next Sunday; she's got the whole day off, and Max an' all, and he's driving her.'

'Does it say all that? Read it out, girl.'

She held up the paper before her face and looking at the large letters, read very slowly:

'I will be at my aunts' on Sunday next: Max is driving me. I would very much like to see you, Jinnie. Very sincerely, your friend Jane Caplin.'

Her head bounced now as she grinned from ear to ear and said, 'There! There, 'tis the first letter I have read. But I've read the Bible. This was easier, though, 'cos Miss Caplin has written in big letters.' She turned the page round and held it out for both of them to see.

'Who are her aunts? And where do they live?'

It was Bruce she answered, saying, 'At the bottom

of the bank, where you met us. Further back along the road, up the side way. 'Twas the last place we passed before we came on you.'

'What's their name?' he asked softly.

'The Miss Duckworths live there.'

'What, Ma?'

'The Miss Duckworths, and they are ladies.'

'Well, Miss Caplin's a lady,' Jinnie put in, looking from one to the other; then addressing the missis, she said, 'Can I go? I mean on Sunday?'

'Yes, you can go. Of course, you can go.' It was Bruce speaking, but he turned to his mother, adding, 'Can't she?'

'I suppose so.'

'I've been six weeks here and had no time off, missis.'

'Six weeks?'

'Aye, yes, it was six weeks yesterday.'

'Well—' the woman now shrugged herself back into her pillows, saying, 'If you want to go jaunting you'll have to look a bit tidier than you are: you'll have to get that print of yours washed again, and your hair washed an' all. It's like a doormat on the top. Do you ever comb it?'

'Oh aye, missis. Yes, every night I take out my plaits and I comb it. But then I have to sleep on it.'

Bruce was smiling at her, and what he said to her implied a question: 'Perhaps after seeing them you won't want to come back.'

'Oh yes, I will. I like it here. When we're on our own, I like it. It's good. Yes, I like it up here.'

He stared at her for a moment before suddenly turning to go to the door, singing quietly: 'The sky is high, the air is free, come, my love, and live with me on this barren rock above the sea.'

Oh, he had a lovely voice. But what a strange song.

87

She turned eagerly to look at the missis, only to see the woman with her head bent on to her chest and a hand across her mouth. And so she went swiftly to her, saying, 'You feeling bad, missis? You want to be sick?'

It was some seconds before Rose Shaleman sighed and dropped back on to the pillow.

'I'm all right, girl. I'm all right. Make a pot of tea. I'm all right.'

Slowly, Jinnie turned from the bed and went towards the fire, pushing her bucket aside as she did so. She was puzzled. There were things about the people of this house that puzzled her, things she didn't understand; although one thing she did understand, and that was very clear: Mister Bruce's singing had upset his mother. The meaning in it she must have taken to heart; the words must have reminded her of something. She had never seen her face so waxen.

Oh, but she now had something to look forward to: on Sunday she would see them, Miss Caplin and Max, the two people so dear to her. And yes, she'd wash her print frock and iron it beautifully; she'd press the three pleats in the front until they were like knife edges; and she would wash her hair an' all. It hadn't been washed for weeks, and Miss Caplin would be the first to notice it and would say, 'Why haven't you washed your hair, Jinnie?' She'd go up to that pool. Oh, she didn't mind what might happen now, she had Sunday to look forward to.

The sun was hot on her neck as she bent over the bank and lathered her hair in the water. It was the most wonderful feeling. Through the hanging threads she could see the ends trailing away. They looked like bronze or gold. Yes, gold. She was glad she had lovely hair because she wasn't pretty, not really pretty. The bit of broken mirror hanging in the scullery used as a shaving glass by the men told her that her eyelashes, like her hair, were long; and that she had a nice mouth. But she didn't have rosy cheeks, and pretty girls always had rosy cheeks. She had very little colour in her face at all. To her it was all of a sameness, a creamy-white, pallid-looking sameness accentuated by the brightness of her hair.

The lathering done, she swished her head in the water, then scooped handfuls over the back of her head to get the soap off. It was blue mottled soap she had used, the same kind as she used to scrub the floor, the same soap they all used, a rough soap. Miss Caplin had once given her a tablet of lovely soap for a Christmas box. Oh, it had smelled nice, and had lasted for months, because she had used it only on her face.

Sitting sideways on the bank now, she screwed her hair into a tight rope and squeezed the first shower of water out of it; then picking up the coarse towel at her side, she began to dry her hair. She rubbed until her arms ached; strand after strand of hair she dried with the rough towel.

She sat back and propped herself up on her hands and let her hair fall around her like a cloak, and as the sun beat on her she knew that her hair would soon be dry. Now and again she would lift one hand and disturb the spread in order to get the underneath dry. She could also feel the sun beating on to the top of her chest where she had turned in the collar of her dress, a nice and unusual sensation. She hadn't felt so clean, so relaxed or so happy for a long time. This time tomorrow she would be with Miss Caplin and Max.

She did not know for how long she had been sitting in this relaxed state when, with a start, she looked up to where she could glimpse a section of the rough road that passed the farm which supplied them with milk, and which eventually led to the village from where it branched off to Allendale.

She reassured herself that nobody could see her, for she would be hidden by the gorse and bushes. She was settling back again, when once more she became alert, this time because of the neighing of a horse. The sound came from a distance; but it had broken the peace of the afternoon. What if it was Mr Hal and he had been watching her?

Well, where could he watch her from? He hadn't a horse. She felt uneasy. She gathered up her soap and the towel, and as she got to her feet she was glad she hadn't taken off her boots and stockings to go into the pool, for, apart from her hair hanging down, she would have been showing her bare legs . . .

She had no sooner entered the door of the cottage than she knew somebody had been riding past, and that must have been the young master from The House, for there, on the table, was a large basket of fruit. But sitting at the table was the dreaded Hal.

She hadn't seen him for some time, at least not since the night of the stabbing; and now he turned and glared at her. Bruce, who was also in the room, exclaimed, 'By! You've made that into a busby. It'll take some brushing down.'

'Go and plait your hair, girl!'

She looked towards the bed and said, 'Yes, missis,' and hurried through the scullery and up into the roof space, and there, taking a dry but worn scrubbing brush, she went to work to flatten the busby, as Mister Bruce had called it.

It was a full half-hour before she came down the steps again and into the kitchen, to be greeted by the missis with, 'Mash some tea, girl, and butter those pieces of pastry you made yesterday.'

Making no reply, she went about obeying the order, all the time listening to the talk across the end of the table between the two brothers. 'You want to think twice about the sea,' Bruce was saying; 'there's some tough'uns man those ships.'

'Tell me something I don't know, and tell me I can't take care of meself.'

'Oh, you can take care of yourself all right; that's if it's man to man; but if it's man to gang and a few belaying pins are flying around, you couldn't do much about it. And I'm told they're clannish on some boats.'

'Since when do you know anything about boats?'

'Oh, I've been to Newcastle a number of times. I've even been on board one or two of them. And from the bar-talk around the quays, you can believe at least half of what they say about the conditions.'

'My! My! Clever bugger, as always.'

'I keep me ears open.'

'That's enough!' broke in their mother. 'That's enough, the both of you. You know what it'll lead to. If you, Hal, want to go to sea, you go to sea. Anyway, you'll probably save yourself a bit of money.'

'Oh, about money, Ma. I want to have a talk with you about money.'

'Well, it won't be now, lad, you'll talk to me about money.'

Rose Shaleman now glanced towards where Jinnie, her head bent, was piling the scones on a plate. And a silence fell on the room.

After Jinnie had poured out the tea and put the plate on the table, the missis said curtly, 'Have you ironed that dress of yours?' and she replied, 'Not yet, missis.'

'Well, go and do it now else it'll never be done. I don't want you to look like a rag-tag when you go down there tomorrow.'

She had hardly left the room before Hal, looking at his mother, said grimly, 'Has the dear little girl been invited to a party?'

'Some such.'

'God! Where?' He was sitting back in his chair, his eyes wide.

''Tis no party,' put in Bruce.

'Well, if it isn't a party what is it?' and Hal mimicked his mother, 'Have you ironed that frock yet?'

'She's going to visit two people she knew in the workhouse. They're coming up to the Miss Duckworths.'

'She's going down to the Miss Duckworths! Her? They won't let her in the door, those two old hoity-toities.'

'Well, apparently their niece has some kind of a position in the workhouse, and has kept an eye on the lass from the time she first went in after her father died. And there's an inmate there, a man who did the same.'

'Well! well! well! Did she let him touch her?'

'Keep your dirty mouth closed, and look at your wrist and remember all women aren't alike, all girls aren't alike; and by God! if you met that fella, if you said as much as a wrong word against her, that would be as much as your life would be worth. I'm telling you that.'

'Oh, a bruiser, is he?'

'No; you could say he looked to me like one of those gentle giants you hear about, and he talked like one an' all. I've never seen a man the size he is, I'm telling you; I wouldn't like to be the one to upset him.'

'My! my! She would seem to have as much protection as a brothel mistress.'

At this, Bruce sprang up from his chair and cried angrily at his brother, 'Why the hell don't you go to sea and stay there, or better still, get yourself into a brothel and be a madam's man; you seem to know so much about them.'

'I've told you!' The voice came sternly from the bed now. 'Now, I'm telling you, please stop it! Both of you, I'm feeling bad.'

Hal, too, rose to his feet, saying now, 'Anyway, on Monday I'm starting in the mine again, at least for a time; I only came up to tell you that you might have to put up with me company for the next few days; not for many, I hope, just as long as it takes for a certain boat to have her backside scraped; then I'll be back to as it was in the beginning, is now, and ever shall be. So long, Ma.'

She did not look at him, or speak, and he left the room, slamming the door after him; but his voice could be heard speaking to his father in an exchange that was anything but friendly.

Rose Shaleman now looked at her younger son who was standing and gripping the back of his chair, the while muttering, 'I wish to God something would happen to him before I take it into me own hands,' and she said pleadingly, 'Bruce . . . Bruce, for my sake, don't traffic with him. Look; now that Mister Richard's back, before he returns to college or some such, university you said it was, well, get some running in with him. He'd like that. He said so, didn't he? Get yourself up early in the morning. You always felt better when you ran first thing. It didn't seem to affect your day's work or the tramping that you had to do. For my sake, lad, try it.'

He turned to her now, saying softly, 'All right, all right; don't fash yourself; but brother Hal is a foul-mouthed, dirty individual, and mean with it. Da's mean, but he can't hold a candle to Hal.'

93

'Yes, I know, I know. Anyway, it's strange how things work out: everybody gets their just deserts in the end.'

'Oh, don't be silly, Ma.' He turned away from her now. 'Are you getting your just deserts?'

'Yes, lad. Yes, if you only knew, I'm getting my just deserts.'

He looked hard at her, and when she returned the look without speaking, he seemed to fling his body around, and he too went from the room, and again the door was banged. Rose Shaleman lay back and closed her eyes tightly as she said, 'Yes, everybody gets their just deserts.'

The sun was shining, the sky was high, and there was a light breeze blowing; her heart, too, was light and she was ready to go down the hill. Jinnie was standing in the middle of the room, her print dress standing away from her thin body; her two plaits hanging down her back, were tied with tape close to her head to keep them in place and the tapered ends were turned upwards, each secured with a small piece of ribbon. Her straw hat was sitting straight on the top of her head; her eyes were bright, her face was smiling; she was looking at her mistress and saying, 'Thank you for the grapes, missis; I'll tell the ladies you sent them, and they're sure to be pleased.'

'Turn around.'

When she turned round she was facing Bruce, and he looked at her tenderly, saying, 'You look bonny and very smart.'

'When the tinker man comes round with his wares, you'll have to buy yourself a piece of long ribbon for your hair. It'd look better than that piece of tape at the top.'

She was again looking at the missis as she said, 'I'll do that, missis; yes, I'll do that.'

'Well now, get yourself away. And you say they're leaving about four? Well, you leave shortly after, and give the ladies my respects.'

'I will, missis, I will.'

As she passed Bruce, he said quietly, 'Enjoy yourself, girl,' and she said, 'Yes, mister, I will.'

'You know exactly where to go?'

'Well, it was that turning off just before we met you that day.'

'Yes, that's it; I know the cottage well.'

As she passed through the doorway Rose Shaleman's voice followed her, saying, 'Keep your stockings well up, girl; I think you need new garters.'

'Yes, missis. Yes, missis,' and she half turned her head to glance up at Bruce; and he exchanged a smile. And presently, as she walked away over the plain towards where it dropped quite steeply in three stages towards the road, she knew that he continued to watch her.

She had the desire to run, to skip and run; in fact, she did just that down the first hill. The second was covered with patches of scrub, and she had to walk carefully here to prevent her dress from being caught in the brambles.

She had almost reached the bottom when something did catch her dress, and not only her dress but her whole body, and she found herself being lifted from her feet and unable to scream. There was no knife to hand this time as she looked up into the infuriated face of Hal Shaleman. His nose was almost touching hers, a hand was tight across her mouth and his knee was across her thighs as he ground out into her face, 'For two pins I'd slit your throat this minute; I could, and no-one would know who had done it, for you wouldn't be found for a long time, and by then you'd be rotten, you little workhouse snipe, you! You know that you've changed

95

that house up there, you know that? I never had much of a welcome; now I get none. My dear brother's for you, isn't he? Oh yes, yes.' Her quivering nostrils were drawing up his spirit-sodden breath. She knew whisky when she smelled it; many admissions got drunk on whisky before they came into the workhouse.

'Beautiful hair you have, lass, beautiful hair.' He was mimicking now. 'Well, we'll see who's got beautiful hair after I've used my knife.'

When the hand was released from her mouth, she was about to let out a high scream when she was thrust around and her face pressed into the earth; and then her whole being was screaming as she felt the knife going through a plait, right up close to her head. But then the sawing motion was checked by the sound of a dog's bark near at hand, and as the animal came bounding through the bushes Hal sprang to his feet; and the next minute she was alone, with the dog licking the side of her face. Then in answer to a whistle, it bounded away again.

Slowly she pulled herself up on to her knees, and as she did so the plait fell from her shoulder and on to the grass. Grabbing it with both hands, she held it out from her, staring at it as if she were looking at an idol, and she might have been, for all she could say was, 'God. God. Oh God. God, God.' Then she was running, the plait gripped in an outstretched hand as she cried aloud.

She reached the road; then, like a wounded animal, she flew along it until she came to the turning; and she couldn't have missed it, for there was the horse tethered to the grass verge and the cart near by; and further up, there was the cottage.

The Miss Duckworths were very refined maiden ladies, both in their late seventies. They had been gently bred, but had been deprived of love by socially conscious parents, and they each knew what they had lost, as did their niece, Miss Caplin, whose generosity had enabled them to live in this cottage, otherwise they might have found themselves under her care in the workhouse.

The cottage was small. It had a sitting-room, a bedroom, a kitchen and an outhouse and was the property of their niece. It was her salary that sustained them, for their father, like her own, had been so self-indulgent that both families had been ruined; and such were the circumstances of Miss Caplin's family that it was only the fact that this cottage had been left to her by her godmother that saved it from being classed as part of her father's estate. So, here they sat, the three of them, at the circular lace-covered table enjoying their after-dinner cup of coffee. Miss Isabel had made it and served it in tiny blue china cups. They were saucerless, being old china. Near the door, and seeming to dwarf them and the room and the cottage itself, sat Max. His coffee was in a mug, and to the side of the mug was a plate on which was a thin slice of cake, and as if he were a gentleman who had been fastidiously brought up, he sat breaking off small pieces of cake and placing them in his mouth, but never while he sipped the coffee.

There was a large smile on his face and every time he caught Miss Caplin's eye it seemed to widen. Then in a flash, as if by lightning, the whole atmosphere of the room changed, for there came a hammering on the door, and when Miss Caplin rushed to open it there fell into her arms her dear child, holding in one hand, of all things, one plait of her hair.

The two old ladies were on their feet, as was Max, all asking questions at once: 'What is it? What's happened? Tell me, child. Tell me! This is an outrage. Your hair! Your beautiful hair! Isabel, did you ever see anything like it?'

'No, Connie; no, I never did. Oh, what is it, child?'

97

Miss Caplin, her voice soft, now said, 'She'll tell us shortly, Aunt; she'll tell us shortly. Let us sit down, please.'

The old ladies turned and together pulled a basket chair towards Jinnie, still trembling from head to foot, and Miss Caplin, crouching in front of her, asked, 'Who did this, dear? Who did this?'

'Hal. Hal.'

'Was he the y-young man who met you?'

'No, no.' She looked up into the dark, blank countenance of Max and said, 'No, not that one. No, Max, not that one. That's Bruce. He's nice, good. No, the brother.'

'Let me have your hair, dear. Come along and loosen your fingers, let me have your hair.'

Slowly Jinnie's grip slackened from around the plait, and Miss Caplin handed it to Max; then addressed Jinnie again: 'Now tell me quietly what happened. Quiet now. Quiet;' then looking at her aunts, she said, 'Is there any more coffee left, Aunt Isabel?'

'Oh yes, dear, yes; yes a lot, a lot. Oh, of course. Of course.'

It was some minutes later, after having persuaded Jinnie to drink a full mug of coffee, that she said, 'Now, my dear, tell me what happened, right from the beginning. Stop trembling and hold my hand. Don't exaggerate, mind. You know what I mean, just tell us the plain facts.'

So, after a number of gulps and taking a long indrawn breath, Jinnie related the events that had transpired from her using the knife on Hal. Then, as if she were recalling an afterthought, she also told them about knocking Pug Shaleman off his stool. 'He was all right to me after that,' she put in. 'He's not a nice man, though, not like Bruce. Bruce is nice.' And Miss Caplin looked up to her aunts and explained, 'He is the young man who met Max, the one I told you about, and Max felt she would be safe in his keeping.' She now glanced to the side where Max was standing, the plait of her hair now wound round his wrist like a snake; but Max made no response; he just kept his eyes tight on Jinnie's face. And Miss Caplin said quietly, 'Am I to believe you actually stabbed the man with your knife, and that it had to be cauterised; I mean, actually burned with the poker?'

Jinnie nodded twice before she muttered, 'Well, he was handling me and he was going to do bad things. And today he said he was going to slit my throat and bury me where I wouldn't be found until I was rotten. It was, as I said, the dog who saved me.'

They were all startled now when Max cried to her, 'Come! Come!'

As he held out his hand Miss Caplin rose swiftly, saying, 'No, Max. No.'

'Y-y-yes, Miss Caplin. Oh y-y-yes, this . . . time, Miss Caplin. This time. Come!'

When Jinnie obediently slipped from the chair, Miss Caplin delayed her while addressing Max again, saying, 'Now, Max, please; you mustn't lose your temper. You know that it will spoil everything; you'll never be allowed out again.'

It would seem impossible for the man to grow any taller, but his head seemed to pull up from his huge shoulders, and he looked down on Miss Caplin and said, 'Not tied. Not tied, Miss Caplin. Not mental.'

Miss Caplin bowed her head and closed her eyes for a moment as she muttered. 'I know that you're not registered mental, Max, but you were found to be unable to look after yourself and . . .'

'Look after myself? Well . . . well, Miss . . . Miss Caplin. Oh yes, c-c-can work on farm. Been . . .

99

been' – he now thumped his forehead with his fingers – 'thinking – yes, thinking – tired of workhouse.'

Miss Caplin pushed Jinnie to one side and stood in front of Max, saying, 'If you do anything bad, Max, you will be held in there for life; and perhaps not only in the workhouse. You understand? Killing someone isn't going to . . .'

Max's eyebrows moved upwards and his mouth opened wider; then he said, 'Not k-k-kill; no, not kill . . . j-j-just give him a lesson.'

'Well, it all depends upon what you mean by giving him a lesson; you're a very strong man, you know, Max.'

'Yes, I know. Good; yes, good. Come,' he said, and gently thrusting Miss Caplin aside took Jinnie's hand and pulled her forward. Then looking at the three helpless ladies, he said, 'Be back. F-f-fetch her back soon . . . soon.'

'Where do you expect to find him?'

'Don't . . . know. Try house. Not there, b-b-bring her back; then . . . then try inns myself,' and he thumped his chest, repeating, 'Myself . . . I go round t-till I find him. Come.'

As he pulled Jinnie forward, she cast a glance at Miss Caplin and said by way of comfort, 'He'll be all right. He'll be all right.'

Some way along the road, Max said to her, 'Up the hill?'

'Yes, Max.'

They had reached the second rise when he stopped his long striding suddenly and, looking down on her, said, 'Tired?' and she lied quietly, saying, 'No, Max.' Nevertheless, he stooped and lifted her up and carried her until they reached the plain, and there he put her down and they both gazed towards the speck of huddled buildings in the distance . . .

In the kitchen, Rose Shaleman was resting on her elbow and looking towards the ladder leading to the loft, she turned her head to Pug, who was standing by the table: 'What's his hurry now?' and Pug replied, 'Only he knows, but he's certainly got a reason.'

Her voice still low, she addressed Bruce: 'What d'you think?'

'Couldn't say, Ma, couldn't say, only something's happened.'

'Sam Valasquey after him?'

'Could be. I'm told he didn't sign on the boat yesterday,' Bruce said and his father nodded, and Bruce asked his mother, 'Are you going to give him anything?'

Before she could answer, his father said, 'No, begod! she's not.'

'He's due a bit.' Bruce's voice was low.

'He's due nowt, and that's what he's getting . . .' Pug stopped abruptly when Hal appeared on the ladder, from where he dropped a canvas bag on to the floor, followed by an overcoat. In the room, he stood buttoning up his short jacket and saying, 'Well, what about it, Ma? I've got to be off.'

When she did not answer, he demanded, 'Come on! Come on! There's quite a bit of mine under your tick, and you know it.'

'Well, whatever's under that tick, lad, stays there. You've had all you're getting out of this house.'

'My God!' Hal glared at his father. 'What have I ever got out of you, you undersized little squirt of a man? I've never even had a civil word from you, as a bairn or a lad, or a man. You've got a lot to answer for, you selfish, misshapen little bugger that you are.'

'Enough of that!' This had come from Bruce, and Hal turned on him, crying, 'You've had it easy, lad, you know nothing about it. You weren't pushed into

101

the mine before you could hardly crawl just to keep his belly full and her nursing herself. You've always nursed yourself, haven't you, Ma?'

The look that Rose Shaleman cast on her son was sad, but nevertheless she confirmed what he said: 'Yes, Hal, I've always nursed meself because I've had to.'

'Had to, begod! Laziness. Other women have dropped dead working, but not you . . . nor you!' And he jerked round to his father now. 'If you hadn't got him' – he was now thumbing towards Bruce – 'you'd be in the workhouse. And he's staying here only because of her,' and he nodded towards his mother. 'You telling me what's mine and what's not mine, you've never earned a penny in your life. You're like your people before you. I didn't know them but the whole village did, and I've heard of them and had them cast up to me, and I've worked twice as hard as any other man in that bloody hell hole, aye, and drank twice as much as any other man, and whored to prove myself. Well, I'm going now, and I don't know when I'll see you ever again, any of you, but before I step out of this pigsty I want me share, and I want it now, quick!' At this he straddled a chair, and it was just as Rose Shaleman was about to beckon to Bruce to see to his brother that the door was kicked open and so startled all of them that they gasped audibly, for there stood the biggest man any of them had ever seen. He was filling the doorway, but more than that he had to bend his head well in front of his shoulders before he could enter the room, pressing the bedraggled and weeping Jinnie before him.

'In the name of God! what's this? What's this?' Rose Shaleman cried.

The only answer they heard was the man saying to Jinnie, 'Wh . . . which one did it, Jinnie? Wh-wh-which one?' Her finger trembling, she pointed to the man straddling the chair with his mouth now agape and his eyes wide with fear, which he was experiencing for the first time in his life as he watched the great fellow unwind the plait of hair from his wrist.

Max turned Jinnie about, then held up the plait to the nape of her neck, telling his gaping audience, 'He . . . he did this. Was . . . was going to k-k-kill her an' all, he was; but first he . . . he did this.'

'God in heaven!' It was a whimper from the bed. 'Oh, you didn't! You didn't! And oh! dear, look at the sight of her.' Then, 'Dear God!' the woman screamed as the big man lifted Hal bodily from the chair and shook him as a dog might a rat.

'Stop him! Stop him!' Hal, too, was screaming; but neither Pug nor Bruce moved as they watched the man bring a crashing blow across Hal's face, and when his head swung from side to side as if it would roll off his body there was a combined intake of breath in the room like air being drawn through teeth. Then, to their fear-filled amazement they saw the big man reach up to one of the hooks fixed in the ceiling and lift down the ham that was hanging from it.

Next, Max ripped the buttons off the coat that Hal had fastened a few minutes earlier, then unbuckled Hal's belt and fastened it tighter, making him gasp, and held him head high, slipping the back of the belt over the hook, and there left him hanging and screaming, flailing his arms and legs.

'Th-th-that's it, scream. This . . . this child screamed. She . . . she rushed in screaming' – he was now deliberately addressing the woman in the bed – 'be-be-beside herself, beautiful hair gone.' And he picked up the plait of hair from where he had dropped it on the table, turned to Jinnie who was standing pressed against the stanchion of the open door and said, 'Knife . . . where's knife?'

'Please! please! Max, don't. Don't. No! please. 'Tis all right now. 'Tis all right. It will grow. 'Tis all right.'

'Do no harm . . . j-just knife.'

She stared at him a moment longer, then she pointed to the drawer in the table; and from it he took out the large gully which was used for cutting the bread and the meat. Then, holding the plait again on the table, he cut off about an inch from the thick end, and as it spread he gathered it up in his fist and, reaching up, rammed it into Hal's gaping mouth.

'It'll kill him; he'll choke. He'll choke,' Rose Shaleman screamed; and Max turned to the woman in the bed, saying, 'P-pity then, missis, 'cos . . . 'cos I haven't f-f-finished yet: said I'd leave a m-mark for all to see, and I w-w-will, one he w-w-won't be able to hide.' Then looking at Bruce, he said, 'Razor?'

'What? Oh man, no!'

'Not . . . not kill him, no. Nor . . . nor blood him either, just . . . just razor.'

'No! please. I . . . I understand how you feel; I feel the same too. I promise you he'll suffer for this more than he has already, but please! please don't . . . don't mark his face. Please!'

'No, no, not . . . not on the face, no; razor.'

Bruce looked to his father – there was a plea in his eyes – but Pug shook his head; the man was obviously just as afraid of this huge beast of a man, as he thought of him, as was his swinging son.

'You . . . you mean to cut him?'

Max shook his head vigorously, saying, 'No. No mean to cut him. No, just razor.'

Bruce could still not comply with the demand. It wasn't until his mother said, 'Give him the razor; I know what he's going to do; give him the razor,' that Bruce went to the far side of the fireplace where, underneath the cracked mirror, a wooden box stood on a small cupboard, and from it he took a razor which he handed to Max.

After pulling open the blade, Max stropped it on the palm of his hand; then he gripped the forelock of the thick black wavy hair of the dangling figure and proceeded to dry shave the rest of the head until there was nothing left but a small tonsure on the crown.

Rose Shaleman's face was tightly pressed into the pillow; one hand was covering her eyes, the other gripping the edge of the bed. Pug was standing, his eyes wide, his mouth agape, as if he couldn't believe what he was seeing. Bruce was not looking at the proceedings; his head was bowed. Strangely, there was no sound in the room. It could have been that Hal was frozen in terror, and likely he was.

The gruesome business over, Max released his hold on the body and left Hal swinging gently to and fro, his arms and legs no longer flailing but hanging limp. When he began to splutter and the hair sprayed from his mouth, Bruce looked at the big man who was now returning the razor to its case, and he said grimly, 'You finished?'

'Yes, fin-finished,' only to add, as if in an afterthought, 'for a time. She'll not come back until . . . he goes; and I'll not go' – he waved his hand as if into the distance – 'I'll not go until . . . he gone.'

'You . . . you could be had up for this.' It was a mutter from the small man, and Max, looking down on him in disdain, said, 'Yes, had up . . . with police in court. Good; I like in court . . . tell of attack,' and he thumbed towards the dumbfounded Jinnie, standing with her hands pressed tight across her mouth as she watched the bald, dangling figure. She did not take her eyes off him until Max's hand came on her shoulder and pulled her to the front of him and said, 'She used knife to . . . to save herself, yes, t-tell in court; then this,' saying which he bent forward and with his other hand took up the depleted plait from the table and, gripping the thick end, he swung it until once again it was twisted around his wrist. As he entwined the two ends he was nodding at the little man again, saying, 'Get me had up . . . that p-p-please me, yes.' Then with one hand on Jinnie's shoulder and the other indicating her, he said, 'Like . . . like d-d-daughter, mine . . . my d-d-daughter,' and pressing Jinnie before him, made for the door. And they were gone.

Stunned, Bruce did not spring forward towards his brother; his actions were slow as he mounted the table; and it took all his strength to hoist Hal upwards in order to release the belt from the hook. The result was, they both fell into a huddle on to the table.

Rose Shaleman was now sitting on the side of the bed and groaning audibly: her son was more bald than on the day he was born, for he'd had black hair even then. 'Oh, Hal . . . Hal,' and there was pity in her voice. But he made no response.

He could not stand without the aid of Bruce's arm around his shoulders, and although Bruce felt that his brother deserved all he had received, nevertheless it was so extreme that he could not but feel deep pity for him, for he had been proud of his hair, as Jinnie had been proud of hers. But then to go and cut off a plait . . . Why hadn't he cut off both of them? And how had she got away? Hal had come in in a scurry, almost running. Likely, someone had disturbed him, for, God above! he would surely have done to her what he had tried before.

After throwing off Bruce's support, Hal now stumbled

towards the scullery, and there sluiced the remaining hair from his mouth, before returning to the kitchen and making directly for the shaving mirror, to stand for a full minute amid a weird silence before saying to Bruce, 'Take the razor and finish it off, will you?'

'I . . . I couldn't do that, Hal.'

'Well, I suppose I can do it myself.'

'Here, give it to me. Sit down,' said Pug.

After a moment, Hal obediently sat down and Pug Shaleman shaved off the remnants of black hair.

When Hal remained sitting in the chair, his mother said to him, 'What are you going to do, lad?'

'What am I going to do, Ma? What I intended to do when I came in here, leave . . . but . . .'

'But, lad?'

'Oh, this.' Hal patted his very tender scalp as if he was used to the feel of it and said, 'Oh, there's been bald men before me. I saw a young one the other day, couldn't be past his middle twenties and all he had at the back was a ring of hair. It runs in families, you know.'

This attitude of his brother maddened Bruce, and he yelled at him, 'Stop playing the big bugger! You deserved all you got. It was a filthy, dirty trick to cut off her hair.'

'Was that all I did, just cut off her hair? Well, let me tell you, brother' – Hal's tone changed now – 'she's damn lucky she got away with one plait missing, for it was half my intention to do her in. So there you have it! Nobody, old or young, big or little has used a knife on me before, at least, no female, and by God! I wasn't going to let her be the first. The workhouse brat! She's a vicious little bitch, and I did to her what she did to me, and if she only knew it, she owes her life to a dog that heard her squeal.'

They looked at him in disbelief now; all pity for him

was fading or had already gone. They all realised he was quite capable of having finished her off.

'Well, I'll take me share now, Ma,' he said. 'That's what it was all about, wasn't it, when that mad imbecile put in his appearance?'

'There again you're making a mistake, Hal: that fella's not daft. To my mind he's wiser than most, although it's only the second time I've met him. I'd look out for him. By! yes, I would; I'd look out for the rest of the time you're in this quarter.'

'Well, if you want me out of this quarter' – Hal turned to his mother again – 'let me have me cut.'

'No!' It was his father denying him again.

'Well, you try to stop me taking it, Da, just try.'

At this Bruce stepped to the bed and placing a hand on his mother's side, he said, 'Move along, Ma,' and, silently, she obeyed. He then turned up the top thin tick and groped beneath it until his fingers came into contact with a chamois leather bag, which he pulled out and handed to his mother.

'You should mind your own bloody business. There's none of yours, none of yours in there,' said Pug.

'There's as much of mine in there as there is of his,' Bruce said, thumbing towards Hal. 'And let me tell you, Da, there's not a penny of yours in there, because you never earned a penny of it. But give him his due' – again he was thumbing towards Hal – 'he paid his whack all that long time you spent filling your guts with beer, using money made from your private deals that should have gone into the pot. We lost more than a sheep or two during that time, didn't we, Da? Hal kept us going then, while I slaved on the farm here for nothing. I call it a farm, and it should be a thriving business if it had two people working on it. And do I receive any wage? I haven't baccy or beer money; but from now on things are going to be different. Count out twelve, Ma.'

At this, Hal's voice came from behind Bruce, saying 'Make it twenty.'

'You're getting twelve, and you can thank your stars you're getting that much. And while you're on, Ma, give me three; I need new boots and breeches.'

Obediently the sick woman counted out twelve sovereigns from the bag; then another three.

The twelve Bruce took from her in one hand, the three in the other, then turned to his brother and handed him his share, saying, 'I don't begrudge you that, Hal.'

'Huh! that's good of you, I'm sure. That's very good of you, brother. If I was getting me due it'd be three times that.'

'If you were getting your due you'd be in hell,' put in Pug.

Bruce looked from his father to his brother, and it came to him to ask how two people could be so alike under the skin and yet hate each other; and the answer was, he supposed, because they knew each other like no-one else did.

They watched Hal pick up his cap from the table and put it on his head, pulling it well down at the back to save it slipping over his brow, and a strange feeling caused his hands to remain on the cap for a moment before he grabbed up the holdall from the floor, and the coat with it, then made for the door.

There, he stood quietly looking out on to the open plain for a time. It must have been all of two full minutes before he turned, his eyes flicking from one to the other, and said, 'Going to make you a promise: I'll be back one day. Aye, I'll be back one day. I'm going to spend me time working out a plan of what I'll do when I come back. Every day I breathe from now on I'll work towards it, and I hope you'll all be here when I return to this set of pigsties. Your time, Ma . . . no; your time's run out, has been for years, but I've got no pity for you 'cause you never had any for me, had you? I was the thing that brought you to this hovel and you took it out on me. Oh by God! you did. You thrashed it out of me: you shook it out of me until me teeth rattled. Oh aye, until me teeth rattled. Then you pushed me into the mine to get me out of your sight. No shepherding sheep for me. Oh no, the mine it was; you got good money in the mine, you could starve depending on sheep, couldn't you, Ma? Couldn't you, Da? But when the bonny boy came along things were different, weren't they? And you know, Bruce, I should have hated you, yet I never did. Didn't like you much but I never hated you, not like I should have, knowing what I did, at least going by the gossip in the village and which reached as far as the market place in Hexham. Did you ever hear of a fella called The Penny Verse and Tuppenny Painter? You will one day. Aye, you will one day. Goodbye then, all; but don't forget what I said,' and his voice dropping, he added, 'I'll be back and the way I feel at this moment it'll only be just; God sparing me. Oh aye, that'll be the day.'

There was a moment of utter silence before he turned and walked through the doorway.

Bruce remained by the window until his brother had disappeared from view. His father had been talking, talking, talking, but none of it had penetrated his mind until he heard him say, 'You shouldn't have given him any; he must have had some stashed away, he had something to lift at the day of the pays and he didn't come and hand you anything then to push into the bag, did he? No. Did he bring anything once a month out of his subsistence pay? And since leaving Beaumont's he's

IIO

been paid weekly at the drift this new fella's making. I know that, 'cos Peter . . .'

'Shut up! for God's sake, Da. Shut up! If you're so concerned about money, why the hell don't you earn some? Yes, I'll say what I've been thinking, just that. And another thing, you've lost a son. Oh, you didn't care for him, nor he for you, but you've lost a son. And what actually frightens me is how little you have in that mind of yours. You have just seen a giant walk in here, hang up your son on a meat hook, gag him with a mouthful of hair, then shave him to the last few hairs on his head, and it hasn't affected you, has it? No, it hasn't. The only thing that's in your mind now is the fact that he got twelve pounds and I've got three and knowing inside yourself that you haven't the pluck to brave Ma and demand a cut – not a share, 'cos you haven't earned it – just a cut.' He looked at his mother now and said, 'I'm going down to bring the lass back; that's if she'll come. I wouldn't blame her for preferring the workhouse, but whether she comes or she doesn't, I'm speaking to the two of you now: there's going to be changes here. Oh aye, changes; big ones.'

4

The tallyman spread his wares on the waterproof sheet
in which they had been wrapped: strings of beads, and
rings and brooches and pendants, studded combs and
earrings; pearl necklaces and ruby hair clips. Absolutely all genuine, he emphasised, as he looked into
Jinnie's bright face, then from her to Rose Shaleman,
who was propped up in the bed now and smiling as
she confirmed his statement: 'Absolutely genuine. Oh
yes, yes, tallyman, I'll stand by you in that, absolutely genuine.' And then they laughed together, the
fat man saying, 'Well, I do my best, Missis Rose, I
do my best. And you should know for I've visited you
twice a year now for how long?'

'Don't ask me to reckon, tallyman.'

Jinnie raised her eyes from the gleaming display,
looking from one to the other, and smiling widely, she
said, 'Is that your real name, Mister Tallyman?'

'No; my dear; and it's a wrong name for me. A real
tallyman is a man that hawks goods round houses and
sells them for twice their value because he has to take
payment for them just so much at a time . . . you know,
what a body can afford. A tallyman, my dear, sells dry
goods, tools and bedding and such. No, I am not a
tallyman, and I don't know how I came by the name,
really, for I have no connections going back with tally-
men or gypsies. Perhaps . . . yes, I think perhaps I come
of tinker stock. I suppose you would call me a tinker.'

'Oh.' Her mouth was wide now. 'My dada was a tinker.'

'Never!'

'Yes. Yes, we had a horse and cart and he sold pans and kettles and fireside things and cooking tins, all things like that.'

'Never!'

'Yes. Yes, he was.' Then her face losing its smile she said, 'He died when I was seven.'

'Oh. Poor man.'

'I'm glad you're really a tinker, Mister Tallyman.'

When the laughter subsided, the tallyman, wiping his eyes, said, 'And how old are you now, me pretty dear?'

'I am gone fifteen.'

'Fifteen. My goodness me! fifteen, and you so tall. I would've said sixteen . . . seventeen, wouldn't you, Missis Rose?'

'No, I wouldn't, tinkerman, for sometimes she talks and acts like a twelve-year-old.'

When Jinnie lowered her head Rose Shaleman said, 'Now get on with your choosing else we'll get no work done today. You want something nice for your Miss Caplin's birthday, don't you?'

'Yes, missis.' She picked up an embossed oval locket and, turning towards the bed, she said, 'That looks lovely, doesn't it? She would like that.'

'See if it opens properly and the hinge is all right.'

She did as she was bidden, and looking up at the tinker, she said, 'It swings nice.'

'Of course, it does, me dear, of course it does; I never sell anything that doesn't swing nice, not in lockets.'

'How much is it?'

'Oh.' He handled it now, saying, 'It's a beautiful piece and it's heavy, but it needs to go on a chain and unfortunately I haven't a chain with me today. I have a new supply coming in though. When is this needed for the special lady?'

'Oh, towards the end of next month.'

'Towards the end of next month. Oh, I'll have them in before then. Oh yes. But I may not be up this way.' He now turned towards the bed, asking, 'Will she be going over to the August fair in Allendale?'

'No, she won't, tinkerman, she's got too much work to do here instead of going to fairs, but my son will be at the fair; he'll be taking down the sheep and pigs.'

'Well, then, he can pick up the chain for the little lady' – he now patted Jinnie on the top of her head – 'and I can tell her she's not missing all that much; there are much better fairs during the year. It's only held for horses and pigs and such, a chance for the farmers to get rid of their remnants. I never think much of the August fair, although, mind, I can look back to a time when it drew people from far and wide; but those times will never come again; even the ordinary fairs are getting thin.

'Oh yes, they are, because who wants to pay toll money for their carts on the new roads? And then there's this railway; they've got it as far as Catton now and I think they intend to go over the hills with it. My, my! the changes we've seen; but life goes on, and me . . . I try to brighten it with me wares as I go on along the way. So, my dear, you're going to have the locket. But we haven't discussed the price. Can you afford it?' He again turned to the bed: 'Can she afford it, Missis Rose?'

'I should think she can; she gets well paid; there's not many get a shilling a week and their keep, not these days.'

'A shilling a week?' The bushy white eyebrows went up to meet the fringe of white hair and the man repeated, 'A shilling a week? Oh well, then I have no hesitation in stating the price, but before I do, I am going to tell you it's worth twice as much as I'm asking; oh yes, it is worth a crown of anybody's money; but because you are a new customer, my dear, I will split it in half and it is yours for half a crown; two shillings and sixpence. Now, there you are.'

'Hold your hand a minute, tinkerman.' Rose Shaleman had pulled herself up on the pillows and she was wagging a finger at him: 'That same locket has jumped sixpence in six months, if I've got any eyes in me head.'

'Oh come! Come, Missis Rose! I've never cheated in my life. That isn't the same kind of locket as I used to sell for two shillings. Look, take it into your hand and see.' He held it out to her. 'Look at the embossment around it, and open it. It can hold two articles: a strand of hair on one side and a little picture of a dear one at the other. You see there's clasps at both sides. Oh no, I could never let this go for less than two . . . well, say two and threepence.'

'You don't change, tinkerman, not by a farthing you don't change. All right, girl, give him his two and threepence, and then you have your present for your miss. Now, tinkerman, we don't want any more jewellery or fancy bits and pieces, but I would like to see what you've got in your ribbon bag.'

'Oh, my ribbon bag. Yes, yes. Now, funny thing, I have never thought of showing you my ribbon bag, not for years, but then, of course, you haven't had a pretty little miss running your homestead.' The man now bent down and from a knapsack lying on the floor he lifted up a bag and proceeded to shake its contents on to a corner of the table.

'There's a sky full of colours for you! Now, what's your choice?'

''Tisn't my choice, tinkerman, I'm past choosing ribbons. Take your pick, girl.'

'Me, missis?'

'Well, who else? Is there any other girl in the room?'

Jinnie bit on her lip, then eyes wide, she stared down at the galaxy of jumbled ribbons and slowly her hand went out and she drew upwards a yellow ribbon.

'Why a yellow one, girl? I thought it would be blue or pink.'

Jinnie turned and looked at her mistress, saying, 'Just like the sun.'

The tinkerman nodded his head in agreement as he said, 'You're right, me dear, you're right, 'tis like the sun. And this one is of such a quality that it will never fade; there'll be no sunset for that ribbon; it will always remain bright, and it will shine brighter when it adorns your beautiful hair.'

'Enough of that, tinkerman, her head'll be turned soon enough. Now, girl, make the tinkerman a cup of tea and butter a wad of that flat cake you made yesterday.' And Rose Shaleman's voice dropped to a whisper as she added, 'She's a good little cook, none better.'

And in a similar whisper, the tinkerman replied, 'Oh, I'm glad to hear that. By the look of her I think she'll be good at everything she tackles. Intelligent face, that's what I say she has, an intelligent face. Bonny yes, but sensible for her years.'

Jinnie's ears were burning: she had never listened to praise such as this in all the months she had been here; in fact, she had never in her life been praised by anyone, not even by Miss Caplin. Advised, cautioned yes, but never praised.

By the time Jinnie had mashed the tea and buttered a generous slice of oven-bottomed bread, the tinker had rolled up his goods and was sitting at the far end of the table chatting away to the woman in the bed, and she had no sooner placed the mug and plate before the old man when her mistress said, 'Take a can to the mister.'

This order was surprising, for it was the first time she had been told to carry tea to her master in the afternoon. In the morning yes, but never in the afternoon.

Once the door had closed on Jinnie, Rose Shaleman settled herself into a new position in the bed so that she could look fully at the tinker, and she said, 'Well, give us your news. What's the latest in your travels?'

'Well now, Missis Rose, I wouldn't know where to start. The world's going topsy-turvy, you know, really topsy-turvy, but some things remain the same, for instance, you know Hannah Brown?'

'Yes, I know Hannah Brown, tinkerman. Don't tell me . . .'

'Yes, I'm going to tell you; her fourteenth last week.'

'Never!'

''Tis a fact; her fourteenth, and all alive but one, and there's eight of them still at home.'

'In those three rooms?'

'In those three rooms, and as happy as a dog with two tails. The child was eight pounds and a boy, another one to tip up his earnings in a few years' time. And she'll be alive to receive it, for she's as healthy as a hog that's been brought up on milk and eggs, and she's forty-six, if a day. And that, Missis Rose, is a good thing. You know, all the years I've been travelling, I've never found big squads among people with money. I've only once heard of a squire who managed ten; for the rest it's one or two or three. Well, you've got to go no further than Towbridge House and the Baxton-Powells: two, Master Richard and Miss May, and the boy not of the strongest, as everybody knows, and it is said that there's a marriage in the offing for him – the Rowlands are returning this weekend from Scotland, I understand. A Hall it is, twice the size of Towbridge House. The maids could hardly look at my wares this morning, there was so much fuss and bustle going on. But then I suppose you would have heard about it before now with your son being a friend of Mister Richard. Now, I've always thought, Missis Rose, that that is one of the strangest friendships I've come across. Of course, it was only allowed, I know, because one saved the other's life; usually there's a small hand-out and that's that; but those two, well, I understand they still run on the hills together.'

Rose brought her chin tightly into her neck and there was a hint of annoyance in her tone as she said, 'I see nothing strange about their friendship. The House owes my son a great deal; but for him there wouldn't be an heir.'

'Oh, I quite agree with you and I've said as much, yes I have; I've said as much to the cook there, and before today: I've said, say what you like about it being odd that the young master should run the hills with the likes of . . . well, I mean, with an ordinary farmer's son and insists on doing it when he knows it annoys his mother and father.'

'Who told you that?'

'Oh, my dear, my dear Missis Rose, you get to hear all things in the kitchens of the great; and it isn't today or yesterday he was told to give up his running, supposedly because of his health. You know, he had rheumatic fever?'

'Nobody better than me knows that he had rheumatic fever, and nobody better than me knows that if it hadn't been for my son, who nearly died himself, he wouldn't be here today to get married, or anything else.'

'Missis Rose' – the white head was shaking from side to side – 'I've said those very words, those very very words I've said: I've said that the master and mistress should go down on their bended knees that they've got a son to run the hills, no matter who with. He's a gentleman, Mister Richard, a real gentleman, he knows he owes this house a debt, and he keeps on paying it in his own way, so I understand: you're not without your baskets of fruit or your butter at times. You don't need eggs. Oh no; you don't need eggs.'

The countenance of his customer told the tinker that it was time to take his leave; but he couldn't be dismissed so lightly. As he lifted his bag on to the table and buckled the leather straps together he said, 'You won't have heard from your son, I suppose? Being on a cargo boat like *The Admiral*, it'll be some time before he gets a letter to you, for I understand what's already out there just plies back and forward between the islands. Must be wonderful, that, to be aboard a ship that goes from one island to another.'

'How d'you know, tinkerman, that he's on a ship called *The Admiral*?'

'Oh, my dear Missis Rose, they were chatting about it in the King's Head the last time I was in. They were saying how funny it was that one man from these parts should choose to go to sea while another, Sam Valasquey, should suddenly decide to stay ashore. Now there's a bruiser of a man for you. I could never stand that man; most uncivil; a heathen of a man, really, and only too willing to use his fists, so that his poor wife almost always has both eyes looking the same colour. And why? Why?'

'Good day, tinkerman, but let me tell you you're on the wrong track this time.'

'I am? You mean . . .?'

'I mean nothing, but I know what *you* mean and I repeat, you're on the wrong track. Good day, tinkerman.'

'Good day to you, Missis Rose. I don't suppose I'll

119

be this way again until the New Year, but until I see you again, I wish you well.'

She did not return his farewell, and after the door had closed on the old man with his pack on his back, she lay back among the pillows and sighed deeply.

The tinkerman was her only means of getting news of the outside world, but he always managed to irritate her one way or another: another time, his barbs would have been against Pug.

Jinnie did not re-enter the house until she saw the tinker leaving, and when she did go into the kitchen she went straight to Rose and in a soft voice she said, 'Thank you so much, missis, for that lovely ribbon. I'll always keep it for special days.'

Mollified somewhat by Jinnie's attitude, Rose Shaleman nodded her head and said quietly, 'Well, you'll likely have a lot of special days now that you'll be able to see your Miss Caplin. You've got Bruce to thank for that, for he's been going out of his way on a Sunday to take the cart all the way round the top road and down to the Miss Duckworths, but I won't have that big fella up here, you understand?'

It was some seconds before Jinnie answered, 'Yes, missis, I understand;' but she was brave enough to go on and add, 'But I'd still like to see Max at times; so if you don't mind, some Sundays I'd rather go down.'

'Oh, get about your work, girl!' Rose Shaleman made an impatient movement with her hand and Jinnie turned somewhat sadly from the bed. Her mistress's attitude towards Max dimmed some of the wonder from the happenings of the day, and they had been wonderful, for hadn't she been able to buy that lovely locket for Miss Caplin, and hadn't the missis bought her that golden ribbon? She put her hand up to the back of her head now, where her single plait was pinned flatly against it. She ignored the plait but fingered the hair growing down towards her shoulder. It was growing fast, as Miss Caplin had said it would if she brushed it night and morning, and she did so then and any other spare minute she had, for she'd never feel whole again until she had another plait hanging down her back, at least at night time; but how long that would take she didn't know and even Miss Caplin couldn't tell her.

5

After a long dry spell it had rained unseasonably for
three days and nights and now the whole world seemed
sodden. The ground outside the cottage was like a
quagmire. The pigs were up to their haunches in
glar. The hens were bedraggled and their laying
had gone off. Inside the cottage there were lines
of old and sodden linen from underwear to top
coats stretched across the scullery, and the fire in
the kitchen wasn't drawing because the top of the
chimney was so damp. Dampness wasn't the word that
could be applied to Bruce's condition: having again
been soaked to the skin, he was changing into clothes
which were still damp. Jinnie was feeling absolutely
worn out, not only with the work in general but
also with having to contend with the fire to keep
it going. And when eventually her frustration caused
her to remark, 'It's bad coal this, there's no roundies
in it at all,' neither Bruce nor his mother made
any comment; although Rose Shaleman wanted to
say, 'Have you any idea, girl, what roundies or
the best coal cost for a load?' But Bruce began
to cough and she said, 'Look, take a drink of hot
ginger before you go out, you don't want that cough
to hang about. Girl, put the kettle on and make
Mister Bruce some hot ginger.'

'I don't want any hot ginger, Ma; I've filled myself
with hot ginger these past days, and what good has it

done? What I want is a set of dry clothes. And she's right, it's poor coal; but I'll tell you this much, Ma, the next lot I bring up won't be poor: if they ask treble for it, you'll have to stump up.' He turned now and abruptly he said to Jinnie, 'Pour me out a drop of broth.'

His mother's voice was placating now as she said, 'Must you go up there again?'

'Ma' – the word came slowly now, as if he wanted to drum something home – 'they're taking shelter in every nook and cranny. I've got half the number I want down. I've only one pair of legs and one pair of hands and the dog's only got four feet. What's more, when I've got what I want of them down I have to get them ready for market. You're not going to get good money for animals looking like drowned rats. And don't forget what you tend to point out every year; our survival through the winter depends on the August sale; and by the look of what I'm bringing down from the hills tells me that this coming winter's fare will be meagre if it weren't for double the number of your porkers we have this year.'

When she made no remark whatsoever he turned to the table and lifted up the bowl of broth Jinnie had placed there, warming his hands on it before putting it to his mouth and gulping down the contents.

He now pulled on a steaming greatcoat, then his cap, and lastly he took up a hessian sack from the floor, punched one end of it into the other until it formed a hood, which he then pulled on to his head over his cap and went abruptly out again into the driving rain.

Jinnie's body was tired and her mind weary. She had never experienced weather such as this. She didn't recall this kind of weather when she was in the workhouse. If it rained or snowed she had always been dry, sometimes cold, oh yes, often cold, but dry. There was a difference between being cold and dry and cold and wet. But here, by night-time her clothes would be wet, and she would be longing for sleep, only to be brought awake by the feeling of the damp pallet. It seemed years ago since a week on Sunday when Miss Caplin had come up here. The sun had been shining then, and it had been quite warm; and Miss Caplin had told her the great news that Max had applied to go out to work on a farm. She had stressed he had no real need to apply, that in fact he was free to go at any time: after all, he wasn't certified and, what's more, he had paid well for his keep with hard work. Anyway, Miss Caplin had taken it upon herself to write to a farmer in Weardale. His advert had appeared in the newspaper. Apparently he had a hill farm and wanted help but the advert stated that the applicant must be experienced in some form of farming. Miss Caplin had added quietly that she had described Max's impediment and his outsize stature, but added that these were compensated for by his intelligence on the one hand and his colossal strength and appetite for work to be of use on the other. The only disadvantage to Jinnie was that she would see less of him then than she did now.

The air of the room was heavy with the smell of sweat. She put her hand out and supported herself against the iron plate under the mantelshelf. If only it would stop raining and she could get the clothes dry and this room clean. She found the heat from the iron plate comforting to her hand, which was red and swollen. She was about to warm the other one when her mistress's voice brought her upright: ''Tis no time for dreaming, girl,' she was saying; 'if you want to be near the fire put the bellows to it; then get another pan of broth ready, because that's the best thing for anybody in this weather, and, if I know anything, Bruce'll be back before long. This is the third day of it and he can't stand much more. He's strong but he's not a horse.'

It was as if her mistress was talking to herself, and apparently she was, for she began muttering and her words became indistinct to Jinnie; in fact, all sounds became indistinct as she prepared the vegetables for the broth. These she scooped by the handful on to the ham bones which had served as the basis for the broth over the last three days. As she did so she thought: back in the house, after they had made the first broth, they used to throw the bones away. There must be nothing left in these, and it came to her that the bones were like herself, there was nothing left in her either. A few days ago when it had been dry and warm she had lain in bed one night and wondered if anything really nice would ever happen to her, and from somewhere deep within her had come the question: What did she want? What would she like to happen to her in a nice way? to which she could find no answer. Yet there was in her a strange desire, a longing for a little bit of wonder to come her way; but since the rain she had become more convinced that nothing nice would ever happen to her: she'd work in this house until she was old and like her mistress, and every day would be the same. Nothing seemed to change here. The place was enveloped in melancholy and she could see no escape from it.

Such were her thoughts until the clock on the mantelpiece showed six o'clock, and it was almost at that precise moment that the door was pushed open and Bruce staggered in, pressed the door closed, leant against it for a moment, then would have slid down to the floor had not his father, who was coming down the room carrying the empty soup bowl, flung it on the table and pushed himself against his son while crying to Jinnie, 'Give a hand here!'

When, between them, they went to place Bruce in a chair and saw immediately there was no way he could support himself, Jinnie cried, 'Lay him on the mat, mister. Lay him on the mat.'

Rose Shaleman was sitting on the edge of the bed now and she called to them, 'Don't let him lie down in those wet things, strip his coats off.'

And this they did, but only after much effort. When they laid him back on the mat his breath was coming in such short gasps that Jinnie imagined he was choking, and, jumping up, she ran to the bed crying, 'I must have a pillow!'

Her mistress almost threw the pillow at her, and when Pug raised his son's shoulders so that Jinnie could place the pillow in position, Bruce began to cough, and such was the tearing sound that Jinnie screwed up her face against it; then it was she who almost choked on a gasping cough as she looked up and saw her mistress hanging on to the edge of the table. She appeared to be so tall, almost as tall as Max, and she too was gasping as she addressed her husband, saying, 'Get him out of those wet trousers, man; and you girl, go up aloft and drop his hap and biscuit bed down and any clothes that you see lying about.'

Jinnie scrambled about in the roof space which, although much bigger than her own, was still cramped, and grabbing up the damp quilt she flung it through the hatch and on to the floor; there followed oddments of clothing, and lastly she dragged the pallet bed to the top of the ladder and slowly eased it down the side. She waited until it fell with a quiet thud on to the floor, then she was almost sliding down the ladder again, only to stop at the bottom: Bruce was lying quite naked and his mother, from a chair pulled to the side of the table, was yelling at her husband, 'Rub him hard! It's no good just drying him, rub him hard, get the blood flowing. Girl!' She had not directly addressed her, but Jinnie, keeping her eyes averted from the prone figure, darted to her side, saying, 'Yes, missis?'

'Pull the bed tick up here, then go and take the top sheet off my bed and pull it over. Be quick!'

Jinnie was quick, and when the sheet was placed over the tick Rose Shaleman said, 'You got a dryish blanket up there?'

'Not bad, missis.'

'Well, fetch it. Go on, quick!'

It seemed only seconds before she was back in the kitchen, the blanket held in her hands, and her mistress was shouting at her, 'Well, don't stand there with it; get down and wrap him in it.'

Her master had already wrapped some of the bottom sheet around his son and all she had to do was to lay her blanket hap on top of him; then she was tucking it in all around him.

Bruce had had his eyes closed most of the time, and now when he opened them he seemed to be looking up into hers and he muttered, 'Drink.'

And she, scrambling to her feet again, said, 'Yes, Mister Bruce; yes, I'll have you a hot drink in a couple of shakes.' Then of a sudden she stopped, saying, 'But how will I get to the fire, missis?'

Rose Shaleman didn't say, 'Well, step over him,' but looked down on her son for a moment, then said to her husband, 'Pull the tick towards me at the bottom; leave it so his head and chest are near the grate . . .'

A half hour passed, and although Bruce had been given another hot ginger drink, and pieces of flannel, wrung out in boiling water, had been placed on his chest, he still showed no improvement, more the reverse. Between gasps of racking coughing, he was talking to Mister Richard and using strange words as if he were reciting poetry, between times berating Hal and his father. Rose Shaleman looked at her husband and said, 'He's bad, he needs a doctor.'

''Tis just a heavy cold,' said Pug.

'Heavy cold be damned, man! He's had colds before, but never like this. If pneumonia sets in that'll be the finish of him. Andrew Stevens went the same way in this sort of weather, and he was the same age, so get your coat on and get down to the village or along to the Stevens'. Ask them to send one of the others down to the village or into Allendale, or wherever the doctor is stuffing himself with his high living, because he'll still be at it, if I know anything.'

'I could never find me way down there: it's coming on dark and me legs wouldn't take me; I'm slithering outside as it is. He'll be all right.'

'Be damned to you, Pug Shaleman, for a dirty little coward! You always were and you always will be.'

'All right. All right.' He was yelling at her. 'If I go, who's going to look after him?'

'The girl can do what has to be done.'

'It wouldn't be decent, woman, it wouldn't be decent.'

His wife now stared at him in silence for a moment, her mouth agape, and now in a strange and low voice, she said, 'God above! I can't believe me ears. You! you above all men talk about decency connected with man, woman, or child.' She now gripped the edge of the table and pulled herself round to say to Jinnie, standing wide-eyed, 'D'you know where the Stevens's farm is?'

'I've never been there, missis, but I've got an idea. It's on the road past the pool, and when Mister Bruce' – she inclined her head to the heaving figure on the floor – 'when he brought Miss Caplin and me up he pointed down the hill into the valley and said that was where we got our milk from. There was a road went off.'

'D'you think you could find it?'

'Aye, missis. Oh aye, I'll find it.'

'Well, hap up as much as you can, girl, and get away. Say to Mrs Stevens I sent you, say that my Bruce is very sick and would she oblige me by sending one of the men for Dr Beattie.'

'Yes, missis, yes.'

'Take your clogs off – you'll lose them in the mud before you get halfway down the bank – put your boots on and put a sack on your head, not your hat; your hat's no good the night.'

Jinnie now dashed into the scullery and up into her loft, and there, grabbing up her coat and her boots, she came down the steps again, put on the coat, slipped out of her clogs and laced up her boots; then from a cupboard, she plucked out a piece of the rough linen she had brought with her from the workhouse and, folding the square crosswise, she put it on her head and tied a knot underneath her plaited coil: she couldn't bear the thought of the dirty hessian sack, when it should become wet, sticking to her hair. Then running into the kitchen, she said, 'I'm off, missis.'

Her mistress said no word, but gave her a sharp nod.

Outside, head down, she began to run, past the pigsty and the barn; she then scrambled crabwise up the hill until she reached the rough road. Here the wind was stronger, driving the rain into her face, each drop as cold as an icicle. She tried to run holding the sack well forward over her brow, but this impeded her balance.

Presently, above the whistling of the wind and the beating of the rain, she thought she heard the neighing of a horse; but on turning and peering back, she could see no sign of one so she stumbled on.

She had almost reached the place where the road leading to the farm diverged when she was startled out of her wits by the sound of the screeching of wheels, which lifted her into the ditch with fright. She knew she was lying against the bank, her face pressed tight to the earth, and when a hand came on her shoulder and a voice said, 'What on earth are you doing out here, girl?' her mouth went into a gape and she slumped against the wet bank and peered up through her dripping eyelids at Richard Baxton-Powell.

He had taken hold of her hand and had pulled her on to the road, and again he was asking, 'Why are you out here?'

'I . . . I was going for a doctor, sir.'

'Oh; is Mrs Shaleman worse?'

'No.' As she shook her head the sack dropped from her shoulders, and now, seeing that the white cloth she was wearing over her hair was getting soaked, he pulled her towards the carriage door, then almost roughly he put his hand under her oxters, saying, 'Get up there a moment,' only to add quickly, 'Oh, I'm sorry, May; but she's drenched. And anyway, I can't stay out in this.'

In the dimness of the carriage Jinnie made out the figure of an elegantly dressed young woman who was staring at her none too kindly, and she said, 'I'm sorry, ma'am.'

'Well, who's ill?' Richard demanded.

'Bruce. Mister Bruce. He managed to get into the house before collapsing. He's lying by the fire now. He's very bad, sir.'

'Bruce? But . . . but why were you on this road going for the doctor?'

'To ask Mr Stevens to send a man for him.'

'Oh, I see.' He now turned and looked at his sister and explained, 'She's from Bruce's place.' But the reply to this came through tight lips: 'I gather as much; then let her get out of the way.'

'How can I, May? She's wringing and she's some way to go over those fields to the farm. Look, I'll drop you home, then go and pick up the doctor. It's as little as I can do.'

'I think I've heard that phrase before with regard to the person in question. And I don't have to remind you that if you don't get back to the Rowlands' for dinner, Mother'll have something to say to you, more than she has already, and that's not to mention Father, with regard to that abode. To my mind this whole thing is becoming a bone of contention; a debt is a debt but once it's paid, it's done with.'

'Shut up!' The words were softly said but nevertheless uttered emphatically, and Jinnie realised that this gentleman's continued association with Bruce must be causing much trouble at The Manor, and so, quickly, she put in, 'Look, sir; I know me way and once I get off the road I'll soon cover that field,' and she put her hand out to open the door. But his voice stayed her. 'Sit where you are,' he said, not in a kindly tone, but in one of command. Then he pulled down the window and shouted to the driver, 'Tim! Make for The House. We'll drop Miss May off; then we'll drive to the village to pick up the doctor.'

'As you say, Mister Richard. As you say.'

The words seemed to be wafted into the carriage on a gust of wind; then the window was closed and Jinnie found herself jolted back in the seat; and as the carriage moved on she remembered the sack and was about to remark that she mustn't leave it behind, when she thought the better of it.

The young lady was muttering something but the noise of the carriage wheels blotted out the words until her voice rose and she said, 'You'll go too far one of these days; Father won't stand for it.'

There was no answer forthcoming but Jinnie could see that Mister Richard had thrown one leg over the other, which she took as a sign of him being annoyed.

Presently, she felt the slowing down of the carriage and when it seemed to turn she was jolted again; then the horses trotted a short way before they stopped, and Mister Richard, opening the door, said to her, 'Stay where you are.' Then he held out his hand to help his sister alight; and Jinnie had been quick to note that the young woman made sure that her cloak and dress did not come in contact with her own long and sodden coat.

Left alone, she looked through the window and saw in the light of a bright lantern a flight of steps leading to the house, and a man dressed in a green breeches suit holding an umbrella over the young lady as she mounted the steps.

Now Mister Richard was shouting up to the driver: 'Turn them round, Tim; I won't be long.'

Although it was only five minutes before Mister Richard reappeared, to Jinnie it had seemed an age, and she felt she could have reached the farm by now.

'We needn't go as far as Allendale,' Richard was calling up to the driver. 'I understand we might find him in the village; he left here only half an hour ago.'

The door was pulled open now, and then he was sitting opposite her in the grey light and she was experiencing the most odd sensation and recalling how, only last night, she had lain in bed and asked herself if anything wonderful or even just nice would ever happen to her, and here she was riding in a carriage with a gentleman sitting opposite her. She was no longer feeling wet or sodden; in fact, her body was experiencing a warm glow. Mister Richard was nice, he was kind; in a way he wasn't unlike Mister Bruce, only Mister Bruce wasn't so polite as Mister Richard, nor did he look so smart; and he hadn't the same accent. Well, he wouldn't have. And yet he didn't speak rough. Oh no; it was surprising that Mister Bruce didn't speak rough, not like Mister Hal or his father. And sitting there musing and half asleep she thought, well, wasn't it wonderful to know three nice men. Max of course would always come first, then Mister Bruce, and now Mister Richard.

The swaying of the carriage was like being rocked in a cradle, she imagined. She felt comfortable and warm and so tired. She wasn't actually aware of the carriage stopping, and so when she opened her eyes and heard no sound about her, she closed them again.

It was some time later when she jerked them wide to the sound of a strange voice saying, 'Why d'you concern yourself? They are scum up there.'

'They are human beings in need and you're a doctor.'

'Look, Mister Richard; if it wasn't who you are, and I have great respect for your father and your lady mother, I would tell you where you could go to at this minute, and that lot up there too, but as it is, I'm not taking my horse and trap out this night. If you take me up you'll bring me back.'

'That's agreed. Well, then, will you get in or d'you want us both drenched?'

That the doctor was surprised to drop on to a seat opposite a white-faced girl with a plait over one shoulder in tangled disarray and with a white cloth hanging round her neck, was putting it mildly; and his eyes travelled down her greatcoat to where it was dripping water on to her boots.

Richard had taken his seat when the doctor demanded, 'Who's that?'

'She's the little maid from up there.'

'A maid up there? Who would stay up there? A maid?'

'Yes, you've said it, doctor, who would stay up there? She's been up there for some months now. And if I remember, and Bruce is right, it's two years or more since you last visited the place, and all you did was leave tablets.'

'What more could anybody do? She's on her last legs. She has been for years now; I'm surprised she's still here. She'll go out like a light one day.'

'Yes, she'll go out like a light one day.'

The doctor's voice rose above the grinding of the wheels and the horses' hooves as he cried, 'Don't take that attitude with me, Mister Richard. I know these people better than you do.'

'That you do not, doctor; at least not one of them.'

'Oh, we're on about the saving of life again. That kind of thing's happening every day, and the debt doesn't go on for ever. If a man is rescued by a cannibal it doesn't mean that he can let the cannibal eat him by way of thanks.'

Jinnie was very wide awake now and aware once again that she was at the centre of trouble; but then she heard Mister Richard laugh as he said, 'That's a very good simile, doctor. Indeed, I must remember it.'

There followed a silence apart from the noise of the vehicle; then, as if the conversation had never been interrupted, and in a more moderate tone, the doctor said, 'You know, Mister Richard, people can't understand you running the hills with young Shaleman.'

Mister Richard did not reply, and a silence again seemed to weigh on Jinnie, making the journey seem never-ending. And the silence wasn't broken until the driver shouted, 'Whoa there!' and she realised that they had reached the cottage.

Jinnie sat still until the doctor had descended from the carriage, and then she was checked from alighting herself by Mister Richard's voice calling to the driver: 'There's a barn further along, Tim; see if it will give the horses a bit of shelter until we are ready.'

When the man replied, 'Yes, sir,' Jinnie imagined that the carriage was about to move on, and so, seeming to decline the outstretched hand, she jumped. Unfortunately her feet landed in a pool of muddy water which sprayed over the legs of both the doctor and Richard, and the older man cried at her, 'You stupid girl! Look what you've done,' as he pulled off a glove and whacked the front of his trousers back and forth.

Jinnie looked at Mister Richard's legs. His trousers were of some dark material and his shoes made of a fine leather and they too were bespattered with the muddy water. Again she heard that long intake of breath.

She ran to the cottage and thrust it open; and although she was used to it, the stench of wet clothes and body odours hit her like a wave. Her mistress was still sitting in the chair, bent over, with her hand on her son's head, while her husband was bathing Bruce's chest with a piece of hot flannel.

'What's this? What's this?'

At the words, Pug Shaleman jerked round, and his wife said curtly, 'Well, doctor, you can see for yourself, if you look closer: he's in a bad way.' She had never liked the man: she would never have sent for him for herself, and it must be all of two years since he was last up here. 'He can't last like this, his chest is bursting,' she added.

The doctor dropped his bag on to the table. He had not removed either his tall hat or his overcoat, because he could see nowhere suitable to lay them; then he went towards the hearth, where first of all he touched Pug with the toe of his shoe, saying, 'Get up out of that, man,' then, turning to Rose, said, 'and move back, woman.'

He did not kneel down but dropped on to his hunkers and, lifting Bruce's hand, he felt his pulse, after which he turned and looked up at Richard, saying, 'Hand me my bag, please,' and having been given it, hesitated whether or not to put it on the floor. He finally did; and extracted from it a stethoscope and began to sound Bruce's chest. After a moment he returned the instrument to his bag; then to no-one in particular he said, 'Pneumonia. What he'll need is a cage.'

'A cage?'

He straightened up and looked at the woman of this place, as he thought of her, and said, 'Yes, Mrs Shaleman, a cage over his head and chest to keep in steam.'

'Oh, that. Well, we can soon fix that up.'

'I'm glad to hear you say so. It's a pity you didn't think of it before. Also, it's a pity he hadn't seen to his own condition before, for I should imagine he's been like this for some time. And I must tell you plainly, if he gets through tonight he'll be lucky.' He lifted his bag and replaced it on the table, and from a small cardboard box he took ten tablets and placed these on the table in single file, saying, 'If he should need them you will see that he takes two a day.' Then after a moment he said, 'There's nothing more I can do. It's up to God and a steam kettle of sorts now. And, mind, he'll need constant attention all night. Where's your other son?' He was now addressing Pug, who answered him in almost a growl. 'At sea,' he said.

'Oh well, that only leaves you and—' He paused before his gaze fell on Jinnie again, and to her he said abruptly, 'You'll have to keep awake or take turns; it's up to both of you now; I can do no more. And as for you, Mrs Shaleman, I'd advise you to get back into bed before you need a night watch too; you're only a hindrance where you're sitting. You know that, don't you? That chair you're on will probably be needed to help make the tent.'

He now picked up his bag and made for the door, saying to Richard, 'We'll be on our way. I had to break an evening's engagement for this, so you'll oblige me by getting me back as quickly as possible.'

Richard stood for a moment and looked from one to the other in the room: to the mother of his friend, then to the undersized father, then to the girl, that slip of a girl, and lastly he looked down on to his friend before turning abruptly and following the doctor out.

He had not uttered a word since he had first entered the room.

If Mrs Rowland was annoyed by the fact that her future son-in-law – which state was not yet known to the man in question – carried his charitableness to exaggerated lengths she showed no hint of it; in fact, she welcomed him in as she always had done, giving not the slightest indication that she had noticed his bespattered trousers and shoes. Her daughter took after her, for Lillian greeted him in the hall with a low tinkling laugh as she said, 'You're very wise to make it late, Richard; Miss Bristow and Mr Williams have finished their duet, and Colonel Falconer has gone over his army exploits yet again. Anyway, we have held dinner until you should arrive home. Your mother and May are in the drawing-room, but your father has escaped with mine to the smoke-room.'

Lillian Rowland was nineteen years old. She was plump and pretty and, like her parents, a Christian of the highest standard. Like her parents, too, she had never missed Mass and she believed firmly in life everlasting, of course as she had known it on earth, and that all this was guaranteed to her through the Church.

The affinity between the Rowlands and the Baxton-Powells was close in all ways, for were not the Baxton-Powells High Church; in fact, so high that as far as they themselves were concerned, there seemed to be little difference between the two denominations, certainly no impediment in the coming together of the daughter of the one house and the son of the other? The parents of both these young people were agreed on this. If the matter of marriage had still to be voiced it was certainly understood by all concerned.

The dinner, as usual, was excellent, perhaps made more so by the fact that, although religion played a great part in the life of the Rowlands, it didn't mean that it was fortified only by ethereal spirit, oh no; Mr Rowland enjoyed his whisky, Mrs Rowland was partial to port; and as for Lillian, she loved sherry; but of course, none of these natural tastes was indulged in during Lent. Later, it was agreed that the whole evening had been so very enjoyable.

When it came to Richard saying goodbye, he kissed Lillian on the cheek, and she returned the kiss in the same way; then linking her arm in his, she walked with him down the steps. The rain had stopped and there was a full moon, the light from which was outdoing the lanterns.

When the carriage door had closed on Richard, Lillian called through the window, 'Will you be at the Wisdons' tomorrow, May?'

'No; I'm sorry, I forgot to tell you, Lillian, we are going by train into Newcastle tomorrow.'

'Oh, how exciting. We'll have to make up a party one day and all go in.'

'Yes; yes, we will.'

The goodbyes flowed back and forth now; then the carriage moved away, Richard pushed up the window, then lay back against the leather headrest and waited for the reprimand. But it was not forthcoming until they reached the house, when it was very brief: 'I will see you in the morning, sir,' Mr Baxton-Powell informed his son, and without waiting for a reply, ushered his wife away hastily up the stairs.

However, May seemed to be determined to express her feelings, for after handing her cape and hat to the manservant, she said, and in a polite tone, 'Can you spare me a moment, Richard?'

Richard followed and, after closing the door behind him, was greeted with: 'You know, you won't get away with it this time; Father really is wild.'

'Away with what, May?' His voice sounded tired.

'Your escapade tonight, playing the good Samaritan.'

'No; I won't get away with it, not if you grow expansive on the matter.'

'I won't have to; they must have drawn conclusions from your clothes; as no doubt did Lillian and her dear mama, not to say her father. I bet he's over here tomorrow to see Father, determined to get to the bottom of it, and why you should be so concerned for that dirty little brat of a girl. And they've always objected to your running the hills with that fellow up there. You know that. They would accept your running with Tim for he is a household servant, but not when you take up with a person who isn't even a farmer. As I understand it, they live up there like prehistoric animals.'

'Yes, they do live like prehistoric animals, May; you don't know you're born. A flick of fate and you could be that young girl up there living in that stinking hole; and it *is* stinking. I hold out no excuses for the father, for he's twisted in mind and body, and the mother is not far behind him, but that's been through illness; and her elder son has always been a drunken bully; but Bruce is a different kettle of fish altogether. I don't know how he came to be bred of them, because he's a highly intelligent fellow, and something of a poet too.'

'A what?'

'I said he is a poet, and I mean a poet: he can hardly write, but he can turn his own thought into magic lines. I, too, have a love for life, for the open spaces, for the beauty of nature and for lovely things, and I would know nothing about them at this moment if it hadn't been for Bruce Shaleman. He saved my life at the risk of his own, and no matter what you or Mother or Father say, or anyone else, I owe him the debt of my life, and this knowledge didn't come instantly, I can tell you. It came when I was lying on my back for a year and I recognized taste, smell, touch and sight in a way that I'd never done before, and all through his visits during that period. And it was he who got me on my feet again; nobody expected me to walk. And, also, I had lain in that gully expecting to die and go into nothingness, yes, nothingness, not heaven with a halo waiting for me as they would have had me believe.'

'Oh, Richard,' May's voice was a plea now, 'please don't turn away from your religion, too; it would break their hearts.'

After a moment he said quietly, 'No, I won't turn away, I'll play the hypocrite, as I've been doing for some time now, because between you and me, May, I don't believe a damn word of it, all the gospels, all the preaching.'

'Oh, Richard.' Her voice came as a beseeching whisper and he went and sat beside her. Putting an arm around her shoulder, he said, 'I'm sorry. I'm sorry, May. I don't want to distress you, but as a result of that accident that's how I feel. You know, during that year I lay on my back, I seem to have lost all my youth; I have never felt young since. And I know I've got to face up to myself. My body isn't strong because of this chest business, and I take the easier way out because I can't bear hurting people.'

She now patted his hand and said, 'I'm sorry I went for you, but I do love you, Richard, and I am concerned for you.' And she added, 'But I would ask you to keep the better side of your nature to the fore, and don't hurt the parents,' in reply to which, he smiled at her, saying, 'What the eye doesn't see, the heart doesn't grieve over, so I'll practise my hypocrisy.'

Timothy Riley was what was known in the Baxton-Powell family as an all-rounder, although mainly he was Master Richard's man. His parents had died in the Baxton-Powells' service. They were both elderly when he was born and they had occupied what was known as the Back Lodge Cottage. The cottage had once been a farmhouse and so had stables attached, and even now the every-day carriage and two horses were stabled there.

George Mather, the main carriage driver, had also suffered badly from the wet weather, and he had been ordered to bed with a severe cold. Tim had been detailed to pick up Master Richard and Miss May from the station at Haydon Bridge. It was part of his duties to see to Master Richard's wants last thing at night and first thing in the morning, but on this night he was detailed to help the yard man rub down and bed the animals and dry off the main carriage so that its high varnish would not be marked with dried raindrops.

Knowing this, Richard had told Riley not to bother with him; he would see to himself. He had given this order in the hearing of his father, but had then made his way to the yard through the side-door, calling Tim aside and giving him a new order, which was to go to his cottage but not to retire to bed until he returned.

Timothy Riley had ceased to be surprised at anything his young master said or did, and because he considered that most of what Richard did was right, he felt no strain in sitting up awaiting his arrival.

His fire was burning brightly, his pipe was drawing well, and he had just stuck the poker into a mug of beer when a knock came on the door. Jumping up, he immediately opened it and for a moment showed some surprise to see how his young master was dressed, for he was wearing high boots and a large cape over his topcoat, with an earflap cap on his head.

'Have you any spare sheets, Tim?'

'Sheets, Master Richard, bed-sheets?'

'Yes, of course: bed-sheets, and what goes with them, pillow-cases and towels.'

'Well, yes, yes,' he said, somewhat bemused; 'there's a drawer full of them in the next room. They never cleared them after Dad died, and I've got my own share, which are changed every week, top and bottom. At least, they give them to me to change.'

'Tim – ' Richard's voice held a note of impatience as he said, 'I want two pairs of sheets, pillow-cases, some towels and any food that you've got to spare, and now.'

After one keen glance at his master, Tim hurried out of the room, to return shortly with four sheets, four pillow-cases and three towels. These he dropped on to the table and, placing his hands flat on them, he looked at Richard and said earnestly, 'You're not going back up there the night, sir, surely? It's killing out.'

'No such thing; the moon's shining and it's drying up quickly. Anyway, since you ask, that *is* where I'm going.'

'Well, if you're going, I'm goin' an' all.'

'Oh no, you're not! I'll have enough trouble crossing country myself without looking after you. You know you hate walking, at least on the hills.'

'I've done it afore with you, sir.'

'Well, you're not doing it tonight. Now look, have you any spare food?'

'What kind, sir, meat, milk?'

'Anything.'

Tim pulled open the cupboard door to show three shelves well stocked with bread, butter, meat pies and bottled fruit, and standing on the front of one shelf was a meat dish holding the remains of a piece of sirloin. Lifting this up, Tim said, 'The only real meat I have is that, sir; and Cook gave it to me for Betsy, but I thought I should keep it. There's a nice bit on it.'

'Well, cut if off then, wrap it up in a handkerchief and give me whatever else you have in there: butter, tea, sugar, and cheese, et cetera. I'll see it's all replaced later.'

This Tim did; but all the while shaking his head, and saying, 'You'll not get this lot up there yourself.'

'You've never seen me pack a knapsack. Wrap them up singly so the sugar won't spill.' And Richard added, 'Don't worry about losing your handkerchiefs, there's plenty more. You know where they are. Now, let me see.' He unrolled the canvas bag he had brought with him; then spreading the sheets, pillow cases and towels on the bottom, he laid the food on top; then before he went to pull the flap over, he said, 'There's nothing else you've got to spare, I suppose?'

'No; no, sir. The only things you haven't got are eggs; and they've got plenty up there, I should imagine, but no milk.'

'Milk? Dear, dear! But I can't carry milk.'

'Tell you what, sir. I've got a couple of tins of condensed milk in the back here. I never use it 'cos it's sweet like. It's got sugar in. You have to dilute it.'

'Let's have them, Tim.'

When the knapsack was strapped up, Tim said dolefully, 'If it starts raining, sir, all that stuff could get sodden long before you get there.'

'Not the way I mean to carry it, Tim,' and at this he unclasped the neck of his cloak, saying, 'Give me a heave up on to my back with it.' He slipped his arms through the straps, then pulled on his cloak again, saying, 'This is mackintosh, so nothing'll get through it. It never has. I often bless Mr Macintosh. Now, listen, Tim. I'll be back about seven. Get a bath ready for about then. See to my room; I mean, remake the bed and so on, as usual, and lay my striped serge out for tomorrow. We are due to go into Newcastle.' He had nearly forgotten about this arrangement, which he had meant to get out of, but he had the feeling that if he complied willingly, it might take the edge off his father's tongue in the morning.

'Sure you'll be all right, sir?'

'Tim, how many times before have you let me out of the side door on nights like this; even on occasions dropped me from the window? Do you remember the time it was on to the conservatory roof? My hat! It was a miracle I didn't go through, but I slid down like an eel on to the ground and was away.'

'Yes, sir, and left me with my heart in my mouth. But this night is different. The ground is still sodden; there'll be gullies full of water, and you can never trust a moon like that. Anyway, be careful. And, sir, let me ask you not to cut across country, but to keep as much to the high road as you can. It's not much further, and it'll be safer in the long run.'

Richard paused a moment, then nodded at his man, saying, 'Yes, you're right, Tim. All right, I'll do as you advise. Be seeing you in the morning.'

Tim pulled open the door and Richard edged his way outside. Then, humping the load further on to his shoulders, he hurried away. And Tim, his head shaking, watched until he had disappeared from sight.

The sweat was streaming down the faces of both of them: Pug Shaleman had taken off his shirt and vest and was standing in his trousers; Jinnie's apron had long been discarded and the front of her print dress was unbuttoned almost down to the curve of her breasts. Her underclothes were sticking to her; she had even discarded her stockings and clogs. For the countless time she took the steaming kettle from Pug's hand and refilled the two basins under the blanket that was covering the chairs, and whisked it back and forth above Bruce's chest.

The skin on his chest was scarlet, as was that on his face. Whether what little steam that came from the basins was doing him any good could not be known for he was still gasping for breath. At times his coughing would bring him up from the floor.

It was about one o'clock when his mother, pulling the blanket aside, looked through the bars of the chairs down on her son and, knowing that he could not last much longer in this condition, dragged herself from the chair and went back to her bed, where she lay staring at the ceiling.

When her husband came to her side and, wiping the sweat from his face with his forearm, croaked, 'He can't last,' she answered quietly, 'I know.'

'I've done all I can.' His tone was apologetic, and she answered again, 'Aye, I know;' but when he added, 'I'm beat meself. I don't know how much longer I can stick on me legs,' her voice was curt as she said, 'You'll stick on your legs till he goes,' and at this he turned away from her to go back to the fireplace and assist Jinnie by once again lifting a kettle from the fire and handing it to her . . .

When the door was thrust open and a big humped figure appeared, the cry Rose Shaleman let out drowned those of her husband and Jinnie, for it was as if the black-cloaked figure was the devil.

'Oh, I'm sorry. I'm sorry. I should have knocked, but I didn't want to disturb anybody.' Richard's voice trailed away and he looked from where Rose had slumped back into her pillows to Pug Shaleman, kneeling bent forward, his hand covering his face; and as for Jinnie, having just refilled the two basins, she had just dropped the kettle, luckily with only a little water still in it, but enough to splash on her arm, causing her to cry out again.

Richard had thrown off his cap and cloak and lowered the knapsack on to the table and dropped into a chair, saying, 'How is he?'

It was Rose Shaleman who answered, 'Bad, sir; very bad. I don't think he can last much longer.'

Richard left the table and, kneeling by the chairs, he threw off the blanket; and when he saw the condition of Bruce's upper body and face he cringed inwardly and bit tight on his lip. Then in a voice of authority, he said, 'He's had enough of this; take all this stuff away. Then you, girl, empty that knapsack and get me the sheets and towels.'

When the towels were put in his hand, he took the softest and began gently to dry Bruce's face and upper body. Presently, he said, 'Take out a sheet and hold it before the fire,' and it was Pug Shaleman who obeyed this order.

Then, to Jinnie's amazement, Richard said, 'Have you got a tin opener?' and when she replied, 'Yes; yes, sir,' he ordered briskly, 'Open a tin of condensed milk, put four spoonfuls into a mug and fill it three parts with boiling water, then bring it here.'

She obeyed these orders exactly and when she brought it to him he rose to his knees, took off his overcoat, then drew out a small silver-topped flask from an inside pocket and, unscrewing the top, poured a good measure of brandy into the hot milk. He then knelt down by Bruce's head and, slipping an arm under his shoulders, he gently raised him, saying, 'Come on, fellow, drink this.'

Bruce's parched lips made no movement to sip and when Richard poured a little of the milk into his mouth it immediately caused a bout of coughing. At this, Richard handed the mug back to Jinnie and, taking the towel

147

again, he began to massage the upper part of Bruce's chest.

It wasn't until the fourth attempt that Bruce could swallow the milk laced with the brandy, after which Richard said to Pug, 'Help me to turn him over and get this wet sheet off him. And you, girl, put the dry one in a roll and push it underneath him from yon side, understand?'

'Yes, sir, mister;' and although she said she understood what was required of her, she tried to keep her gaze away from the naked body she was handling.

This was the second time she had looked upon Bruce's naked body, and the sight was disturbing her. However, the business was soon over, and Bruce was not only lying in dry sheets, but also his breathing seemed a little easier. The damp blanket Richard threw to one side and said, 'Pass me my greatcoat.' This he placed over the sheets; then swinging round, he pulled his cape from the chair and laid this half-way up Bruce's body, so that it could be tucked under his feet. Then taking up the softest towel of the three, he again began to wipe Bruce's swollen and contorted face.

For a time there was only the sound of the agonized breathing in the room, that is until Pug, who had been sitting at yon side of the fireplace, fell on to his side and awoke with a start, saying, 'I'm sorry but I'm . . . well, I feel all in.'

'Yes, you're bound to,' said Richard. 'I would go to bed: there's nothing you can do for some hours yet. I'll call you if necessary.'

He stood up and looked towards the bed, saying, 'I'd advise you to do the same, Mrs Shaleman. Once the fever reaches its height, I'll let you know.'

'Yes, sir. Thank you, sir.'

Richard now turned his head away, partly with

embarrassment and disgust, when he saw the small man crawling over his wife to the far side of the bed. Then he looked at the slim girl hanging a thin blanket on the rod. She had to double it so that it would not cut out the heat from the fire; and bending down to her, he said, 'I'm going to sit here' – he pointed to a chair that was near Bruce's head – 'Would you like to go to bed?'

'Oh no, sir. Oh no; no. Not when Mister Bruce is like this. I can keep awake; you'll probably want help. I'll sit here, near the fire.'

He smiled at her gently, thinking, Not for long, you won't, because her eyelids were already drooping and her face looked utterly weary. He could see no place for her to sleep, except on the bare floor.

His eyes took in the knapsack on the table, and, calling her to him and with a wag of his finger, he whispered, 'Take the rest of the stuff out of the bag. Put it in a cupboard; then bring the bag to me and I'll show you something.'

Quickly she did this, and after she had handed him the knapsack he took the straps and tucked them in, then folded it into a short form of pallet, saying, 'You see, the bottom's quite stiff. It isn't very long, but if you lay it alongside the wall there and put your feet towards the fire, you can curl up on a good part of it. And look, take that towel, the big one, and roll it up and make a pillow of it.'

She stared blankly at him, her mouth slightly agape, for she said, 'What if you want help, and the kettle, and . . . ?'

'I won't need the kettle, not for a while, since you've made up the milk. I'll wake you if I need you.'

She stared at him for a moment longer; then taking the knapsack from him she turned about and laid it down against the wall as he had instructed, and for the first time he noticed her hair. One bedraggled plait was twisted on her head above her ear, making her head appear lopsided, so that he noticed the hair growing in straggly ends on the left side of her neck. Good gracious! he almost exclaimed aloud. She had only one plait, the other had been cut off. Why? Who had done such a thing? She had had beautiful hair: he had once watched her washing it in the pool, and afterwards it had fallen like a cloak about her. He recalled the day when, out riding, he had reached the end of the ridge, when the light hitting the top of the hill in the far distance made him draw the horse towards the broken wall bordering the ridge, and he had taken from his pocket the book which he always kept there. It was no larger than four inches long and three wide. It had a pencil in the slot of the cover and, over the years, he had used many such for sketching parts of this attractive countryside. Later, in the deep winter months, or when his bones ached too badly, he would transfer special sketches to canvas and the memory would be reproduced in oils. But this day his hand became still on the book, because out of the corner of his eye he saw a small figure bending over the pool below, with its hair floating out on top of the water. For a moment he thought someone had drowned, and then he felt further amazement as he watched two hands come up and massage the scalp, then sway the head backwards and forwards in the water. Suddenly the head came up and back and the naiad that she represented at this moment now began to dry her long tresses with a towel.

He recalled that he almost prayed that his horse wouldn't neigh or make any movement, because he knew that never again would he see a picture so perfect and innocent.

The next toss of the head had sprayed the hair around

the small shoulders, and it fell like a cape on to her hips. Following this, she put her hands behind her flat on the grass and still with her legs tucked beneath her she leaned backwards, her face turned to the sun. He recalled the tight restriction that had gripped him by the throat, and he had known he must move away for he was experiencing pain, a pain evoked by unusual beauty.

But could this be the same child? No, this was no child, this was a girl, soon to be a young woman. But look at her, half her hair gone and in such a bedraggled state! Well, what could you expect from anyone living in this hovel? And for a moment he thought of the maids in his own home, and he knew that even they would scorn to take her place, even the meanest of them.

Yet when he saw her lying with her head on the rolled towel on the knapsack, the damp hair on her forehead, her cheeks streaked with dirt, the red and swollen hands now joined together on the makeshift pillow near her face, the hidden beauty of the water nymph remained.

When Bruce moaned and his chest heaved painfully, Richard dropped on to his hunkers and raised him up, saying, 'Spit it out, Bruce. Get rid of it. That's it. That's it,' and his own words took him back down the years to the time when he lay like this, coughing as if his heart would burst, and his godmother, one Lady Hannah Bolton, uttering those same words, 'Get it up, boy. Get it up. Spit it out.' He recalled now, with an inward smile, that his godmother had been a disturber of the peace, for she had stayed with them for two months during his bad period, and had succeeded in upsetting the whole household. As for his mother and father, they were worn out by the time she left in order to go on one of her arranged tours. Poking her nose in, she called it, and she had poked her nose into many countries. The only thing that seemed to prevent her from entering a country was a revolution; an ordinary war she could take in her stride. No-one had known his godmother's real age, but he guessed it must have been fiftyish. He knew now what he didn't at the time she had nursed him, the reason for her interest in him: it was because he was like his grandfather and she had, let it be whispered, in her early years been that gentleman's mistress. It was a buried secret in the family, because his grandmother, he was told, had taken to her bed on hearing of the liaison. How shocked his parents would have been if they knew that he had received the news from Lady Hannah herself.

And now her voice seemed to have taken over his own as he laid Bruce back and, his face hovering over the sweating distorted features, he said, 'Now listen to me, Bruce: you've got the will, you must use it. D'you hear me? Oh, you can hear me. Look – ' his voice was a whisper but the words came strongly, 'who am I going to run with if not you? Who can I talk to, if not you? You've got a mind, a poetic mind, and I've told you till I'm tired that you've got to learn to write. I'm going to see that you write. You hear me, fellow? I'm going to see that you write. Now it's coming up to the testing time.' Yes, that's what his godmother had said, and he repeated it, 'Bruce, hear me! It's coming up to the testing time. Make an effort.' Then once again he was holding him up and using his godmother's words, 'That's it. It's better out than in. Get it all up.'

Following on this bout, Richard drew himself up on to the chair again and other than periodically wiping the sweating face and rubbing down the heaving chest, and easing drops of brandy and milk down his friend's throat, he did nothing more.

He had been sitting on the chair with his legs wide apart so that he could bend easily, but at what time he crossed his legs and put his right forearm on top of them while his other hand lay on the edge of the seat, he didn't know, but he was amazed and not a little ashamed when, blinking his eyes, he opened them fully to realise he had dropped off to sleep.

Gasping himself now, he looked down on to Bruce. He pressed his eyeballs with his finger and thumb for a moment, then when he opened them it was to see Bruce lying quietly looking up at him.

He was on his hunkers in an instant and, putting his hand on the still sweating brow and stroking back the wet hair, he said, 'Good. Good. You've made it.'

Bruce was now moving his swollen lips and when on a croak he brought out the word, 'Dry,' Richard said, 'Right. Right; I'll get you a drink,' and he rose to his feet and went to the table.

There was still some cold condensed milk in a mug. His nose wrinkled at it for a moment, but it was either that or water, and he decided there was more substance in the milk, and he made certain there was more when he added drops of brandy from his flask.

Bruce actually gulped at the liquid, then lay back and closed his eyes for a moment.

'Go to sleep.' Richard's voice was low, and when Bruce lifted a weary hand towards him, Richard clasped it and their gaze held. Then, like a child, Bruce closed his eyes, turned his head to the side and went to sleep. Again Richard sat in the chair and he, too, after a time, went to sleep and did not wake until the cock crowed . . .

Later, while he was walking back home, he stopped suddenly to look up at the lightening sky. There was a strange feeling on him: he should have been feeling tired, but instead there was a feeling of lightness as if a burden had been lifted from his shoulders. And it came to him that that was exactly what had happened. For years now he had been paying the interest on a debt which he imagined could never be cleared: his friendship and running the hills with Bruce had been obligations expected of him. But after what had happened this night he could, in all honesty, now tell himself that he had given Bruce back his life and in doing so had expiated his own debt.

If he hadn't been aware of the atmosphere prevailing in the breakfast-room, May's quick glance and raised eyebrows were a clear warning that there was trouble ahead.

'Good morning, Richard.' His mother's voice was cool, icy cool. His father gave him no greeting, but when he stabbed yet again at a kidney that would not remain still on his plate, he said to Pearson, who was about to serve Richard, 'Tell Cook from me that I like my kidneys cooked but not to the extent of being so hard that they can bounce off the plate.'

'Yes, sir. Will I remove them? There are some others.'

'Can I expect the others to be any better? Take them away!' He thrust his plate at the butler, causing the offending kidney not actually to bounce from the plate but roll around what was left of the bacon, eggs and sausage, the master's usual breakfast.

When the butler had left the room Mr Gregory Baxton-Powell looked at his son and said, 'I'd advise you to eat a good breakfast because you'll need it to fortify you against what I have to say to you,' and at this he thrust his chair back, got to his feet and, pointing a forefinger at his son, added, 'I give you fifteen minutes. I'll be in my study.'

'If I'm to eat this good breakfast, Father, it'll take me more than fifteen minutes. It would ruin my digestion to gobble,' a remark which brought a scathing glare from his father as he left the room.

'Richard!' It was his mother's voice, now high and commanding.

'Yes, Mother?' he said quietly.

'Don't you dare be so facetious when answering your father. You're an ungrateful individual.'

'Yes; yes, Mother.' He had now pushed his chair back and was on his feet, and in as angry a voice as hers he said, 'Yes, I'm an ungrateful son. I should go on my knees every morning at prayers and ask God to make me good and dutiful in the only way that will make you and Father happy. Of course, I won't ask God if I shall be happy or even if Lillian would be happy. That's beside the point, I suppose. Nothing else matters so long as this High-Church house is joined to Rome, and for my pains I can be assured of being cosseted for the rest of my life in high style, can't I, Mother? It will be a payment for the attention I've been given all these years and for being unable to take up a profession. Of course, one doesn't recognise painting as a career; it's only people in the low dives of Paris who paint.'

'Yes; yes, you are right, Richard. And perhaps that's where you'll find yourself in the end, the way you are going.' And at this, his mother rose from the table and marched from the room, leaving May to say, 'Oh, Richard, you have done it this time. Why did you have to stay the night up there; you did stay the night, didn't you? Mother went to your room early on; then she cornered Tim, but he's like a clam where you're concerned; knew nothing, nothing. What time did you get in?'

'Oh, around seven, I think.' He sat down again.

'What were you doing all that time? Surely you . . . ?'

Richard banged down his knife and fork, and now leaning slightly towards her across the table, he said harshly, 'May, I was trying to save the life of the man who once saved mine.'

Her voice was quiet too as she said, 'Well, did you?'

He let out a long sigh before he said, 'Just; but he's still got some way to go, just as I had after my do. But there are no nurses and doting parents to see to him.'

'There you are, then; you must give Mother and Father credit for how they felt and thought when you were ill.'

'I do. I do, May; but . . . this marriage business: to tell you the truth—' his voice dropped and he repeated, 'to tell you the truth, May, I'm afraid to marry.'

'Why?'

'Because . . . well, just think back. Two years ago I felt as fit as a fiddle, and although I did not relish this business of taking up law, what happened? Six months on my back again, almost having to learn to walk once more. This thing's with me for life.'

'It isn't. The doctor said you'll grow out of it.'

'I was near death's door on and off for weeks, so I'm told, after Bruce brought me in. You see old men sitting at cottage doors, their hands on top of a knobbly stick. They are riddled with their rheumatics. Well, I'm not an old man, I'm a young man and I'm troubled with something similar, and if I were to marry Lillian, just imagine what would happen if I took ill again. One family is bad enough to put up with, two would become unbearable; but I am to believe that everything is being done for my own good.'

'Well, it has been and still is. You've got to see it that way.'

He took another mouthful of bacon, then muttered, 'Well, if I could go for a few years clear I might feel different about it. But it isn't only the marriage business,

May, and you know it; it's because I will not break my friendship with Bruce Shaleman. And you know, it isn't only because of the debt I owe him, for if he was a dear brother I couldn't think more of him.'

'Oh, Richard' – May tossed her head from side to side now – 'for the life of me I cannot see what you find in him. He's a very ordinary-looking man and he's not even a farmer, he's shepherding most of the time, and his people are noted for their . . . well, lazy ways. If only they had been at least respectable and tried to make something of that place up there . . . but as far as I can gather it's . . . well, it's a dreadful hovel, and you have said so yourself.'

'As far as you can gather, May, yes, it is a dreadful hovel, and compared to this house, it's a pigsty, but of late the young girl has made a difference to the place. I should imagine she works unceasing inside and out. As I think I've said to you before, May, it's all a matter of environment.'

'I don't agree with you, Richard: it isn't just environment, it's a matter of getting down to work and making the best of what you've got, being respectable.'

He cut her off here, saying, 'Getting down to work, May?' He now poked his face towards her. 'Have you ever washed a cup in your life or polished a shoe? Oh, May. And being respectable, you can only be respectable when you've got something to be respectable about. Anyway, the quarter of an hour was up some time ago, so wish me luck, or perhaps *bon voyage*, I might be sent on a long holiday for my health once again, and if I am I'll welcome it.'

'Oh, you are ungrateful, Richard, and weak. I've got to say it; you're ungrateful and weak.'

He was at the door when he turned and there he

6

The sun was at its height. It had been shining for the
past three days and had dried up the mud beyond
the rough flags that bordered the cottage. What was
more, both the room and the scullery were free of wet
clothes, and yesterday Jinnie had tackled and managed
to get dry an enormous amount of washing, including
the beautiful sheets that Mister Richard had brought
them. One had been patched darned, but they were
still beautiful; and they were so white. Bruce had lain
in them for three nights by the fireside. On the fourth
night she and the master had replaced his pallet in the
loft, and how Bruce had managed to pull himself up, she
did not know; but he hadn't come down at all the next
day and had eaten hardly anything. However, yesterday
he had managed the climb, and again today; and now he
was sitting outside on a kitchen chair, his head leaning
against the sun-warmed stone, his gaze cast upwards
into the clear unclouded sky.

He was aware of Jinnie flitting in and out of the cottage
and surprised to hear her humming gently to herself.
He raised his head and when she went to pass him, he
stopped her, asking, 'What's that you're singing?'

'Singing? Oh, I don't know, Mister Bruce, just a
tune, I don't know any words to it. Like the organ
on a Sunday in the dining-hall: they used to take the
services there and a man used to play the organ both
before the preacher came in and after he had gone.

It was nice, and everybody sat quiet. Well' – she laughed now – 'you weren't allowed to speak to each other. On a Saturday afternoon, the married couples could during visiting times. It was odd, though, some didn't, they just sat there . . . mute.'

He stared at her. She seemed to have altered over the last few days. How long was it since he knew he couldn't go on? A week or so; but before that he had known what was happening to him. She must have had to look after him in every way. Dear Lord! in every way. His father had been there, but not all the time, as she was; nor had he tended him, as she had. He said, 'Are you tired?'

'No, Mister Bruce. No; I'm not tired, not any more. I was a bit a few days ago but it went off. One night I had eight hours bang; I was dead out. After that I was all right.'

There was a pause before he asked, 'Are you happy here?'

And she, too, paused before answering, while she looked away, right away over the green to the far distant ridge before she muttered, 'Yes; yes, I am now, because you're better.'

He didn't know why he should go on to ask her: 'What would have happened if I hadn't got better, would you have stayed?' And without hesitation she said, 'No. No, Mister Bruce, no.'

'Not even to look after my mother?'

There was another pause before the answer came: 'I couldn't have, I couldn't have stayed . . .' She didn't add, 'because, you gone, I would have been left alone with just the mister.'

'About Max. You did say he was going to get a job on a farm?'

'Yes, I did; and he's got it; he goes in a fortnight's

time. But it's a long way off, and although I'm glad for him I'm sorry for meself.'

'He's a lucky man is Max.'

'Yes, I think he is, Mister Bruce . . . I mean, to get the job.'

That wasn't what *he* had meant, but she wouldn't understand. He continued to look at her. Yes, she was changed, and it had occurred apparently only in the last few days. His eyes hadn't been open enough and so he had missed the butterfly emerging from the chrysalis, but his thoughts, nevertheless, told him that its wings would still be wet and fragile and it would be some time before they became strong enough for it to fly; but when it did it would be exceedingly beautiful. What was she now? Fifteen? Well, give her two years . . . yes, two years, and what then?

'Will I make you a cup of the coffee that Mister Richard brought you?' she now asked.

'Yes; that would be good, but make enough for four this time.'

Her face straight, she now bent towards him and in a low voice she said, 'Well, it won't last long at that rate, and then you'll go for me, saying I've had it on the sly,' smiling mischievously at him, and his eyes twinkled back as he said, 'Well, I know you do; you're not to be trusted with coffee.'

She straightened up. 'Oh you! Mister Bruce,' she countered, and turning, she almost danced into the cottage. Again leaning his head back against the wall, he did not, however, look up into the sky, but away to the hills to the right of him, and his thoughts touched on more mundane matters at the sight of his father coming out of the pigsty, and he considered, It'll take something stronger than coffee to get me on my pins for Wednesday. If I'm not we're going to be in the cart unless – his thoughts checked – unless he can see to them. He can see to the pigs all right, but what about the sheep? It's a good job I got most of the flock down ready for market. Otherwise, we would have been in a fix. Anyway, there's five days to go; we'll wait and see. I could always sit on the cart and let him do the herding; but that'll be only part of it, for you need legs when you get there, and also a voice to bargain for a decent price.

Jinnie was handing him a mug of coffee and saying, 'It's got a lovely smell, hasn't it? Makes you think of foreign places, like the missionaries went to. The missionaries used to come to the workhouse and talk about the foreign places.'

He smiled as he said, 'Yes, the aroma sets fancy free.'

'What was that, Mister Bruce?'

'I was saying that the smell of coffee makes your thoughts wander.'

'Does that. It does that.' Her voice had dropped; then she said, 'The missis said you could get drunk on it,' and she turned and skipped again into the cottage; this time returning with a tin mug full of the steaming liquid.

At the far end of the barn Pug Shaleman had made a kind of armchair for himself with some empty crates and a couple of bales of straw, and to the side of it was a low table holding pieces of wood and whittling tools. And he was sitting there now; and he turned as Jinnie's voice came to him, saying, 'A drink of coffee for you, mister.' As he took it from her he sniffed the mug and said, 'Oh, that again. Kindness will never cease,' and she replied flatly, 'Well, there wasn't a lot; there was only one packet; I think it was a half pound.'

'Kept for special occasions. Is this a special occasion?'

She was backing away from him as she said, 'I don't know, mister, only that it's a nice day, and on nice days people are generally pleasant.'

This remark must have left him speechless, because he sat with the mug in his hand and his mouth slightly agape until she was out of sight. Getting too big for her boots, that one. Yes; yes, indeed. Things hadn't been right since she came into the house. For two pins . . . but his mind at this point did not tell him what he would do for two pins; instead, he gulped at the coffee.

Bruce was still sitting outside at three o'clock in the afternoon. He had fallen asleep, his head to one side and resting against the stone wall, one hand holding the seat as if to prevent himself from sliding off. The other arm was hanging limply down by the side of the chair.

'Don't wake him, there's plenty of time. I'll wait out here if I may have a seat.'

Jinnie dashed into the cottage room, and as she went to lift a chair she turned her face towards the bed and in a loud whisper she said, 'It's Mister Richard.'

'Yes, I can tell that, girl.'

Outside, Richard took the chair from Jinnie, straddled it, then leant his arms on the back and asked softly, 'How long has he been asleep?'

But before she had time to answer, Bruce's throaty voice came to them, saying, 'She doesn't know, and I don't know, but I'm awake now, for who could sleep with all this narration going on?' He opened his eyes now and smiled as he looked at Richard, and he, smiling back, said, 'How're you feeling?'

'Much better. Oh, much better.'

'Can I get you a cup of tea, Mister Richard?'

'Yes, Jinnie. Thank you. That would be nice and re-freshing, for that sun is never moderate, it's one extreme or the other. We shouldn't grumble though, for I think these will probably be the last sunny days we'll have this year. At least,' he added now, 'at this end.' Then abruptly, he said, 'I'm off to Brighton tomorrow.'

'Brighton?'

'Yes. I was to be sent either to Switzerland or to Germany to do penance, but not France, because I might paint there. My godmother has a house in Brighton. It's really her main base. She has a place up in Scotland too, but the south is much warmer.'

'I thought she was touring in India?'

'So did I; but something's brought her back. I had a letter last week and she was apparently asking me to go down to see her and to stay for a while.'

'Will your . . . people be going down with you?'

'To my godmother's?' Richard's laugh rang out. 'Oh no; she's a firebrand: they dread her visits; always have done; although, as I remember, they've only ever been short, much too short for me. I seem to be the only one she doesn't swear at. No; I think my parents would rather take a tour to India themselves than go to Brighton.'

'She sounds interesting.'

'That's just one of the words you can put to her, Bruce. I think you would like her.' He now turned to look through the open doorway, to where Jinnie was mashing the tea at the cottage table, and bending towards Bruce, he said, 'I've never asked, but I'm interested to know how she came to lose the plait. Was it anything to do with—' His voice dropped to a whisper, 'Your brother and his quick departure?'

'Yes, everything;' and more quietly still, he said, 'I'll tell you later.'

After Jinnie had brought them out each a mug of tea and they had drunk it, Bruce pulled himself up from the chair, saying, 'I'd better get some practice in with these legs before market day.'

'You'll never be able to go down on market day.'

'It's only . . .'

'Yes, I know it's only a few days off. Couldn't your father see to it?'

'I don't know. With someone with him, yes; but on his own, I doubt it. There's the herding, although that could be seen to, but there are other factors too. Anyway, let's walk a while.'

'You're not fit to be up yet, never mind walking.'

Bruce made no comment on this, and they walked slowly over the flat plain.

They had walked some distance before Richard said, 'You were going to tell me about Jinnie and the hair.'

'Oh, that! Well, if it wasn't for the fact that she's lost half of her bronze beauty the whole thing could be laughable, like a farce. You see, it started the day she entered the house: she knocked my father off the stool on to his back.'

'She what!'

'Just what I said.' Bruce was smiling now. ''Twas the funniest thing I ever saw enacted in that kitchen. Apparently she will not be touched in certain places and he had made a grab at her backside; and after she had dealt him a blow with her forearm, she explained in no small voice that she wasn't going to be handled by anyone. That was the word she used, "handled", and with emphasis. Apparently at her previous place, the boss of the house had tried it on in the middle of the night, and that was that. Anyway, that was the first we heard of her objection to being handled, and from then everything went smoothly until Hal came home. Well, I did my best to warn him off – you know Hal – but one night he went up her ladder with the intention of . . . "handling" her; and what did she do? She stabbed him.'

'She stabbed him?'

'Yes, in the arm, with a sort of dinner knife. Her father, who was a tinker, so I understand, carried this little pouch around with him with a knife and fork and spoon in it. That's the only thing she's got that belonged to him. But she wouldn't have had that if that Max fellow I told you about, the huge fellow, hadn't rescued it after her father died. Otherwise, it would likely have gone in the incinerator. She can tell some amazing tales about what happens not only to their clothes but to the inmates of the workhouse themselves.'

'Was he badly cut?'

'Yes, he was. What is more, part of the knife was rusty and that could've meant trouble later on, so I had to take the poker to it.'

'You . . . you actually cauterised it?'

'I had to, or get him to a doctor – ' and now slanting his gaze towards Richard, he said, 'and you know what it's like getting a doctor up here, don't you?'

Richard ignored this statement, but said again, 'Stabbed him? You can't imagine her doing such a thing.'

'Oh, *I* can. There are two Jinnies inside that budding exterior. The day she arrived she looked like a child, but only for a short while. Anyway—' his voice altered now as he went on, 'Hal is a spiteful devil; I could say he is evil; and he meant to do her in, and so he waited his chance. She was all tidied up one Sunday to go down to the Miss Duckworths, who happen to have a niece who is a seamstress in the workhouse. Anyway, big Max apparently gets leave once a month to take Miss Caplin to visit her aunts on her day off, and there was our Jinnie going joyfully down to see them all. You see,

166

she has a great feeling for Miss Caplin. But there was Hal waiting for her.' He nodded and went on, 'He must have been waiting for her in the copse down the hill. Whether or not he intended to kill her, I don't know; but he certainly meant to take her down. The beauty of her hair must have enraged him enough to drive him to cut off her plaits. He had managed one plait when a dog sniffed them out and this must have frightened him off. And there she was running like a wild thing down to the Miss Duckworths. Well, what followed you really wouldn't believe, but to give you it in brief, the big fellow brings her back right into the kitchen.

'There we were, the three of us, sitting, and Jinnie points out Hal, and Max picks him up, gives him a blow in the face that should have broken his neck, then gets him by the belt, hoists him up like this' – he now demonstrated, putting both hands above his head – 'steps on to the table and hangs him by the belt from one of the bacon hooks. And to repay him for what he had done to Jinnie's head, he shaved him bald. Then he takes Jinnie away again.'

'It's almost unbelievable,' said Richard.

'It was more unbelievable seeing it played out. Anyway, he was for going to sea. He had talked about it for a long time, besides which there was an irate husband in the village on the hunt for him; so he went to Newcastle the same day swearing that he would come back, and he will. That's one thing I'm sure of. What he would hope to achieve, if that big fellow's still about, I don't know. Of course, there's always the shotgun.'

They were walking on again and had gone some way before Richard said, 'Do you mean to say that Jinnie won't allow anyone to touch her at all?'

'Oh, touching and handling are quite different things in Jinnie's mind – I've seen her jump into Max's arms in greeting. When she says "handled" she means something else, you know.'

'Oh yes. Yes, I see. But she looks so thin, so fragile, and she'll likely grow into a very pretty girl.'

'She'll never be pretty, Richard, beautiful yes, but never pretty.'

Richard gave a short laugh as he said, 'Yes, there *is* a difference.' And he paused again: 'Dare I ask if you've got a feeling for her?'

'Oh yes.' The answer came promptly. 'Always have, from when I first brought her over this plain. Sometimes it's that of a brother, sometimes that of a father; and now and again, of something else too; but I doubt if the latter will ever come to anything, for she'll never see me in that way.'

'How on earth d'you know?'

'Oh, I know. I am in a way like her Max, who is a sort of protector, a friend. Anyway, whatever feeling she has for me I'll make sure I don't spoil it.'

'But if you . . .'

'Look, Richard; let's forget about Jinnie and her . . . what would you call it? I can't think of any name for it except nicety, and that isn't right, is it?'

'No, it isn't right.'

'Well, anyway, what I want to know is how long d'you think you'll be in Brighton?'

'Oh, just so long as I can stand it; for about a month, I should say. Perhaps not that long; she may decide she's going to Timbuktu. Of course she would want me to go with her, as she always does, but this time I have the excuse that we're all going to France.'

'Well, you know, Brighton will do you good. After your trip there last time you felt much better.'

'I didn't, not really. I never feel so well as when I'm out on these hills.'

They were nearing the cottage when Bruce stopped and said, 'I've never thanked you for the other night. If I'd been left to the care of me da and Jinnie, I'm sure I wouldn't have made it.'

But knowing what he had already decided in his mind, Richard did not answer for a moment; when he did he said, 'Well, that makes us about quits,' and they walked on in silence until they reached the cottage when Richard said, 'When we come back from France I will likely be engaged to be married.'

Bruce turned and looked at his companion but Richard was staring straight ahead and he added, 'It's expected of me; that's if my health keeps up.'

'Is it Miss Rowland?'

'Yes, it's Miss Rowland. Well?' The word was a question and now Richard stopped and, facing Bruce he said, 'I, I don't feel ready for marriage.' He tossed his head to one side now and said, 'Candidly, Bruce, I'm afraid I . . . well, I won't be up to it, because there are times, and you know this, that I'm as weak as a day-old kitten. All my brave talk has never hoodwinked you.'

'D'you care for her?'

'Lillian? Strangely, yes, in a way.'

'What d'you mean "in a way"? You must know if you love her or not.'

'Oh, what is love? It has so many facets. I love my nanny; at my boarding school I fell in love with a teacher, he had blond hair and blue eyes; I love my dog. I love my pony. Oh, how I loved the pony that tipped me into the ravine—' he sighed, and they had covered a short distance before he asked, 'Whom or what have I loved since then?' His head drooped and he gave himself no answer.

'You should marry, and it will be all right.' Bruce put out a hand now and caught Richard's arm and, after pressing it tight, he dropped into the jargon of his class: 'Marriage could be the makings of you, man.' At this, they both stopped and looked at each other and burst out laughing, and their laughter rang clear across the land to the hills, so loud that it brought Jinnie out of the cottage door, and there she stood awaiting their approach. Their faces were bright with their laughter, and hers became bright too, and she said to them, 'An apple a day keeps the doctor away, but a laugh a day keeps life at bay.'

They were standing before her now, their faces no longer spreading laughter, their gaze soft on her, and as if they had but the one voice between them they repeated, 'An apple a day keeps the doctor away, but a laugh a day keeps life at bay,' and they both knew in this moment, though barely conscious of it, that she was the life they must keep at bay.

7

Bruce stood by the cart and looked up at his father, and he had to shout to make himself heard above the combined din of the squealing pigs packed into the back of the cart, all aiming to climb up the high sides of it.

'Mam's given you a sovereign, and let that make do, d'you hear? There's some hard months ahead of us and, as far as I understand, prices are low. It will all depend upon who is there this morning. Avoid Dickinson if you can, because he'll beat you down.'

The reins in his hand, Pug Shaleman leaned over and, his face almost touching Bruce's, he said, 'Who d'ya think you're talking to, a bairn? a lad? I was at this game before you were born, remember; I haven't always been pushed to the side.'

Angry now, Bruce yelled, 'You went to the side because you found it easy; no responsibility, anybody else could take the pull; it was first Ma, then it was me. Look, get down from there.' Bruce put his foot on the spoke of a wheel and as he aimed to pull himself upwards his father thrust him back, saying, 'Go to hell with you! This is still my place, my stock; I can do what I bloody well like with them.' And the horse moved off.

The sudden jerk of the cart almost toppled Bruce backwards and, likely, he would have fallen if Jinnie had not placed her hands flat against his back.

171

After steadying him, she remained standing by his side as they watched the cart joggling over the rough ground, and she said, 'Don't worry, Mister Bruce, Mr Locke will be with him. He's a steady man, is Mr Locke,' and added hesitantly, 'isn't he?'

It was a moment before Bruce answered, 'Yes, Peter Locke's all right in his way, but he won't be selling the stock, nor will he be handling the money. When he once gets the stock into the market his job'll be finished, at least with us. Somebody else will then pick him up to get their stock home. I should have gone in. God! I should have gone in.'

'No, Mister Bruce, you shouldn't. Look what happened to you yesterday with that walking. That kept you lying flat nearly all day, so come on back; it's a long day ahead.'

They were about to turn towards the cottage when Bruce exclaimed, 'He's stopped! What's he want? He's standing on the seat looking back. He's forgotten something; but what?'

'Oh, he's off again, Mister Bruce. Come on; come on back and have a sit down; the sun's warming up now. You've had no breakfast; I'll make some fresh porridge.' And she put the tips of her fingers on his arm and turned him about. They went forward and into the cottage.

Bruce flopped down into a chair near the table and, looking at his mother, he said, 'He stopped at the end of the lane. He must have stood on the seat, because I could see all of him. He stood looking back here.'

'Stood looking back here? On the seat? How long?'

'Oh, just for a minute, perhaps.'

'Could he have forgotten something?'

'What was there to forget? He's got the piglets, he's got the sheep; perhaps he was sorry he didn't take the eggs. But he said, didn't he? that they'd be mulch by

172

the time he got there, even if he'd had them on the seat with him.'

She was now lying on her side, half raised from her pillows by supporting herself with the hand flat on the tick, and she continued to look at her son where he sat, his elbows on the table, his head in his hands, and her voice was quiet as she said, 'You feeling bad again?'

It was a moment before he raised his head to answer her: 'No,' he said; 'not any worse than usual; but I'm worried, Ma. I've got a feeling on me about him. I know I shouldn't have let him go in by himself.'

'Lad, as he's told you many a time, he used always to go in by himself at one time, for his own father was pretty much like he is now, doing anything to get out of work of any kind; in fact, he was worse because he didn't spend any of his time whittling a stool or a bowl or a platter, the only thing he was good at was snoring. Oh, don't worry your head, lad. When it gets a bit warmer get yourself out in the sun and sit there and thank the Lord you're still alive. And I must admit that's only because of Mister Richard, and I've thought a lot about that, y'know. Life's funny: it gives tit for tat: you saved him and he saved you. Tit for tat, that's life.'

The weather had changed again back to drizzle, and by the afternoon the sky had darkened so much Rose Shaleman said, 'Light the lamp, girl.'

As Jinnie did so, she thought to herself that it was the first time it had been lit in the afternoon; the mistress was very mean where oil was concerned; sometimes she even had to grope around the kitchen by the firelight, especially if the men weren't in. But there was very rarely any glow from the fire to give light to the room: if the kale-pot was not hanging above the flame, the kettle on the hob would be obscuring it.

Jinnie gave a pleasurable sigh as she placed the lamp on the table, moving aside the jar of dog-daisies she had picked that afternoon. It was one of the rare pleasures of her life now to slip along to the copse above the pool where, during the seasons, different wild flowers would appear – she remembered her joy at seeing her first cowslips – but she had, until lately, never thought about picking them, in case her mistress should call them falderals. This word had first come to her notice when she had suggested that she cut a bit off the bottom of the window curtains to make a little frill to cover the ugly hooks that pinned them to the window frame: 'We haven't time for your falderals here,' Rose Shaleman had almost barked at her. 'Cut the bottom off to stick on the top? Did you ever hear of it!' Nevertheless, she had made no such remark when Jinnie had first dared to place the wild flowers on the table, saying tentatively, 'I thought you might like to look at them, missis.'

There had been no response to this, but no censure either.

She now glanced to where Bruce was sitting in a somewhat lopsided cane chair. This had been retrieved from the rubbish piled in one end of the barn after Bruce, having lain on the biscuit tick on the floor for three days and nights, found that he still needed support for his back, support which could not be given by one of the straight-backed kitchen chairs. And so, Mrs Shaleman had badgered her husband into raking out the chair and lacing its broken seat with whatever pliable pieces of cane he could find.

Because of the chair's shape, Bruce had to lean back and stretch out his legs; but he was not leaning back now, and his mother must have noticed it, for she called to him, 'It's no use worrying your guts out: drunk or sober he'll be back. Oh yes, he knows how far he can go. Girl, make some griddle cakes and we'll have a sup of tea with it.'

'Oh yes, missis. Yes.'

Jinnie liked making griddle cakes: there was nothing tastier than hot griddle cakes with butter on, and to have a sup of tea with it and the lamp burning brightly and, as today, the fire glowing because the kale-pot was shelved, was grand.

While making the pastry for the griddle cakes she smiled across the table at Bruce, who was now lying watching her, and as she was about to put the griddle on the hot iron plate she said to him, 'Now, don't move your feet, they're not in the way;' but when he drew up his knees, she shook her head at him, and he, smiling for the first time that day, shook his head back at her.

She was feeling happy. The house was quiet without the mister here, and nice and homely. Of course, he spent most of his time outside or in the barn, but then she was always aware that he was about. Now there were just the missis and Mister Bruce, and it was different, lovely.

She made the griddle cakes, and she buttered them; she made the tea; then putting one piece on a tray with a mug of tea, she took it to the bed. Then she gave another to Bruce who, chewing on a piece of griddle said, 'They melt in your mouth. You're a fine cook, Jinnie,' and in reply to the compliment, she smiled widely at him, only for a voice from the bed to say, 'Don't swell her head. That's enough of that,' which took away some of her joy.

A few minutes later, sitting at a corner of the table with her mug and a piece of her pastry, an idea came to her. She wondered why she hadn't thought of it before, but supposed it was because every evening the mister was always in the kitchen. Now that there were only the three of them, and as the mistress couldn't read, and neither could Mister Bruce, which surprised her, how would it be to bring her Bible down and read them a story? She herself was a very slow reader, she had to admit, even having to break up some words; but then she knew all the Bible stories off by heart; well, the Gospel ones, anyway, and she would be able to tell them the story; that's if the missis would like it.

She looked towards the bed and said, 'Missis?'

'Yes, girl?'

'After . . . after I've made the meal the night, and seen to the hens and pig swill and things, would . . .?'

'Yes, would I what?'

'Would you like me to get me Bible down and . . . and read you a story? I *can* read a bit. Well, I'm slow; but you see I could tell you the story. What I mean is . . .'

Only very rarely had she heard her mistress chuckle or laugh, but now her laughter started on a chuckle and it brought Jinnie to her feet to look apprehensively towards Bruce, who also was smiling broadly, as he nodded at her, saying, 'That would be nice, Jinnie. Yes, it would. It would indeed be nice to hear a story. Wouldn't it, Ma?'

The laughter from the woman in the bed died away. Jinnie looked towards her mistress, who was wiping her eyes on the end of the sheet; then, after sniffing several times, she said, 'I wouldn't have said it's any use bringing down your Bible the night, because himself will be back and there'll be lots of things to talk about. But there must be another hour afore the meal and the animals need seeing to, so away up to your loft and get your Bible and let's hear you read. Wonders will never cease.'

After Jinnie had scampered from the room Rose Shaleman said, 'I didn't know she could read, not

176

really. She's spoken of the Bible stories the parson used to tell them and which they had to listen to every Sunday whether they liked it or not, poor beggars . . . but *read*.'

'She's a bright girl altogether.'

'Oh, I give you that. She's bright all right, too bright in some ways, could be cheeky if she was given half an inch.'

'You don't know when you're on a good thing, Ma.'

'What d'you mean?' His mother's tone was tart now.

'Just what I say. There's such a thing as appreciation. She came here, not so long ago, little more than a child; then she became a girl; and I can tell you she won't remain one much longer. And another thing; she's got a thinking mind and, putting her growing and the thinking mind together, she must ask herself why she's stuck here.'

'What's up with you, man? We took her from the workhouse; she was a tinker's girl.'

'Yes, she was a tinker's girl; but you didn't know the tinker and why he was a tinker. By what she has told me, he wasn't a very successful tinker but he was an intelligent one, and he passed a lot on to her. As I see it, it was very unfortunate for her he had to die when he did; but it's been pretty fortunate for us. Just think of the three you had before her. The house has never been so clean for years; nor, while I'm on, I must say it, have we ever eaten so well, either. Her cooking gets better as the weeks go by.'

'My, my! She has found a champion in you, hasn't she?'

'Well, she had to find a champion in somebody, Ma, 'cos she didn't find it in your elder son or your husband, and if I remember, right from the beginning you haven't done much yourself to encourage her to stay.'

177

'Well, well! Do I smell a rat?'

He pulled himself up from the basket chair and put his hand out and gripped the edge of the table to steady himself, saying, 'No; you don't smell any rats, Ma, but if you're not careful you might again smell the stink of that bed you're lying in; and this kitchen will become the pigsty it was before; she's got friends down below and she could up and go the morrow and get service in some decent place.'

There was a telling silence before his mother spoke again, when, quietly, she said, 'What's come over you? You never used to go on like this.'

'No, perhaps not. What maybe it is, I've grown up too; grown up to the fact that I've been a damn fool to spend all me years up here. If I hadn't, I would have taken the offer of Arthur Wentworth, when I was twelve, to work on his farm. I know now that life would have been different. D'you know something, Ma?' He bent his body towards her. 'That girl, as you keep calling her, knows more about the outside world than I do; she knows more about people and their ways; aye, and what they think.'

'You're thinking of taking her on, aren't you? And I suppose . . . oh yes, you could do worse. She'd keep you clean and snug and well fed.'

'For God's sake, Ma! Sometimes . . .' He broke off as the door opened and Jinnie entered, and she, seeing him standing by the table, said quickly, 'You want something, Mister Bruce?'

And at this he turned from the table and flopped into the chair again and lay back before he answered her, saying quietly, 'No, Jinnie; just to hear you read.'

She put her Bible on the table, then pulled the lamp towards her; and, opening the small book, she thumbed through it before saying, 'I'll read you about Jesus going into the desert and being tempted by the Devil. It's the first story in the New Testament by Saint Matthew. Parson McKane went all through the Testament; Matthew, Mark, Luke and John.' Then on a little giggle she said, 'There are some funny rhymes about Matthew, Mark, Luke and John.' But she went no further, realising that this was no time to bring in funny rhymes.

And so she began to read: 'The Gospel according to Saint Matthew.' She now flicked her eyes upwards, wetted her lips, and began in earnest: 'Then . . . was . . . Jesus . . . led . . . up . . . of the Spi . . . rit into the wil-der-ness to be temp-ted of the Devil.' She now looked up and smiled from the one to the other as if very satisfied with her progress; and when neither of them made a remark, she went on, 'And when he . . . had fas . . . ted forty days and forty nights, he was after . . . wards hungered.' Again her eyes flicked upwards before she continued, saying, 'And when . . . the . . . temp-ter . . .' But Bruce's voice broke in quietly, saying, 'You're a good reader Jinnie, but you could tell the story yourself just as well.'

'You think so?'

'Yes; like you told me about the one where the farmer lost one sheep and he was sorry about it, likely afraid that, as you said, it wouldn't find its way back, so he went out and searched for it.' And here she nodded at him, saying, 'Yes, I liked that one about the lost sheep. Well, then, about Jesus going up the mountain. In one of the other Gospels they say it was a desert and there was nothing to eat there at all, but that he was praying all the time, and when he got very famished the Devil appeared and he said, "Look, if you're so hungry and you're so well in with God—" Yes; yes, that's what he did say, that's how Parson McKane told it; Parson Freeman said the Devil said something

179

different; but anyway, what he did say was, "You see them stones? Well, you being so clever like, why don't you turn them into bread . . .?"'

'Well, why didn't he?'

Jinnie stared wide-eyed towards Rose Shaleman as she replied quickly, 'Well, 'cos it would've been a sin and Jesus was up there to get away from all sin, and he told the Devil where to go to. At least, that's how Parson McKane told it: "Get off with you about your business," he said. But the Devil wasn't finished with Jesus and the next thing he offered him was to be a kind of boss of all the towns roundabout, and the cities an' all, everything, and when Jesus would have none of it, what d'you think the Devil did then? He put it to Jesus that if he bowed down to him he would give him everything he wanted, everything.'

'Lucky fellow.'

'Aw! Ma.'

'All right, I was just saying he was a lucky fellow. Go on, girl.'

Jennie hesitated for some seconds before she started again: 'Well, God was very very pleased with Jesus' – her voice was very low now – 'and He gave him food for his soul.'

'Food for his soul?' The words had come from the missis. 'Where did he keep his soul? You're just making this up, girl. I think we've heard enough.'

'I'm not making it up, missis; He did give him food for his soul and his soul is next to his heart. Parson McKane said the soul is so near the heart it's almost one, and he always said that people should look to their souls more than to their bodies. I wasn't making it up . . .'

Bruce had risen from his chair again and he said, 'No; you weren't, Jinnie;' then almost glaring now across the lamplit room to his mother, he said, 'My mother is an ignorant woman. But it isn't her fault; she never had the chance to listen to a parson, as you did. And I enjoyed your telling. And you read fine, but go now and put your Bible away, then see that the hens are all in, for who knows when Mr Fox or any weasel will pass by.'

She made no retort to his light chatter, but went quietly from the kitchen; and he was about to resume his seat again when his mother's voice rasped at him, 'It's come to something, hasn't it, when you can insult me in front of a workhouse skivvy?'

Bruce reacted so quickly, she hitched herself away from him.

'Ma,' he said, his tone deep with anger, 'for two pins I'd send her packing down to her friends: and me, I would take to the road; even feeling as I do I'd take to the road; but before I left this quarter I would call in on Nellie Kingsley and tell her you'd be glad to have her back, gin bottle an' all. Now mind you, this is no idle threat. I can't do it at this moment because I'm in no fit state, but I'll soon be me own man again; and I'm warning you, it could happen just like that,' and the crack he made with his fingers caused her eyes to blink. 'I've stayed with you because you were a sick woman, but sometimes I have to wonder just how sick you really are.'

Her voice came as a whimper now, saying, 'What's come over you? You never used to be like this to me.'

'And you never used to be like the way you are now, Ma.'

She whimpered again, saying, 'It's just that since she came into this house, you've changed.'

He drew himself up, and it was a second or so before he said slowly, 'Yes, perhaps you're right there, for she

181

brought something with her, not only cleanliness and a smattering of comfort that she scraped out of this hovel, but she brought another world with her. All right, it might have been a smattering of the workhouse world, but unconsciously she must have studied all the people she met, even in there, and is able to describe them in the same way as she related that bit of the Gospel the night.' He now shook his head. 'Oh, Ma, you would never understand.'

As he turned away her voice, high now, cried at him, 'No! I'll not understand, because every time I look at the back of her head I can see my son swinging from that hook' – she pointed to the ceiling – 'brought low, made to look like an idiot by that ugly beast. I know what he was, no-one knows better, but I bred him and to see him treated less than a man – in fact like some animal in the slaughterhouse – did something to me. So there you have it. And another thing I'll tell you: I always made more of you than I did of him because I wanted you by me side; but now I know you're farther away from me than he is, and he's away across the sea. Even Mister Richard didn't make the difference in you that she has.'

'Perhaps it is as I've said before, Ma: I appreciate a clean room and a decent meal now and again, something I've never had, not even when you were about.' And on this he turned and went down the room, though not back to his seat: he opened the kitchen door, and when he closed it behind him it wasn't gently.

Outside, he stood looking up into the sky. The darkness was coming sooner than usual, bidden by the dullness of the day, so his deeper thoughts told him; then leaning for support against the wall of the cottage, he began vigorously rubbing at his legs, telling himself he must pull himself together, he must get outside and walk . . . walk, walk and get himself as far away as possible from that room.

He straightened up now, and walked past the pig-sties, noting that the three large pigs, amid loud grunts, were now licking the remains of the swill.

When he came to the barn he stood with his hand on the stanchion and looked into the dim length of it. It was a good barn. The far end was warm and snug. Oh yes, his father had made another house for himself. But there would have to be changes. Tomorrow morning he would tell his father that if he wanted to spend his time in the barn, well and good, but that he must turn it into a workshop. He was very handy at making those little crackets, and there would be a ready sale for them in Hexham, as well as for other odds and ends. Well, instead of just putting his hand to work between dozing, he'd be earning his keep. And if he didn't like that, then he could attend the sheep, those on the lower hills. He had lived on his bad leg for far too long.

The sound of scuffling round the corner of the barn brought him walking again, and in the distance he saw Jinnie grabbing the cock by its tail, then expertly holding down his wings, and by the time he reached the crees she was pushing him in.

She had seemed unaware of his approach, yet she spoke to him without turning her head, saying, 'He does this every night, y'know. He gets to the door after they're all in, then turns and looks at me and hops off again. I'm sure he does it on purpose, that it's a kind of game.' She now closed the door of the hen crees and slipped the peg into the staple; then brushing her hands one against the other, she turned to him and looked at him squarely for a moment before, without any lead up to the subject in question, she said, 'The missis doesn't like me reading, does she?'

For a moment, he was slightly taken aback and he found himself stammering: 'W-w-well, she doesn't understand the B-B-Bible.'

'You don't much either, but you're not nasty about it.'

'How d'you know I know nothing about the Bible?' There was a surprised note in his voice.

'Well' – her head wagged – 'you've asked me to tell you the stories I know from the Bible.'

'Yes; yes, I have, because I like to hear the way you tell them. And let me tell you something, miss' – he now bent towards her – 'your stories are not always true, I mean they're not always really right.'

'Oh yes, they are. Parson . . .'

'Yes, I know all about the parson, but you've got a wonderful imagination, Jinnie, and you paint your words.'

'Paint me words? I don't paint me . . . what d'you mean, paint me words? Tell lies?'

'No, no; it's something to be proud of, having a good imagination and putting a different meaning on things.'

They were walking away from the hen enclosure now and after a moment she asked quietly, 'Where did you learn about the Bible?'

'Oh, for a short period, very short period, I went to Sunday school; then came the time with Mister Richard, and I saw him pretty often. He taught me, yes and pretty often, for nearly two years. The second year he was taking lessons again. And, you know, his family is very church-going; everybody in the house gathers between the hall and the dining-room for prayers before breakfast, and it's the same at night.'

'Really! Every day?'

'Yes, every day.'

'Oh.' She was smiling now. 'We only had it on a Sunday; and some people didn't like that. I did. Well, not listening to sermons, but the reading and the stories.' She glanced at him now, saying, 'And . . . and that's where you learned all about the Bible and things?'

He laughed outright as he said, 'Learnt *all* about the Bible, Jinnie? I'm afraid not; I listened and I took in bits and pieces, snatches.' Then his voice trailing away, he said, 'I suppose I could've learned to read and write if I'd merely . . . well, mentioned it, but likely Richard thought I could already. Yes, that's it; he thought I could. Well, now he knows differently.' And he sighed.

They were nearing the corner of the barn when the neighing of a horse came to them, and they looked sharply at each other, and it was Jinnie who said, ''Tis the Mister; he's back early.'

Her words were significant, and Bruce thought, Yes, he's back early, early for him.

He hurried forward, she by his side, and when they reached the cottage door they both stood peering into the distance to see a man driving a horse and trap come out of the gloom.

Peter Locke waited to pull the horse to a standstill, when he himself was looking down on to Bruce and the young girl, and he said, 'Hello, there. Aye-aye! I suppose you're surprised to see me, and driving a trap? Mr Stevens said to me, "You'd better take it, Peter, 'cos you've got a long trek back after you've been up there. And you're the one that seems to know more about it than most; so you'd better put it over like . . . what y'know about it, if you see what I mean."'

He jumped down from the trap, saying, 'Can I hitch her to anything? 'Cos I can't stay long, and I wouldn't want her to go jaunting off in the hills on her own. That would put the finish to a very odd day, wouldn't it?'

'What are you talking about, Peter?'

'Well, give me a chance, Bruce, to get inside; I'm not going to go over all this twice.'

Bruce had taken the reins from the elderly man and hitched them to a post near the door. Then the three of them made their way into the kitchen.

Rose Shaleman was already sitting bolt upright in bed, and her greeting was, 'What do you want, Peter Locke?'

'I want nothing, missis; I've just come to tell you something.'

'Sit down.' Bruce pulled out a chair, and Peter Locke said, 'Ta, Bruce. Ta. I always get off me legs when I can.'

'What d'you mean, tell us something? Where's Pug?'

'Well, you know as much as me at this minute, missis, where your husband is. I can only tell you where I left him; and that was on the station, Catton way. He had booked to Newcastle, but would have to change at Hexham, I told him that.'

'You told him what? What in the name of God are you on about?'

'Shut up! Ma, and listen. Go on, Peter.'

'Your husband's gone off, missis; where, I don't know, but he's made it plain to everybody that he's off, and for good. He was questioned when it came to selling the cart and horse, but, as he said, Mister Richard was doing you all fine, and because Bruce wasn't yet fit to manage, he was going to send up another man. But few believe this, because they know who holds Mister Richard's purse-strings: his old man.'

'What you on about, Peter? Mister Richard was due to leave last night.'

'Oh yes, that's what I'm meaning; that's what your da said, but that it had been all arranged beforehand.'

'God almighty!' The cry came from Rose, and Bruce saw his mother flop back on the pillows. He stood looking down at the drover as he asked, 'And he sold everything?'

'Oh yes, naturally. Well, the stock was for sale, wasn't it? But I didn't think he would get rid of the old cart and horse. I couldn't see any need for that meself; neither could Mr Stevens; but at five pounds for the horse and three pounds for the cart . . . of course, as you know yourself, they both had had a lot of wear. Oh aye, a lot of wear.'

Jinnie was standing at the end of the table, her hands gripped together, and she watched Bruce pull out a chair and almost drop on to it.

Rose's voice came from the bed now like a deep croak, 'What did he get for the stock?'

'Oh' – Peter Locke's voice was airy – 'you wouldn't believe it. Everybody around thought it would be low, but no, there were some good dealings the day; the good lambs went a guinea a head. And then there were twenty-five piglets. Pug took out the odd one, and the other two dozen went to Carters of Hexham.'

'What did he get for them?' Again Rose's voice came from the bed.

'Now, missis, I'm not sure; I wasn't there at the time. But prices seemed to be very good the day, and I wouldn't be surprised if they fetched ten shillings each. Although what he got for the lambs was surprising, and fifty of them, besides the few old sheep, he would probably have picked up nearly eighty pounds. You did have them down on the bottoms for a time, and that would have put a bit of weight on them.'

'He'll come back; and just wait till he does!' Rose Shaleman's words were weighed with threat, and Peter Locke stood up, looking from one to the other, and said, 'I wouldn't bank on it, missis. You could have; but in the bar he played the big fella and stood a round of drinks, and then brought out all that about Mister Richard; and later, after he sold the cart and horse, too, it was evident he was going to do a bunk.'

Bruce's voice was low as he asked, 'Did he say anything to you? I mean, leave a message of any kind? You said you saw him on the station.'

'Well, he said a lot of things I couldn't really make sense of, but he did say he was heading for Norfolk eventually. Had some people there once, he told me. He give me me due, but not a penny over, and him with his pockets weighed down, as they could never have been before in his life.'

There came into Bruce's mind the picture of the small figure standing up in the cart and looking back towards the huddle of buildings. He knew now that it had been his way of saying goodbye to them.

Peter Locke was addressing him across the table, saying, 'He's left you in a nice hole, anyway; you not right on your pins yet and with a long winter ahead. Scurvy trick, I call it . . . scurvy. But he's not much of a loss, I would say.' And with this he rose, adding, 'After I drop the trap I still have a long haul. I must be off.'

When he turned and made to go out, Jinnie sprang to the door and pulled it open, and when he came abreast of her he stopped and looked at her and said, 'You're growing, lass, aye, noticeably growing. Bonny with it. Good-night all.'

'Good-night, mister.'

Bruce followed Peter outside, and after the drover had mounted the trap he said to him quietly, 'Thanks, Peter.'

'I wish it could be something different you were thanking me for. I reckon he took a tidy pile with him;

but you know, Bruce, it won't last for ever, and you'll likely be hearing from him again. You can't really see any relatives in Norfolk or anywhere else greeting him with open arms. Well, I'll be off . . . Get up, there! . . .'

As Bruce entered the kitchen Jinnie was screwing the kettle into the heart of the fire, and she turned towards him saying, 'I'll make a strong cup of tea eh, Mister Bruce?' but before he could answer her his mother yelled, 'You'll make no cups of tea until you're told, girl; and you'll be lucky if you get a cup of tea a day after this.'

Bruce's voice was almost as loud as his mother's as he countermanded her order: 'You make a cup of tea, Jinnie, and now; and a strong one; I need it.' Then he walked towards the bed, holding up a hand to stop the tirade he knew was coming, and said, 'Now listen to me, Ma. He's gone. I doubt if he'll ever come back. For my part I hope he doesn't. Yes, I know he's taken what would have got us through the winter and a bit to put by—' He paused, and bending towards her, he said, 'Now let me have that bag from under your tick and we can do some counting.'

'No! Leave it to me; I'll dish it out.'

'Oh no, you won't,' and suddenly he tipped up the edge of the mattress and dragged out the chamois leather bag causing his mother to fall flat back on to her pillows. 'I struggled all me life for that,' she moaned. 'It was to put me away decent. I've always wanted to go decent. And the rest was for you.'

'Me? Well, let's first see how much there is, Ma,' and he added slowly, 'Don't worry; I'll see you go decent, money or not.'

With his forearm he slid the crockery and oddments on the table towards the lamp, and after he had emptied the contents of the bag on to the table, his mother leant from the bed to peer at the not so small glittering pile of sovereigns, all the while shaking her head at the prospect of seeing her scrounged and scraped life-savings about to be disposed of.

Bruce began to count.

Altogether there were fifty-four sovereigns, twelve half-sovereigns, four crowns, sixteen half-crowns, and seven pennies. He stood back and let out a long slow breath before he said, 'Sixty-three pounds, seven pence. My! My! With what has already gone my impression was, Ma, that there should have been around the thirty left. Well now, as far as I can see, we needn't worry.'

She was sitting back on the bed, her head on her chest, but when he said, 'I think five pounds would see you nicely away, Ma, wouldn't it?' her head sprang back and she said, 'You'll not leave me with just five pounds. Oh no; you'll not do that.'

'All right then, we'll double it.'

'It's *my* money; it's what I've scraped and worked for and . . .'

'Ma, you've never in your life worked for a penny of that money. If everybody had their rights you know who would have that money at this minute? Hal, for since he first went up into that mine as a lad you saw to it that he tipped the lot up. In fact, you made your yearly journey on the Day Of The Pays to see that he wasn't dragged down into the town and into the bars, and spend what you considered to be yours. Then there was the head of the house; he used to work at one time, remember?'

'He's never worked for years.' Her voice was like a bark now.

'No, but when he did he, too, tipped his money up. You saw to that, Ma. As for me, I have never had wages to tip up. But I was being fed. You once said to me that you had paid for me in suffering. I didn't understand it

190

at the time, I do now, though only up to a point, for there was very little suffering on your part. I was the one who did the suffering, and that at the hands of your husband, Mr Pug Shaleman.' The last few words had been ground through his clenched teeth; and now, his whole body shaking, he pulled a chair towards him and sat down. His doubled fists on the table, he said, 'It seems to be a night for plain speaking, so let's have it, Ma.'

His mother was sitting bolt upright on the bed now, pointing past him and yelling, 'Get out of here, girl! Get out!'

Quickly, he turned and checked Jinnie's departure, 'Stay where you are, Jinnie. Stay where you are. Everyone except me seems to have known for a long time who I really am, so we'll get on with it, Ma. From what I understand, Jinnie, my father was a man of some culture. He must have been to write poems, for he made his living at it, a penny a rhyme, tuppence a song, which he both wrote and sang. He could also draw and paint.'

Jinnie said not a word, just stared at him, and he turned back to his mother and said, 'I've been sick of that being thrown at me in different ways over the years. At first I couldn't understand it, I couldn't understand it at all; until one day I began to sort myself out, when I realised I had nothing in me of Pug Shaleman and very little of Hal; and it's many a year now since I thanked God that you had your fling with the travelling poet. To my mind it's the one good thing you've done in your life, because for as far back as I can remember, most of the time you've lain on top of the bed or under the sheets.'

Rose Shaleman looked at her son. If she had loved anybody in her life she had loved him. She remembered the day he was conceived. It was very hot; the sweat had been running down her breasts and she had opened her blouse to give her skin air. She was attending to the fire when the Penny Poet appeared in the doorway. She knew her face was red and her hair was straggling about her. It was the third time he had called in on his yearly round, and, she recalled she had been about to speak about the weather when he said, 'Don't move; stand just like that, your hand to your hair, like that, yes.' And then he had whipped a coloured crayon and a large pad from a side pocket and had made a drawing of her. It had taken only minutes; and when he handed it to her saying, 'It doesn't do you justice, but I've caught something,' she couldn't believe she was as bonny as the drawing showed. He had said her eyes were lovely but lonely. Over the years she had kept the sketch hidden here and there. It was lying under the newspaper that lined the bottom drawer of the chest, only she could hardly make out her face on it now.

On one of his visits she saw him looking at Hal as he ran in and out of the cottage. She had said to him, 'Do you paint children?' and he had shaken his head, telling her that children were most difficult to paint; only real painters could paint children and he wasn't a real painter. She had contradicted him here and said she thought he was a lovely painter, and he had said it wasn't true, but if she called him a lovely poet he'd kiss her.

He would say odd things like that. She couldn't remember how on that day they came to be sitting close to each other as they drank their tea, or when his fingers began to trace the contours of her face, but she did recall when his lips fell on her eyelids. She had never known anything like it. She had thought often since it may not have been love but it had certainly been beautiful. It led to this very bed where she was lying now, dying of a heart problem.

When the child came she felt that Pug knew from the minute he looked at it that it wasn't his. Things had never been good between them because of the conditions on which he had taken her, and of the man himself, and from that time they had worsened.

She had waited for the poet's return, but he had never come. She recalled that when Bruce was about seven years old Peter Locke, being up here one day, looked at her and said, 'He reminds me of somebody; the cut of his chin and his fair hair.' Then he added, 'We never get that songster round these days, do we? Likely he's gone back to Ireland. His name was Bruce, too. I've never known a man attract the women as much as he did. In the town they would be round him like flies. It was open doors for him. Oh yes, open doors for him; but he never bothered. It was thought he wasn't made that way; but you never know, you never know, do you, Missis Rose?' he had said.

She had never liked Peter Locke. He was nosy; he knew too much about everybody and everything. Nothing seemed to escape him. And yet it couldn't really escape the eye of anybody who had seen the poet painter that her child was the image of him. Therefore, she loved Bruce, that is, right up till lately she had loved him, because he had loved her. Oh, she knew he loved her; and he had looked after her, that is until that girl came on the scene. Oh, that girl! She had an influence on him. And yet she herself had liked her when she first came; and there was no doubt about what he'd said that she'd made a difference in the house. But then the house wasn't the point; it was the difference she had made in him. Just look what he was doing about the money. She couldn't believe it.

He startled her by saying, 'We'll have to buy a new horse and cart, that'll be twenty pounds, at least.'

'But Peter said he only got eight for the old ones.'

'Yes, Ma; he only got eight for both the cart and the horse, and he was giving it away because together they were worth twice as much as that. Anyway, we'll say twenty; and then ten to put by for you. That leaves forty odd. Now, if we're careful, thirty would get us through the winter, and the remainder . . . well, I may have to pay out for a little help now and again until I get right back on me feet, because if it gets around that I'm not able to tend far and wide up there, others will help me, as they did Jim Beckett. Those Scots are still long-rangers, and they've got cats' eyes, so they can travel at night. If you remember, Beckett lost fifteen at one go.'

'They should've all been marked.' It was a mutter from Rose, and he said, 'Yes, Ma, they should've all been marked years ago; and if your husband had been any good they *would've* been marked. I've only one pair of legs and one pair of arms and I'll have to get help, for the time being anyway.'

'And how d'you expect to pay them?' She was barking at him again. 'You heard what that sneaking little squirt said the last time he was up here; farm workers all over the place are asking for more.'

'They're out, Ma, to get enough to eat, not for big money, just enough to eat. Anyway, we won't go into the condition of farm workers at this moment.'

A small voice came to them from the far side of the room, saying, 'I . . . I've saved me wages and you can have that. And I don't need to be paid until you're on your feet again.' Jinnie's voice trailed away into silence.

The fire crackled and the lamp spluttered twice before Bruce, turning to his mother again, said, 'Well, Ma, what d'you make of that offer, eh?'

On receiving no answer, he turned to Jinnie and said, 'Thank you, lass. Thank you, lass. I'll not forget your offer, ever. And if it should turn out we're hard-pushed, I'll take you up on it. Now,' his voice dropping, he said, 'get yourself off to bed. There's another day tomorrow.'

'Good-night, missis.'

She was answered by a grunt from the bed.

'Good-night, Mister Bruce.'

'Good-night, Jinnie. Good night.'

When the door had closed on her Bruce turned to the table again, picked up ten sovereigns and put them into the leather bag, which he then handed to his mother. She had watched the proceedings, and now she demanded, 'And where d'you think you're going to store that?'

'Where I can lay me hands on it at any minute and not have to ask for it.'

'You're playing the big fellow all at once, aren't you?'

'And not before time, Ma. Not before time. But if you want a different arrangement, just let me know.'

He now gathered up the rest of the money and thrust it into his coat pocket and immediately felt the weight of it. As he made for the ladder leading to the loft she said, 'What if he was to come back?'

'Then you'd have him all to yourself, Ma, because I would go.' His foot was on the bottom rung of the ladder when he stopped and, turning his head towards her again, he said, 'And I'd take the girl with me; at least as far as the bottom of the hill, because I wouldn't like to hear of her being imprisoned for stabbing your husband to death for, as you know, she doesn't like being handled.'

Jinnie spent a very restless night. After she had climbed the steps to her pallet she had lain awake for hours, and as the night wore on she became more and more aware of the change in herself: she could understand very clearly why her mistress had, of late, shown evident dislike of her. It was because at one time she must have had all Mister Bruce's attention: she had been his main interest, and she had played upon it; but since she herself had appeared on the scene and he had been so thoughtful towards her, the missis must have built up a resentment against her. And all that money in the bag. The only time she herself had turned the tick she hadn't seen it. The missis must have had it hidden in her nightdress.

As sleep at last began to overtake her she made up her mind about one thing, if the missis kept on going for her when there was no need, she'd make a stand and point out to her that it wasn't a very nice job having to see to all her dirty bed needs, and so she should be grateful they were done for her. Yes, she would; that's what she'd say to her; and also that she thought that there were lots of things she could do for herself if she had the mind. Yes, she would dare to tell her that, too.

The cock woke her up at half-past five, and as she lay struggling out of sleep she recalled her thoughts of the earlier hours with regard to her attitude towards her mistress, and sleep left her. She realised she was still of the same mind and also that she wasn't, as she put it to herself, like the person she had been yesterday morning at this time; for one thing she felt older . . . Her mind checked her thoughts here . . . perhaps not older, just different, because she realised she wasn't afraid any more, and she *had* been afraid of so many things; she had been afraid of having to return to the house, of men and their hands; but her main fear since coming here had been that of her mistress. Now she was afraid of her no longer. It was an odd feeling, the loss of that fear, for it was making her dress more slowly, not drag on all her clothes anyhow so as to get downstairs quickly and see to her mistress and her bed needs. Oh, those bed needs.

When she arrived in the kitchen, a lighted candle in her hand, it was to see Bruce descending the ladder.

He didn't speak to her on his way to the scullery, and the door had hardly closed on him when Rose said, 'See to me, girl, I'm wet.'

She was about to jump round in her usual scamper, then stopped herself and, going to the fireside, she took up the bellows.

'Girl! You heard me.'

'Yes, missis.' She did not turn round, but kept applying the bellows to the damped-down fire as she said, 'I'll be with you in a minute, when I get the fire going and the kettle on.'

'Girl!'

From the tone of her mistress's voice, she knew that she was now sitting up, but she still took no heed until the flames were well spread over the top of the small coal, when, after brushing down her apron, she made for the bed, there to be greeted by an infuriated woman who did not speak but who raised a hand to strike her, only to be checked by a yell: 'You do, missis! Just you hit me once! that's all, and out I go and nobody'll stop me, nobody, Mister Bruce or nobody. I'd rather go back to the house this minute. Oh yes, I would.'

Rose Shaleman was now lying back on her pillows gasping, her hands pressed tight against her breast. On the sight of her Jinnie omitted a smothered 'Oh my!' and dashed to the chest of drawers, grabbed the bottle of pills, shook one out, then dashed again to the water jug on the delph rack and spilled most of it as she tried to fill a mug. Then she was at the bedside again and hardly aware that Bruce was by her side.

After a moment, he pressed her away, saying, 'Make some tea;' then to his mother he said, 'Just lie quiet. You're all right. You're all right.'

He took hold of his mother's hands and held them until her breathing became easier; then he said, 'Go to sleep now. You'll be all right.'

Jinnie had made the tea and as she handed him his mug, he said, 'Drink yours, go on. She'll be all right.'

'I . . . I shouldn't have yelled, but she was going to hit me.'

'You did right there. Anyway, she was due for a turn. I expected it last night and was a bit amazed when it didn't come. When things happen up here they happen, don't they? and all at once.' He gave her a wry smile; but she couldn't answer it, she was still shaking, not only from the threat of being struck but from the realisation that if her mistress had died she would have been to blame.

After they'd had their breakfast together Bruce said, 'I'll see to outside while you carry on as usual in here, and when she's ready for changing I'll give you a hand: the mattress will have to be turned. Now don't worry.' His voice was very low, and he put his hand up towards her but didn't touch her. 'The air has been cleared: we all know where we stand. Things'll be different from now on, I don't know how, but just different. Come on now; take that look off your face, and just remember you'll soon be going to see your Max and Miss Caplin.'

Yes, yes; it wouldn't be long now before she would see her dear friends. She hadn't thought about them since last night . . .

It was just turned seven in the morning. She had scrubbed the table, the chairs and the kitchen floor and, throughout, her mistress had slept. She was now about to pick up a very heavy clippy mat which lay on the grass, getting the wind through it, as she put it; but it would have taken a very strong wind to raise the matted rags that had gone to make it. She had just gathered it in her arms when Bruce's voice, from some way behind her, said, 'What's that?' He was pointing ahead, and on the sight of two vehicles she dropped the mat, saying, 'It's the cart and Patsy.'

Bruce said nothing; he just stood staring at the approaching vehicles. Presently he went forward and as he passed their old cart he said to its driver, 'Hello, Roy,' and the young Stevens boy answered, 'Hello, Bruce.'

Mr Stevens himself was seated in the smart trap and he said briefly, ''Morning, Bruce.'

'Good-morning, Mr Stevens.' They looked at each other in silence for a moment before the farmer said, 'Bad business, yesterday, real bad business. I thought there was something in the wind, but what could I do? He put about this tale about you being all set up and so on . . . well, I know you're friends with Mister Richard, but as I know that family a bit I could never see him having enough of his own to set you up. He depends on his father, doesn't he? Anyway, when I heard Pug was going to sell the cart and horse I knew there really was something wrong: people don't get rid of their only means of transport. That was one thing that came to me mind. The other was, if you were going to have a new set-up you could always do with an extra old girl like that in front, 'cause there's quite a bit of work in her yet, and in your cart; and to let it go for eight pounds, well . . . Anyway, Bruce, you can have her back for what I paid for it. That's fair, isn't it?'

'Indeed it is, Mr Stevens, and I'm more than obliged to you.'

'How are you feeling?'

It was a moment before Bruce answered, and then he said, 'Well, to tell you the truth, I'm still somewhat shaky. I would never have believed a cold like that could have taken it out of me as it has done.'

'Oh, that couldn't have been just a cold. As I understood things at the time you were lucky you got through it. Pneumonia can finish off the strongest, and if you do pull through, it takes its toll on your pins for some time. Anyway, how are you going to manage?'

'Oh, we'll manage all right. Now I've got the cart back, half my troubles seem to be over.' He gave a short laugh as he added, 'The small half anyway.'

'You'll need help of some kind because, as you know, your lot like to stray.'

'Yes; that's what worries me. But I'll manage.'

'Well, if you say so, Bruce, I'll take your word for it; but if I can be of any assistance in any way, you just have to say.'

'Oh well,' Bruce came back quickly now, 'it's strange but I've been thinking it would be a help if we had a cow; not a spanking one, just an old one that would still give us enough milk to carry on and perhaps get a little butter and cheese from it.'

'Well, that's a good idea, and it should happen I'll be sorting out shortly, and I'll think of you along those lines.'

'Thank you, Mr Stevens; I'm more than obliged to you because the sky was very dark this morning, the clouds low, no break in them anywhere and I couldn't see how they were going to lift, but now the sun is almost shining.'

During Bruce's last few words the farmer had looked up into the sky and was now saying, 'Bright enough down our way;' then, his brows shooting upwards, he laughed and said, 'Oh. Oh yes; I see what you mean. I see what you mean, Bruce. My missis said you've always had two languages and I think she's right. Anyway, shall we get down to business?'

'Of course. Of course.'

Bruce now hurried into the house, went up the ladder quicker than he had done for some time, came down again, and when he handed the eight pounds to his benefactor he said, 'I would not have thought any less of you, Mr Stevens, if you had asked twice as much.'

'Anybody else, man, and I might have. Oh yes, I might have. And if it had been your brother, or the old one himself, I still might have, but you yourself have always sold good stock, because you've looked after them, and you never haggle on a private deal. Of course' – he put his head back now and started to laugh – 'I remember once, when you were just a nipper, coming down with three chickens and saying to me, "We don't want for them turnips. Don't mind taties but not turnips."'

'I said that?'

'Aye, you did. And I can remember wanting to scud yer ears.'

He pointed now to where his seventeen-year-old son Roy was talking to Jinnie and he said, 'He's not losing any time, is he? Never does where lasses are concerned. Can talk the hind leg off a donkey yet we can't get a word out of him when he's in the house. But she's grown into a bonny piece, that one. Lovely head of hair, at least . . . well, old Peter told me half of it had been chopped off. Something to do with Hal.' His eyes narrowed now as he looked down on Bruce and asked the question point blank, 'Was it Hal up to his tricks?'

'Yes, Mr Stevens; you could say it was Hal up to his tricks, but he got more than he bargained for in the end.'

'There were some funny tales going about after he left, very funny, and unbelievable really, and not all to do with big Sam. No, no.' He paused now as if waiting for Bruce to clarify matters, but he was saved from this by the horse suddenly throwing its head up and letting out a long neigh, and the farmer, pulling on the reins, shouted, 'Whoa! there. Whoa! there;' then he added, 'She's very fresh and not used to the trap. Just got her a few weeks since. Feel she had been a bit of a racer. She came with a pack from over the border, so perhaps somebody found their stables had one horse fewer.' He laughed. But then, his voice rising to a shout, he cried, 'You! Roy, come on. Stop your gossiping,' and, backing the horse away from the old cart, he turned her; then experienced quite a business holding her waiting for Roy to jump up beside him. His last words shouted to Bruce were, 'If we can give you a hand in any way, we're just down below. Don't forget, just down below.'

Bruce caught up with Jinnie as she led Patsy towards her old stable, and he said, 'Take her on into the barn. There's more room there to unharness the cart.' Then he stroked the horse's muzzle, saying, 'Hello there, Patsy, old girl. Am I glad to see you back!' And as if the animal understood him, it replied with a gentle whinny.

A short time later, as they walked back towards the cottage Bruce smiled at Jinnie, saying, 'Roy's a nice boy, isn't he?' to which she answered simply, 'He seems all right, but I wouldn't really know as that's the first time I've really spoken to him. He asked me if I go to the barn-dances, and I said no, because . . . well, I didn't know what a barn-dance was. What is a barn-dance?'

He stared at her. Of course she wouldn't know what a barn-dance was; they didn't talk about such things in the kitchen. He himself had only ever been to two. The first time he had sat on a bale of hay all evening and nobody had been able to get him off it. The second time, several people did get him up from a bale of hay and each of them, as he had pointed out, afterwards wished they hadn't. He had learnt over the years that some people danced in their cottages to tin whistles, one-string fiddles, melodions, accordions and the like, and, everything else being missing, a Jew's harp. But there never had been any dancing in their cottage. As for musical instruments, not even a Jew's harp: and so strange, when he cae to think about it, his supposed father, who could whittle most shapes, had never made either Hal or him a little whistle or a flute.

So he explained to her what a barn-dance was, and finished with, 'You must go one day. He'll take you. Oh yes, he'd be delighted to take you.'

She looked ahead as she said dreamily, 'There was a girl in the house. She used to clog-dance. Once she wanted to show me, but I didn't like it. It was sort of ugly and noisy. But there was another girl, who slept in the end bed, who could play tunes on a comb, and I can an' all.' She turned a bright face towards him now and he said, 'You can?'

'Oh yes; a bit of paper on a comb. And I can play hymn tunes.'

'Then you must play for us some time.'

The smile slid from her face as she muttered, 'No; I don't think I could; 'cos the missis wouldn't like it.'

He did not contradict her and say, Oh yes, she would, but when she asked, 'Will it be all right for Sunday for me? I mean, to go down and see Miss Caplin and Max?' he was quick to answer, 'Oh yes. Yes, of course. Rain, hail or shine, you must go down and see them.'

She stopped with her hand on the sneck of the door

8

It was six days later and Bruce had just harnessed up Patsy to the cart in readiness for driving in to Allendale to replenish stores for both the kitchen and the animals, when Jimmy Dixon's hired cab arrived at the door, having come all the way from Haydon Bridge, and out of it stepped a policeman and a man in plain clothes.

On the sight of them Bruce brought Patsy to a standstill and hurried towards them. The policeman was a stranger to him, as was the other man.

'You Mr Bruce Shaleman?'

'Yes; yes, that's me.'

'We . . . we understand your mother's alive but not well.'

'That's right.'

'And her husband . . . well, do I understand he left some days ago?'

'Yes, six days gone.'

It was now the man in the plain suit who asked, 'Would it be possible to have a word with your mother?'

'Yes; yes, come in.'

Bruce pushed open the door and entered the room, calling loudly, 'Ma! There are two men here to see you.'

Rose Shaleman pulled herself up on the pillows and peered down the room, and when she saw the policeman her hand went to her mouth.

The two men stood by the side of the table and both

looked around the room before the policeman said, 'This is Inspector Morris from Hexham, missis. I'm afraid we have bad news for you.'

She said nothing, but waited.

The policeman now looked at the Inspector and he, after clearing his throat, said, 'Your husband, Mrs Shaleman, died yesterday morning in South Shields Infirmary. He had been found near the waterfront, badly beaten and stripped of most of his clothing, right down to his boots. He was revived for a short time and was able to give his name and address. I understand his last words expressed the desire that he be taken home.'

Rose Shaleman now made a strange noise in her throat, then she said, 'South Shields? All that way? Why? Why South Shields?'

Before either man could give her any answer Bruce put in quickly, 'We . . . we understood he was going to Norfolk.'

'Norfolk?' The Inspector raised his eyebrows. 'In that case, South Shields was somewhat out of his way.'

A long pause followed this remark before the policeman, turning to Bruce, said, 'The body's in the mortuary but it will have to be removed shortly. Will you make the necessary arrangements?'

After again casting a critical glance around the room, the Inspector continued, 'If it would be easier for you, arrangements could be made with an undertaker to bring the body directly to your nearest cemetery. This could save you a lot of journeying and trouble. Of course, it's up to you as to whether you make the arrangements yourself. Otherwise he would be buried in a general grave.' Out of politeness he had omitted the word 'pauper's'.

'Oh. Oh, thank you. Thank you, I'd be glad if an

undertaker could deal with the matter,' Bruce replied.

'Well, that being so, we will take our leave.' And turning again to the bed and in a sympathetic tone, the Inspector said, 'We're very sorry for your loss, Mrs Shaleman. Good-day to you.'

She gave him no reply, nor to the policeman when he added his sympathetic comments.

Outside, the inspector brought up the matter of finance with Bruce. 'Of course,' he said, 'you understand it will cost more than an ordinary funeral: it's a long way and it'll need to come by train and there'll have to be pall-bearers too.'

'That's all right. The bill will be met, and on the day the undertaker finishes his job.'

'Oh well, that's good to hear. It will likely take three or four days to arrange but you will be notified when they are due to arrive.'

Without further words of farewell or commiseration the two men left.

As Bruce made to re-enter the cottage Jinnie came out of the scullery and hurried towards him, although she did not speak. It was he who said, 'You heard?' and she nodded. He knew she couldn't say she was sorry, no more than could he.

'Go and hold Patsy for a minute, would you?' He indicated the horse, who had wandered and was nibbling at the grass. 'She'll get so full she won't want to move.'

He now went into the cottage and straight to the bed. His mother was sitting upright, her clasped hands beating the hap, and the expression on her face was one he hadn't seen for a long time. In fact, he didn't think he had ever seen her look so sad.

'Awful way to go,' she said.

'Yes; yes it was.' His own voice was low.

'You'll . . . you'll put him away decent?' It was a plea to which he responded quickly, 'Of course, Ma; yes, of course.'

'You . . . you can have what's under the tick.'

'Oh, Ma,' he said, shaking his head. 'Don't worry. Just leave that where it is; what has to be done I'll see to. If our belts get very tight later on, I can come to you.'

'Aye. Aye.' And then she added, 'They must have beaten him up. And what was he doing on the sea-front in Shields? Shields is a long way off.' She was looking up at him appealingly now, and he answered her quietly, 'Not today, Ma; not with the trains running. And he's been gone, you know, for nearly a week.'

She was nodding again. 'I forget about the trains. He must have been badly knocked about to die like that. And you know, Bruce' – now she gulped in her throat – 'I've wished him dead for years. Oh aye, I've wished him dead for years; but not to go like that; I meant he should just go in his sleep, sort of. I've never been sorry for him in me life, but I'm sorry for him now. You . . . you know what I mean?' She put out her hand to him, and he took it and patted it as he said, 'Yes; yes, I do; and I feel the same, Ma. I too have wished him out of the way more than once but, as you say, not in that way. But don't worry; I'll see he has the best that can be bought.'

'You will, sure?'

'Sure. Oh yes, sure, Ma.' And he laid down her hand; then went out of the room.

He walked until he came to an outcrop of rock, and there he sat down.

Yesterday, the man he had assumed for many years to have been his father was still the man who had run off six days ago with the earnings of six months' hard graft, *his* hard graft, and he only had to call up the image of him to feel his fingers clutching his throat. He knew too that his mother would have done the same then, had she the strength; yet here, today, both he and she were consumed with pity for him. From the very beginning, she had apparently resented the nearness of his body yet now her pity was oozing from her like a soft mantle and enwrapping him almost in love.

Such were the effects of death.

9

Jinnie stood before her mistress. She was wearing a long grey coat, her polished boots and her flat straw hat. Rose Shaleman looked her up and down before she said, flatly, 'You look tidy enough.' There was no censure in the remark, yet neither was there a trace of kindness. It was a tone that expressed indifference. Yet when Jinnie said softly, 'I won't go if you think it shows disrespect, missis, with the Mister not being buried yet,' she was told, 'Oh, you needn't worry your head about that; your visiting won't make any difference one way or t'other,' only for a note of interest to show itself in Rose Shaleman's voice when she asked, 'You've got the locket for her?'

'Oh yes. Yes, missis.' Jinnie put her hand in the pocket of her coat and brought out the small cardboard box, saying, 'I'll have to tell her I'll get the chain for it later.'

'Aye, well, mind how you go, and mind your manners.'

Jinnie stared at her mistress for a moment before saying, 'Goodbye then, missis. I'll not stay all that long.' She felt obliged to say this, because for the first time in days Rose Shaleman had spoken civilly to her. And so she added, 'I've laid your tea and Mister Bruce's and I've wrapped up the oven-bottom bread so it won't get . . .'

'All right. All right. Now get yourself away. Go on. Go on.'

Jinnie took two steps backwards saying again, 'Good-bye, missis.'

Rose Shaleman gave no further farewell but watched her until she had passed through the doorway when she lay back on her pillows, muttering to herself . . .

Jinnie hurried in the direction of the barn, but as she passed the boiler-house Bruce's voice hailed her. 'You're off, then?'

Laughing, she turned and went into the steamy room, where the pig food was cooking in an iron boiler. The walls were covered with odd pieces of harness. In the middle of the room was a bench like a butcher's block, and Bruce was seated there. He had been about to press the large curved needle through a thick leather strap.

She watched what he was doing for a moment before she asked, 'The leather's dried, hasn't it?'

'Yes, you could say that, Jinnie; it's dried all right.' And he withdrew the needle from the hole it had made and he looked her up and down, as his mother had done; although what he said was, 'You look bonny; and you're excited, aren't you? Well, it's something being invited to a birthday party.'

'Oh, it won't be a party; just a cup of tea and a piece of cake. The Miss Duckworths are very old, you know.'

'Yes, I know.' He laughed now. 'But they weren't always old. I remember them chasing me when I was a lad.'

'Did they?'

'They did indeed. I was scrumping their apples. I remember one collared me and said, "You must come and ask if you want any."'

'And did you?'

'No; there was no fun in asking.'

She looked at him intently now before she asked, 'You still feeling tired.'

211

'No, no; I'm fine.'

''Twas a long day yesterday, going all the way into Hexham.'

He smiled at her, saying, 'I was on the cart.'

'Yes, I know; but it can be long, with having to wait about an' that. Did they bring him to Hexham in a glass coach?'

'No; in the guard's van. Now, forget the funeral and get yourself away.'

She smiled now, as she backed from him, saying, 'I wish you were coming with me;' then, biting on her lip, she turned and ran from the room. He stood up and, through the murky window, he watched her as she ran for some distance before stopping to straighten her hat, then walk sedately on. He continued to watch her until she disappeared beyond the ridge. It was as if she had floated into the air like the ethereal creature she sometimes appeared to be. But what was he thinking? Ethereal? Practical would be a more apt word . . . Yet, he didn't know. She was a gentle creature, until she was provoked. And he had seen the result of that, when rather than anything ethereal, she was more like a gale of wind creating havoc.

He smiled to himself as he went back to the block. He picked up the needle and continued to mend the worn-out harness, and as he sat there he wondered how they were now going to survive the winter after having paid fifteen pounds for conveying Pug's body to Hexham; and this would be only the beginning.

An hour later he had finished his mending and went indoors, where he put the kettle on and brewed a pot of tea. He did not, however, speak to his mother, nor she to him until he handed her the mug and then, as if she had picked up his thoughts from the swill-room, she said, 'Fifteen pounds! Daylight robbery.'

' 'Twas a double journey, Ma.'

'Double journey or not, fifteen pounds!' Then, as an afterthought, she said, 'How are you feeling?' to which he answered, 'Not so bad. But don't worry, everything'll be all right.'

'All right, you say—' She took a drink from her mug, then she continued, 'All right, you say. You don't look fit enough to walk the flat, never mind the hills.'

He picked up his mug of tea and went to the door, which he had just opened when his mother demanded, 'Where are you going now?'

'I'm going nowhere, Ma; I was just going to stand here and drink my tea.'

After a short silence her voice came again: 'You never sit with me now. I hardly ever see you, except when you come in to eat or to go to bed.'

He looked towards her and said, 'Ma, you want it all ways: you want me up the hills to see to our living, you want me outside, and in the kitchen here; not to talk, no, or discuss anything, no, just to moan. And you're never alone for long, anyway. Jinnie spends most of her life in this damn kitchen or the scullery, and a big slice of that time is taken up attending to you. So there you have it.'

He did not walk away from the door but stood looking out over the plain. Suddenly his eyes narrowed as he spotted two figures far away in the distance but coming his way.

He took two quick steps back into the kitchen, placed the mug on the table, then hurried out, ignoring his mother's querulous enquiry, 'What is it now?'

He went some little distance before his shortened breathing caused him to stop, when his eyes stretched wide and he muttered, ' 'Tis her and the big fellow. Well, well; what now?'

Jinnie was still some distance from him when she called: 'Hello, Mister Bruce; I've brought Max to see you,' and after hurrying towards him, she continued breathlessly, 'He . . . he's got something to tell you . . . to ask you. Haven't you, Max?'

'Y-y-yes, Mister Bruce.'

Somewhat puzzled, Bruce looked from one to the other, then started to laugh, and he said, 'Well, if it's good news I'd like to hear it. Come on back to the house.' But even as they made their way towards the cottage he was telling himself he'd better not take the fellow in there or he'd have his mother screaming; and so, he led the way to the barn, and there said, 'We can talk here;' but even as he said the words his mind took a wild turn and thought, Surely he's not come to tell me he's going to take her away, and that with Miss Caplin's approval!

He waited for Max to speak, but Max was looking about him and to no-one in particular he said, 'N-n-nice barn.'

'Well, will you tell him or will I?' said Jinnie now.

'You st-st-start. I say l-l-later.'

'Well' – she had now turned to Bruce – 'it's like this. You know I told you Max had got this job on a farm? Well, he doesn't start until the New Year. There's a cottage and the man won't be out until then; I mean, the other man. And so, as Miss Caplin says, at the moment, Max is as good as his own master, at least until then. Well, he can leave the house, the workhouse, any time. The farmer there has been very good to him and he put in a good word to the guardians for him.'

At this Max said, 'Yes, to the guardians. They all . . . right to me.' He grinned now, a wide toothful grin as he added, 'Not always . . . all right . . . guardians.'

Bruce nodded understandingly; then he looked at Jinnie again and said, 'Well, go on.'

'Well, then, that's it, you see; he's got nearly two months and he wants to come and help you.'

'Oh dear.' Bruce now shook his head, then to Max he said, 'That's very kind of you, Max; but I'm sorry to say I can't afford to employ anyone at present.'

'Not em-ploy. No money . . . just eat and . . . sleeping,' and saying this, he flung his arms wide to take in the barn and on a deep laugh he said, 'Best bed . . . hay bed.'

'It's very kind of you, Max, but . . .'

'Oh, Mister Bruce, he'd love it. And . . . and he'd be such a help. He can do all kinds of things. The farm at the house is quite big, with pigs, chickens, ducks, cows and sheep.'

'Sheep?' Bruce looked down at her now.

'Well, not as many like you've got, but there were a good few dozen.'

Bruce now looked at Max and asked, 'You've dealt with sheep?' and Max nodded, then said, 'N-n-not on hill; on fells. And I l-l-lambed and clipped.'

'You can shear sheep?'

'Huh! Huh!' The big head bounced. 'Frederick show me.'

Bruce now looked to Jinnie for confirmation, and she said, 'Frederick was the man who came to shear the sheep, and he showed Max how.'

Turning fully to Bruce now and lowering her voice as if Max were some distance away, she said, 'He can turn his hand to most things. Miss Caplin said the Master didn't want to let him go, but the farmer put a good word in to the guardians, as he said, and they can't keep him because they haven't got a paper on him. Well, you know what I mean.'

No, he didn't know exactly what she meant, except perhaps that he wasn't certified.

The two men now stared at each other and one part of Bruce's mind was saying: Yes, he is ugly but he's a splendid creature, nevertheless, and should be as strong as a horse. I really shouldn't look a gift horse in the mouth. But the other part was saying, But there's Ma. Just think what she'll say. She's never forgotten the last time she saw him. But then she needn't see him: he wouldn't be in the house at all. She would have to be told, though. Oh yes; she'd have to be told. What was he saying? Was he saying that he had already decided? Yes, he supposed he was. This was a gift from the gods; a man who didn't want paying and could turn his hand to anything; even if it was only for the next couple of months until he got on his feet again and before the winter really set in. He glanced from Max to Jinnie. They were both staring at him, a plea in both faces. That was another thing: she loved this man; he was like a father to her. His presence would make her happy, if nothing else did.

'All right; we can but give him a try.'

'Oh! Mister Bruce.' She had hold of his hands now, her face reaching up to his, and for a moment he thought she was going to kiss him. But then she turned and flung her arms around the big fellow; and he held her; and as Bruce watched the embrace he knew a moment of aloneness that he had never experienced before. It was as if he had never known either Richard or her, or, worse still, having known them, had lost them. And then the big fellow was standing in front of him, his hand extended.

When his own hand became lost within the tough palm and was shaken vigorously, yet without a hurtful grip, and the stilted voice came to him saying, 'N-n-not sorry. Regret no,' he found himself responding warmly, answering: 'No, I'm sure I'll not be sorry, Max. When can you start?'

'Wednesday.'

'Wednesday? Good.'

Bruce watched his new assistant turn and look about the barn as if he were viewing a new house, and when he said, 'Must go. Miss Caplin . . . back before dark.'

'Yes, yes of course.' And Bruce looked at Jinnie and said, 'Are you going down again?' and she answered, 'No. No, we had tea and birthday cake, and Miss Caplin was so pleased with her locket.'

'So she should be; it was a lovely locket.'

Jinnie said, 'I'll . . . I'll set Max on his way, just a little bit, and then I'll come back and see to the missis.'

'But there's another good two hours yet before dark.'

'I know. I know, but it doesn't matter.' Then again lowering her voice, she said, 'It's so kind of you, Mister Bruce, 'cos I know you'll have to face the missis, and she won't be for it. But she needn't see him, need she?'

They both turned and watched Max as he walked well outside the barn entrance and looked about him, and he answered her, also quietly, 'No, she needn't see him; but, as you say, Jinnie, she's still got to be faced . . .'

Fifteen minutes later he faced his mother with the news, and the yell she let out caused him to screw his eyes and turn his head away as he listened to her tirade: 'You mad? D'you want us to be murdered in our beds? He's not safe. He'll do for you first chance he gets.'

He rounded on her then, crying almost as loudly as she had done, 'The only thing he'll do for me, Ma, is to help me over a very, very bad patch. I'm not yet fit to shepherd the hills; I'm not even fit enough, let me tell you, to keep walking about here. I'm aching from head to foot; all I want to do is to lie down . . . somewhere

217

. . . anywhere. The alternative, Ma, is to sell up and then you'd have enough to keep you in a back room down in the village, with someone like Mary Fanny Cook to see to you. There'll be no Jinnie down there to answer your beck and call. Yes' – he jerked his head down to her – 'that's what I could do; sell up. And the quicker the better for me.'

Her voice came back at him, deep and flat, and holding a touch of disdain as she said, 'You could sell nothing: this place is still mine, and when I go it is Hal's.'

He straightened up and stared at her; and she stared back at him; then her head emphasising the words, she repeated, 'It is Hal's. Legally, you haven't a leg to stand on. You hadn't thought along those lines, had you? If he came back, and he said he would, you couldn't claim a dead hen. He might keep you on as a hand, because he's always hated farming of any kind.'

He stepped back from her as if, in doing so, he would be seeing her in a different light, because he had never imagined her as being capable of venting such spleen: he had always been her first choice because he was the result of the only love she had ever known, perhaps had ever been capable of.

His voice came as a croak when he replied, 'Well, now I know where I stand, Ma, and I'll fit into the post, something between a farmhand and an acting manager. Well, being the acting manager, I'm definitely keeping the big fellow.'

Her voice rising again, she cried, 'You do that and I'll have every word I've said put in writing. I will. I will.'

'Yes, you do that, Ma. Have it put in writing if it'll ease your bitterness.' And he went slowly from the room.

Outside, he stood leaning against the wall of the swill-house. He was feeling so tired and drained that he could have slid to the ground. In the distance, he could see the figure of Jinnie returning from seeing Max off. She was neither walking nor running, but like a child she was hopping from one foot to the other.

On seeing him, she changed her step and began to run. And when she reached him she panted, 'He'll be such a help, Mister Bruce. And you know what I was thinking? He said he could sleep in the barn, but the nights are cold, you know. I tell you what I could do.' She pointed to the door of the swill-room, saying, 'I could clean up in there: take the cobwebs down and do the floor and all that, and he could put in a plank bed.' She paused now and leaned towards him, saying, 'You all right?' and he answered wearily, 'No, Jinnie: I'm far from all right.'

'Oh; the missis went on?'

'You could say the missis went on, Jinnie. Yes, you could say that.' And he pulled himself from the wall, adding, 'You know something, Jinnie? If I had thirty pounds of my own I know where there is a derelict cottage that could be made warm and snug, and it has quite a bit of land around it. I would buy it and take you and Max with me. We might have to eat grass for a year, but I know we'd make a go of it.'

'Oh! Mister Bruce. That would be nice. Oh yes; it would, but—' With a slow shake of her head, she added, 'The missis needs you and she's sick.'

'Yes—' he looked towards the ground as he muttered, 'She's sick,' and he could have added, 'but she's not so sick that she doesn't know what she is doing. And she meant what she said. Oh aye, she meant what she said.'

As she rounded the side of the barn, and carrying a flat straw-lined basket layered with eggs, Jinnie was brought abruptly to a halt. Drawn up opposite the cottage door was a trap, with one man seated in it, another standing by the horse's head. The man in the trap was a parson: his collar, his black garb, his hat yelled that at her; but she did not hurry towards him: she put down the basket, then dashed back the way she had come and into what had once been the cowshed, where Bruce and Max were examining a crumbling wall, and she called, 'Mister Bruce! you'd better come quick. Parson; parson's here!'

'What? Who?'

'A parson. He's in a trap by the door.'

He hurried past her and after rounding the barn, he too hesitated for there was the parson to whom, on the advice of Mr Stevens, he'd had to give a precious sovereign; and for what? for yammering some nonsense about the corpse now being in heaven and protected by angels as he awaited the last day of judgement.

He purposely slowed his step; and it was the parson who spoke first, almost heartily, saying, 'Good-day to you, Mr Shaleman. I am on my rounds of the outposts of my parish, seeing as I am what you would call new to the job, and in visiting you, I thought I would kill two birds with the one stone; introducing myself to your mother as that new parson from down below, and offering her my condolences on her loss.'

When there was no reaction from Bruce, the parson became slightly embarrassed. From his verger he had heard of the extreme poverty of some of these hill farmers. It had been said that church mice had more than this particular family. Yet it was odd that the old man, whom he had buried, had been driven to the cemetery in a glass hearse and he himself had been given a gold sovereign. Normally, he was lucky if he got half that amount, and from those he was well aware could afford more.

However, the outside of this place certainly fitted Verger Wilson's estimation. He would soon see if the inside matched up to it, for the young man who had given him no greeting at all had thrust open the door of the cottage and was now addressing someone at the far end of the room, saying, 'You have a visitor, Ma.'

For a moment, the Reverend Norman Cuthbert stood just inside the room so as to allow his eyes to become accustomed to the gloom after the bright sunshine outside, and when his vision cleared his suspicions were confirmed, for the inside of the cottage appeared to him little better than the outside. The place was sparsely furnished, and he noticed that although it was clean it offered not the slightest trace of comfort.

He now looked up the room to where a woman was sitting in a wall-bed, and he was about to speak when she said, 'He sent for you?'

'No-one sent for me, Mrs Shaleman, but I thought it was time I made your acquaintance and offered you my condolences on the loss of your dear husband.' He watched her flop back on her pillows, then he turned quickly to see the young girl, the one who had been carrying a basket of eggs, pushing a chair towards him, and he said, 'Thank you, my dear.' Then turning back to the woman in the bed, he asked, 'Is this your granddaughter?'

'No; she is not my grand-daughter; she is a maid.'

'Oh.' He half turned and watched the girl going out of the room, and when he turned to the woman again she was staring at him, her eyes wide, her mouth slightly agape, and when she said, 'How did you know I wanted you?' he paused for a moment, then said, 'I . . . I wasn't aware that you wanted me, or you needed me, but the spirit is a very mysterious thing. It is, as it were, God's messenger. Now—' He was about to bend towards her but was checked by the strong body odour emanating from her, and so he remained seated upright; but his voice had a confidential note to it when he said, 'Is there something you would like to tell me?'

'Yes. Yes, there is. I . . . I didn't know how I was going to get either you or the doctor. I want a letter written; but it's only to be read after I am dead.'

'Oh, you mean a form of will?'

'Yes. Yes, I suppose that's it, a form of will.'

'Well, now, I take it you can't write yourself?'

'No, I can't.' She could have added, 'I wouldn't be asking you, would I, to write me a will if I could write meself?'

'Have you any paper?'

'Paper? No. No, we have no writing paper.'

He sighed deeply before he said, 'Well, all I have on me is a notebook. Is it going to be very long?'

'No; just a few words.'

'Oh, well.' He now thrust his hand into an inner pocket of his black open coat and withdrew a large notebook from it, and he had to flip over a number of pages before a blank one presented itself, and then he said, 'Well, what would you like to say?'

'I would just like to say who I'm leaving the farm to when I go. It is my farm at the moment.'

'Oh, well . . . well now, give me your full name.'

She gave him her name, Rose Ann Shaleman, and when he asked, 'The name of your farm? It's just slipped my mind,' she replied, 'Tollet's Ridge Farm.'

This done, he now prompted her: 'Tell me what you want to say.'

She came back sharply at him, 'I've just told you, it's to do with who I want to leave the farm to.'

He sighed deeply, paused a moment, then said, 'I shall

write: "I, Rose Ann Shaleman, of Tollet's Ridge Farm, wish to leave the said farm and land and stock to my son—"' He now looked at her and asked, 'What is your son's full name?'

She told him, and he wetted the pencil lead on his tongue before writing the name on the paper in block letters; then below that he wrote: 'Signed this 14th day of November 1871 in the presence of the Reverend Norman Cuthbert'. Then he looked up again and said, 'As this is a form of will there should be two witnesses to your signature.'

'Why?'

'Oh; without going into the legal details, I only know that it is . . . well, a law, and makes the bequest valid, if you follow me.'

She didn't follow him, and she only knew that she didn't want anyone else to be aware of the details, and she voiced this by saying, 'I don't want that splashed around. I thought that you, being a parson, would keep it secret.'

'And it will be kept secret, Mrs Shaleman, until the time comes for it to be read. My verger is outside; he is my driver too.'

'You've got a driver? How did you come?'

'A sort of trap; a light brake, really.'

'And you've a driver?'

His tone was sharp now as he answered, 'Yes, Mrs Shaleman,' but he did not go on to explain to her why he had a driver for a trap-cum-small-brake, although it was already known in the parish that he had had a serious accident with a horse and therefore did not trust them. He hadn't let it be known that the horse had really been but a donkey and that it had happened during his early childhood, but he had never been able to overcome the fear of animals since.

'Will he spill it about?'

'If you mean, will he talk about what is in this will, the answer is no, because he won't read it. All that is required of him is to write his name at the bottom. Now do you understand?'

She did and she didn't, but she lay back now and he rose and went to the door, and lifting his hand to his verger, who was talking to the son of the house, he beckoned him. And when the man entered the room he, as his master had done, paused for a moment to get used to the gloom. Then he made his way behind the minister to the gaunt woman sitting on the wall-bed, where the minister said, 'This is Mrs Shaleman, Wilson, and she would like you to sign your name to this document.' He now held the notebook out to the man, but kept his hand over what he had written, and pointing with the forefinger of his right hand he said, 'Write your name there.'

'Write my name?'

'That's what I said: just write your name there. That is all that's required of you.'

George Wilson picked up the dangling pencil and in a large sprawling hand he laboriously wrote his name, and he had hardly finished putting the long stroke attached to the end when the notebook was almost whipped away from him and the parson said, 'That'll be all; I'll be out in a moment.'

'Just as you say, Parson. Just as you say.' The man gave one hard look at the woman in the makeshift bed, before walking with slow strides down the room and out into the fresh air again, his whole mien showing his protest. He'd have something to tell his missis, all right, when he got home the night.

Back at the bedside, Parson Cuthbert now very carefully tore the leaf from the notebook, but as he went to hand it to her she pushed it away, saying, 'I can't keep that; I've nowhere to put it. Anyway, I don't want anybody to see it.'

'Then you wish me to keep it in my care until . . . ?'

'Yes. Aye, of course that's what I wish. No other way, is there?'

He folded the piece of paper with the perforated edge and after placing it carefully into an inner pocket, he said, 'I shall see that it goes into an envelope and is sealed.'

At this, she let out a long slow breath and said, 'Oh. Well, thanks. Thanks very much. That's off my mind.' Then pulling herself upright, she said, 'The girl will make you a cup of tea.'

'No, thank you. No, thank you.' He busied himself now returning the notebook to the inner pocket of his plain coat; then, as he was in the process of buttoning it up, she asked, 'Would you like a few eggs, then?'

'Yes. Yes, thank you very much, Mrs Shaleman. Yes, I'm very partial to an egg.' She put out a hand as if thrusting him aside and, leaning out of the bed, she called, 'You! girl.'

As if she had been waiting for the command to come in and to make tea, Jinnie appeared from the scullery, saying, 'Yes, Mrs Shaleman?'

'Pack up half a dozen eggs for the parson.'

Jinnie paused as if surprised by the order, but then turned and went out, and the Reverend Norman Cuthbert said the words to himself: half a dozen eggs. Really! A dozen and a chicken, he would have thought, at least, if not a suckling pig, for they couldn't be that hard up if they could afford such a funeral as they had given the old man after bringing him all the way from South Shields, which he heard would have cost them nearly twenty pounds; and this after the old man had absconded with the market takings. There was something fishy here.

His voice held a distinctly cold note as he bade her his farewell: 'Good-day to you, Mrs Shaleman. I'm glad to have been of service to you.' He stressed the words, then added, 'I'll remember you in my prayers.'

'I'm obliged,' was her only answer.

The parson lost no time over his departure; yet he hesitated before climbing into the trap, for he had glimpsed a very large figure of a man standing near the girl. He had no recollection of anyone so big in the parish; still, he wasn't going to enquire further. All he wanted to do was to get away from this mean and miserable place, and he promised himself it would be a long time before it saw him again.

Bruce stood apart, watching the trap disappear into the distance. She had done it then. But how had she got in touch with him? She had seen no-one from outside. Was it by chance that he had come? Well, if it was, it was strange, for she must have carried out her threat: the verger had been called in, and it would have been to put his cross to something. Being a verger, he probably could write.

Well, he knew one thing: if she could make her plans, so could he, for he had no intention of slaving on until she died; and afterwards, when Hal returned, as he likely would, he could sell up.

When Jinnie's voice at his side said, 'He wasn't over-pleased with half a dozen eggs; he never even said thank you,' he made no comment; but when Max said, 'P-p-parson, ch-ch-church beggars,' he nodded at him, saying, 'You're right there, Max. You're right there.'

Max now continued the conversation they had been having before the arrival of the visitor. 'C-c-could build that wall p-p-proper. Good for cow. Good for cow and next-door dairy.'

At this Bruce laughed ruefully, saying, 'Yes, good cowshed and dairy; all we want now is the cow.' He patted Max on the arm, adding, 'It's a good idea, Max, but we'll leave it for the time being.'

'There were several cows at the house, and a dairy,' put in Jinnie. 'Three of the girls worked in the dairy. But' – she now pulled a face – 'nobody in the house saw a bit of butter or cheese; it was sold, but only after them up top had their share. It would be nice to have a cow, Mister Bruce.'

'Jinnie!' There was a reprimand in his tone, and it was enough to make her say, 'Oh yes. Yes, I'm sorry. I know. It was just that I thought, with Max being here, he's so handy, turn his hand to anything, he can—' She looked at her self-appointed guardian with admiration, and he modestly tossed his head, saying, 'Not . . . not everything, no. Things I want to do, but can't.' He now wagged his fingers. 'Write. Y-y-you know, write.'

'But you can read. You can read well.'

Bruce's interest was momentarily aroused, and he looked at Max and said, 'You can read but you cannot write? How comes that?'

'D-d-don't know. Writin' all m-m-mixed up. Letters won't f-f-fit.'

Bruce sighed and smiled at the big man; then said to him, 'Well, you've got much more in your head than I have, Max, because I can neither read nor write.'

'Try. Try.'

'Oh, there's no time; never has been. And no need. Well—' He jerked his chin upwards as if in denial of his last statement, then added on a laugh, 'When I'm older and have plenty of time, I'll start then.'

'T-t-too late.' And on these words Max turned away,

and Bruce, looking after him, thought, an amazing fellow, really amazing. He's got a mind, and yet look how he's placed. Why? Oh, for God's sake! he said to himself; let's keep off the whys and get on with the job, and with this thought he said briefly to Jinnie, 'You'd better go in and carry on as usual.' And to himself he added, 'We'll both carry on as usual, for the time being at least.'

IO

November had come in with wind and sleet showers. Towards the end of the month it snowed heavily and lay frozen for three days; then followed a thaw and intermittent rain that took them into the first week in December. In the second week, the weather changed again, this time to frosty nights and mornings, and a modicum of weak winter sun.

A week after Max's arrival, Bruce had been able to take him up into the hills and show him the ropes of getting the sheep down from the high fells and also of controlling Flossie. It was strange, Bruce found, that here was this man who stammered on every other word yet who could whistle perfectly, and he was quick to learn the different notes to which the dog answered.

Flossie had taken a liking to the big man to the extent of following him each night to share the warmth of his sleeping quarters in the swill-room.

Max had made the room as comfortable as possible. He had constructed himself a plank platform on which to lay a home-made tick full of straw. He had also built a rough open cupboard to hold his two changes of under-clothes, a number of coloured handkerchiefs, a new cap, and a long hand-knitted muffler. On another shelf he kept his Bible and a number of old exercise books, which were covered mainly with his efforts at writing, some old newspapers and three-year-old magazines. His

Sunday coat and other oddments of top clothing were hanging from nails in the wall.

Altogether Max was very pleased with the accommodation. As he had pointed out to Bruce, after lying in the twelfth bed, the one that was farthest away from the door, since he could remember, this was a private domain, and he was very grateful for it.

After the sheep had been brought down to the lower pastures, there was much less work to do, so Bruce let Max carry on with his suggestion of making the old cow byre fit to be used again; although where the money to buy the cow would come from, he didn't know.

Max spent much of his time on the building next to the byre, and, whenever possible, Jinnie would visit him. These, of course, had to be flying visits because, these days, the missis was keeping her on her toes. One day, Jinnie had dared to protest that she had the chickens to see to, and the missis had shouted at her, 'You don't keep dogs and bark yourself. You brought him here to work, so let him get on with it. He eats enough for two, so let him work enough for two.'

There were times when Jinnie came to wonder how it was possible to feel sorry for someone and hate them at the same time.

Yet these days, on the whole, Rose Shaleman was much quieter. There was no longer a nightly conversation with her son. When she had bad breathing attacks, he would still see to her, but afterwards he no longer sat with her until she went to sleep. He would say, 'You'll be all right now,' and leave her. And what conversation she had with Jinnie was always in the form of either an order or a reprimand.

At one time, Rose might have thought that if Bruce married the girl he could do worse; but no longer, not since she had brought that beast to the place. He was just another throw-out from the workhouse, as Jinnie was.

The Shalemans could, by no stretch of the imagination, claim any prestige in the farming world, but they had survived on the sheep, and independently; and no matter what the general opinion was, they hadn't risen from hinds either; in fact, right back, one of their ancestors had owned Valley Farm.

Rose Shaleman was now asking herself why the girl should be wanting to change her half-day off from a Sunday to a Saturday, and further, why she wanted to go down to the Stevens's farm. She had said it was to ask Mrs Stevens how to make a Christmas cake. Rose couldn't come back at her and say, 'Why didn't you ask me?' because she had already admitted to the girl that she was no hand at any kind of cake-making. And now, there she was off on the cart with that weird individual.

She strained to sit up in bed and through the window just managed to see the high back of the cart disappearing. She lay back on her pillows and for a moment was consumed with a feeling of loneliness, which led on to bitterness. It seemed as if those two had taken over the place. She wished she was dead.

The thought brought her up from her pillows and almost aloud she said, Oh no, I don't! She was afraid of death and what lay after. For a moment she wished that Hal was back . . . But then she mustn't be here when Hal came back. He was too much, was Hal.

231

Jinnie took the seat Mrs Stevens offered her, a padded black oak settle set at an angle to the roaring fire that fed two ovens; and there were two hobs, on one a kettle, on the other a large black pan. Her eyes were wide, her mouth slightly agape. She had never imagined anything like this farm kitchen, every corner of which was bright. On the mantelpiece were several pairs of shining brass candlesticks. The wall above was thick with pewtered plates, and to the far side of the fireplace from where she was sitting, an oak dresser stood, bright with china of every description. To her amazement she saw that apart from a cooking table a long oak trestle table stood at the far end of the large room, and positioned around it some chairs. Four black rafters crossed the ceiling, each one heavy with cuts of ham. The floor was flagged, but smoothly flagged, and there, beneath her feet, was a rug, a carpet rug, a real carpet rug.

'Now, you can have tea, coffee or a glass of ale,' said Mrs Stevens.

'What? Oh. Oh, I'm sorry. Thank you. I'll have coffee, if I may.'

The small woman laughed as she leaned towards Jinnie, saying, 'You were miles away, lass.'

'No, no, Mrs Stevens, I wasn't miles away; no, I was right here, 'cos I've never seen such a beautiful room.'

'Oh. Oh now; well, that's nicely spoken.' The little woman seemed to bounce to the table now, and as she began spooning coffee from a caddy into a tall jug she said, 'Well yes, yes, you're right. I'm very proud of my kitchen; I have a place for everything and everything in its place. What's that you say?' She turned again and looked at Jinnie, whose head was now moving slowly as her eyes were taking in every item in the room, and after a moment she answered, 'I said I could live in this room for ever.'

'Huh! No, you couldn't, girl; no, you couldn't. I have to get out of it at times. I look forward to my breaks on market day and my chapel on Sunday and my meetings once a week, because, you know, there's an old saying that you can get too much of a good thing, and if you're wise you don't take too much of a good thing when you know you've got it.' Then, her voice changing, her hands became still and looking at Jinnie with pity in her gaze, she said, 'I've never been up there, not for years and years, not since I was a girl, but I understand you've got it rough.'

All Jinnie could answer to this was, 'I . . . I like the open air.'

'Well' – again the little woman was laughing – 'you'll get plenty of that up there, and it's cheap. But now you tell me what you want to know. It's about a cake, isn't it?'

'Yes. Yes, Mrs Stevens. Well, you see, when your son came up for the eggs he asked if I was baking for Christmas, and he said you made grand cakes. Well, I . . . I don't know how to make a Christmas cake and I would like the men to have one. So I asked him, if I came down, would you tell me how.'

Mrs Stevens stared at the young girl: she was a bonny lass; over-thin perhaps, but you couldn't get away from the fact that she was bonny. And by! she must have had a time of it up there, the tales that Roy had brought down

233

since the agreement about exchanging oats and taties for eggs and such like. She herself had always refused to keep hens, too much bother and little result. As for pigs: no, she didn't like pigs either. They'd kept some when she first came here, but that was years ago. She had soon made her new husband understand that she would never attend to pigs or chickens; the house was her concern, that, and supervising the dairy. Oh yes, the dairy. And he had seen it her way, for now they had a real fine herd of cows and the best horses in the district.

Charlie had a soft spot for young Bruce up there. He'd always liked Bruce, and yet he had hinted at things about him. Couldn't believe he was a son of Pug Shaleman. Hal now, yes; he was Pug all over again. Anyway, he was out to help Bruce, and he was tickled to death by Bruce's new help and he had said, laughingly, that if Max could wrestle he would make a fortune at the games.

And then there was this girl and her Roy. He was struck on her, was Roy; but if she was to speak the truth she wasn't for it. The lass was bonny all right, but she was from the workhouse, and supposedly from the tinker's clan. Well, that meant the gypsies, didn't it, or their like? Yet, as Roy said, she was well spoken and worked like two donkeys up there. And yes, she would have to, looking after that lazy trollop, for Rose Shaleman had never liked work, and if everybody took to their beds when they felt off-colour there would be such a to-do in farmhouses, wouldn't there? And then there was Mister Richard going up there. Funny thing, wasn't it, a friendship between the high and the low? Yet if it hadn't been for Bruce, Mister Richard wouldn't be here today. Still, she knew it wasn't looked upon with favour by Mister Richard's people, and this she could understand, oh yes, because she was feeling the same about her Roy and this lass sitting here, for this lass was, in some way, beginning to touch her own life.

She said now, 'It takes a lot of ingredients, you know, to make a Christmas cake; and it should have been made weeks gone and wrapped up and put away in a tin.'

'Really?'

'Oh yes. Oh yes; must be two months since I made mine, half a dozen or more of them.'

'Half a dozen Christmas cakes!'

'Yes. And don't look so surprised; they get through them, not only the family, but the people who drop in here, especially at New Year.' She went on, 'What kind of an oven have you up there?'

'Oh, it's only small compared with these.' Jinnie pointed to the black-leaded oven doors.

'Dear, dear! A little oven.' Mrs Stevens now handed Jinnie a cup of steaming coffee, which didn't fit in with *her* idea of coffee, for surely that was cream floating on the top; and when she was then handed a plate of stottie cake, the little woman said, 'Now, get that down you, and then we'll talk business.'

It was only a few minutes later when the business began with the farmer's wife pulling up a chair towards Jinnie and saying, 'Now this is how it's done.'

Five minutes later Jinnie asked pointedly, 'But how much would all that cost? There's such a lot of fruit and fat needed, and you say it must be butter; and beer an' all.'

'Oh, I don't rightly know, lass, I've never reckoned.' Mrs Stevens looked at Jinnie with a touch of pity in her glance, and then said, 'I tell you what, my dear, I'll give you a Christmas cake as a present for yourself.'

'Oh! Mrs Stevens. Oh! how wonderful. How good of you. Oh, but I could pay, I could pay you something.'

'Have you enough money to pay me, lass?' There was a look of amusement on the face that was pushed close to

235

Jinnie's, and she said, 'I . . . I've got thirty-four shillings left, but . . . well, I had two pounds, but I spent some on a present for Miss Caplin and a reading book and some notebooks for Max, and . . . well, I'm sort of saving up for something for Bruce. I want to buy a cow.'

At this Jinnie had to put her hand out quickly to prevent the little woman falling off her cracket, because she was shaking so much with her laughter, and it was a surprisingly loud and boisterous laugh to come from such a small frame. It was at that moment that the door opened and the farmer himself appeared, and Jinnie noticed immediately that he was in his stockinged feet. And there was a broad smile on his face as he said, 'Tell me what's tickling you, woman. I haven't heard you laugh like that for a long time.' At this his wife turned round to him and she gasped and swallowed deeply before, pointing a thumb back towards Jinnie, she spluttered, 'She wants to buy a cow . . . a cow. She's got thirty-four shillings saved up. Did you ever hear the like?'

'Well, missis—' He looked towards Jinnie now, his face a beam as he said, 'You have to start somewhere. So you've got thirty-four shillings, lass, and you want to buy a cow? Well, if you ever want to buy a cow of good stock this is the place to come. But how long d'you think it'll take you to save up enough to buy a cow?'

'I . . . I don't really know; I haven't talked about it to anybody because I . . . well, I thought that with Max mending the cowshed and the place next door that could be a dairy, because back in the house—' and she looked from one to the other as if she had to explain the word – 'workhouse, he looked after the cows; and there was a dairy there and I just thought how wonderful it would be for Mister Bruce if I could get a cow. I wasn't meaning one of yours, Mr Stevens.'

She looked at the big bony man who, hands on knees, leaned towards her. 'I meant just sort of a . . . an old one, well, you know, that wasn't giving all that amount of milk and was nearly finished, and well, just to give him a start. I thought, well, Max could milk it; and then I knew that was silly, 'cos Max leaves us in the New Year.'

'Oh, he does, lass, does he?'

She nodded. 'Yes, he's got a situation over in what he calls Weardale, and a cottage to himself. It'll be very good for him. But I'll miss him; and so will Mister Bruce, because he's done such a lot of work up there mending things that you never thought could be mended. He's very handy, is Max.'

'Yes; yes, I know that; I've just been talking to him along there. I've left him with our Roy. He could show one or two of our men some ropes, I think, if only he could talk straight. Roy seems to have got the hang of his lingo, but I can't. Roy says he's got it all up top. 'Tis a pity he's going. Would you still want a cow if he left?'

'Oh yes. Yes; I want it for Mister Bruce, 'cos he's finding things rough. I mean, not that it would help straight away, but later on, if we could make butter and cheese for market.' Her voice trailed away. 'Oh, we wouldn't want to upset you in the market.'

Again the farmer's wife started to laugh, and at this her husband said, 'Give over, Dilly. Give over; this is serious business.' And now he sat himself down by Jinnie's side, and when he put an arm round her shoulders his wife said, 'Take no notice of anything he says from now on, girl, because he's quite capable of promising you a cow if you'll run off with him.'

At this his red weather-beaten face was thrust towards Jinnie's, and he said, 'Would you run off with me?' and she, joining in the joke, said, 'Yes; yes, Mr Stevens, for a cow; but it would have to be a good one, not one I would get for thirty-four shillings.'

Now the man took his arm away from Jinnie and lay back against the settle, and he was roaring with laughter as he said, 'She's all there, this one, isn't she? I can see what our Roy means.'

'Shut your mouth, you big galoot, and I'll tell you what you can do. You can go down to the cellar and bring up a couple of bottles of my home-made wine, a parsnip and an elderberry. Yes, that's it, a parsnip and an elderberry; and on your way back pick up a pound of butter from the dairy and a shive of cheese; and if you can remember all that, put it in a basket.' He got up from the settle and, looking down at Jinnie and without any laughter on his face, he said, 'You really were saving up to buy a cow?'

'Yes, Mr Stevens.'

'And, as I understand it, you get a shilling a week?'

'Yes.'

He shook his head; then turned away and muttered something that Rose Shaleman had muttered once before; 'He could do worse.'

Jinnie could hardly believe her eyes when she saw the big, beautifully smelling Christmas cake, the slab of butter, the shive of cheese that must have weighed all of two pounds, and the two bottles of wine, as well as a big, round stottie cake.

As Mrs Stevens was packing them in the basket she said, 'One of these bottles is for the big fella outside; and you'll give him a share of this other, won't you?'

'Oh, I always halve what I have with Max,' she said; 'always. He's . . . he's like a father to me; he's always looked after me, Mrs Stevens.' She was feeling teary; she did not know whether it was because of her talking about Max caring for her, or for the kindness of this little woman in heaping this wonderful food on her.

As Mrs Stevens was lifting the basket from the table, she said, 'Is this too heavy for you to carry to the cart? I'm not letting that big fella in here with his outsize feet. Look; you take the two bottles in your arms and I'll take the basket.'

As Jinnie went to follow her, she said, 'Mrs Stevens.'

'Yes, lass?' The small body was turned towards her.

'I'll never forget this visit, and I'll never be able to thank you enough. I wish there was something I could do for you, but I know there isn't, or ever will be but . . . but I thank you.'

'Oh, lass, lass. 'Tis nothing; absolutely nothing. When you have plenty, as we have, you don't miss it; though of course it would be something if we had very little. That's how our parson often puts it; and he's right. Now come along; I don't want you to shed any tears on my behalf: you've got to get back up on that farm and start saving more for your cow.' And again Mrs Stevens was rocking with her laughter; and when they got into the yard, there was Max standing by the cart with Roy at his side, and Roy, turning to his mother, asked, 'What's so funny? I want a laugh an' all.'

'You'll laugh later on, lad, when I tell you; or then, on the other hand, you mightn't. Here, girl! give me those bottles.' And now she turned to Max, saying, 'And you, big fellow, take them and push them down the side there . . . That's it. And be careful of them.'

Max now took the basket from the woman, who hardly came up to his chest, and placed it between a sack of potatoes, two sacks of oats and some bales of hay, then turned to see Roy hoisting Jinnie on to the seat.

Lastly he bent down to the farmer's wife and, his

mouth agape for a moment, he brought out the words, 'Th-th-thank you;' and she was checked from answering by his struggling with the next word, 'Gr-gr-grateful. Wish I could stay . . . help with h-h-horses, big horses . . . shires.'

'Yes, indeed.' Charlie Stevens was nodding at him. 'Yes, shire horses, the best,'

'Y-y-yes, straight furrow.'

'You said it, man. You've said it, straight furrow. I understood that all right. Yes, indeed.'

Max went round to the other side of the cart and after seating himself, he looked across Jinnie to Roy, who was reaching up to Jinnie, saying, 'Give it a thought;' and she answered, 'Yes; but I don't think so.'

Max jerked the reins and the horse moved forward, and Jinnie turned in her seat and waved to her benefactors.

They had gone some way before Max asked, 'What's he want, that Roy?'

'He wants to know if I would go to the dance in the New Year; they're having it in their barn; but I said I didn't think so.'

'Why not? Nice f-f-fella.'

'Yes, he is; but how could I go to a dance, Max? I can't dance; and I haven't a dress or shoes or any- thing, have I? But believe me, oh please, Max, believe me, I'm quite satisfied as I am.'

'No . . . nobody satisfied . . .'

Back at the farm, Mr Stevens said to his son, 'What were you asking her?'

'Just if she could come to the do in the barn, Dad.'

'And she said no?'

'Along those lines.'

'Aye, well.' The farmer made to move off, saying, 'Time will tell. But don't forget you've done a bit of near courtin' down in the town; Jeanie Brown, Mary Cotton and Bella.'

They both swung round now as the wife and mother, making towards the house door, said in no small voice, 'Flibbertigibbets, the lot of them! Flibbertigibbets! Here the day and gone the morrow. Anything with breeches on.'

After banging the door behind her she stood for a moment, slightly bewildered as she asked herself: was she, after all, *for* that girl? No; no. Men. Men. Let her get on with some cooking.

Back in the yard her husband and son were pushing at each other, the while aiming to still their laughter.

Before taking the basket into the cottage, Jinnie gave Max the bottle of elderberry wine; she thought it might be nicer than parsnip. Her immediate greeting from Rose Shaleman was, 'What have you got there?'

'Just some things Mrs Stevens gave me for Christmas.'

'Gave you for Christmas? *You?* If she was sending anything up here it would be for me. So what do you mean by *you?*'

'Just what I say, missis. She gave them to me because I offered to pay for the ingredients to make a cake. She wouldn't take it; and she said I had to have these and share them with Max.'

'God in heaven! girl. You'll try my patience too far one of these days. All that lot! Is it butter and cheese?'

'Yes. Yes, it is butter and cheese, and two cakes.'

'And you say she gave them to you?'

'Yes, she gave them to me; and she wouldn't take the money for them. I offered it. And she said I could share them with Max; but I'll share them with all of us.'

After a long pause Rose Shaleman said, 'Give me that bottle here.'

Slowly Jinnie picked up the bottle and took it to the bed, and when her mistress demanded, 'What make is it?' she asked, 'Parsnip.'

'Parsnip?'

'Yes; that's what she said, parsnip.'

'It's a wonder she gave you that; it's the nearest thing to whisky, they say. And she only gave you the one?'

'No; she gave me two; one was for Max.'

At this the woman grabbed the bottle from Jinnie's hands, saying, 'For two pins I would hit you with this bottle, girl. A bottle for Max? a whole bottle for Max, and there's two of us here! I mean three if you want your share, and there's only one bottle?'

Jinnie stepped back from the bed and dared to shout at her mistress, 'You're the most ungrateful woman I've ever met in my life. There was nobody as bad as you in the workhouse. If it wasn't for Mister Bruce and the plight he's in, I'd walk out of here the morrow. Do you hear? Yes, I would. And from what I gather, Mrs Stevens would find me a decent place somewhere. So look out, I'm telling you. Look out, missis.' And she swung about.

She did not go to the table but went outside again and along to the stable where Max was seeing to the horse, and without any lead-up, she cried at him, 'You're leaving here, Max, and so would I if it wasn't for Mister Bruce. I'm telling you, so would I. That woman in there is so ungrateful; she's awful, awful.'

'She's sick . . . lonely . . . lonely.'

'She's not so sick and she's not so lonely. If she was lonely she would want friends, and I could be a friend; but she's awful to me. Never a civil word. Oh, Max, how wonderful it would be to work for someone like Mrs Stevens.'

Max went on brushing down the horse while saying, 'Few and f-f-far between, the Stevens.'

She sighed now, and said, 'Perhaps you're right. But the others couldn't be worse than her in there.'

'Go b-b-back. Be sorry for her.'

'Oh, Max!' There was a note of impatience in her voice now. 'It's all right you talking; you haven't got to be in there with her.'

'No.' He gave a small laugh now as he turned to her, saying, 'G-g-go barmy.'

'Well, what d'you expect me to do? I'll go barmy too before long, I'm telling you.' And abruptly she turned about and went back to the cottage; there to be met by the demand, 'Bring me a cup, girl;' and when she reached the bed, instead of handing the cup to her mistress she placed it on the stool that was always to the woman's hand; and when she was ordered, 'Give me a shive of the Christmas cake,' she boldly said, 'I'm not opening that till Christmas; I'll give you a piece of the currant flat cake.'

'You! girl.' The neck of the bottle rattled against the edge of the cup and Rose Shaleman paused for a moment before pouring herself out almost a full cup of the wine.

Jinnie was still at the table cutting into the stottie cake when she heard the sharp exclamation and, looking towards her mistress she saw her screw up her eyes while drawing her lips inwards, so demonstrating the effect of her first drink; and when she placed the flat cake on the stool, her mistress was again drinking from the cup. Then her mouth opened and Jinnie could hear the woman's tongue clicking against the roof of her mouth and the sound caused her own nose to wrinkle. At the same time she snatched up the bottle from the stool; and the yelling of 'Girl!' did not stop her from taking it to the table, from where she looked at her mistress and said, 'It's to be shared. And it was meant for Christmas; and you've already had more than your share.' Then she placed the bottle on the delph rack and placed the cake next to it; the rest of the good things she put in the cupboard.

She had taken off her hat but not her coat; and now she grabbed the hat and went out into the scullery. There she stood for a moment panting with vexation. It was her leave time; she needn't have come back until just afore dark. Well, she wasn't going upstairs to change her frock and then get started again with the meal; she'd take a walk until the light faded and let that one back there stew in her own bitter juice. She'd walk as far as the pond.

Ramming her hat on her head, she went out and to the stable again.

Max wasn't there, but she could hear him in the hen cree and she called, 'I'm going for a brisk walk.' He had been bending over a hen and he straightened his body and called back to her, 'Oh, good. W-w-walk it off.'

She knew what he meant all right, and she repeated to herself, walk it off; yes, but I've got to go back into it; and still mumbling, she started to climb to the path that led between banks of frozen brushwood to the surroundings of the pool.

She stood looking down into the water. It was very still, but had risen considerably during the past two months, because of the rain and snow. The hill beyond, which lay in deep shadow, was still tinged with frost and this went up to the railings that bordered the short section of the coach road above. The land to the left of the pool rose steeply and in the still clear light she could see a distant rise tinged with snow. It was the rise that Bruce had told her was only the beginning of many more, and if the sheep never went any further than that they were all right. He had brought the last of them to the lower land yesterday and was out there now seeing to them.

Max had said to walk it off, but perhaps she hadn't walked far enough because she was still feeling angry inside, and the pool and its surroundings weren't helping her today. Back in the summer, whenever she could escape for a short while, she had come running along the path to this spot and had sat by the water's edge for a few minutes and dreamed; but as the seasons changed, something seemed to change in her too so that now there was no comfort to be found within herself. She was turning away to retrace her steps back to the farm when a voice, apparently from above, hailed her and she quickly turned to look up the hill to the coach road, to see Mister Richard seated on a horse.

'Hello! there,' he called.

'Oh; hello, Mister Richard. You're back, then?'

'Well, if I'm not' – his voice came to her – 'then somebody's impersonating me.'

She laughed outright, and he called, 'Stay there, and I'll come down.'

'But . . . but how?' She could see no possible way to bring the horse down the hill; and he called to her, 'Further along; there's a cut.'

Yes, she had noticed a narrow cut leading up to the road but had never investigated it, and when she reached the place it was to see the horse negotiating the cut very carefully, so that it appeared to be dancing.

Then he dismounted and stood before her saying, 'Oh! you *have* grown. How many months is it since I last saw you?'

'Almost three,' she said.

'Good lord! yes, it *is* almost three months; but you've certainly grown in that time. How's everybody?'

'Oh now, what can I say, Mister Richard?' She shook her head. 'You do know that the mister died?'

'Yes. Yes, I heard of that.'

'Well, since that, something nice has happened.'

'That's good to hear. Tell me.'

'Well, you know Max? You saw him once; the big fellow. That's what Mister Bruce calls him: the big fellow.'

'Yes; yes, Max, your guardian.'

'Yes; he's always been my guardian. Well, he works on the farm now.'

'Here? With Bruce?'

'Yes, but only for a time: he's got a job in Weardale, and it seems very good. He starts in the New Year.'

'He was in the . . . I mean, he's been able to leave the . . .?'

'Yes; yes, sir, he was able to leave the workhouse. He's not simple, or anything like that, far from it. He's what you would call very intelligent.'

'Yes; yes, I understood that from something Bruce said. By the way, how is Bruce?'

'Well—' she turned her head slightly to the side and looked away from him as she said, 'you know he took a long time to get over that dreadful bout; and he would never have got over it if it hadn't been for you.'

'Oh, that's nonsense.'

' 'Tisn't nonsense. Oh!' She now bowed her head and said, 'I'm sorry.'

'What on earth are you sorry for? And why are we standing here jabbering? Let's get to the farm and say hello. Oh, dear.' He was looking along the flank of his horse now and he said, 'The three of us can't walk on this path; one of us has got to ride.'

'Oh, it's all right, sir.'

'No, it isn't all right: I meet a fair maiden who has lost her way. What kind of a cavalier am I to leave her stranded? Would you care to ride on my horse, madam?'

Her head deep on her chest, her shoulders shaking

with laughter, she muttered, 'I saw a play like that once back in the house. They used to come at Christmas, and it was just like you said, the hero found this . . . this lady was lost and he puts her on his horse and took her back to the castle. But,' she now spluttered, 'it was all very religious: I think he was out to save her soul, and he was really an angel in disguise and the castle was heaven.' She now looked up at him, her face wet with tears of laughter. 'Those of us who had laughed got into trouble next day.'

He too was laughing now as he looked down at her, and he said softly, 'Oh Jinnie, that was very funny. I'm sure I would've laughed too. Out to save her soul. Dear, dear.' Then his voice changing, he said, 'But I have found a lady who is lost and I'm going to ask her if she will do me the honour of riding my horse back to her castle.'

'Me ride the horse?'

'Just sit on the saddle like this.' And before she knew what was happening, he had taken her under the oxters and hoisted her on to the saddle; and still holding her, he said, 'How do you feel?'

'Frightened. It's very high.'

'Hang on to the pommel.' He pointed out the front of the saddle, then assured her, 'Don't worry, you won't slide off. Anyway, if you do, it won't matter because you'll only be trodden underfoot by the horse.'

Oh, he was funny; and so different. She couldn't have imagined that he would joke like this.

When her body began to rock with the motion of the horse she bit tightly on her lower lip; but as they neared the farm she thought, and regretfully, what a pity the path wasn't longer. She had been so miserable, so tired and fed up with everything, and now she was feeling happy, strangely happy . . . that was until they came into the clearing, there to see Max and Bruce standing together, their expressions showing amazement mixed with disapproval, until, bringing the horse to a standstill, Richard said, 'We couldn't walk abreast, so I hoisted her up there.'

He reached up and lifted her to the ground, saying to her, 'Don't expect that to happen every day. Go on with you and get away inside and out of the cold.'

His tone could have been that which he would use to a child, and laughing, she looked towards Bruce and Max, before slowly walking away, and with her departure the look on the faces of Bruce and Max changed. Bruce, thrusting out his hand, said, 'When did you get back?' And Richard, shaking the hand warmly, answered, 'Last night; and it's good to be back, I can tell you. How are you?'

'Oh, I'm fine. And you?'

'It's a long tale, as usual, but not so much about me as about Mother. She was pretty groggy while we were away, and that kept us stuck in the same place for more than a month.'

'You know Max?'

'Oh yes. How d'you do, Max?' Richard said, although he didn't hold out his hand to the man, whose height and breadth made his own dwindle.

'Well . . . sir, v-v-very well,' Max answered.

'Good. Do you like it here?'

'Oh . . . yes. More . . . more than like.'

'Well, I'm surprised at that,' said Richard, and pointing to Bruce, said, 'working under a boss like him.'

And Max, picking up the jocular tone, replied, 'You're r-r-right, sir. Hard boss. Big stick,' and when Bruce aimed to push him away none too gently, they both laughed, leaving Richard feeling, for the moment, he was being left out of something. What, he could not rightly put a name to, as he witnessed the obvious affinity there was between his life-long friend and this new fellow, this very strange new fellow who, being stuck with such an impediment was nevertheless not without a wit of his own, workhouse product as he was.

'Come on,' Bruce said; 'let's go into the barn out of this wind; I want to hear all your news.' Then, turning to Max, he said, 'Walk Mister Richard's horse for a time. We won't be long.'

At the far end of the barn they sat on upturned boxes facing each other, and, laughing now, Bruce said, 'Privacy. We never could talk indoors, could we, either here or at your place?'

Except for the death of his father, Bruce's news was the same as always. He was unable to speak of the change of feeling between his mother and himself, and so he ended his short recital with, 'Now, what's yours?'

'Well; first of all,' Richard said emphatically, 'I'm not going to be pushed into this marriage. All right, I shall marry some day, and it will likely still be Lillian. And yet, I have to wonder what difference marriage would make in our lives anyway – we'd never be free of either family. You've no idea, Bruce, of the closeness between them; it's extraordinary, even though they are of different religions. Even the recent papal declaration of the infallibility of the Pope on his personal immunity from error in faith and morals hasn't loosened the tie, as would have been expected. You know, Father and Mother were as excited about it as Lillian's people were. They all went to Mass together that morning. I was conveniently unwell. I can't help but say it, Bruce, but I think it's weird.'

'About you being unwell: how are you these days?'

'Oh, as fit as a fiddle. I always am when I'm back here in the hills.'

'No, you aren't.'

'Well, most of the time. There's only one other place I'd like to be, Bruce; that's in Paris. There's a marvellous quarter there for painters; and they're so helpful to each other. I think it's the only place in the world where you could live on a pittance. By the way, I heard a bit about your father absconding with the money. How're you fixed now?'

'Oh, I'm all right,' Bruce said; 'we'll survive.'

'Jinnie tells me you're soon to lose your new hand.'

'Yes; and that's one thing I'm sorry for. But I can't employ him. The fact is, he's working for nothing now, but he insisted on staying under those conditions.'

'Working for nothing? Not many in his position would do that today. The farm workers are at it again, you know. They're gathering strength as they get together. Not that it'll do them much good; but I'm sorry for them. It wouldn't be so bad if they were provided with decent living quarters.'

Bruce laughed, saying, 'Such as I provide for mine? Max is sleeping in the swill-room; from his own choice, I may say.'

They were outside the barn now, and they stood looking to where Max was walking Richard's mare up and down by the cottage, and Richard said, 'Look; I know we've been over this before but, on this occasion, why don't you accept a little help? I've had quite a bit from my godmother; I don't have to depend entirely on the powers that be, so who's to know? And you could keep him on.'

'Yes, Richard; we've been over this before, and I have to say again that it's more than kind of you, but as I've also said, I'm not starting on that tack; I value too much what is between us.'

'Well, you don't value it any more than I do; but in

a matter like this I don't see why you can't accept just a little help; in fact, treat it as a loan: you could pay me back later if it niggled you so much to be beholden to me.'

'Oh, don't be silly. It isn't a case of that, and you know it; but look . . . all right, when I reach rock bottom, I'll yell for help. As it is I've worked out that I can manage until my two lady friends and her husband decide to supply me with another litter. There's quite a market, you know, in that direction.'

Richard sighed and said, 'I'm not so ignorant of farming as not to know it'll be a matter of months before you could rake anything in from them,' to which Bruce had no answer; and so they walked to where Max was now holding the horse still.

When Richard took the reins from Max, he did not address him but just nodded to him; but once mounted, he looked down at the big fellow and said, 'Goodbye, Max;' and Max replied, 'Goodbye, sir.'

'And the best of luck in your new position.'

'Th . . . thank you, sir.'

Bruce walked alongside Richard's stirrup until they were well past the cottage; and then looking up at him he said, 'You intended to go this way?'

'Yes; I've been out for some time. She's had enough.' He patted the horse's neck; then looking down at Bruce, he said, 'You will miss Max when he's gone.'

'Yes, I know; in more ways than one.'

'Well, it's up to you: you can keep him if you like, you have a choice.'

'Oh.' Bruce now stepped to the side, saying, 'Get yourself away; I'm not going through that again.' Then he added quickly, 'Will you be at home for the holidays?'

'Oh yes; I hope so. And for some good long time afterwards if I have my way; so, be seeing you soon.'

'Yes; yes.' Bruce watched him tap the horse with his heel, setting the animal into a trot; then he immediately turned about and went back into the cottage.

As soon as he opened the door the broadside came at him: 'Been enjoying yourself out there? Glad you've got something to talk about. And I'm not allowed to see your visitors these days, am I?'

'Well, Ma' – he was hanging his cap on the back of the door, and he stayed his hand on it as he looked down the room towards her – 'they would have nothing to talk about if they came into this house, now would they?'

'Well, who's to blame for that, eh?'

He was about to go towards the fire to warm himself when he caught sight of the bottle on the delph rack; and he turned to look enquiringly at Jinnie, who was standing at the far end of the table working up the pastry for the dumplings; but she kept her eyes fixed on her work as she said, 'Mrs Stevens gave me some things for Christmas instead of giving me the recipe for the cake, as I asked her. She gave me a cake and some currant stottie bread, together with butter and cheese and a bottle of wine.'

'Two bottles of wine.' This came from the bed. 'Your creature outside has one to himself, and this one is supposed to be shared.' But Jinnie immediately put in, 'The missis has had her share; you can see by the bottle,' and she thumbed over her shoulder.

He walked slowly to the delph rack and lifting the bottle up to the light, he commented, 'And a good share, I'd say.' Then looking towards the bed, he said, 'You've certainly wetted your whistle this time, Ma.'

'And who has a better right, I ask you; it was never meant for her; Dilly Stevens isn't so free at handing things out.'

'Well, she has been on this occasion, and for the time being I think you've had more than your share. I

252

suppose Mrs Stevens meant it for Christmas?' He had turned towards Jinnie. 'Isn't that so?' and she muttered her answer, 'Yes, it was for Christmas.'

'Well, we'll keep the rest for then, shall we, Ma?'

He walked to the cupboard and after placing the bottle inside, he closed the door, then tapped on it twice, saying, 'See you on Christmas Eve.'

No remark on this was forthcoming from Rose, and he went towards the fire and, bending, held out his hands to the flame that was escaping from beneath the bottom of the iron pan of stew bubbling in the heart of it. He glanced back at Jinnie, saying, 'Did you enjoy riding on the horse?'

The question brought her hands to a standstill before she said softly, 'Yes; but I never asked.'

'No, no; of course you wouldn't.' He straightened up suddenly and, now turning his back to the fire, asked, 'Did she charge you for the Christmas cake?'

'No. No, she charged me for nothing. She was most kind.'

'Where's the cake?'

She jerked her head backwards, 'On the top shelf of the cupboard.'

He was about to mount the steps to the loft when his mother's voice called, 'Here! a minute.'

His hands remained on the rung of the ladder for a moment before he turned and walked slowly to the bed.

Rose Shaleman did not speak immediately, and as he looked at her he realised with some surprise that she was slightly tipsy: her eyelids were blinking rapidly and her mouth was opening and shutting, and her body seemed to be . . . the only word he could think of was 'bristling', her shoulders hunched, her hands gripped into tight fists as she said, 'It is only parsnip wine.' And her head began to wag now, and she put a hand to her mouth and wiped the spittle from her lips before she went on, 'I'm not as black as I'm painted.'

The remark in itself was another surprise, and to this he answered, 'Nobody is, Ma; nobody ever is.'

'Well, you're acting as if I am.'

'Well' – he paused – 'that's your own fault, Ma; you haven't been very pleasant of late.'

'I'm pleasant to them that's pleasant to me.'

To this he had no answer, and she now began to pick at the quilt with her finger and thumb, a nervous movement, and her voice was low as she said, 'I've got something to tell you; but it's got to be when—' She motioned towards the table before adding in a mutter, 'It's got to be when we're by ourselves. Will you stay in the morrow?'

'Yes; for as long as you wish, Ma.'

Her head nodding, she leant towards him, saying, 'Just a little drop of that wine; it's eased the pain' – she patted her chest – 'better than any pill, and it's been bad today.'

She was indeed tipsy. He had the desire to laugh at the thought that she could be nicer when she was drunk than when she was sober.

Of a sudden, there came into his mind the picture of a woman lifting her skirts up to her knees and dancing when there had been no-one in the house but he and Hal; and he could faintly recall Hal's yelling at the woman and she boxing his ears. How old would he have been then? Three? Four?

He backed a step away from her, saying 'Ma, you'll have your share at Christmas; I think you've had enough for one day, don't you?'

'What d'you mean, enough?' Her voice had changed, her body had stopped its jerking, she was stiff again. 'I had two drops in a mug.'

'Well, by the look of the bottle the drops were big drops, Ma, so settle yourself.' And he turned quickly and made for the ladder, her voice following him, the words so muddled he couldn't make them out, other than that he knew they were abusive.

Up in the loft he threw himself on his pallet and, bringing a forearm across his eyes, he let out a long slow breath. He was tired. He had lost two lambs today, and he was afraid it was a sign of footrot. If he cleared anything next year he'd put up some windbreaks, because even on the lower ground it was hellish for the lambs. Money. Why couldn't he bring himself to take up Richard's offer? But no; that would spoil things. He was so glad he was back; yet what was it he had experienced when he saw him leading Jinnie on his horse? As with many of his other emotions, he would not dissect this one, for he couldn't possibly think it touched on rage; never towards Richard. But the feeling had passed when Richard condescendingly sent her scudding away as he would any servant girl.

Servant girl. It was odd, but he himself never looked upon her as a servant girl: rather, he saw her on an equal footing with himself, and as someone he imagined would be permanently in his life.

12

The moon was shining, lighting up half the room and just touching the wall to the side of Rose's head. It had moved a lot, she thought, since she had fallen asleep after that last pain. Her head was aching; her mouth was dry, and she needed a drink. It wasn't water she wanted, it was another drink of that wine. Before, it had eased the pain and she felt good after drinking it.

Bruce had said she was tipsy. That was nonsense; you couldn't get tipsy on home-made wine. Well, not drunk-tipsy. She looked towards the window again. It was a nice night but frosty, and she was cold; cold inside, cold all over. She must have a drink; but he had put the bottle in the cupboard and she'd never manage to get to the cupboard. Yet, why not? She'd got as far as the table the other night, hadn't she?

She threw back the bedclothes, then sat on the edge of the bed for some minutes before she began to pull herself upright. If she could get to the table and into the moonlight she would be all right.

With an effort, she reached the table, and leaned on it, gasping for breath.

Minutes passed before she was able to pull herself upright and edge round the side of the table until she was opposite the cupboard. And now she turned her back to the table and leant her bony buttocks against it, her breathing coming in gasps. She looked towards the ladder: she had better be careful or he would be down.

It would take four steps to reach the cupboard. After another effort, she reached it, then slumped against it; but now she had to step back to open it. More minutes passed, and then the contents of the cupboard were revealed by the moonlight, the bottle of wine gleaming before her. She had to stretch her arm right out to reach it and when she brought it down she clutched it to her and was about to turn away when her eyes alighted on the stottie cake.

After grabbing it, she found she couldn't turn around without the assistance of one of her hands, and so she brought the cake to her chest and pushed it behind the bottle.

After some minutes she reached the table again, and rested against it while looking towards the bed; and she knew she couldn't cover that distance again, but there within an arm's length the moon was touching the top of the old basket chair. This she made for, sliding down into it with hardly a sound, except for her heavy breathing.

She lay, her head back, her mouth open, her arm all the while grasping the bottle and the cake to her. Presently she relaxed and allowed the cake to slip on to her lap as she slowly withdrew the cork from the bottle. She put the neck to her mouth and made two audible gulps at the wine, then sighed, tears streaming from her eyes and which she made no effort to wipe away. Why hadn't she thought of making wine out of parsnips? Likely because she knew she was no hand at anything like that; she wasn't another Dilly Stevens. She had always been a Miss Clever Clouts, had Dilly Stevens; and she had won prizes for her efforts at the fairs.

She again lifted the bottle to her mouth and took two more gulps; but this time she didn't lie back: she placed the bottle on the floor, then began to eat the stottie cake. She was now lying relaxed in the chair, and feeling so well. There was a lot to be said for parsnip wine. She no longer had a pain or an ache anywhere. Strangely, she was feeling young again; young enough to dance. She felt sleepy. But she wasn't going to sleep, not so long as there was anything left in that bottle. In for a penny in for a pound. There'd be hell to pay tomorrow, of course. Well, just let them start. She had got one on them, hadn't she? Keep it for Christmas, he had said; and that other skit saying that it had been given to her to share around. Now that she was feeling better she'd get rid of her, if it was the last thing she did. The bottle was again to her mouth, but now it had to be tilted well up.

She was about to take another gulp when she gasped and her left hand clutched at her chest. 'Oh! God. Oh! God. Not that again,' she groaned. She had been all right a minute ago. Fine, fine. 'Oh! God.'

Slowly the bottle slid from her hand to the floor. She was used to these attacks: she had only to lie still and they would go, even without a pill. But this pain was different. She screwed up her face and brought her teeth tight into her lower lip. She'd have to call for help. She'd have to bring him down. What was happening to her? She put her fingers up to her mouth; then through her glazed vision she could see that her hand was covered with blood. Her lungs. It was years since she'd bled. It had been the heart that was out of sorts, just out of sorts. Oh . . . h! There was a yelling in her head, but it made no sound outside her lips, and although she tried to call out, the words were strangled in her throat.

When she toppled forward it was a slow movement: her body just seemed to fold up; and then she was lying in a huddled heap on the clippie mat.

When the little clock on the mantelpiece struck twice, she failed to hear it.

*　　*　　*

Jinnie was so cold she put her head under the clothes and brought her knees up to her chin. She didn't want to get up, even though the cock had crowed some minutes ago. It had sounded far away: perhaps it hadn't crowed at all, for it didn't always crow at the same time. Sometimes it had her up half-an-hour before she need be. Oh, if only she could go on sleeping; she'd soon get warm, curled up like this.

When the cock crowed again she slowly brought her head from under the clothes, yawned, shivered, then grabbed at her stockings that had been laid across the bottom of the pallet. One had fallen on to the floor and she had to rise from under the cover of the hap and her Sunday coat in order to retrieve it.

Back in the bed, she pulled on her stockings and her elastic garters and her underclothing.

She did not pull on her bodice and her skirt until, standing as upright as she could, she had shaken her petticoats into place. Finally, she wrapped the woollen shawl, a present from Miss Caplin, around her shoulders, crossing it over her breasts before tucking the ends into the top of her skirt.

She had accomplished her dressing in complete darkness; but now she reached out towards a beam and, taking up a box of matches, she lit the candle that sat in a tin holder lying there.

When she reached the bottom of the steps she shuddered. The place was like an ice-box. She hoped the fire hadn't gone out.

She opened the door into the kitchen, turned towards the fire, but then she was unable to prevent the high scream escaping from her lips, for there, on the mat, lay the missis. She couldn't see her face, only an arm outstretched and clutching a piece of the stottie cake, both covered in blood. A second scream that finished on the yell, 'Mister Bruce!' brought Bruce's head peering through the hatch; and the sight he looked down on made him cry out, 'Oh God above!' Then he was reaching back for his trousers.

Within seconds he was in the kitchen where, grabbing the back of the basket chair, he flung it aside.

When he was kneeling beside the twisted form, there was no need for him to appeal with: 'Come on, Ma! Wake up,' as he knew straightaway that she was dead, and had been for some time.

'Oh God! To go like that.' He looked up at Jinnie, and his voice strangely quiet, he said, 'Go and get Max; I'll need help to get her on to the bed.'

Jinnie remained standing as if she hadn't heard him speak, one hand held tightly across her mouth to prevent herself from being sick; and it wasn't until Bruce said sharply, 'Did you hear what I said!' that she sprang away . . .

She was unable to recall much that happened during the next hour, except that Max had helped Bruce to do what was necessary to lay out his mother; all she had to do was to keep them supplied with bowls of hot water, and then hand them clean sheets. Afterwards, Max came down the room and told her to make some porridge, which she thought was odd. But one thing was clear: the woman on the bed would no longer pelt her with orders, and her going would assuredly change her life. Yes . . . yes, it would.

On his way to tell the doctor of his mother's death, which he realised would come as no surprise to the man, he called in at the Stevens's and told them the news. And Mrs Stevens, knowing it was policy to speak well of the dead, said, 'God rest her soul: she's had a long painful road to travel, and now she can lie easy.'

Mr Stevens was more to the point: walking with Bruce to the cart, he said, 'Well, lad, you're on your own now, and not afore time. She was your mother, but you can't get over the fact that she's been a heavy sack on your back. Now you'll likely be able to get some order into the place and tidy it up a bit. It used to pay well at one time, that place. Oh yes, it did, in your grandfather's time.' Then, as if the thought had just struck him, he said, 'There's Hal. What if he turns up? How will you view that? Have you thought about it?'

'Yes, Mr Stevens, I've thought about it and I know how I would view it;' but he did not go on to explain what he meant, leaving it to his tone to imply it . . .

The doctor happened to be at breakfast, and so Bruce was told to wait in the hall; and when the man emerged wiping his mouth on a large white napkin and asked abruptly, 'Well, what is it now at this time in the morning?' Bruce stared at him and in much the same tone as the doctor had used, he replied, 'I'm very sorry to disturb you at your meal, but unfortunately my mother has died.'

'Oh! When was this?'

'I don't know; I found her dead in bed.'

'Well' – the napkin was again rubbed across the mouth – 'you've been expecting it, haven't you? In fact, in the ordinary way, if she'd had to go about, she would have been dead years ago. She's had it easy, you know, compared with some women. I suppose that's entirely thanks to you. Yes' – he nodded – 'I would say, thanks only to you. Anyway, I'll be up as soon as I've finished eating. There's no hurry. Your next caller'll be the undertaker, I guess. Are you going to give her a big splash, like your father's?'

Bruce's tone was grim as he answered, 'No, doctor, I'm not going to give her a big splash.'

'Well . . . well' – the man was shaking his head now – 'that's sensible: your father was sent off like one of his betters and he had never done a decent day's work in his life.'

Bruce did not make the expected reply to this, but pulled on his cap, saying, 'Good-morning, doctor,' then walked out . . .

The undertaker said, 'You're not going to put her away like her husband?'

'No; she is not going to be put away like her husband. I've just told you that. I want a plain wood coffin and an ordinary hearse.'

'Pall-bearers?'

'No, thank you; my assistant and I and two friends' – he was thinking of Mr Stevens and Roy – 'will do the necessary once we reach the cemetery.'

The undertaker pursed his lips and ran his fingers round the high collar of his jacket as he stared at the young man. He was curious to know about his change in fortune, for he had certainly spent on his father's last journey, and so, in an offhand manner, he said, 'Well, we'll have to see when we can fit it in.'

'I want it done on Tuesday.'

'On Tuesday? It's Christmas week and we're already . . .'

'I want it done on Tuesday. If you can't manage that day, I can go to your opposite number who deals with the workhouse. I understand he puts them away as decent as possible. And what is more, I should like to know your charges now, to see if I can meet them; unless, that is, you'd like to be paid in kind with eggs, pork or lamb.'

The outcome of that terse conversation was an agreement that the hearse would be at the house at one o'clock on Tuesday, the undertaker giving himself the last word as he saw his unwelcome client out, 'weather permitting.'

On his way back, Bruce called at the parsonage, only to be told by the verger that the parson was on a visit to The Hall, and so Bruce said, 'Will you please tell the parson that my mother has died and I wish her to be buried on Tuesday?'

'Oh, Tuesday! Tuesday? Oh no; we're up to the eyes on Tuesday.'

Looking the man squarely in the face, Bruce said, 'I have seen the undertaker and he will be at the house at noon . . .'

''Tis Christmas week, and there's lots to be done: I have the whole church to decorate, then there's the children's do and Parson won't . . .'

'You tell Parson what I said. You always have help in digging graves, don't you? Well, you won't have to dig far for this one, because she'll be on top of her husband.'

'Still, it's got to be opened up.'

He nodded at the man now, and then said stiffly, 'Till Tuesday.'

As Bruce went through the lych-gate the verger shouted, 'Parson'll have the last word,' and so he turned again and called back, 'Yes, he will, and to you if the coffin is left on his doorstep!'

As he urged the horse up towards the coach road he thought it was a wonder that neither the undertaker nor the verger had asked on the reason why he was insisting on his mother being buried on Tuesday; and it was just as well, because he would have had to say that beyond Tuesday he would be unable to stand the stench of her; it was bad enough now going in and out of the kitchen and seeing her lying there.

They could no longer eat in the kitchen and he had made arrangements with Max to move the table into the scullery. Of course, the fire would have to be kept going, for that was their only means of cooking and hot water. He could not imagine how some people were able to stand the corpse laid out in the coffin and kept on the table for days so that visitors could pay their last respects to the body, more often than not already in a state of decomposition.

And poor Jinnie. She had been sick first thing this morning and had been unable to swallow a mouthful of porridge. Anyway, her tasks in the future would be much . . . What was he thinking about? Jinnie will go. She'll have to go; at least Miss Caplin will see to it. Tomorrow's Sunday, her day for visiting.

Oh no. Oh no. But yes; they wouldn't let her stay with a lone man out here in the wilds. If Miss Caplin didn't do something about it the workhouse crowd would; she'd been here only a matter of months, hardly a year yet. But had they any claim on her now? She was fifteen.

He slumped in the seat. It seemed he had known her for years. It was as if she had always been here, her freshness wiping the dreariness of his life away. The thought of that place without her was unbearable.

The day he had first led her over the plain to the house she was like a young child. Now she was a young girl, and something more. But the purity she had brought with her as the child she still retained. Of course there was a way out, but it took two to cover that way. She wasn't yet sixteen, in fact she wasn't much over fifteen. Was it fair to tie a young spirit like hers to that stone cage?

With Max gone, he'd be alone up there just waiting for Hal's return. God above! yes, Hal's return, and to his farm. He jerked almost savagely at the reins.

Jinnie was sitting on a straight-backed chair, her head bowed and her hands tightly gripped between her knees.

Miss Caplin was sitting opposite her, and the Miss Duckworths one on each side of her.

Miss Caplin was saying, 'Don't you see, my dear, it wouldn't be allowed? It . . . well, it would be considered improper.'

'Very improper.'

'Oh yes, very improper.' The two lace-capped heads were nodding in unison.

'You are fifteen, Jinnie, and if it came to the guardians' knowledge; well, I don't know what the rules are exactly in a case like this, but I think that you might be considered to be still under their jurisdiction until you are sixteen.'

Jinnie's head came up and her hands came from between her knees and one accompanied the protest of her voice as she wagged it towards Miss Caplin, saying, 'I won't go back, Miss Caplin; I won't! I'll never go back there. Never! never! never!'

'All right; all right, my dear. That is the last thing I would desire for you; and I shall make it my business to get you a new place. And should they take up the matter I will tell them you'll be my responsibility and that you could stay here. Couldn't she?' and she turned first to one and then to the other of the Miss Duckworths, who again nodded in unison, saying, 'Of course, yes. Yes; delighted. Oh yes, delighted. There's a little room off. It is very sweet and . . .'

'He'll be so alone.' Jinnie's voice was very low now. Her eyes were blinking to keep the tears back. 'He's lonely, and it'll be awful up there by himself with nobody to cook or do for him.'

'He can always engage an older person. A married woman, for instance, could go up each day. I understand that was the arrangement before you arrived.'

'He couldn't engage anybody; he hasn't any money.'

'What?'

'I don't know how he'll get through the winter. I'm not taking a wage, and neither is Max. It cost quite a lot to bury his father; but now that he's got to bury his mother too, I don't know what he'll do.'

There was silence in the room for a moment; and then Miss Caplin rose to her feet, saying, 'Well, that doesn't really change the matter at all; only that one is deeply sorry for him and the predicament he finds himself in. It's you we must be considering, dear. You see, if you had parents they could decide whether or not to allow you to stay alone with a man in that small cottage, which has really only one room.'

'It hasn't; it's got the scullery, too, and that's quite big; and I sleep above that. And Mister Bruce is nice and he's good and he would look after me. I mean, he wouldn't let anyone get at me.'

Miss Caplin closed her eyes for a moment: she wanted to say, 'We're not afraid of who else might get at you, my dear, it's what Mister Bruce himself might decide to do when he has you there alone;' but what she actually said was, 'Anyway, it will be all right for the next few days . . . well, up to the New Year when Max leaves. But afterwards you'll have to fall in with the new arrangement, dear.'

An idea striking her, Jinnie bounced to her feet, saying, 'Look; could I not go up every day and come back here to sleep at night?'

'Oh no! my dear, not in the winter. Those hills to climb and that long stretch, oh no! It's as much as you can do now in the daylight; but it doesn't get light until late, and then it gets dark so early. To do that twice a day . . . No! dear. No; it's as much as a man would be able to do.'

'I . . . I could.'

Ignoring this remark, Miss Caplin went on, 'You can go back now, my dear, and tell him what I have said. If he wishes to discuss it, then he must come straight down because Mr Beaney's cart will be here to take me to the train at three o'clock.'

'Yes, Miss Caplin.'

The day was solemn; it was damp and cold, a dead day; and this was how she felt inside too as she made her way back to the farm. She should be sweating, for she was hurrying so much.

It seemed that Bruce had been waiting for her: there he was, hurrying to meet her while she was still some distance from the house.

'Cold?' he enquired briefly.

'Freezing. It's this damp.'

'Yes, it gets right through you. Well, what did she say?'

She had walked some steps with her head down, before she muttered, 'I can only stay on until Max goes in the New Year; and then I've got to go down and live with the Miss Duckworths until I get a new place.'

He said nothing, but the chill inside him deepened.

Of a sudden, she stopped and, looking into his drawn face, she said, 'Oh, Mister Bruce; I don't want to go; I don't want to leave you; you'll be all alone.' Then she made her characteristic, impatient movement of her head, and her voice was loud as she said, 'I don't know what they're all on about, I really don't, because you're like a brother to me. You always have been from the time you met me down there.' Now she was thumbing back over the road she had come. 'You would never do me any hurt, I know that, not like others. You're like Max; you would look after me. I've tried to tell her but—' She turned away now and began to walk on, and he hesitated a moment before following her.

Look after her like Max did? Well, hadn't that been

his intention from the first, when he used to think of her merely as a child; and she was little more now in many ways, and yet . . . as old as the hills in others . . .

Max was waiting for them. His welcoming words were, 'You see Miss C-C-Caplin?'

She nodded.

'Everything all . . . all right?'

She shook her head before hurrying past him and through the scullery door, and he, looking at Bruce, asked, 'What the matter?'

'They are not going to allow her to stay here after you go.'

'No? W-w-why?'

Bruce now walked towards the barn, with Max close by his side and his face showing concern as he waited for the answer, which Bruce did not give until they were inside the barn. There, turning to Max, he said plainly, 'She'd be living alone with me. And that's not to be thought of, is it? And this I can understand. Miss Caplin is going to get her another job.'

Max stared at Bruce; then he said quietly, 'No life a-a-alone, sp-sp-specially up here.'

'Oh, I'll get used to it. Don't worry your head now.'

Max turned and stood staring out through the open barn door for some time, before he emitted loudly, 'Sol-sol-solution.'

'What did you say?'

Max turned quickly to Bruce, saying again, almost shouting now, 'Sol-solution. I got it. I go down to Miss Caplin n-n-now,' and he gently thumped at Bruce's chest, and said with assurance, 'Everything all . . . all right. You see. I go now.' And he made hastily for outside, saying, 'Ch-ch-change my boots and c-c-coat.'

Bruce now ran after him and, pulling him to a standstill, said, 'Look, Max; it's no good. Anyway, why all the fuss? I'm used to being on my own; I'm a shepherd, aren't I?'

Max stared at him for a moment before repeating flatly, 'Going to change boots. M-m-must hurry . . . else Miss C-C-Caplin gone.'

A few minutes later, Bruce and Jinnie watched Max go into a lolloping run across the plain. Neither of them spoke, not even when Jinnie turned and went into the scullery, where, after closing the door, she stood for a moment looking towards the stone steps, and they seemed to remind her she must go up there and change her clothes . . .

Having done so, she sat on the edge of her pallet, her arms hugging her knees, rocking herself. It was a dreadful place up here, and it was a dreadful place downstairs, but the kitchen had become more so since the attitude of the missis towards her had changed. She couldn't help thinking it, but she was glad she was dead. And yet, it was because she was dead that she herself would now have to leave Mister Bruce.

She was brought from her musing by the sound of a loud thumping on the door.

As she scrambled down the steps and opened the kitchen door, it was to see the man who had driven the parson to the farm some time ago; and he said to her, 'Where's Mr Shaleman?'

'He's along there working in the barn.'

'Go and fetch him, then.'

'Wait a moment.' The parson spoke as he descended from the trap. 'I'll see him myself.'

At the door of the barn, he called loudly, 'You there! Mr Shaleman.'

Bruce appeared at the far end of the barn and called back, 'Good-day, Parson. Have you come to see my mother?' There was a surprised note in the question and the answer he was given was sharp and brief: 'No! I have not come to see your mother' – he could have added, he had seen her once and that was enough – 'the dead are dead and should be left in peace; we don't believe in wakes.'

'I wouldn't expect you to.' Bruce was now standing in front of the parson as he added, 'Yet one never knows, with your Church and Rome hand in glove.'

'Mr Shaleman, I have not interrupted a very busy routine to make this journey to discuss theology with you, about which I am sure you know nothing whatever, but to remind you that I have been here before and it must have been a matter of interest to you when my verger was called into the cottage. Perhaps you are not aware that it needs two signatures to make a will legal. Your mother made a will, verbally, that is—' He now thrust his hand into his pocket and pulled out the envelope, which he now handed to Bruce, saying, 'There it is.'

Bruce took the envelope, but did not open it immediately: he just looked at the parson and said, 'Well, I'm not surprised. I've been expecting something like this. I think I know what's in it.'

'Oh, you do, do you? Well, then, in that case your mother wasted her time, and mine also. And lastly, Mr Shaleman, I would thank you not to leave impertinent messages with my verger.' And on this the irate parson turned and marched smartly back to the trap, leaving Bruce with the envelope, his jaws clenched.

He did not open it until he had returned to the other end of the barn and seated himself on a box; nor did he put his thumb under the envelope to roughly open it, but, taking a penknife from his pocket, he inserted it in the flap and slowly cut it open.

He drew out the perforated sheet of paper and stared

at the words. Then his teeth clamped together as a wave akin to shame swept through him: Why hadn't he taken advantage years ago of Richard's offer? Because of his damn silly pride, that's why. But what had he to be proud about? Nothing in the world. He could have learned much even from Max these past weeks or from Jinnie these past months, but no . . . no, he was too big in the head; and so he'd have to go and ask her to read it. Anyway, it was only Jinnie; she'd understand.

He met her coming towards him from the cottage, and when she said, 'He didn't come in to see her,' he made no comment but took her arm and led her back to the barn. Handing her the letter, he asked, 'Will you tell me what it says, Jinnie?'

Jinnie looked at the small squiggly handwriting; then she began laboriously to read:

'I, Rose Ann Shaleman, of Tollet's Ridge Farm, wish to leave the said farm and land and stock – '

She paused, and then went on,

' – to my . . . son, Bruce Arthur Shaleman.'

Jinnie now looked up into Bruce's startled face and smiled widely before finishing,

'Signed this 14th day of November 1871 in the presence of—'

She again looked at Bruce, saying on a laugh, 'His name's all squiggly, but I can make out the Rev . . . erend something, and then the verger's name.'

She laid the paper on her lap and, putting both hands out to him, she said, 'It's yours! The farm's yours. A little while ago, I thought, if Mister Hal comes back – oh, I hoped he wouldn't – but if he did, the farm would be his.' But seeing Bruce place a hand across his forehead, she said, 'What is it? What's the matter?' His face had almost blanched. 'Is . . . is it the shock?'

His hand dropped from his forehead and he said, 'Jinnie, she swore to me that she was going to leave it to Hal. In any case, you know, Hal is the rightful heir, and he could still claim it. You see, Jinnie, I am not Pug Shaleman's son and the farm was handed down from his family. But it isn't that which upsets me; it is because she wanted to leave it to me and, as she said, she wasn't as black as she was painted, and she was aware that I would be thinking the worst of her.'

When his head drooped, she quickly put her arms about his shoulders, and drawing his head into her small breast, she stroked his hair, saying, 'Don't worry about having hated her, because I've hated her as well. I know she was ill but at times she asked for it. Oh yes, she asked for it, so you shouldn't blame yourself. Come on. Come on.' She lifted his head, and now she was cupping his face in her hands, her bright eyes looking into his, and she said, 'It's yours. Nobody can take it away; that is a real will.' She pointed down to the box on which she had laid the paper. 'And you know something? You must keep it in a safe place, because if he was to come back' – she straightened up and her own head drooped – 'everything would be worse than it is now.'

He sat staring at her: she had laid his head on her breast; she had held his face between her hands. She wasn't a child any more, she was a young girl, older than her years, but her very actions had proved that, if nothing else, she looked upon him as a brother. She had handled him in a way she objected to others handling her . . . oh yes, indeed, she thought of him as her brother.

* * *

It was almost dark when Max returned to the farm. A light was showing from the small window of the scullery, and when he went in it was to see Jinnie, an apron over her best coat – in fact, her only coat – and a shoulder shawl covering her head and ears, standing at a rough-made bench and pounding dough in a large brown dish.

Since her mistress had died she had refused to work in the kitchen. It was enough for her to hurry in to keep the fire going, but on each flying visit she was freshly conscious of the woman in the box on the wall-bed. Whenever possible Bruce himself would do this chore, although even he was reluctant to go into the kitchen.

'Wh-wh-where is Mister Bruce?' asked Max.

'He's along yon end, knocking up a kind of trestle table instead of this,' she said, pointing to the rickety bench.

'C-c-come on.' Max put out his long arm and tugged her from the table, while she exclaimed, 'Wait a minute! Wait a minute! Max. Look; I'm all covered in dough.'

He allowed her to wipe her hands before he again tugged at her arm, when she said, 'What is it? What's the matter?'

'W-w-wait. Not w-wasting two breaths. C-c-come,' and he hurried her out and along to the barn.

Bruce was working by the aid of an oil lamp. He turned at their approach and, looking at Max he said quickly and abruptly, 'Well?'

'Y-y-yes, well. All is well. Miss C-C-Caplin agrees. S-s-says authorities have n-n-no juris . . . diction – b-b-big word that, eh?' He grinned from one to the other. 'Miss C-C-Caplin uses b-b-big words.'

'Well, for goodness sake! Max, spit it out. What did Miss Caplin say?'

'I'm trying to t-t-tell you. She s-s-says, if I stay on here, s-s-so can Jinnie.' And he pulled Jinnie towards him and, gently touching her bright face, he said, 'As l-l-long I'm here, y-y-you can stay.'

'Hold on! Wait a minute.' Bruce was holding up his hand. 'What d'you mean, as long as you're here? You'll soon be gone.'

'Not be g-g-gone. Miss Caplin, she write and t-t-tell them, I'm n-n-not going. Circumstances' – he grinned widely now as he nodded his head to imply that that was another big word – 'ch-ch-changed. So all is . . . v-v-very well.'

Bruce sat down on a box and he looked up at the big fellow and, slowly shaking his head, said, 'You shouldn't have done that. It was very good of you, more than good, but you know how I'm placed: I can't offer you anything like a wage until the spring, if then. It'll all depend on the market. You're a fool, you know.'

The change in Max's countenance was evident to both of them and after a moment he said, 'Don't c-c-call me that, Mister Bruce, n-n-not even in fun.'

'Oh, I'm sorry, Max.' Bruce was standing in front of him now, his hand on the big man's shoulder. 'It wasn't meant that way; it was . . . well—' He moved his head as if searching for a word, and it was Jinnie who put in, 'Endearment. Yes, Max, it was an endearment, because nobody would ever put that word to you.'

'Oh yes, Jinnie, many put that word to me; f-f-fool and idiot.'

'Oh no. What can I say?' said Bruce, apologetically. 'Well, I know this and I would bet on it; you have more sense and knowledge in your head than three farmers I could name in the valley, not to mention this one standing before you.'

Max turned away in evident embarrassment, muttering, 'Everything all r-r-right now, then. So l-l-let's get on with s-s-some work.'

At this, Jinnie put out a hand and patted Bruce's arm, and she smiled widely, her gesture confirming that, from her point of view, everything would go well from now on.

13

'So you're going to do it?'

'Yes, May; I'm going to do it,' replied Richard.

'I'm glad.'

'Strangely, so am I.'

'And about your painting. Will you go wholeheartedly for that, or into the office, as is being proposed?'

'Well, what do you think? I'd go mad sitting in an office all day.'

'But you know what the doctor said about the lead in the paint.'

'Yes I know, and I agree with him, and lead poisoning is something to be taken very seriously. I had never thought of it before – few painters do, I'm sure. I always thought that when I felt rotten it was due to the aftermath of the fever still hanging about me; and because my heart seemed to be all right, that puzzled me.'

'Well, I always thought your water colours were superior to your oils, anyway.'

'Did you?' He smiled at her gratefully, then said, 'But there's something very relaxing, you know, in slapping lumps of paint on canvas, and the beauty of it is you can go over your work again and again, whereas with water colours one splash and it's done. At least' – he nodded at her now – 'this is what all the books tell you: get it down first time clear, otherwise the result will be mud. Well, a short time ago, you know the one I did of the early morning in the forest with the deer coming through the trees and a shaft of sunlight hitting them, I was trying to get that early light mist effect. I didn't get it; and if I went over it again once, I did so ten times, and you've seen the result. You live and learn. Anyway, I'm off into town now to do a bit of shopping.'

May had been sitting on a couch near the fire and she stood up and, her voice changing, she said, 'You're not going to stop off on your way and attend that funeral, are you, Richard?'

He was half turned from her, and he didn't answer her for a moment, and when he did he said, 'I've a damn good mind to.'

'You'll only upset them if you do and everything is going so smoothly. Anyway, you half promised last night.'

'No, I didn't; I just didn't answer.' He now swung round to her. 'Anyway, Bruce has been my friend for years, so I should show some respect.'

May shook her head in a show of irritation, then said, 'All my life, at least, my adult life, I've heard the same arguments between you and them, and I can see their side of it, Richard. If they were prosperous farmers, there would be something to be said for your side of it, but by all accounts they're below ground level.'

'That's not his fault.'

'Well, you want things to go smoothly from now on, don't you? They'll accept your position, I know, whether you take up Papa Rowland's offer of a junior partnership or take up your art seriously. I'm just pointing out that they are falling over themselves to meet you half-way. They are more than fond of you. And they are not the only ones.' These last words prompted him to go and put his arm around her shoulders and to kiss her, saying, 'And that feeling's reciprocated twofold, May.' Then, slightly embarrassed, they broke apart with her

277

saying in quite a motherly fashion, 'Get yourself away. Get yourself away; but—' and the sudden appeal in her voice caused him to hesitate as he reached the door— 'do be a good boy and keep the family peace. And remember there's Lillian now, and she's no longer just Lillian. You mustn't forget that. You know what I mean.'

His tone was clear and definite when he said, 'Yes, I know what you mean, May.'

The morning following the funeral, Richard was riding to the farm, when from a distance he could see some activity outside the cottage. He drew his horse to a momentary stop before going on again. To the three people awaiting his arrival he called, 'Why the bonfire?' which was giving off thick grey smoke from the flocks of the bed tick and other pieces of bedding. 'You're making a clean sweep?'

'You could say that,' Bruce said, 'and not before time. I think you'd better take the horse along to the shed next to Patsy's stable. They can talk to each other. That's if you're meaning to stay.'

'No; I'm sorry, Bruce; I've just called to bring these.' He indicated the bags hanging over the saddle. 'If you don't mind I'll take them along to the barn, and him with me—' he patted his horse's neck. 'He doesn't like the cold either.' Then, as if just becoming aware of Max and Jinnie, he said, 'Hello! there.'

It was Max who said, 'M-m-morning, sir.'

Jinnie, who had been scrubbing a wooden chair, did not respond to his greeting, but she looked up and smiled at him, a smile which seemed to hold him still for a moment. Then jerking the horse forward, he said, 'Come on. Let's all go into the shelter.'

He dismounted just inside the barn and hooked the reins over a staple in the wall. Then, after taking the bags from the saddle, he walked beside Bruce and Max to the far end of the barn and dropped the bags on an upturned box.

He was about to speak when his attention was caught by Jinnie. She was standing apart. She did not appear her usual chirpy self; her look was pensive; and the thought flashed through his mind that she was beautiful; and it wasn't a childish beauty either, or that of a young girl. He had noticed before that her skin still retained its creamy tint of youth; the wind up here had not seemed to mar it, as work had her hands.

He now took a prettily wrapped parcel and handed it to her, saying, 'Happy Christmas, Jinnie.'

Quickly, she glanced at Bruce as if for permission to accept the present; then looking back at Richard she took the parcel from him, saying, 'For me?'

'Yes—' and he looked about him, saying, 'there's no other young lady here, is there, who could wear what's inside that?'

Then not waiting for her thanks, he drew two more parcels from the first bag and handed one to Bruce and the other to Max.

Bruce muttered softly, 'Thank you, Richard;' but Max, holding the parcel across both his hands and smiling broadly, said, 'My thanks, s-s-sir. F-f-first present I've had wr-wr-wrapped up . . . in my life.'

'Well, don't keep it wrapped up,' Richard laughed back at him, 'none of you,' he added. And amid laughter each undid his parcel. It was Bruce who first exclaimed and in admiration.

'Oh my! a real gansey.'

'Well, jersey or gansey,' cried Richard now, 'put it on and see if it fits. If not, I can have it exchanged, so they tell me.'

'If it doesn't fit,' said Bruce slowly, 'I'd want to

279

keep this just to feel it.' His hands stroked the soft woollen garment. He'd had ganseys before, but not like this one. They had been fisherman's ganseys, made with coarse wool for rough wear.

All attention was now turned on Max, who was holding a very fine thick tweed waistcoat at arm's length, for such it looked at first glance; although it was a waistcoat with a difference, because it had long, soft leather sleeves and leather buttons to match.

'That was the largest in the shop, so I can't take it back, Max, and ask for it to be exchanged. You'll just have to lose some weight.'

Max had risen from the box on which he had been sitting and, walking towards Richard, he put out a hand, his other forearm pressing the waistcoat to him, and almost with a break in his voice he said, 'S-s-sir, I have never seen anything l-l-like it, and I thank you m-m-most warmly.'

'Oh.' Richard, slightly embarrassed, laughed as he said, 'It's only a waistcoat, but I liked the look of it, as I did Bruce's guernsey.'

They now all turned and looked at Jinnie, and Bruce exclaimed loudly, 'Haven't you opened it yet?'

'Yes; I've opened it, but I haven't taken it out of the paper because you two were so busy admiring yourselves.'

This was greeted with a burst of laughter, and Bruce cried at her, 'Get on with it! you cheeky monkey. All you want is attention . . . well, we're all attention now, so get on with it.'

Slowly and in amazement she lifted up a fur hood and held it in one hand while the other picked up a pair of fur-lined gloves. She sat gazing down at them for a moment before she lifted her eyes to Richard's. Her lower lip was trembling but she was unable to speak.

It was a moment before Richard said, 'I had to guess your size . . . I mean, with the gloves.'

No-one spoke while she laid down the gloves and, opening the hood, pulled it on over her head. It had a fine, pink flannel lining which was continued as a tie under her chin, although she didn't make it into a bow. She picked up the gloves and drew them on her fingers. They were tight at first, but she stroked her fingers in as any lady might, and the three men sat watching her.

Her attire could have been regarded as grotesque: her feet encased in ugly block-toed working boots, the long, dull grey coat covered with the work-spattered apron, while above it the face with cream-tinted skin enhanced by the long dark lashes of the clear green eyes, all framed in an expensive, brown-fur hood lined with pink flannel, the hands, in the matching gloves, held up now, palm upwards, as if for inspection by the audience.

As the hands dropped down to her lap and her head slowly bowed, Max was talking in his mind – and with no stammers – if only he had money; his child was so beautiful.

Bruce's thoughts were revealing in that they held a slight touch of resentment. Richard shouldn't have done that. Such a present was so out of place for her. Just look at her coat and boots. And if she had to have anything in the way of clothing, he was the one who should have provided them for her. Items of that quality would put ideas into her head.

Looking up at Richard, Jinnie found she still couldn't find any words, although her thoughts were running wild. He was so kind, and he was beautiful; oh yes, so beautiful. Ever since he had lifted her on to his horse she had been unable to get him out of her mind. But then her voice seemed to be forced from her by Bruce saying, 'What's the matter with you? Have you lost your tongue?' And she finally did speak as she continued to look at Richard and said softly, 'Thank you. Thank you so much. They are lovely . . . lovely.'

It was almost on the tip of Richard's tongue to say, 'And you're lovely too;' but instead, turning abruptly from her, he picked up the other bag and said, 'Odds and ends of Christmas fare for the table,' and handed it to Bruce.

It was all Bruce could do to say, 'Thanks. Thanks.' For some reason he couldn't quite fathom, this further gift had intensified his resentment.

They were walking back towards the end of the barn and Richard's horse, the while thanking him again for his kindness, but, as perhaps could have been expected, he did not discount their thanks by saying, 'Oh, it is nothing,' but after taking the horse's reins from the nail, he mounted the animal, then looked down on them and, with a quizzical smile on his face, he said, 'I've had my own Christmas present, I am engaged to be married to Miss Lillian Rowlands. The wedding is to be next June. It hasn't been made public yet, but I'm telling you because you are my friends.'

As he turned the horse and left the barn, Richard waved aside the congratulations from the two men, and he did not notice that Jinnie remained silent; but Bruce did, as he also noticed the stricken look on her face. And he thought, Dear God! she surely wouldn't be so silly; not Jinnie. But then she was still a young girl, and all young girls were silly.

He turned to Max and said, 'Well, that's no surprise. It's been hanging fire for a long time. But I don't suppose it will make all that difference to him; except, perhaps, that both families will now have a stronger claim on him, if that's possible . . . It says something for being independent, even if you do have a hungry belly.'

282

He felt himself almost pushed aside as Jinnie passed him and hurried out on her way to the cottage.

From the first time she had seen him and had experienced that strange pain in the middle of her chest, she had known that what had entered her head was but a crazy idea. She might not have seen him for weeks or months, but the very sight of him would revive the feeling, bringing it out from its night-time hidden chamber, when the fancy and fantasy would take on a kind of reality. But the reality had today been given real life when he had presented her with this wonderful gift, because for a moment she had imagined that no man would give such a present to a girl he saw only as a maid. He was a gentleman, but with a difference: had he not already made a friend of Bruce, and Bruce was not a gentleman? And so, why not also make a friend or more of her?

In that fleeting moment it had appeared feasible; whereas now all she could think was, she wanted to die; and immediately she asked herself why she was staying on at this place, because it was awful. One thing was sure: she would not wear his hood and gloves, ever.

PART TWO

I

It was now July 1872 and a great deal had happened since Christmas, on this hill as well as in the valley. Here, at the farm, alterations to the buildings were immediately noticeable.

In the farmhouse itself, the recess that had held the bed had been extended to make a room as large as the kitchen. It had its own fireplace on the far wall, as well as a loft above, in which a person of normal height could stand up.

The pig-swill room remained as it was, as did the sty and the barn, although around the corner were two new cow-byres and beyond, a stone building had been converted into a dairy. But these changes seemed insignificant when, on entering the cottage, one found oneself in what was really a thirty-foot room, with a fire and a cooking oven in the kitchen area and with an open fire at the far end, with the whole of the floor space covered either in rope or cocoa matting. The stone walls had been plastered and lime-washed and the two windows, the larger of which was in the extension, both sported brightly patterned cotton curtains. The room was sparsely furnished, but nevertheless there were signs of comfort in the newer part with two worn, chintz-covered armchairs and a backless settle seat placed against the fireside wall. This was four feet long and had a thick, comfortable pad on it. This too was chintz-covered but gave evidence of much wear, being patched at the corners. It had at one time graced another farmhouse kitchen, as had the other odds and ends. But odds and ends or not, they could not at this time have brought more delight to Jinnie had they been pieces worthy of the name of antique.

The sleeping arrangements, too, had been altered. The loft above the new room took two pallet beds comfortably, and was shared by Bruce and Max, although Max could not stand up straight in any part of it. However, this did not deter him from appreciating his new quarters.

As for Bruce, he was glad to have Max's company at night, for he had grown very fond of the big fella.

What was strange, although Bruce never referred to it, in case by doing so he should check the flow, was that Max's stammering and incoherence was now hardly noticeable. Perhaps it was because the man was happy.

But in spite of the apparent well-being of the farm, money was still very tight. And yet Bruce would have been content but for one concern. And the name of that was Hal.

For months now he had tried to prepare himself for his brother's return. Moreover, one thing was sure: whatever had happened to him on his voyages would not have lessened his hatred of either Max or Jinnie. Then, there would be the question of the real ownership of the farm, for no matter what his mother might have wished, or indeed expressed, Bruce felt that Hal could legally claim ownership. And the worry had really come to the front and taken on the shape of fear when, two days before, he had heard through Peter Locke that *The Admiral* was due in.

Although he had no assurance that Hal was still on this particular boat, nevertheless there was the possibility that he might be, and that once it touched harbour he would make straight for the farm. And so he had thought it wise to put Jinnie and Max in the picture. If things did come to a head, Jinnie could go down to the Miss Duckworths. As for Max, he had already earned himself the name of an excellent handyman, and could easily obtain temporary work elsewhere . . .

He had been up in the hills for most of the day, and being back in form, he was now blithely running with the dog, his dread almost forgotten in these moments of exhilaration. But, on seeing two figures making their way down from the road to the pond, his dread was overshadowed by a feeling of anger.

What the hell does he think he's up to! And she, the little bitch, must know what she's doing. I'll have to come into the open with her. I will! he thought.

He pulled the dog towards him and sat down on an outcrop of rock. He'd have to wait until they were gone . . .

Had arrangements gone as planned Richard would have been married the previous June; but fate had arranged otherwise; after a happy day in Newcastle, shopping for the new home, situated just outside Hexham, the two families were in the Rowlands' carriage bowling homewards when Henry Rowland fell sideways across his wife's lap with a stroke, as a result of which, four days later, he died.

Between them, his wife and daughter had kept a continuous vigil at his bedside; and although both were devastated by his loss, it was the condition of the wife that concerned everybody, for she demanded her daughter's presence night and day. Of course, there was now no thought of a June wedding. It must be put off for a year, Henry Rowland's widow insisted. When Richard had dared to suggest that six months might be considered enough mourning time, Evelyn Rowland was aghast, and showed it. She would be unable to go on if her daughter lived all that way from her.

What Lillian Rowland's true thoughts of the matter were, no-one knew. From her earliest days she had loved their neighbour's son Richard, and just as her mother thought his proposal was long overdue, so did she. And so, when he actually did ask her to be his wife, it had come as something of a surprise, for on his part, there had been no particular show of ardour as he led up to it. Nevertheless, the days of her engagement had been the happiest she had known in her life, for he had been most caring of her, and because of it the days had flown.

In these present conditions, the waiting seemed interminable, but just bearable; that is, until her mother suggested that they could be married in February, providing they made their home with her, permanently.

It was this suggestion that had driven Richard to Paris.

As for Lillian herself, her one desire, apart from actually being married to Richard, was to get away from the stifling atmosphere of a house of prayer, as her mother's had become.

From his viewpoint, Bruce thought that should those two down there get their heads together, he would certainly tell her something when he had her alone: he would warn her she was playing with fire; but he would not raise her foolish hopes by telling her that Richard was going through a very tense period and that he was now in two minds about the marriage, a doubt engendered mostly, he thought, by Mrs Rowland's determination to keep her hold on her daughter.

Becoming impatient, he continued his way down to the farm, circumventing the pond and the pair still standing there, seemingly engrossed . . .

At the farm, he found Roy Stevens talking to Max, and, straightaway, Bruce asked him, 'Did you not see Jinnie on the way up?'

'I didn't come up that way, Bruce. I've been over to Timpson's.' He thumbed in the opposite direction.

'And you walked all that way?'

'No; the nag's round the corner. But I thought I'd drop in and tell you he's got an old cow that could give you a start. She's still giving a good measure each day, and he's wanting space, as he's starting up a new herd. I told him you were on the look-out for something more than reasonable' – he stressed the last words – 'and he said you should pop over.'

'Oh; thanks, Roy. That was good of you. Well, we've got the space and Jinnie's picked up enough knowledge from your mother and Bessie Singleton to make butter in her sleep but, as they say, the theory's all right, it's the practical that gives you change for a shilling.'

'Yes, you're right there; but she'll make butter, all right. I wanted to have a word with her.'

Bruce paused for a moment before he said, 'She should be here shortly; I saw her coming along the top road.' He didn't say by whom she was accompanied and they both laughed now as Max said, 'I'll need white coat now; always have white coat when milking.'

'And you'll need the white cap and boots to go with it,' put in Roy; 'you can't milk a cow properly unless you're wearing the proper clothes!'

The joviality ceased as Jinnie appeared from behind the barn. She was alone.

No-one who remembered the girl of fourteen arriving at the farm in 1871 would connect her with this tall, slim young woman. Although not yet sixteen, she would pass any day for twenty. Her face was beautiful, her skin perfect; these spoke of youth, but it was the

291

eyes that suggested her maturity. Her hands, too, were smoother. As the rough work was now mostly carried out by Max, Jinnie's main employment, in which she showed great pride, was cooking the meals and taking care of the inside of the house.

'Hello, Roy,' she said; 'I've just been down to your place.' Her voice too had changed, having lost its high, sharp twang. Now it was rather low-pitched and some-what mellow, as if she had been taking elocution lessons. 'How did I miss you?' There was a touch of anxiety in the question.

'Oh, I've been over to Timpson's, and I'll likely get it in the neck when I get home. You can never get away from there, you know, once you get in their kitchen: I'm stuffed up to here' – he patted under his chin – 'with cake and home-made wine, and I bet that'll kill me tomorrow, if not before, because it hadn't been standing long enough, it was too fresh. Anyway, I must get back now.' He moved from one foot to the other with his eyes still on her, then added, 'I'll go and get my nag.'

As the young fellow disappeared around the barn, Bruce said softly to Jinnie, 'Go and have a word with him.'

'I've had a word.'

'Look!'

'Oh, all right.' She swung about and walked away in an obviously disgruntled manner.

'Nice fellow . . . Roy.' – Max nodded in Jinnie's direction – 'What d'you say?'

'What d'you mean, what do I say?'

'Just that. It would be good thing. He's only son; he have farm of his own some day.'

Bruce sighed, a long slow sigh; then he nodded and said, 'Yes; yes, you're right.'

'Know I am. Yes; know I am.'

'Yes, of course you would be,' Bruce almost shouted. 'You're nearly always bloody well right, at least you think so, where she's concerned.'

Max had not moved an inch while looking down into the eyes of the man he thought of as his best friend and quietly he said, 'No. But I know her.' Then his tone taking on a more serious note still, he added slowly, 'Best for everybody's sake, Roy is. Everybody's. You know what I mean?'

Bruce knew very well what he was suggesting, but he said, 'No, I don't know what you mean; and I don't want to hear what you mean. Sh! Here they come.'

Roy was leading his horse and Jinnie was walking by his side, but they weren't talking, and it wasn't until they were abreast of Bruce and Max that Roy said, 'I'm trying once more to get her to come to the dance, but she keeps saying she can't dance. Well, she'll never learn if she doesn't come, will she? And anyway, there'll be no experts there.'

'Why don't you go?' Bruce was looking straight at Jinnie now, and she answered promptly, saying, 'Because I can't dance. And anyway, I have no—' she did not say, 'desire to go to the dance or anywhere else with Roy,' but added lamely, 'I have no suitable shoes.'

'We get you suitable shoes.'

'You'll do nothing of the sort, Max. Anyway—' looking at Roy now, she smiled, saying, 'we'll see. We'll see. I'll go if he goes,' and she pointed to Bruce, who said immediately, 'Very well, yes. It's a long time since I've been to a dance. Yes, I'll come too. So it's a deal, Roy: we'll be at the barn-dance.'

'Good. Good.' Roy was smiling broadly now. Then turning to Jinnie, he said, 'But I'll be seeing you before that; 'tis not for another month or so.'

'Yes, yes,' she said briefly.

Roy mounted his horse and with a 'Tara! then,' trotted off leaving the three of them standing watching him for a moment, until Bruce turned to Jinnie saying, 'Why don't you go to a dance with him; he's asked you often enough? You go into the farm, you have tea there, you're always chatting with his mother.'

Jinnie's face seemed to stretch: her mouth opened wide and she cried, 'Oh you! You're a dumb-head. And you an' all!' she included Max in her tirade. 'Yes, I have a cup of tea with his mother and I let her talk and talk and talk because she likes talking, and I take down the eggs and I get the butter in exchange, and the cheese and so on, and sometimes he walks back with me and carries the basket. Well, as far as I can see that's enough, because I just need to go alone with him to a barn-dance and what kind of construction would be put on it then, eh? I'd be courting, because that's the term, isn't it, around here? They walk out up and down the lanes on a Sunday, and then they take them to a barn-dance and their death warrant's signed, or whatever you like to call the marriage licence. The reason why I've refused Roy's offers is because I don't want to give him the wrong idea. He's a nice fellow; I like him. I like to be in the kitchen with his father and mother and listen to all the talk being flung back and forth, but that's as far as I go. Do you understand, both of you? I am not for courting Roy Stevens!'

The two men now exchanged glances, and the expressions on their faces were similar. One retort from them could have been of laughter, another could have been of amazement, for here was a young woman definitely speaking her mind; but neither of them was given a chance to express an opinion, for she flung around and went into the cottage, banging the door shut behind her.

With the sound of the door being banged there arose in Bruce a feeling of righteous anger. What was she, after all, he asked himself, but a girl? She wasn't even sixteen, yet she was already talking like a fully fledged woman, and a knowledgeable one at that. If she had taken up with Roy he would have had to bear it, but as she didn't want to take up with Roy she was still open to anybody, and that particular anybody was a man out of her class. She must put him out of her mind. No matter what difficulties he was now experiencing, he would eventually marry, and it certainly wouldn't be her.

He almost bounced into the kitchen, and he too banged the door after him.

She was standing at the far side of the table. She had taken off her light sun bonnet and was now fastening an apron around her blue print dress, and without warning he began pelting words at her: 'What d'you mean, miss, by acting so big and grand you can turn your nose up at a good fellow like Roy, while at the same time walking secretly with a man who you know is going to be married and can never, never, never be anything to you?'

His teeth were clenched as he glared at her and the fact that her face was now almost devoid of colour did not stop him from going on: 'And what's more, you've only got to be seen walking with that certain gentleman more than once and your name will be mud; and so much so that Roy wouldn't look the side you were on if he knew of it. And who d'you think you are, miss, to take up this stand? You came from the workhouse; you came into this very house a little whipper-snapper of a girl. Granted you worked, but let me tell you something: if I was anybody but the man that I am you'd either be gone or you'd now be in the family way, or you'd be married to me. Now, Miss High and

Mighty, think on those things; and if you should want to leave here the door's open. In that case I could have a wife tomorrow; but as long as you are here and in this position I cannot take one: there would be no room for two of you. Now what d'you think about that, eh? I'll repeat: as long as you are here I cannot take a wife, because she wouldn't put up with you in this house; and there are two girls in the village just waiting for me to speak, and neither of them acts like a slut; they know their place.' He stopped, gasping for breath as if he had been running, while he continued to glare into her wide-eyed, stricken face. Then flinging his body around, he stamped out and almost collided with Max, who muttered, 'H-hold on a minute. Steady on. You hit her hard . . . very hard. But I know . . . Mister Richard not g-g-good for her. Come on.' He now put an arm around Bruce's shoulders and led him towards the barn.

The emotion in Bruce that was now replacing his anger warned him with a touch of shame that, like any woman, he was near to crying.

In the barn, Bruce sat with his head in his hands; that was until Max said, 'All bad things come together. P-P-Peter called; says, Hal's boat in. L-l-lying outside last night.'

Jerking up his head, Bruce exclaimed, 'It's in! *The Admiral*?'

'Yes. So he'll be up soon. You must expect. I do. And if he stays we go, her and me. I'm sorry. Very . . . very.'

Bruce drew himself up from the box. That's all he needed to know: Hal was back. Life would never be the same again anyway: as Max had said, she would go and he would go. Well, in that case, if something wasn't worked out between them, he could see himself leaving, too. And after all, that wouldn't be such a bad job.

Max was saying something, quoting from the Bible again: The thing they feared had come upon them.

And indeed it had; what with one thing and another it had come with a vengeance.

2

Four days had passed and Hal had not showed up. Nor had there been any talk of him being in the village, although his lady love's husband was at sea again.

The harmony had gone from the long room in the farmhouse. Jinnie cooked but she did not sit down to have her meal with Bruce and Max. She cleaned the place and baked and washed as usual; and twice she had had further straight words with Bruce. On the first occasion she had said, 'I'll be seeing Miss Caplin next Sunday and will arrange about getting another place,' and had added tartly, 'so there'll be no obstructions to your courting.' She had stressed the last words; but he had given her no reply whatever; he'd just looked at her sadly, because all he wanted to say was, I'm sorry I said what I did, but it's because I love you. Don't you see? But as those words were impossible to utter he had turned and left the room. Next time she spoke to him had been very much to the point: 'I read in a newspaper in Mrs Stevens's kitchen that there is a position vacant on a farm near Haydon Bridge. I think I am due for a day off. I would like to go on Thursday and see about it, if that's all right with you,' to which all he could find to say, and with his head shaking in desperation, was, 'Oh! Jinnie. Jinnie.'

It was around nine o'clock in the morning, just as he was making for the hills, that he was hailed from the coach road by Geoff Taggart, who took the letters around. The man was shouting, 'One here for you, Bruce; a letter!' He was waving it, and when Bruce reached him the man handed him the envelope, saying, 'You don't often get post; and that looks a business one an' all. Name at the top; look.' He pointed.

All that Bruce said was, 'Thanks, Geoff. Thanks,' then turned slowly away and walked back towards the farm; at least, until he was well out of sight of the postman, who must have been disappointed at not learning the contents of this important-looking letter.

Bruce now stood and slowly put his finger under the flap of the envelope. It was tough paper and he had to press hard to get it open. Then, from the envelope he withdrew a piece of thick writing paper, and his eyes narrowed as he attempted to read the printed words. Over the past year he had learned to read and write, but found the reading much harder than the writing. And slowly he made out the name of the firm of solicitors at the top of the letter; then he read:

Dear Sir, Having ascertained that the parents of Harold Shaleman are now deceased and that you are the only surviving member of that family, we are pleased to inform you that if you will call at the address above at your convenience, you may hear something to your advantage.

Three times he went over the words before, calling Flossie to him, he made his way back to the farm and, going straight to the hen crees where he knew Max would be working, he called to him, 'Here a minute!' and when Max had come to the wire gate he handed him the letter, saying, 'Read that.'

Max could read well, although he couldn't transcribe on to paper what he was reading, but the joyous sound he made was evident that he understood every word and implication of the letter. 'Something happened to Hal. You go right in today?'

'Yes; of course.'

'Come on; sh-show it to Jinnie.'

'No. No.'

'But y-yes. Come on.'

After pushing a hen back into the wired enclosure, Max caught hold of Bruce's arm and hurried him along the front of the buildings to the cottage door, and when Bruce was again for pulling back, Max opened the door and almost thrust him inside; and there, staring at the startled face of Jinnie, he said, 'R-r-read that. Read.'

Slowly Jinnie took the letter from him, and after she had read it she looked up at Bruce and said, 'You've read it?'

'Yes.'

'I'm glad.' She nodded at him. 'It could mean that he's . . .'

'Dead.' Max almost spat out the word; then he repeated, 'Yes, dead. Good thing. Bruce must go into N-N-Newcastle now. Make cup of tea, eh?' His smile was almost beguiling as he gazed down at her: it was begging her to be her old self, and for a moment she was, as she said, 'Yes; yes, I'll make some tea.'

'I'd better go and wash and change,' Bruce said as he hurried out. And when the door had closed on him Max went up to Jinnie and in a quiet voice he said, 'Very sad. Very sad, 'cos he cares for you. Yes, yes, he does. Love you, but you never love him that way.'

She drooped her head, saying now, 'Oh, Max, I . . . I feel dreadful. Dreadful. I'm sorry; I . . . I can't think of him in that way. As you are my father, he is my brother.'

'Very loving brother. You . . . we both owe him lots.'

'Yes, I know. I know, and I'm sorry for what I said, too; but it's done now.'

'Needn't be. Needn't be. Now Hal gone.' He put up his hand as if calling on the gods and looked up towards the ceiling as he said, 'Praise be the L-Lord if it be so.' It was one of those times when she might have laughed outright, but instead all she said was, 'I . . . I can't help how my heart feels, Max. I've tried. Oh yes, I've tried again and again, telling myself I'm stupid, silly; but it won't listen to me. I know . . . I know more than anybody, you or him, that nothing can come of it.'

'Oh, my dear. My dear.' He drew her towards him and pressed her head against his shoulder and patted her hair as he said, 'Heart awful thing; c-can't rule it. My heart ache one time, f-f-for children I would never never have, then God gave me you. I was man of twenty-seven when I first saw you.' Then pressing her from him, but still holding her, he smiled widely as he added, 'You were k-k-kicking the labour mistress. They had just taken your papa's cart and horse away, but God gave you to me then.'

'Oh! Max. Max.' She was sobbing openly in his arms. 'Oh! Max; Max, I'll never leave you. Wherever I go they'll have to find a place for you.'

His face now straight, he said, 'And leave him alone here? No, no; he's my friend. He's been very g-g-good to me. If you go into service it must be on your own.'

Noticing Bruce descending the steps from the loft, Jinnie drew away from Max's hold, quickly wiped her eyes with her apron, then attended to the making of the tea.

Although the clothes that Bruce was now wearing were well-worn, the tweed jacket almost threadbare at the elbows, he still looked a very presentable young man. His body was lithe, his head was well set on his shoulders, and his clean-shaven face, if not handsome, was pleasantly featured; and all was not lost upon Jinnie as she glanced at him, and she wished, really wished, from the bottom of her heart that she could have loved him with the love that he deserved, for she owed him so much.

Bruce drank the tea, wiped his mouth on the pad of his thumb, pulled on his cap, then as casually as he could, he said, 'Well, I'm off.' And at this Max said, 'I'll be walking on c-c-cinders until you come back.' But Jinnie said nothing. She only hoped that some good fortune would come his way and compensate him, if love could be compensated.

Bruce sat in the office of Walters, Claire and Fowler, Solicitors. It was a well-upholstered office, all the chairs being covered in either leather or hide, and the desk, behind which sat either Mr Walters, Mr Claire or Mr Fowler, was very deep and wide. It too had a leather top.

'Your name is . . .?'

The thin man with the grey hair leant forward across the desk towards Bruce, and Bruce replied, 'Bruce Shaleman.'

'Yes, Mr Bruce Shaleman, I'm Mr Claire and I'm very pleased that you have called. But may I ask if you have anything that can prove your identity?'

Bruce's answer was terse as he replied, 'None whatever; only that's my name and I received a letter from you asking if I was Mr Harold Shaleman's brother. You had our address, although not the full one: it is Tollet's Ridge Farm, The New Coach Road, Whitfield.'

'Would that be Hexham way?'

'No, sir; quite a way beyond and beyond Haydon Bridge and Langley. Catton and Allendale are one way,

Whitfield t'other. Above that. Yes, way above Whitfield. Do you know that part, sir?'

Mr Claire cleared his throat and said, 'I have been almost as far. Yes, as far as Catton. That is the terminus of the train, isn't it?'

'Yes, sir. Just beyond.'

'Have you anyone who could vouch for your identity?'

'Yes. Oh yes; a man of substance, too, Mr Richard Baxton-Powell.'

'Oh, you know the Baxton-Powells?'

'As I've said, I'm well acquainted with the son, Richard, sir.'

'Oh. Oh, well; they have offices in the city, so we could soon verify that, couldn't we?'

It was a moment before Bruce answered, 'Yes, sir; you could, and the sooner the better, I would say.'

The grey-haired man now glanced towards his partner who was sitting at the end of the table writing, and he said, 'Do you think we could go ahead now, Mr Fowler?' And Mr Fowler, raising his head for the first time, looked straight at Bruce and muttered something that could have been, 'Yes, Mr Claire, of course;' then continued with his writing.

Mr Claire was addressing Bruce again, saying, 'It is a most strange story. I am sure you don't know as yet that your brother died at sea.'

'No; no, I didn't, sir. When was this?' Mr Claire again looked at Mr Fowler, and without raising his head Mr Fowler said, 'Off the Island of Jamaica, on May the second of this year, 1872, and he was buried at sea.'

Bruce's attention was all on the man at the end of the desk now. He seemed a queer fellow. All the time he was talking, he was continuing to write rapidly. This was what solicitors did, he supposed.

Mr Claire brought Bruce's attention to him again, saying, 'Well, Mr Shaleman, I will put it to you as plainly and as shortly as possible. For the full details you must see Captain Thomas Stoke, Master of *The Admiral*. He knows quite a bit about the matter; but the First Officer, Mr Carter, will take you deeper into your brother's life and his business. It is a very strange business, but it has netted you, Mr Shaleman, what to my mind is a small, though not so small, fortune.'

Bruce said nothing: he just stared across the desk at the man and waited.

'Before the boat left the last port of call, your brother put into the Captain's care a box containing five hundred pounds and valuables; jewellery, in fact. The Captain and his First Officer brought the box to me and asked for our advice. I suggested it be opened here in the presence of witnesses and when the contents were revealed, I suggested the money be banked at Lloyds, and the valuables left in the safe here for the present until we ascertained their value. Now, if I may suggest to you, I would go to where *The Admiral* is berthed and if the Captain and the First Officer are at liberty, I would invite them to a meal, and there I am sure you will get the whole story. Then, perhaps this afternoon, you will do me the honour of returning here at three o'clock, at which time I will take you and introduce you to the Lloyds Bank manager and also ask for a valuer to be there to give you an idea, even a rough idea, of what you can expect from the four pieces of jewellery that are deposited over there—' His hand pointed to the safe in the far wall.

Bruce made no murmur of reply. Five hundred pounds and jewellery. From where, in God's name! could Hal have got five hundred pounds honestly? And jewellery. Jewellery! He must have been robbing somebody. And yet this man was telling him to take these two gentlemen, a Captain and his First Officer, out to a meal and all he had on him was one pound three and sixpence.

As if the man at the end of the table had been reading his mind, he raised his head for a moment, stopped the movement of his pen, looked at his partner and said one word, 'Advance;' then he resumed his business, and Mr Claire said cheerfully, 'Oh yes; yes. You will be needing an advance, Mr Shaleman. Let me see, would ten pounds be in order?'

'Yes, sir. Thank you; that would be in order.' How was it he was able to answer so calmly? His voice certainly wasn't conveying his thoughts, which were in a racing jumble. He now watched Mr Claire bend to the side, open a drawer and take from it a box which he placed on the desk. From the box he extracted a chamois leather bag and, pushing it across the table towards Bruce, he said, 'I think you'll find the required sum in there.'

'Thank you, sir.' Bruce put the bag into his pocket; then, pushing his chair back, he stood up and his voice still not sounding like his own, said, 'Until three o'clock, then.'

Mr Claire now half rose from his chair and rang a bell on his desk, and when a door opened he said, 'Will you see Mr Shaleman out, Williams?' The clerk did not answer but inclined his head towards Bruce. However, when the door had closed on them, Mr Claire turned to his partner and said, 'Well, what do you think?' and the mutter came back, 'Honest, poor and half-fed. Could pass if he was dressed in a decent rig.' Then, looking towards the wall in which he had indicated the safe, Mr Claire said, 'I wonder how that fellow came across that little lot in there. I wouldn't like to guess at its worth.'

To this Mr Fowler muttered, 'Never got it by honest means, you can be sure. Stolen stuff. No other way for a sailor to come by that. Still, no business of yours; no business of mine; but don't let Stoneford rob him: he'd take your eyes out and come back for the sockets, Stoneford would; beat you down. Don't have it.'

'There's always Fielding; he's ready to take anything.'

'Yes, so are the police. Don't trust him as far as I could toss him. Get as much as you can from Stoneford.'

'You're right there; yes, you're right there.' Mr Claire now rang the bell for the next client, who, he expected, would prove only half as interesting as the one just gone . . .

When Bruce found *The Admiral* he was surprised at the smallness of her. He had expected to see a very large boat. Men were busying themselves on her deck. He made his way between piles of ropes and odd crates, and then he was standing at the end of a short gangway facing a man, who asked, 'Aye; what you after?'

'I wish to have a word with the Captain or the First Officer.'

'Oh. Well, come over and take your choice. You're not after wanting to sign on, are you? 'cause this is the wrong place.'

Bruce could smile at this and say, 'No; I'm not wanting to sign on, thank you.'

The man now called across the deck, 'Bloke to see the Captain;' then turning to Bruce again, he added, 'Lucky to catch him on board. If it weren't for the tide the night, you wouldn't have seen hilt nor hair of him.'

The second sailor eyed him up and down, and realising from his clothes that he was of no account, and being curious, he said, 'What you up to with the Captain, then?'

'That's my business.'

The man seemed nonplussed for a moment. The tone of voice didn't go with the fella's rig-out, and he said, 'Come on with ya, then;' and Bruce went on with him, and down an almost vertical ladder to the deck below. That he did so with such agility surprised the man. They now went through two narrow corridors before the man stopped, knocked at a door, and at the sound of a grunt opened it, to reveal two men examining some papers spread out on a table. One of the men turned towards the sailor, but it was his companion who said, 'What is it?'

'Man to see you, Captain. Says he's not for signing on.'

'All right, Spears.'

At this the man backed and pushed past Bruce, and the First Officer said, 'Come in, and close the door,' then demanded, 'What's your name? And what's your business? We're busy.'

'My name's Shaleman. I understand that my brother died on this ship.'

The two men now stared at him, and it was the Captain who said, 'Oh! Shaleman. Oh yes; yes. Come in. Come in. Sit down. We've been half-expecting someone to come about that.' He glanced at the First Officer, then added, 'You've been to the solicitors', then?'

'Yes, sir. I've just come from there. They suggested you had a great deal to tell me and that we might do that over . . . well, a bite to eat.'

The men now smiled at each other but it was the First Officer who said, 'That's a very good suggestion, isn't it, sir?' and the Captain answered, 'Very good indeed. But to my mind it's as well not to have to talk business of any kind in eating houses; too many loose ears about. We'll definitely have a meal with you, sir, but that can be later. At the moment I suppose you want to know how your brother came into his small fortune.'

'Yes, sir, I do. It would be helpful because I can't imagine my brother having that amount of money at any time.'

'He never played cards with you at all?' It was the First Officer speaking to Bruce who shook his head and said, 'No; we lived on a farm up in the hills; we never had much time for card playing.'

'Well . . . well, where do we start?' said the Captain. 'Really, we should have the Second Mate here, but he has already gone on before us to Scotland; we sail for the Clyde tonight, you know. We're picking up our next cargo from there. But the Second Mate could have put you in the picture much better than either of us. As it is, I think I'll leave it to Mr Carter here to tell you what he knows; and I think he'd better start at the beginning.'

The First Officer now cleared his throat as if about to make a speech, and then he said, 'Well, Mr Shaleman, you know your brother's character and temperament better than anybody, I should say; and if you were truthful you might add he wasn't an easy fellow to get along with.'

'You're right there, sir.'

'Well, now that's out of the way, I can say he had a pretty rough time when he first came aboard this ship. You see, we are very proud of our crew, most of them having been with us for years, some even from boys. I am just putting you in the picture that when your brother came aboard he was for using both his fists and his tongue, and neither of them was a match for those of some of the crew; and so going out to the Indies was rather a rough passage for him, with one exception. We had a man aboard who was a bit of a magician. Oh, that's wrong, Captain, my saying Samson was a bit of a magician, he *was* a magician.

308

The Captain here had picked him up from one of the Islands four years previously. He was a good worker but he was a better entertainer; he could do anything with cards . . . and rats. He could be in his bare pelt up to here' – the First Officer now put his hand around his waist – 'and his breeks would just reach his knees, he would never touch them but he'd bring a rat from behind his back and tweek its whiskers. To say that he was feared is putting it mildly: sailors don't usually like weird or odd individuals, so he hadn't any friends on board, a lot of admirers you could say, but no friends; until your brother appeared, that is. Your brother did not seem to be afraid of him and all the hocus-pocus he got up to. You could say now that he cultivated him in order to learn his tricks, and the tricks he did learn best were those that can be achieved with a pack of cards, because Samson – that's the nickname the men gave our odd man – could win every hand he played, without anyone being able to detect a cheating move. We've sat in, haven't we, Captain?' He looked at his superior, and the Captain nodded, saying, 'Yes; many a time.'

'Anyway, it didn't make the men like your brother any better when he became a mate of Samson. When we reached some of the islands the Captain did not allow any of the crew to go ashore. The women were rotten, as was the food and drink in some of these places, but there was one particular town where leave was always granted. There were many whites there, mostly settlers on the outskirts, but the town itself was run by half-breeds, and there were three main gambling saloons. But, as Samson said, he never allowed himself to win more than ten of the island's golden coins in any one game, an insurance for getting out alive. But ten of these coins apparently were not enough to satisfy your brother. And although he *was* your brother I must say that he was like a ferret in his actions. He managed to unearth the fact that some private gambling games went on outside the town, and for pretty high stakes; and that the planters would sometimes play all night. Then, one day, a strange thing happened: Samson jumped ship when we were berthing at one of the islands. He had given no reason to anyone that he was going, except that on the day prior to his disappearance he told one of the stokers, 'Hal man unlucky,' which the stoker found very strange, because everybody knew they were mates. In any case, you don't talk about being unlucky aboard any ship. Once a man gets known as a jinx, there's trouble all round.

'Anyway, when we next made a port where the men could go ashore – quite a civilised place, really, even though the town itself was run by half-breeds – your brother went on shore leave by himself. No-one ever went out of his way to seek his company, and on this particular night, when he returned about two in the morning, one of the men, being awake, noticed that he seemed very pleased with himself. By the way, you knew, of course, that he kept his head shaved, didn't you?' He looked towards Bruce, and Bruce nodded at him, saying, 'Yes. Yes. Almost bald.'

'He was very touchy about it when he first came aboard and resented being called Baldy. That was the start of his bashing period, I think. Anyway, two days before we left port he was out again late at night; in fact, it was about four in the morning when he returned. He was carrying this small steel box; and early the next morning he came to the Captain here, didn't he, Captain? in this very cabin. I was here at the time, as was the Second Mate. We were doing much as we are doing now – going over our course – and he asked if the Captain would keep the box in his safe and if he could tell him how to get a sum of money forwarded to Newcastle. The Captain suggested that since they were preparing for a home run, it would be quicker to take it with him. At first, he didn't seem to take to this idea, but I pointed out to him that with the kind of banking arrangements to be found in the islands, it might be a long time before he saw his money. At the time I did not add "if ever". Consequently the Captain persuaded him to leave the money with the box. Your brother then left the cabin and returned with the steel box in which he said he had placed money and property. And being of a deceitful mind himself, and believing that everyone else was of the same nature, he had sealed the box with red wax in a number of places, with the key hanging from a piece of string attached to it.'

The Captain himself now took over the story: 'I detected a great bitterness in your brother,' he said. 'From when he first came aboard it was as if he was fighting something or someone, and on the day he brought the box and I asked him what he intended to do with the money when he got back home, he said, "I've got what you would call a mission to perform, Captain. Oh yes, I've got what you would call a mission to perform." Now, I have repeated the words as he said them. And he went on, "If you've got money you can bring things about." I recall there seemed to be an implied threat in the words; I felt he had it in for someone and he was going to make them pay. Am I right?'

'Yes, sir. Yes, you are right."

'Well,' the Captain now turned to his officer and said, 'Carry on and give Mr Shaleman the rest. There's not much more to tell.'

So the First Officer took up the tale again, saying, 'We didn't know till later that after coming aboard with his spoils that night he was sick, and two or three times more before we sailed, and that during that time he never left the boat. We were two days out when he went down with a fever. We haven't a doctor on board, but our Second Mate is very knowledgeable with herbs and such, and he has books on different diseases. From these he could find nothing, but his own opinion was that the man had been poisoned. And poisoning wasn't anything new in the islands. To confirm this he found a mark like a puncture on your brother's body. Death comes in many strange ways in the islands, and here was a sailor who was winning too much money and they couldn't prove he was cheating. It is now evident, of course, that he must have been in a position to play for high stakes to win whatever was in the box. Or else, as has happened to many a man, he would have found himself trussed up and thrown into a stinking hole to die there slowly. It has been known in those parts. Anyway, his ills were short for within five days of his acquiring the fortune we buried him at sea.'

There was a pause during which Bruce thought, Dear God! What a way to go! But then, if he hadn't been poisoned when he was, he could have seen to it that Max and Jinnie were taken care of, as he had promised. He wouldn't have needed to go further than Newcastle Quay to find somebody to do his dirty work, especially if it promised to pay well.

'Now, the box,' the Captain was saying. 'I was of two minds what to do with it: either hand it over to the shipping company or to the police. But then I thought of the solicitors Walters, Claire and Fowler. I knew them as being very good at straightening out sticky matters.

'Well, now you know them. And they have been fortunate in tracing you, because your brother left his correct address when he signed on. And this doesn't always happen, you know, when a man doesn't want to leave a half-pay note to some lady. And Mr Claire told me it didn't take much investigation after that to discover that your parents had both died whilst your brother was at sea, and that you were the only known relative.

'Now the time's getting on. Have you to go back to see Mr Claire?'

'Yes, at three o'clock. But about the meal . . .'

'Well, perhaps we just have time to push in a bite.'

It was exactly three o'clock when Bruce was shown into the solicitors' office accompanied by the Captain and the First Officer, and what struck him immediately was that Mr Fowler was still seated in the same place, and still writing. It was as if he had never moved.

After some pleasantries were exchanged between the Captain and Mr Claire the box was brought from the safe and placed on the desk. It was small, not more than six by five inches and apparently made of steel.

Bruce uttered no word until the box was opened and the four pieces of jewellery displayed on the desk, and then all he could say was, 'Oh my!'

And Mr Claire repeated the words, then he added, 'Their brilliance is startling, isn't it? They must have been intended for a lady with a very delicate hand, because the rings aren't all that large, nor is the bangle.'

At that moment there was a tap on the door, then it opened and the clerk announced, 'Mr Stoneford.'

'Ah! Good-day to you, Mr Claire,' cried the newcomer.

'And good-day to you, Mr Stoneford. We have the display all ready for you.'

313

The visitor said nothing, but nodded to the Captain and the First Officer, then with a smile on his face, he turned towards Mr Fowler, saying jovially, 'That law book not finished yet? My! my!' and at this Mr Fowler raised his head and said, 'Never will be if I'm interrupted with such trite remarks.'

'Never changes, does he, Mr Claire?' His hand went out to the jewellery and he said, 'What have we here? My! my! Two rings, a bangle and a necklace all to match. Why, if they're as good as they appear to be, somebody is going to be warm for the rest of his days. Now who, may I ask, is that?'

It was the Captain who now put in quickly, 'Mr Shaleman here,' indicating Bruce, 'is the heir to these articles. They were left by his brother.'

'Oh. His brother? Was his brother a sailor?'

'Yes. Yes, he was a sailor.'

'Well, well! That speaks for itself. And you want me to look them over?'

'Yes, of course, man. And not so much palaver.' Mr Claire's voice was terse.

Mr Stoneford now took from his pocket a jeweller's glass; and the first piece he took up was a ring.

There was silence in the room as they watched him examine one piece after another. Even Mr Fowler's eyes were on him as they waited for his verdict, and when it came there was a concerted gasp as, looking at Bruce, he exclaimed his opinion in one word: 'Fakes.'

At first Bruce didn't take this in; well, not as quickly as both Mr Claire and Mr Fowler; and it was Mr Fowler who said, 'Never! Never! Stoneford. They're set in gold. Don't tell me otherwise; I know gold.'

Now Mr Stoneford's whole manner changed, and his voice had an angry note to it as he barked at Mr Fowler, 'I am telling you, and I'm not charging for telling you, either. Take them to someone else: Gibson or Rowe. They'll give you a fair answer. But if they say the same as me, then I think it would be only fair of you to bring the deal back to me. Of course, you could ask them what they would offer. I wouldn't mind that. They'll likely offer you only the price of the gold settings, which really are beautiful in themselves. But I think they might still command a good price as they are, because the glass has been expertly cut. I'd like to bet that whoever owned them thought they were genuine enough. But at some time or other the stones have been replaced: glass, however well cut, would not originally have been put into settings like these.'

He now thrust the bangle towards Mr Fowler, saying, 'You think you know a bit about jewellery, don't you? You always have done. But what you recognised in this lot was the old settings.'

The man's voice changed as, turning to Bruce, he said almost sadly, 'I'm sorry. I wish it could have been otherwise. But at the end of the day you still won't be out of pocket.'

'Well, what you never had, sir, you never miss,' Bruce said.

The man smiled back at him and said, 'Well, that's the way to look at it. Whatever you get for the pieces will depend on whether or not you are short of cash at the moment. Imitations sold in a group like this could fetch . . . well, a hundred and twenty-five to a hundred and thirty pounds.'

'Oh my God!' burst out Mr Fowler.

'You choking, Mister Fowler?'

'Yes, I'm choking, Stoneford. You giving a lie to your profession . . . a hundred and twenty-five to a hundred and thirty pounds indeed! I suggest that, having given us your evaluation, you leave the matter in abeyance for a time, and we will come back to you.' He now addressed his partner: 'Yes?' and, as if he were but a junior clerk, Mr Claire repeated, 'Yes, Mr Fowler . . . Yes.'

Mr Stoneford's anger was concealed by a tight smile and the thin tone of his voice as, looking from one to the other of the partners, he said, 'I am quite used to your courteous manner in our dealings, and also matters being left in abeyance, only for you to call in the old firm again, and so I shall await your pleasure, gentlemen.' And he now turned towards Bruce and, the smile still on his face, he said, 'Goodbye for the present . . . I almost said "sailor", but that was your brother, wasn't it? I am sure we shall be meeting again shortly,' and on this and ignoring both the Captain and his First Officer, he walked smartly from the room, leaving an uneasy silence, which was eventually broken by the Captain who, replacing his cap and straightening his jacket, said in a brisk tone, 'Well, I think our part in this business is over, don't you, Mr Claire?'

After clearing his throat, the solicitor said, 'Ah, yes. And I thank you. I am sure Mr Shaleman is very obliged too.'

'I am indeed. I am indeed,' Bruce put in hastily, and he held out his hand to one after the other of the men, and with no further ado they left the room.

For a moment, Bruce stood staring at the door; then quickly turning to Mr Claire, he said, 'Could I have fifty pounds, please?'

'Fifty!' exclaimed Mr Claire, and he too glanced towards the door before adding, 'You wish to compensate them with fifty?'

Before Bruce could answer, Mr Fowler, head up now, said, 'Yes, fifty, Mr Claire. I think they've earned it. Mr Shaleman, I would say, is lucky that his brother was on that particular boat, and not on some that we know.'

Bruce almost grabbed the wash-leather bag Mr Claire had taken from the bottom of the box saying, 'You'll find fifty in there,' and without even thanking the solicitors, was out of the door and into the street, just in time to see the two nautical figures disappearing around the corner.

After sprinting down the street and calling the Captain's name, he brought them to a halt. Pushing the bag into the Captain's hand, he gasped, 'Fifty pounds there! Share it, please.'

Both the Captain and his First Officer, smiling now, said in unison, 'That is indeed kind of you.'

'No; it isn't, not at all. I'm no fool, because I realise that in another ship and under similar conditions, I would never have seen a penny of this money.'

It was the First Officer who answered, 'Well, I must admit, you're right there: if the Captain had not been a God-fearing man, it would have been split long before now.'

Again they were shaking hands . . .

Back in the solicitor's office, Bruce found Mr Claire dressed for the street. The solicitor said briskly, 'Well, let us go to the bank, Mr Shaleman, with the money. The trinkets will remain in safe keeping here, if you are agreeable.'

'Yes; yes, Mr Claire. I leave things entirely in your hands.'

The lamp was lit, the fire at the far end of the room burned brightly. Bruce was sitting in the armchair to one side of it and Max and Jinnie on the couch at the other.

Since arriving home, he had talked more than ever he had done at any one time before. He had related to them everything he had experienced and, as in a story, he had kept news of the contents of the box to the last, when their amazement was no less than his.

Max was the first to react. Standing now, he said, 'Money good for you, Bruce, but best thing him dead.' And he put his hand out to Jinnie, and she endorsed his words by saying, 'Oh yes; yes, by far; although—' she looked hard at Bruce – 'I'm glad for you; yes, I am.'

Max's head was bobbing now in an effort to bring out something important, and what he eventually said was, 'He would have been m-m-mad when he found out he had risked his life for fakes, and he must have risked his life time and again to g-g-gather up all that money. No wonder he was p-p-poisoned. But thanks be to G-G-God he was.'

Again, in his mind, Bruce heartily agreed with this statement; then aloud, he said, 'And now for tomorrow: we're all going into the city and have a day out; all kinds of a day.' He looked from Max's smiling face to Jinnie's straight countenance as she said, 'No, thanks, Bruce, if you don't mind; I won't go. You two go on your own.'

'We're not going on our own.'

'Well, under the circumstances I can't come with you, Bruce.' She rose to her feet, and her voice rose too as she said, 'The situation has changed, hasn't it? I'll be leaving here shortly.'

'No, you won't!' Bruce too was on his feet. 'You're not going to leave here: we can't do without you. Forget all I said; I was mad. She can't go, can she, Max?'

'No. N-n-no, she not leave. You not go, Jinnie,' saying which, he pulled her down on to the couch again beside him; then holding her close for a moment, he said, 'Bygones be bygones. We be happy here, at least a little longer. Time'll tell . . . what'll happen.'

Abruptly she stood up and, nodding from one to the other saying, 'Good night,' she went hurriedly from the room, only to be followed immediately by Max.

She was washing her hands at the sink when he went up to her, saying, 'You leave, Jinnie, I not go with you. I stay with Bruce. He's a lost man. Lonely, deep-inside lonely. You and me in another place have company; he has no-one; and he's a good man, better than most.' He now wagged a finger in her face as he said, 'If he hadn't . . . been good man you would have been touched before now. You understand me?'

Yes, she understood him and all he was saying. 'Leave it for a day or so, Max, please,' she now whispered. 'Seeing that you know so much, you might as well know that it isn't only Bruce I'm trying to avoid; I must get away from . . .' Before she could go on Max's head was bobbing again as he said, 'That one will be no good for you ever . . . ever. If he weren't to be married, he would not marry you.'

Her face stretched and she wanted to bark at him, 'He would! I'm sure he would. Oh yes, I'm sure he would,' but all she could say was, 'Leave it, please. Leave it,' and she pushed him gently away, and stood, her back to him, her hands in the sink, until he had gone; then she continued to wash her hands, in her mind repeating the words, 'Oh, he would. Yes, he would.'

The next morning, Jinnie's excuse for not going into Newcastle would have sounded plausible to anyone; and so it did to Bruce: she hadn't any proper clothes in which to visit a city: her boots were cobbled, and just look at her coat and her hat. And they both examined the coat that she was holding out to them, then down at her feet, and it was Max who said, 'Right. She's right;' and Bruce, after a long moment of staring at her, said quietly, 'I just wanted you to share all I have with both of you; but as you say, you're right. I can tell you now, though,' and his voice rose, 'today is the last time you'll wear that coat, or those boots, because I'll bring back a rig-out for you. Oh, I can guess your size. I should be able to—' there was a pause before he ended, 'I've looked at you long enough.' Then abruptly he turned and went out, leaving Max to ask her softly, 'You'll be all right?'

'Oh yes, Max, yes. And there's nothing really left to do. I'll take a chair and sit outside. That'll be a change.'

'Yes, yes; or go down to the pool and paddle your feet.'

'Yes. Yes, I could do that. That's a good suggestion. Now get yourself away and' – Jinnie's voice dropped – 'enjoy yourself, and,' she added in a softer tone still, 'see that Bruce does too. I'm sorry for all that's happened.'

Then Max was bending down to her: 'You'll not think of leaving any more?' he asked her anxiously.

'No; perhaps not. Perhaps not.'

'Oh, good, good. Then we are back where we w-were, eh?'

'Nearly.'

His voice sober now, he repeated, 'Nearly;' then he too left her.

Picking up her coat from the back of a chair, Jinnie went into the scullery and hung it on the back of the door; then she returned to the kitchen to stand by the table and ask herself what she should do. It was nine o'clock in the morning. She had been up since six; she had done the necessary chores. She had finished the washing yesterday, and because of the heat the clothes had dried almost as soon as she hung them out. There was a little ironing to be done, shirts and such but she told herself she would leave that till the cool of the evening, because already the day was promising to be as hot as it had been yesterday. She could wash her hair. Yes that was an idea. She put her hands up to the coil on the back of her head where the shorter plait was twisted into the larger one. She would walk down to the pool and do it there. In spite of the heat there should still be enough water running.

She sighed now as she thought how wonderful it would be if she could wash herself all over; but that being out of the question she would give herself a wash down in the cold water from the pump.

The bathing over, she put on a clean shift and only one cotton petticoat; and then she donned her thin print dress that had been washed and ironed so many times the pattern had almost disappeared . . .

She stood in the open doorway, gazing over the open land already shimmering in the heat, and she realized that it was the first time she had been left alone since she arrived here. It was a strange feeling. She missed them. Oh yes, she missed them both, and this prompted her to ask herself what she was really going to do about leaving, only to scorn herself for being a hypocrite: she had known from the first that if she were to leave and go into service elsewhere, she would likely never see Richard again, and that thought was unbearable. She wished he had got married when it was originally planned; but the last she had heard was that he was going to Paris with his sister.

At times she wondered if he knew how she felt about him, for surely the deep pain in her own heart would be expressed in her eyes, although she always managed to smile and be bright when they met. Oh! She flung herself about. Why was she standing here . . .?

She was disappointed to find that the water in the pool had sunk much lower than she had thought, but it was still deep enough to rinse her hair in it.

First, she took off her boots and stockings and, sitting on the bank, she dangled her feet in the water, experiencing the delight of the cold water running through her toes.

Leaning back on her hands, she gazed about her. It was a wonderful day. She only wished she could feel happy, really happy.

After a while, she pulled up her feet out of the water and set about washing her hair. Lying on the bank, as she always did, she leaned over and swished her hair back and forward in the water.

Perhaps it was because the towel was over her ears, as was her hair, that she didn't hear the footsteps, but when the voice said, 'Don't move,' her body actually bounced on the grass, then her hands became still on her head, the towel dangling over her face.

'Just stay like that.' The voice now was coming from the side; then it was right in front of her and saying, 'Lift the towel from your face, Jinnie, but keep your hands there.'

Slowly, she did as the voice requested; and then she was staring directly at him.

He had a notebook in his hand and he was drawing swiftly in it. She remained still, feasting her eyes upon him. He was so good to look at. So clean-looking, and she could pick up the smell of him from this distance. Her heart began to ache again. She watched him turn a page of the notebook, then listened to him say, 'Drop your head slightly to the left side, my dear.'

Did he know he had called her 'my dear'?

She was perched in an uncomfortable position with half her wet hair dangling down the side of her face and her body was stiffening, so that she felt she was going to topple, and so she did, exclaiming, 'Oh, I'm sorry; I was getting the cramp in my side.'

'It's all right. It's all right.' And he did a few more strokes before closing the notebook and putting it in his pocket.

'I'm sorry if I disturbed you,' he said, 'but I went up to the farm. There was no-one there. I stabled the horse and I thought there was just the chance you might be here. Oh, please! don't get up. Don't get up, I'll sit down.'

As he sat down on the grass beside her, she made a frantic effort to plait her wet hair, and he remarked on this, saying, 'It's still wet. Why don't you dry it?'

Then turning to the side, he picked up the dry towel from the ground, saying, 'Here's a dry one. Look; let me do it.'

When he knelt behind her and she could feel his hands gathering up her hair, she felt faint, but the common-sense voice from deep within her said, Take a hold of yourself. It is nothing just drying your hair, 'tis nothing. But it *was* something: Mister Richard was drying her hair; and it could only happen in this isolated place. Would he have done it if either Bruce of Max were here? No; no, of course he wouldn't. Nor would they.

She remained silent; and after a while when he said, 'How's that?' she put her hand round the back and felt her hair, saying, 'I'll . . . I'll plait it now.'

'No; no, leave it loose; the sun will dry it. It's still damp.'

He was now sitting by her side and he asked, 'Why are you down here by yourself? Where are the others?'

'They've gone into Newcastle.'

'Newcastle? Bruce and Max together?'

'Yes; Bruce and Max together.' And she had enough spirit to say, 'Is there anything very strange about that?'

'Yes; yes, there is. I've never known them both be away from the farm at the same time.'

'Well, apparently things have changed. You won't know about it yet, but Bruce will tell you. Hal – you know . . . the brother – he died at sea and' – she paused; should she tell him about the money that had been put into the bank? No, no. Instead she said, 'Apparently he had some wages coming and they told Bruce to collect them, and now he's gone in to spend them.' She smiled as she added, 'Something new for Bruce, for he never has anything over to spend on himself or on anyone else.'

'No. No, I know that. And he won't take presents. But oh, I'm so glad he's had a windfall. I bet he'll bring something back for you.' He was smiling broadly at her, his face not a foot away.

She managed to smile back at him and say, 'I shouldn't be a bit surprised; he's very kind, is Bruce.'

'Yes; yes, he's very kind.' He turned from her now and, drawing his knees up, he put his arms about them and joined his hands together.

She looked at the hands: they were long and slender and beautifully shaped. His trouser legs were hitched up, showing his socks above the tops of his highly polished brown boots. The tops of his socks, which appeared to be made of silk, fell into folds.

She was startled when he said, 'Are you looking at my big feet and comparing them with your dainty ones?'

For a moment she wanted to draw her feet up under her dress: dainty feet that had known only the roughest of stockings, clogs and old boots during their existence. Suddenly he was by her side, his knees touching hers as he said, 'Have you been paddling?'

'Yes. Well, dangling my feet in.'

'Then that's what I'll do too, we'll dangle our feet together,' and before she could protest, he had unloosened the laces, pulled off his boots and then his socks and exposed his very white feet. Then taking her hand, he made as though to pull her to her feet, but when she resisted he said, 'Why not? Look; no-one can see us down here; we are as secret as if we were in fairyland among the pixies. Come on; a chance like this doesn't happen every day.'

No, it didn't happen every day, and she doubted if it would ever happen again, so she allowed herself to be pulled up, and did not resist when he took her hand and drew her towards the bank; and there he sat down. And when his feet splashed the water into spray, hers joined his, and their laughter mingled.

Later, she could not recall how long they sat splashing their feet like two children; she only knew that when they moved away from the pool, he insisted on drying her feet; and during the process they fell into a silence until, as she went to put on her stockings, he said, 'No; leave them be. And let's move into the shade over there; the sun is getting very hot here.' He gathered up his boots and socks and she carried her boots and stockings and the towels, and together they walked into the deep shadow of the copse.

There it was cool and, looking round at the foliage, he said, 'Isn't it beautiful? It's like Arcadia,' and putting out his hand, he now gently stroked her cheek, saying, 'You don't know anything about Arcadia, do you, Jinnie?' and she answered, 'No; it's a new word to me.'

'And you like words. Max says you're always learning new words. What do you get from them, Jinnie?'

She looked down through the cool green light to where their feet were close together and still, and quietly she said, 'The difference in people.'

He stared at her for a moment, the expression on his face puzzled; and then he said, 'Yes. Yes, words make out the difference in people and separate the classes. Is that what you mean?'

She wasn't quite sure about the bit of separating classes, she only knew that how people spoke pointed to how they lived; and yes, she supposed that did put them into different classes.

She did not resist him when he caught hold of her hand and drew himself closer, while murmuring, 'I doubt if we'll ever sit like this again, Jinnie.'

She was gazing into his eyes and he into hers.

'It's only once in a lifetime one touches on wonder and the spell of love. You understand what I mean, Jinnie?'

Yes. Yes, she understood what he meant, but for the life of her she couldn't give him an answer.

'I am to be married very shortly, you know that?'

Still she couldn't answer, but she made the slightest movement with her head and he went on, 'I've been torn asunder lately with my feelings: I . . . I know I must be married, for everyone's sake, yet I can't get you out of my mind. I've . . . I've always had a feeling for you, Jinnie; but recently this has grown and at times has become unbearable when I've seen you and couldn't touch you, couldn't be near you. I had to joke with your two guardians, when all the time I just wanted to talk to you.'

'If you weren't promised in marriage and bound to marry, would you have married me?'

He was so taken aback by the cool question that he dropped her hand for a moment and, sitting back on his knees, stared at her for some seconds before, mumbling, he said, 'Why . . . why, of course, Jinnie. Yes, yes.' Then with more emphasis, 'Yes, of course I would.'

She refused to question the icy dart that pierced her chest during that second of hesitation, his hooded gaze, and then his mumbling . . . he who spoke so perfectly.

But in a low and tender voice, she said, 'That's all I wanted to know, because I've always loved you, Richard. Since the very first moment I saw you I think I've loved you. Yet I've known in my heart it was just like a fairytale, just like this.' But then spreading out her hand, she added quickly, 'No, not like this because this *is* real; my dreams weren't, and I knew that they never could be. I . . . I know you must marry. I've always known it, and I've accepted it, but I just wondered if you hadn't been bound to anyone would you have stooped to me.'

'*Stooped* to you!' He was now gripping both her hands and pulling her close. 'Jinnie. Jinnie, never say that about yourself. No-one . . . no-one would ever need to stoop to you, you're so beautiful, so attractive in all ways: those dreadful clothes, your ugly boots, all these rough things that you've always worn every time I've seen you, couldn't hide your beauty, or cover your appeal, and wherever I am, whomsoever I'm with, your appeal will stay with me.'

Her hands went up to his face now and cupped it, and her lips trembled as she said, 'That's all I wanted to hear.'

When he drew in a long shuddering breath and put his arms around her she allowed her body to fall against his. Then they were lying on their sides.

When their faces were almost touching she felt him stiffen, and when he said, 'I . . . I should go. I must go,' she kept her arms about him and murmured, 'I want something of you to remember, and once you're married you . . . you must never come up here again, for my sake, even if it means breaking your friendship with Bruce. Yes, it would be better all round if you did that.'

'Oh, my dear; you're so wise; yet you're not even seventeen. You've always been much older than your

327

years. Oh, if only things could be different. Oh, Jinnie. Jinnie. Jinnie.'

When his lips fell on hers, they did not make her feel ecstatically happy, but rather she experienced a feeling of satisfaction, as if something she had waited for and dreamed of had at last come to pass . . .

The sun was spangling the shadows when at last he drew her up from the ground and they held each other, swaying as if slightly intoxicated, as no doubt they both were. Her hair had fallen in a tangled mass on one of his shoulders, her face was rosy, her eyes bright. She brought her head forward and kissed him on the lips and said, 'Till my very dying day I'll remember this morning.'

'As will I, my dear, my dear, dear one. Oh' – he was clasping her to him again – 'you're so lovely and so understanding. That is it, so understanding about this whole tangled matter. I don't think there's another young woman in the world of any class who would see things as you see them.'

There was that stab again to mar the wonder of the past ecstasy . . . a mention of class. It was because of class that this would perhaps be the only time in their lives they would come together.

As his hand stroked her neck yet again she said, 'I . . . I must go, really I must. I have chores to see to' – she had stressed the word chores – 'and I'm not sure what time they'll be back.'

'Oh yes; they . . . they—' He relinquished his hold on her and, sitting down again on the grass, he quickly pulled on his socks and boots; then turning from her, he straightened his clothes, dusting down his waistcoat, then his coat and trousers. She too had donned her stockings and boots, and when slowly she walked from the copse and into the harsh sunlight he drew her back into the shade, saying, 'Don't come with me; I want to remember you here; always to remember you here.'

He leant forward and once again they embraced, and now she said, 'Goodbye, Richard;' and after a moment's pause, he said, 'Goodbye, Jinnie, my dear, dear beloved Jinnie. Goodbye.' Then he turned from her and hurried towards the narrow road that led to the farm.

She stood watching him until he was out of sight; then she returned to the copse and lay down on the ground where they had lain together and where she had given herself wholeheartedly to him; no reticence, no shyness until now, as she recalled what had taken place and wondered if she really was just sixteen. Did all girls feel as she did at this age? How were you supposed to feel at sixteen? Surely not as she was feeling now: like someone full of knowledge, strange knowledge, for she had to ask herself, how had she known how to make love with a man?

3

With the high winds and cold driving rains, summer seemed but a memory.

Bruce had brought up an extra ton of coal and also a load of wood so that the two fires could be kept on day and night. He found pleasure in being able to buy extra comforts for the house, almost as much, in fact, as when he bought odd things for Jinnie. But he still retained the vivid memory of the disappointment he had experienced the evening he and Max had returned from Newcastle, parcel-ladened.

He had stood by the table urging Jinnie to unwrap the packages, only to be dumbfounded, first by her hesitation, then by her lack of any appreciation as she unveiled the contents of one parcel after another. And when, finally she lifted up a pair of soft, black-leather shoes, and a cry escaped her, he and Max stood in blank amazement as they watched her fling the shoes along the table, and after them the lovely pink-velvet dress and the green-milton cloth coat with matching felt hat, and all the other bits and pieces of fancy aprons, cotton dresses, and such, before flinging herself round to drop into a chair; and the cries that escaped from her were like those from an animal.

Bruce had taken her by the shoulders and shaken her, crying, 'Stop it! girl. Stop it! What's come over you?' But when the sounds became even louder and more unearthly, Max pushed him roughly aside and his large hand with no light slap went across her face, sending her head wagging, causing Bruce to protest, 'My God! man. No; don't do that; you'll break her neck.'

'Only way, hyst-hysterical.'

And apparently it was the only way, for her voice stopped its high wailing and dropped into sobbing. She then lay back gasping for air, and when Bruce stood looking down at her, shaking his head and saying, 'Well, that's the last time we'll surprise her like this,' Max said, 'Under-understandable: never had decent rags in her life.'

'Yes; yes, that's it,' Bruce agreed, 'yes, I suppose you are right.'

'We should have thought of that.'

He recalled that she had stayed in bed the following day, lying like someone sick; and in a way she had behaved like someone sick ever since.

Later, she had thanked Bruce for the beautiful clothes and for his kindness to her; but apparently they brought her no real joy, for there remained that same sadness in her, and he was pained by the knowledge that he knew what was causing it.

And now the day had arrived. It was pouring from the heavens and there was a wedding in Hexham Abbey, and her pain was at its height.

Neither Max nor Bruce had mentioned the wedding, nor had they questioned the fact that for months now Richard hadn't put in an appearance at the farm; but then it was known he had again been to France and had returned only a week or so ago. It would seem that all the preparations for the wedding had been left to his family, although Lillian's mother had surprisingly got over her bereavement malaise and was once more visiting, so Mrs Stevens had informed Bruce.

She was a little busybody, was Mrs Stevens, but then busybodies had their uses, for he would have known very little about the goings-on in the villages and thereabouts if it wasn't for her, because on market days he would journey either to Allendale or Hexham simply to sell his goods, returning as quickly as possible. He had never yet accepted an invitation to go and spend some of his hard-earned money in any of the bars.

He wondered if Jinnie knew what was to happen this day. Very likely she did, because she took Mrs Stevens her eggs, and Mrs Stevens would keep her there for long periods because she liked her visitor, who was such a good listener.

Of course, Bruce had been quizzed about his windfall: poor Hal to go like that and to be buried at sea; but then one man's misfortune was another's good luck. It was understood he had picked up Hal's full-pay note, as he hadn't left the half-pay to anyone. He was a mean fellow, was Hal, except when paying for his bodily needs.

But Bruce was another mean one, wasn't he? He had never been known to stand anybody a pint, not even himself, and market days were a thirsty business.

So the gossip had gone on, and today its main subject would undoubtedly be the wedding, for anyone who was anyone in the county would be there.

For the last four nights, after going up to her pallet bed under the roof, Jinnie had sat for an hour on end rocking herself. Her periods had always been regular, so after missing a period, she knew what had happened. She had managed to hide her morning sickness from both men, but the period of hiding would soon be over, for the result of that glorious moment was already in evidence, and there was a fear on her, not about having a child, but about the reactions of both Bruce and Max towards

Richard. When Hal had hurt her, Max's reaction had stopped short of killing him, but she dreaded to think what he, and Bruce too, might do to Richard. There was a new pain inside her when she thought of Bruce. He had been so kind; he was still kind. Each day he seemed to be more thoughtful of her. He never went into Hexham but he brought her back some little item that would add to her pleasure in the house, for he knew that now she was taking a pride in it. But what she feared most from him was his scorn.

She knew through Mrs Stevens that today was the great day; and not before time, she had said, for one obstacle or another had delayed that marriage. Of course, Mrs Stevens had put in slyly, it seemed strange that Bruce had not received an invitation, even if it was only to the Abbey, because they had been such pals, hadn't they? Very strange pals, too, because it wasn't often two different classes met as they had.

Sometimes, Jinnie wondered if she really liked Mrs Stevens.

She heard the scullery door being opened; then the clatter of big boots told her that Max was entering the kitchen. He had to push the door open with his back for his arms were full of logs, and as he passed her on his way to the fire at the far end of the room he said, 'It's s-set in again. Did you ever see such weather? I hope Bruce didn't go very f-far up there the day; but likely he did because of the f-foot rot. It's only affected two, but it can spread. That smells nice,' he added.

'It's just hot pot and dumplings.'

'D-do me,' he said, moving towards the table, where he watched her mixing some flour and fruit in a bowl, and he asked, 'What's th-that for?'

'A plum-duff.'

'Oh, plum-duff. I love plum-duff. Plenty of currants in it, though.'

'Well, there's plenty of currants in this one,' she said, smiling at him across the table; then she added, 'There's a cup of tea if you'd like it.'

'When d-did I refuse tea, eh?'

She poured him out a mug of tea, and he pulled a chair out from under the table and sat down. As he sipped it he watched as she placed the pudding into a cloth and tied the ends, and quietly he said, 'Don't be sad, Jinnie.'

She blinked her eyes rapidly, pressed her lips together tightly and slowly shook her head before she said, 'What makes you think I'm sad?'

'Well, I know you, don't I? I know you better than you know yourself. Know lots of you . . . about you.'

When she lowered her head and he saw her hands grip the edge of the table, he rose quickly to his feet and went round to her side, murmuring, 'Oh, me dear. Me dear. Don't cry. I know 'tis a special day for some and a heartbreak d-d-day for others. I know, but l-l-look at me.' He thrust a hand under her chin and brought her swimming eyes on to his face as he said, 'One day you'll be happy, very happy. I know. You still a girl, full of f-f-fancy.'

'No, Max,' she interrupted him; but he put in quickly, 'Y-y-yes, Max; and Max is telling you you've g-g-got to grow yet, both in your body and your mind. We live and learn. I learn y-y-years ago over Miss Caplin.'

'Miss Caplin?' Her eyelids blinked now. 'Why Miss Caplin?'

'Huh!' He tossed his large head to the side and again he emitted, 'Huh! You think I not capable of falling in l-l-love?'

She wanted to laugh: Max and Miss Caplin? Miss Caplin must be nearly twenty years older than Max.

'When I young boy, all limbs' – he now jerked his arms and legs – 'g-gangly they call it, she was good to me. And she was beautiful. M-m-my love for her was hopeless. She could have been my m-m-mother, but she was pretty and kind and I l-l-loved her. I still do, although in a different way. I said before, you know, Jinnie, there be all kinds of love. I l-l-love you. Oh yes, I l-l-love you, but in a different way from that which I l-l-love Miss Caplin.'

Slowly now she dusted her hands one against the other over the pastry board; then turning to him, she put her arms around his neck, and she kissed him on the cheek, saying softly, 'And I love you too. You have been my father, as Bruce is my brother.'

'Ho, ho! Oh, yes; I be your father. Could be your father, yes, yes; but Bruce no brother. Oh no, Bruce no brother. Get into your head' – he now stabbed his finger against her brow – 'Bruce is a man, and a good man, but he is n-n-not your brother.' He turned sharply from her, saying, 'There he is now,' and made quickly for the door into the scullery room, while she took up the pudding from the table and dropped it into the pan of water boiling on the hob, before pulling it aside to make room for the kettle; and she was brewing a fresh cup of tea when Bruce entered the kitchen.

His face was red, as were his hands, which he chaffed together as he said, 'I don't know when it's going to stop; it thinks it's winter.'

'You're cold.'

'Frozen. I don't think I have any skin left on my face.' He rubbed his cheeks, and when he saw her mashing the tea he said, 'Oh, I'll be glad of three pints of that. Next time I go up there I'm taking a can with me. It might only be luke-warm when I get at it, but it'll be something.'

'That's an idea.'

When after a moment he said, 'How d'you feel? How have you been?' she turned sharply and looked at him and asked, 'What d'you mean? I'm the same as when you left this morning.'

'Oh, Jinnie' – he dropped his head – 'let's come into the open. You know what day it is as well as I do. Let's face it: it's over and done with, he's married. The fairy-tale's finished.'

'Oh you! Don't you start on me, please!'

'Oh.' He moved from the fire to go quickly towards her, saying, 'Oh lass; I didn't want to start on you, I just want you to feel I'm with you. I know how you feel because I know how I feel.'

Her head was bent as she muttered, 'Oh, don't. Don't talk so, not tonight, Bruce, please.'

'All right. All right. Here's your guardian angel coming back. He'll knock my block off if he thinks I've made you cry. Come on. Come on. Smile. Please try. We'll both try, eh?'

But instead of trying she said a strange thing. Looking him squarely in the face she said, 'You're too good to be true, Bruce, you know that? You're too good to be true.'

'Me? too good to be true!'

'Yes. Yes, you. Your consideration hurts me, it does really.'

At this moment the door opened and Max, ignoring what he surmised had been going on, said, 'Do you know there's p-p-plum-duff the night?'

'Plum-duff? Oh, I'm partial to plum-duff; but I'm more partial to three pints of tea first.' And at this, Jinnie poured out two large mugs of tea and handed them both to Bruce, managing to smile as she said, 'These are equal to three pints,' at which Bruce laughed.

At the beginning, she had managed to keep her sickness from the men; in any case, when it stopped after a few weeks, it had seemed it might be of short duration; but during this past month she had, at times, felt sick and not a little ill. Only this morning she had been up at five and had managed to get the bout over in the scullery.

This done, she had returned to her bed because, these days, she did not rise before six.

It should happen that Bruce slept in this morning and did not arrive in the kitchen until a quarter past six, being somewhat surprised not to find the fire glowing and the porridge on the boil.

When, a few minutes later he was joined by Max, he remarked, 'She's not up. We've all slept in, I think.'

'Oh, then l-l-let her lie. I'll s-s-see to the porridge.' And he laughed gently as he said, 'It would be f-f-funny if we took her breakfast up to bed.'

'It would that,' said Bruce. 'And she'd likely die of shock.'

But some time later, after they had both washed in the scullery and had their breakfasts, Max said somewhat anxiously, 'Do you think I'd better look in on her? She's never slept in for this long.' Bruce replied, 'I was thinking the same,' only to add in a horrified tone, 'Good God! She wouldn't have done anything silly, would she?'

Almost as one now, they were in the scullery, there to be brought to a halt by the sight of her at the head of the steps, from where she muttered down to them, 'I'm sorry. I slept in.'

Neither gave her an answer; they were staring at her clothes: she was wearing a blouse with the bodice tucked into her skirt, and it was on her waistline that their eyes were concentrated.

Up till then her body had appeared to them to be as flat as a pancake; but here now, beneath the tight waistline, was an evident bulge. It was there one minute

337

and gone the next, for she had flung her strapped apron over her head and was rapidly fastening it at the back.

She had completed the process before she came down the steps and, without looking at them, had walked past them and into the kitchen.

Neither of them had moved, but their gaze was linked by a knowledge that they didn't want to believe, made evident by Max grabbing his coat from the back of the scullery door and rushing out of the far door and into the morning, leaving Bruce standing there looking stunned.

Then, as if he too were in a great hurry, he dashed into the kitchen, snatched his coat and hat from the back of the door and went out that way as if he were not aware of her presence.

When Jinnie heard him calling the dog, she dropped into a chair and wondered how long it would be before the avalanche hit her . . .

The weather had changed again. Although it was still very cold, it was a calm autumn morning. The sky was a clear blue, with no tufted white clouds spun across it; the grass had stopped its urgent upward striving; it was as if its growth had slowed down to meet the stillness; and the only noise from the pigsty was the slop of the food in the trough.

Bruce had intended to make straight for the hills, where he might find comfort to ease the turmoil raging in him. But he realised that he must first talk this thing out with Max.

Max was seated on a stool in the cowshed, his head leaning against the side of the cow, his large hands gently directing the jets of milk into a pail. Only when he was aware that Bruce was standing beside him did he turn his head, but he did not speak; instead, he continued to relieve the cow until he had emptied its udder. Then with a damp cloth he wiped the udders, before rising and, moving the stool with the toe of his boot to one side, he picked up the pail. As he passed Bruce he said, 'Come into the dairy.'

A few minutes later they were facing each other, and it was Max who asked the first question with a single word, 'Well?'

'I can't believe it. I won't believe it; but it's—' Bruce swallowed and gulped before ending, 'it's been staring us in the face for weeks now, her being off colour.'

'Yes, it's been staring us in the f-f-face.'

Bruce now turned and beat a doubled fist against the wall and ground out, 'If he was here I would kill him. I would. I would.'

'Best he's not here, else I would have k-killed him first. But then, thinking back, he's not all to blame.'

'What do you mean, he's not to blame?'

'Well, n-n-not fully. She was ripe; she was ready.'

Bruce's tone was high now as he exclaimed, 'It must have been just before he married. We are in October. He was going to be married, and he takes her. He'd managed to hold out so long, why not a little longer?'

'Well, maybe, b-b-but she's older than her years. She's been with animals for long time, so she knew.'

'How can you say that, Max, when you care for her so much?'

'I can say it, Bruce, because I know her. From seven years old I know her. And she's warm inside, wants to give.'

'Wants to give, be damned. Yet, my God! I could go in there now and punch her silly.' And he flung about again and punched the wall, spitting out the words: 'In the main, as you know, Max, life is dirty, mucky, rotten, but here and there you find something shining on the muck heap, something that somebody's thrown

339

away. That's how I used to see her, somebody who had been thrown away. But I saw her as a shining piece of purity, outspoken, wouldn't be handled.' Suddenly he snatched off his cap and flung it down the narrow room saying, 'Wouldn't be handled! She hated being handled! Look at the night when she first came here and she went for my father; look what happened with Hal because she was handled: you were on the point of murdering Hal for what he had done. No; no, she wouldn't be handled; she would fight anyone who dared to handle her in that way; but she won't have left any mark on him for handling her, I bet!'

Of a sudden, it was as if all the fight, all the blood had drained from him. He leaned back against the stone wall, and so white and limp did he appear that Max went to him quickly and, putting an arm around his shoulder, drew him from the wall and thrust him on to the stool. Then he took a scoopful of milk from the basin standing on the shelf and said to Bruce, 'Drink that. I know how you f-f-feel. I'm s-s-sick to the heart of me at this minute.'

Bruce sat staring ahead of him for some time before he said, 'What are we going to do?'

'Think it will be better to l-l-leave first move to her. It won't be long. I feel she's back there waiting for us. But l-l-look at it this way: she's going to have a child and it will be born here . . . I hope.'

'Maybe, Max. Oh, just maybe. It's just come to mind who'll be given the name of fathering her fly-blow; who else but me? She won't give him away. Now have you thought about that? Be damned if I'm going to take it.'

'Yes, I have. Everybody will c-c-come to it that it's you.'

Max leant his back against the marble slab, folded his arms and stared up to the bare roof that showed the underside of the tiles, and as if he were asking for an answer from them he said, 'Well, who else c-c-could be named? There's only young Roy.' He now looked down at Bruce, adding, 'And you can 'magine what Mrs Stevens w-w-would say to that.' Then shaking his head, he added as an afterthought, ''Tis great pity it wasn't Roy, because Mrs Stevens w-w-would have had them into church before they knew wh-wh-what had kicked them.'

'You know what?' Bruce had got to his feet. 'I've been a bloody fool: I could have put her in the family way time and again, the way I was feeling, but this "brother" business of hers put a check on me more than ten parents could have done, for she would have looked upon it as what they call incest; and that, let me tell you, if you're not already aware of it, goes on all around us all the time. The church covers up a multitude of sins, and when one hears of men like Isaac Tuftacre going round with the plate on Sunday, well, I could vomit: he lives with his sister up on the top, but they've got a lodger as a cover. But it's public knowledge. So, Max' – his voice dropped a tone now – 'you can see how I react to the "brother" bit, can't you? I can understand her looking upon you as a father, but me as a brother . . . well, truth to tell, that annoyed me from the first time she mentioned it, 'cos if there was ever a barrier needed to be erected between us she did it with that word "brother".' Now his voice rose again: 'It's kept her safe, safe from me. I can tell you that. Father of her child indeed!' The last words were full of bitterness. 'If anybody should be father of her child it should be me, 'cos before you came, Max, I looked after her. Before her head became full of him, time and again I could have taken her.'

'You didn't, Bruce, and I very much doubt if you would have, she was too y-young in all ways.'

341

'Yes, yes. Well, she's learnt since, hasn't she? What are we going to do?' There was a note of appeal in the words, and Max said, 'As I s-s-said, l-leave it, let her come into the open, let her be f-f-first to speak of it.'

They had to wait till suppertime. After placing a bowl of stew in front of each of them, she stood gripping the back of a chair and, looking from one to the other, she burst out, 'All right! So you know: I'm going to have a bairn. And before you say anything else' – her voice had risen now – 'I'm not sorry. D'you hear?' She stared from one to the other, holding their gaze, and she repeated, 'I'm not sorry. I wanted something of him, and I got it. Don't blame him: I want this child and I'm going to have it; whether it's here or in the workhouse, I'm having it. The young girls in the workhouse who came in like this would take doses of white mixture every day, line up for it, so as to skite the child out of them. Well, I don't want to skite it out of me, and I'm not taking any medicine or any advice on what to do; I'm having a child, and it's up to you' – she was addressing Bruce pointedly – 'whether I stay here or not.'

Both men were slightly astounded, not only by her manner but at the words she used, such as 'skiting the child out of her'; these were common words used by the lowest of the low. She would have heard them often enough in the workhouse, but she had been out of the workhouse for some time now. She had left when she was fourteen, and she was now sixteen, and although she hadn't listened to any fine talk, there had been no coarse language to hurt her ears; perhaps a plain 'damn', or 'bloody' at times, but to stand there yelling at them about skiting the child out of her! If anything had taken the wind out of their sails, that had.

342

Bruce was for walking out. He pushed back his chair, half rose, but then resumed his seat and said, 'There'll be questions asked as to who is the father of your child. Do you intend to name him?'

For a moment she was stumped: she wetted her lips, her eyelids blinked, then she said, 'No, I don't. And if anyone did name him I would deny it.'

'Then, who, may I ask, is going to have the honour of being its father?'

She stared at him, then at Max, whose eyes were hard on her; then she turned back to Bruce and said, 'They'll likely name you, but I'll deny that an' all.'

'Then that only leaves Max here.' Bruce stretched out a palm towards Max, and at this she cried vehemently, 'Don't be nasty, you! Don't be nasty!'

'Don't be nasty, you say, don't be nasty, when I'm getting the honour of giving you a bairn, because there's nobody up here in line for your suitor, is there? Are you going to try to hang it on Roy?'

Her face hardened now, and her voice too, as she said, 'Don't try to be funny. I have never given Roy any encouragement, ever . . . ever!'

'Well, that comes back to me then, doesn't it?' Bruce was yelling at her now. 'And let me tell you, miss, that I'm not going to take that honour. I haven't earned it, have I? So if anybody asks me who the father is I'll tell them to go down to the house and ask for Mr Richard Baxton-Powell.'

They both watched as her body jerked now and, leaning for support against the chair, she muttered, 'You wouldn't do that?'

'Oh, but yes, I would, because, don't forget, long before he became your suitor he was *my* friend. He sought my friendship, not I his, and what does he do? He knows well how I feel about you but he still takes you

343

like any of the other cheap cows he's been acquainted with. And that's what you've made yourself into: a cheap cow. He would never have married you. What I mean to do, Miss Howlett, is exactly what I've already said; you once name me, or let my name be mentioned without contradiction, and I go down to that house and blow the roof off it with my news that their son will soon be a father and have a bastard son or daughter!'

She was still gripping the chair, but her body was rocking slightly as she said, 'You do that, you do that and I walk out of here and I go back into the workhouse. Oh, gladly; yes, I go back into the workhouse.' And at that she turned from them both and went into the scullery.

During all this Max had not said one word, but had sat there with his head bent.

4

'I tell you she's pregnant, three months gone, if a day; in fact, she brazenly owned up to it. I couldn't help but keep my eyes on the right button of that old coat she wears. It was just a slight bulge, but I kept saying to myself, no; no; no; and she saw where my eyes were. And then as brazen as brass, and as cool as a cucumber she said, "Yes, Mrs Stevens, I'm going to have a baby." Just like that. You could have knocked me down with a feather, I could have fallen to the floor; well, to tell you the truth I flopped on that chair. There she stood, that young piece, and butter wouldn't have melted in her mouth before, would it?'

'Eeh! my!' The farmer pushed his cap further back on his head. 'Can't believe it. Yet at the same time' – his tone changed – 'what d'you expect? She's been up there with Bruce all this time, and she's no girl; she's got a woman's figure on her, and she's only . . . what is she, sixteen? Well, anyway she was ready for it, I would say, and he's kept his hands at bay all this time. I've wondered about it, mind, I have; I've wondered about it because he seemed to care for her.'

''Tisn't him.'

'What d'you say, woman?'

'I said, 'tisn't him; at least, that's what she says, and so emphatically that I can't help but believe her. I said to her, "When's Bruce and you going to be married?" and in that quiet, sort of different voice of hers, she

345

said, "I'm not going to be married, Mrs Stevens; and Bruce isn't the father."'

'Holy cows' udders! She said that?' The farmer's voice was high. 'Then who is it? 'Tisn't the big fellow. Oh no; he acts as her father. And he's a good bloke, that. Who then? . . . No . . . oh no!' He put out his hand to her as if in protest, 'Our Roy?'

She almost sprang from her chair and with a doubled fist she pushed him in the chest, saying, 'Don't talk so bloody soft! Our Roy . . . when would he . . . I mean . . . well, she wouldn't go to the barn-dance with him, she wouldn't go out with him, and he isn't the kind of fellow to force himself on a lass, now is he? Fancy! you saying that!'

'Well, woman' – he looked down at his wife – 'tell me who else there is in this neighbourhood that goes up there. There's only Mister Richard, and she would as soon be taken down by him as by God.'

Mrs Stevens again sat down on the chair, her elbows on the table, her cheek resting on her knuckles, and looking at her husband, she said, 'I don't care what she says, it must be Bruce; it's got to be.'

'Aye. Aye, I think with you, it has got to be; but the question is, why is she denying it?'

They both turned and looked towards the kitchen door that led into the boot-room. After a slight clatter the door opened and their son appeared.

'Dad,' he said, 'Maisie is right off colour; she's almost dry. I think we'd better get Mr Abner to come up to see her.' He looked from one to the other and said, 'What's up? What's the matter?'

'We've had a shock,' Mrs Stevens said; and both she and her husband were immediately amazed when their son said, 'Aye, I suppose you would have, seeing who your visitor was.'

346

His mother was on her feet now, her two hands close joined on her ample breasts, and she muttered low in her throat, 'Oh, our Roy, you didn't . . . you haven't, have you?'

'No!' The shout Roy gave not only made her jump but also jerked the big frame of his father. 'No! I didn't; and no! I haven't, but I wish to God I had. I wish it had been me. D'you hear that, both of you? And if I'd had the chance it would've been, 'cos I've been seeking her for years . . . well, since she's grown up.'

'How did you know, lad?' His father's voice was soothing.

'Because, Dad, I put two and two together; she hasn't been down here for some weeks, has she? and I happened to glimpse her once when I went up there for the eggs. Max saw to me. She was in the house and didn't come out, at least only to the clothes' line to whip something off it; and I saw her.'

Mrs Stevens sat silently now, gazing at her son. This was the reason he had been odd of late, hardly opening his mouth. She had thought he was sickening for something; but thank God it wasn't him. Oh yes, thank God, because after all, what was she? A tinker's lass, and they are akin to gypsies. 'And she says it isn't Bruce's?'

'Yes; that's what she says.'

'Why? How d'you know, lad?'

Roy looked at his father. 'I talked to her,' he said.

'About her condition?' There was a touch of disbelief in his father's voice, and he went on, 'Did she bring it up?'

'No, Dad; I brought it up.'

They both looked at their son as if they were seeing him for the first time, but they were shocked further, absolutely shocked, when he said, 'I asked her to marry me; but she's not going to marry anybody, she said.'

'You what!' His mother's voice was a high squeak, and Roy's, when he answered her, was quite low and calm as he said, 'I asked her to marry me, Mam,' and she could hardly get the words out: 'And where do you think you would bring her, that piece?'

He looked from his mother to his father, then back to her, saying, 'Well, if you wouldn't have had us here there's plenty of jobs we could have got together. She's used to hard work and so am I: I've been well trained.' He was nodding towards his father now. 'And I wouldn't get any lower wages wherever I went, would I, Dad? because as you said, the farm is going to be mine one day and that's what I've got to work for, a meagre wage. Well, there now, you have it.'

'What's gone wrong with you?' His mother's voice had an appeal in it and it was evident she was almost on the verge of tears. 'You've changed. Yes, you have.'

'Perhaps, I have, Mam: I've grown; I'm nineteen, kicking twenty.'

His father now quietly put in a question: 'You mean to say, lad, that you would take her on? Knowing it wasn't yours, you'd marry her?'

The boy's answer was as quiet as before: 'Yes, Dad, I'd do that knowing it wasn't mine.'

'And what d'you think Bruce would have to say about that?'

'I don't know, Dad, what he'd have to say, but the only thing I know is that she swears it isn't his.'

'Well, whose is it then? Do you know?'

'No more than you at the moment;' but he could have said, Yes, Dad; I'm almost sure it's the pampered Mr Richard Baxton-Powell's, he who's never done a day's work in his life except dabble with a bit of paint, all because he's supposed to have recurrences of the fever. Recurrences of bloody laziness is how I see it. I've been

348

made bloody sick at times with your pandering to the Baxton-Powells and the Rowlands just because they're your best customers. I could almost name the day he gave it to her. You would tell me, as Mam would too, to keep me mouth shut, and you would remind me again that they're our best customers.

Roy turned slowly about and went back into the boot-room, and after seating himself on a form and pulling on his boots again, he sat with his hands dangling between his knees for a moment, the while saying to himself, Yes, I could practically name the day when I went up there and I saw his horse in the stable, and I waited and waited, but neither she nor he came back. If it's born at the end of April, that'll put the stamp on it, and there he is roving the world. Touring they call it, touring. I wonder, while he's taking his new bride, if he remembers whoring with a bit of a lass who had likely become fascinated by his looks and his grand manner . . . Lasses are like that.

When the door banged his mother and father looked at each other. They hadn't exchanged a word whilst waiting for him to leave the boot-room; and then Dilly Stevens looked at her husband while the tears ran down her face, and she said, 'I feel that we've lost him, and all through that dirty little trollop.'

Mr Stevens didn't contradict her, but he put his hand on her shoulder and patted it as he said, 'Things'll work out; they've got to. But, Dilly, listen to me: if the worst comes to the worst and she decides to change her mind and take him, they would have to come here, because I can't lose him. He's me only son and . . . and I'm rare fond of him.' There was a break in his voice now as he added, 'You liked the lass. You once said as much that you wished you had a daughter like her. Well, she's slipped up somewhere. You've got to try to get over that, because whatever happens, we mustn't lose Roy.'

5

There had arisen on the farm a kind of mutual understanding: each got on with his own tasks. They would sit down to meals together, when the two men would usually discuss the stock: how many gimmers they could expect to be lambing for the first time come April next; with luck, a hundred or more, provided the winter was kind and there was little foot rot or wet mouth. Only good thing about wet mouth was that it didn't spread like foot rot, but then, it could kill an animal off quite easily.

And Jinnie just listened. She was knowledgeable now about all they were saying; at one time she had imagined their reference to hogs was to pigs, whereas it was referring to lambs more than a year old; and when they were speaking of wethers, it had nothing to do with the climate.

Max was now asking how many sheep Bruce intended to take down to the market next week, and he answered, 'Oh, twenty, at the most; we'll keep the bulk for nearer Christmas when, hopefully, the prices will be higher.'

Max was laughing now as he said, 'I was thinking about P-P-Peter Locke when we were shearing in June, remember? He t-t-told me some tales. Funny one about a farmer over C-C-Corbridge way, who was supposed to get m-m-mortallious the night before market and regularly beat up his wife. He only ever drank at market times, but on market day itself he would stay as sober as a judge so that he could bring his m-m-money home intact. Nobody ever saw him drunk on m-m-market day.'

Bruce laughed and said, 'Yes, I've heard that one before. And he comes out with funnier ones still.' He now looked across the table at Jinnie and said, 'This is a nice pudding. Is it a new recipe?'

'Not by me; I got it off a piece of old wrapping paper. Some newspapers have a Ladies' Corner. There's some more if you would like it.'

'Oh yes, please,' and Bruce handed her his plate on which she spooned a piece of light sponge covered in jam; and she said to Max, 'What about you?'

'Now w-w-why bother asking me; one plateful is like an apple to a horse.'

She smiled as she replenished his plate; then she sat down to finish her own portion, and with her eyes on it she addressed herself to Bruce, saying, 'When you're next in Hexham would you be getting me a cookery book? There's a little shop there that sells them.'

'Cookery book?' He stopped eating. 'Yes. Yes, of course. But . . .' he was about to add, But your cooking satisfies us . . . me. I never knew what it was to have a meal like this until you came on the scene; but that would have sounded as if he were condoning all she had done, and his mind was far from condoning the fact that her belly was swelling daily. And yet he never consciously looked at it, but kept his eyes on her face, and to do that was painful enough, for there was a hurt in him so deep he thought it would be with him for ever. If he could have put it into plain words he would have said he felt despised. A woman might have used the word 'spurned' to express the same feeling, and of course he had been spurned. And yet, on the other hand, she had never promised him anything, had she, so how could he feel spurned? In his world, if a man in his position left a girl in the lurch, it would be said that she had been chucked. But he had never been close enough to Jinnie in that way to be thought of as having been chucked. Yet, as near as he had been, the effect was the same.

It was the following week, and Bruce and Max had returned from market after a good day of selling.

Here and there Bruce had received some hard looks and once or twice a sly smile, but he had ignored them. He'd had little to say to anyone except when dealing over the price for his sheep. He had bought the cookery book Jinnie wanted. It had cost sixpence and the woman had smiled and said, 'Taking it up as a pastime?' to which he had answered in the same vein, saying, 'Something like that.'

As they had driven home, sitting side by side on the high front seat of the cart, he and Max had hardly exchanged a word until the farm came in sight, when Bruce had muttered, 'Heard anything?' and to this Max had answered, 'S-s-same as you, I suppose. He's b-b-back; but then he was bound to come, since her mother died.'

They had passed the cottage door and reached the stables and had drawn the horse and cart to a stop before Max spoke again: 'W-w-whatever we decide to do about him, mind, is going to affect her.'

'He's not getting off with it.' Bruce pulled another bale towards him, and actually throwing it against the barn wall, he growled, 'I'm having it out with him one way or another.'

'One way or t'other,' Max agreed. 'Yes, one way or t'other. Me, I still f-f-feel like throttling him; but that would get us nowhere, except perhaps into j-j-jail. And what we've got to remember now is that with what's c-c-coming, more than ever n-n-now she'll need protection, if she's n-n-not going to land b-b-back where she c-c-came from.'

'Let's sleep on it,' said Bruce. 'But I mean to confront him, by God! I do that.'

They were to know of Richard's reaction the following day. Jinnie had been to the barn to take a can of tea and two mugs for Bruce and Max, who were busily constructing slatted crates to house a number of young pullets that were destined for the Hexham weekly market. Emerging from the barn, she was about to put her head down against the wind when, in the distance, she spotted the horse and rider, and knowing that she would not make the cottage door before he would come abreast of it, she dashed into the stable, next to the barn, and there she stood behind the door, pressed against the wall.

She did not know whether or not he had seen her, but even if he were to look in the stable he wouldn't see her behind the door; but he would hear them in the barn and so would make for there. Dear God. She had her hands tight to her throat now. He had promised; he had said he would never come up here again. Mrs Stevens, in her chatter, had passed on the rumour that he was intending to reside permanently in France, where he had a painting studio, and this had upset his wife's mother and caused her to take to her bed again, permanently this time, for she had died, and that must have been what had brought them back. How long had he been gone?

She turned her face to the rough wall and her fingers clawed at it as she prayed: Don't let them do anything to him. Please God, don't let them hurt him.

And when she heard Bruce's voice yell, 'What the hell

do you want here!' she closed her eyes tight and again she prayed.

Beyond the wall, in the barn, Richard was staring back at the two men who were glaring at him, and his voice had a surprised yet disdainful note in it as he said, 'What do you mean, what the hell do I want here? I could say, what the hell did I ever want here?'

'Yes, you could that. You could that.'

'What's wrong?' He looked towards Max for enlightenment, and Max growled, 'You shouldn't be st-st-standing there asking me that, because let me t-t-tell you, the very sight of you m-m-makes my hands itch to get at you.'

Richard actually took two steps backwards; then, his head drooping for a moment, he shook it before raising it sharply again, saying, 'Oh, she told you what happened then, did she? Well, it takes two to make a pact, you know, of any kind.'

As Bruce made a quick movement forward, Max gripped his arm and jerked him back, saying, 'He's n-n-not worth your spit, Bruce.'

Glaring at his one-time friend, Bruce said, 'No, *she* didn't tell us of any pact, but her belly has.'

'Her . . . her what? Oh no! Oh no!' They watched him cover his eyes with his hand, then drawing it slowly down his face as he murmured, 'Oh! no. Well, after that I can understand how you both feel. But I assure you it had not been my intention to take her; it just happened. And believe me, I did not force her. I know it must sound foolish, but I never thought of the consequences.'

'No, you didn't; you just had your bit of fun and then . . .'

'I didn't have my bit of fun, as you call it; and I can tell you this, she was more ready for it than I was. Oh yes, yes, she was. As I said, it takes two to make a pact

354

and I would never have forced myself on her, never; but to put it bluntly, she was waiting for it, waiting for me to go ahead. Oh yes, she was. And don't come that with me, Bruce, because if there's any punching to do, I can do my share of it.'

When Bruce did not immediately come back at him, he said, in an airy sort of way, 'Look; she knew what she was doing because she talked about class. Yes, she did. She was aware we are poles apart. She was very sensible, always very sensible. We talked about my coming marriage. She said she was quite aware of it but that she . . . well, she was more than fond of me – and yes, I was of her – and she knew nothing would ever come of it. Even if I hadn't already been engaged to be married she was aware that I couldn't have married her. In fact, if I remember rightly, she asked me if I would have married her if I wasn't engaged; and well, what could I say but yes, just to please her? You know yourself, Bruce, you and I had discussed class and all the intricacies of it, and you also know that I have fought it so as to remain your friend, and I might tell you that that's caused hell in my home many a time. And you're a man; just imagine the reaction if I had mentioned her at home, I ask you.'

'You better not ask me anything further,' retorted Bruce, 'but I'm going to tell you something. It was always drilled into me that I saved your life once, but I tell you this now; I'm not going to save your reputation. I've been named as the father, but I'm not going to pay for a pleasure that I've never had, so what are you going to do about it? She's going to have your child. Who's going to bring it up, see to its education, because you'd like it to be educated, wouldn't you?'

In the ensuing silence and in the dim light of the barn, Bruce and Max watched the figure before them blanch and they watched him put his hand out towards a stanchion as if for support, and when he muttered, 'Don't . . . don't do this to me, Bruce, for what has been between us, please! I . . . I will see to it, I mean, maintain it. I can make private arrangements; but don't, please, upset my whole life. I . . . I am now happily married. My wife is young and . . . well, you know, you've seen her. Please, I beg of you. I definitely promise you the child will be well provided for in any way Jinnie wishes. I'll do anything as long as you don't break up my life and that of my family. Oh yes, that of my family. As you know I've depended upon them for everything, but with the death of my mother-in-law, I no longer need assistance from my own parents. There is money for me to use, and I'll use it. I promise you. I will use it in whatever way Jinnie wishes.'

It was Max who noticed her first; then Bruce; and only when their heads moved to the side and they stared towards the barn opening did Richard swing round; and there he saw Jinnie.

She was wearing her old grey coat and it didn't hide the bulge beneath her waist, and his eyes were drawn to it. He stepped sidewards and leaned against the post, and he bowed his head and was about to say something, when her voice came at him, so cool and calm it sent a shiver through them all. What she said was, 'Thank you, Mr Baxton-Powell; but believe me when I say I have no intention of accepting support from you for the half hour of fun we had together on a very hot morning. Things happen in the heat that one wouldn't dream about in colder weather. Don't you agree?'

He had straightened up and was staring at her. She was taller. She was filling out naturally, and she was different. This wasn't the Jinnie that had brought him such joy that morning; this could be a woman of the world of his own class taking the situation in hand, and this irritated him. He wanted to come back at her, saying, 'Don't try to play the lady, it doesn't suit you,' but this wouldn't have been true: she *was* playing the lady, and it *did* suit her. But he didn't like her in this part. That she could play such a part brought a sudden fear to him: she had the power to ruin his life, his marriage. And he had found that he was liking marriage; likely because he realised that he loved Lillian. This girl who had been so gentle, so frail in his arms, so wonderful in loving, he now saw almost as a vixen. And she was speaking again:

'As for the exposure that you fear,' she was saying, 'Bruce knows how I feel about that, so your fears can be allayed in that quarter so long as you—' she stopped and, her head thrusting forward, she ground out, 'keep out of my sight and never again interfere with me or mine.' And she repeated, 'Interfere in any way, you understand?' Then she walked past him to Max and Bruce, still standing close together and, bowing her head, she said, 'Tell him to leave.'

Bruce put his hand on her trembling shoulder and, looking over her head, he said to his one-time friend, 'You heard. And for my part and for your safety, don't show yourself up here ever again.'

Never before in his life had Richard Baxton-Powell felt like a whipped terrier. Although he kept his back straight and his walk firm, he was actually shaking like a leaf when he mounted his horse; and not until he was well clear of the farm and downhill in a shaded lane did he dismount.

Looping the reins of his horse over a branch, he sat on a fallen tree and dropped his head into his hands: Just what had made him go up there? Although he had promised her he would never again do so, he really *had* expected her to be pleased to see him. Had he imagined he'd be able to take her on the side once more? Yes, he had, because he could not dismiss the fascination she'd had for him. But it wasn't to be classed in the same light as the love he now knew he had for Lillian. He had also lost his friend and there was a deep sadness in him about that, for he had nothing in common with any men of his age or older that he knew, not in this country, anyway.

He rose from the log, took the reins from the branch, mounted and told himself grimly that he could not under any circumstances settle here now.

They had gone into the house, she walking between them with her head down and her lips trembling but her eyes dry. She had heard every word that had been said. First of all, she had feared for his safety at their hands, but then, after he had spoken his thoughts of how he must have always considered her, as someone very far below him, even below the servant class in his own home, as a silly girl mostly wearing a coarse apron and clogs or boots and an old grey coat, she was not only surprised and hurt to the core, but also furiously angry. But surmounting all was a feeling of humiliation.

Sitting at the table, her head bowed, there reverberated through her mind the word 'Arcadia', and it brought back the memory of his love-making, at a time when he had seemed like a prince and had made her feel that she was indeed a princess. She could not believe that the man she had just heard speaking could be one and the same as the ardent lover of that morning . . . that morning, that time he had said was so beautiful it could not possibly happen again.

But now, both hate and love had emptied themselves from her. She was feeling utterly degraded and dirty.

Oh yes, dirty; and she said it aloud, shaking her head from side to side, 'I feel dirty, dirty, dirty.'

'Don't talk like that.' Bruce put his hand on her shoulder. 'You made a mistake in thinking he was someone he wasn't: a young god, because of his looks and his voice. I, too, in a way loved him for his looks and voice, but as Max said, he isn't worth a spit. You have lost what you thought was love and I have lost a long-time friend.'

She now raised her head and looked up at him and, her voice breaking, she said, 'I'm . . . I'm sorry, Bruce. I'm sorry for everything. Oh yes, I am. I've been stupid. I am stupid, and ignorant. I only know I've got what I deserved and that I'll have to carry the shame to the grave, as do all those who go my way through ignorance and stupidity and silly dreams.'

'You'll carry nothing to the grave, girl; you have both of us. Your child will be born here and you'll have everything that money can buy. We're no longer short. And there'll be still more if I am to go by the letter I received last week from Mr Claire. As you know I have to go into Newcastle on Wednesday. And so your baby will be born in comfort, and we'll be a family.'

'That we will,' agreed Max. 'Indeed we will. B-b-but now you go up and put your head down for a while; have a little rest.'

At this she rose quickly from the chair, and stood for a moment taking in a deep breath before she said, 'No. No; I'll do some baking. That's the best thing.' Then turning to Bruce, she smiled weakly as she said, 'I'll try some of those recipes in that book.'

'Aye. Yes, do that. That will be nice.'

Bruce turned and made for the door now, beckoning Max to follow him; and when they were outside he said, 'She must have heard every word to go on the way she did, but I'd say it's brought her to her senses. What do you think?'

'As you s-s-say, yes. There wasn't much lost l-l-love in all she said to him, but more like pain. Aye, yes, pain. You know something, Bruce?'

'No.'

'She should have a bed, proper bed when the child c-c-comes. She needs a bed.'

'But where are we going to put a bed? She won't have it in that room, now she's got it so nicely titivated.'

'Well, you c-c-can't see her bringing a child into the world under that r-r-roof, can you?'

Bruce said nothing for a time, but then asked, 'What's brewing in that mind of yours?'

'Another room built on to back towards the pathway, and a n-n-nice big window. Proper built this time, with fireplace.'

'Well, we didn't make a bad job of the other one, did we?'

'Rough walls plastered,' Max went on.

Bruce nodded and said, 'Yes, she will need a bed. Good idea. That's what we'll do. But I think we'd better have a little help, at least for the plastering, roof and windows.'

Max stopped and, a bright smile lighting up his face, he said, 'Wood floor and c-c-carpet on, and proper furniture, and l-l-looking glass,' and he went into a grotesque pose of admiring himself, at which they both burst out laughing.

The laughter came to Jinnie in the kitchen as she prepared for the baking session. Her hands became still on the table, and when her head began to droop she knew she was about to cry, until she heard a stern voice within her saying, 'No more of it,' and as her hands became busy once again she had the strange feeling that time had slipped back and that she was the girl she had been during that first year in this cottage, full of gratitude to the nice man called Bruce; and being that girl, she could now face Miss Caplin.

6

Jinnie was seven months pregnant and feeling very well.
She couldn't describe herself as happy but content, yes.
Everything in the house was running smoothly. At night
she was sleeping in a bed on a flock mattress and in
between sheets and two pillows, their ticks covered with
cases of white linen. The hap on the bed was made of
a primrose print, but what was more astounding, she
could step out on to a blue carpet that almost covered
the entire floor. In the scullery there was a large tin
bath hanging on the wall and on a side bench was an
innovation, a real godsend; a wringer with two narrow
rollers. It wasn't very wide but it pressed out most of
the water from the wet clothes.

Life was good, except on those nights when sleep
evaded her and the feeling of being degraded and worth-
less drove her mind into the depths.

Outside, too, the farm was prospering for not only
did they now have two cows but twice the number of
pigs and chickens, which had meant the building of
new sties and runs. And what was more, Bruce wore
a new tweed suit when he attended the main markets.
This alone would have caused comment in the valley;
but the building of another room for, as some referred
to her, that young slut up there, and it being furnished
with a van-load of new pieces had caused the tongues
to wag unceasing about the size of Hal Shaleman's back
pay. There was something fishy there, if you asked them.

It was very evident who had fathered that one's bairn, but why wasn't he marrying her?

At the same time, the nearby countryside was murmuring words of sympathy to Richard's young bride, who had lost her baby and was still very ill, having undergone an operation when she miscarried, the result of which was she would never bear another child. Such a tragedy, for they had been so happy. And why did it have to happen to the likes of her when that tinker's girl up there, her belly sticking out a mile, so it was said, was as healthy as only those of her tribe could be. What had happened lately to that young bride was surely enough to drive her out of her mind.

And so thought May Baxton-Powell. She said so to her brother: 'Something will have to be done with her, Richard. I think Father should get another man in to see to her, a specialist from Newcastle, because there must be other women who react in the same way after what she has gone through.'

He remained silent where he sat at the other side of the breakfast table. His parents had left the breakfast-room, his father to his study, his mother to her room at the far end of the house, and for which she was thankful, for she was weary with trying to pacify the girl, as she now thought of her daughter-in-law. It had been a great sorrow for them all when Lillian had lost the child, and she had told her that they were all suffering, but that one must face the trials that God put on one's shoulders, and that if you prayed fervently to Him, He always gave you the strength to bear whatever burden you were carrying.

She had been very disappointed at the way her daughter-in-law had reacted to this tragedy: she would not listen to reason; all one could get out of her was that she wanted her baby. It was really a stupid way to go on, when she had been made fully aware that she could neither have her baby nor have another. She herself had explained all this to her and what had been the response? Oh, hysteria, dreadful hysteria, so much so that she did not go and visit her for a number of days, but left her to the nurses. The stupidity of it was that the girl seemed to be blaming her for her loss. Even now the only one she would put up with for any time was May. May seemed to have a calming effect on her. Well, she was glad somebody did because she was becoming tired of the whole business. It seemed to her that the girl was really losing her mind, yet Dr Beattie spoke of it as a natural reaction, assuring them she would come out of it, and telling them he had suggested adopting . . .

In the dining-room May was saying, 'How do you feel about adoption?'

The adoption idea had been sprung upon Richard yesterday, and his first thought had been: Oh no, he couldn't see himself playing father to somebody else's brat. No; what he wanted to do was get her away out of the Bible-chanting, sanctimonious atmosphere and to the open free-living air of Paris, or anywhere else, for that matter.

It was as he had lain awake in the early hours of this morning that an idea had come to him. But straightaway he had pooh-poohed it as an impossibility, because it would entail the disclosure of his escapade, and he could just imagine his parents' reaction to that. But now it was being revived by May's bringing up the matter of adoption again.

And when she repeated, 'I said how do you feel about adoption?' he looked across at her and said, 'I've been thinking about it a lot, May, and it could be the answer. Yet there are others to be considered.' He now rose quickly from his chair and walked across the room to the serving hatch, and pulled the door back quickly as if aiming to surprise someone standing on the other side.

Although the hatch did not open directly into the kitchen, there was a passage and opposite was the kitchen door.

There was no-one standing beyond the hatch, although Eliza Fenwick, the second housemaid was coming through the doorway from the kitchen and she said hastily, 'Were you wantin' somethin', Mister Richard?' and he replied tartly, 'No. No, nothing,' and with that, he closed the hatch none too gently before going back to the table to stand near May's chair and say, 'There is a way out. I have something to tell you. If I . . . we go the right way about it I can adopt my own child.'

May had twisted around on the seat of the chair and she now stared up at him. Then with the flat of her hand she pushed him further away so that she could rise to her feet, and what she said now was, 'You could adopt your own child!'

'Sh! Sh! No need to shout it out.'

'Well, I ask you, Richard.' Her voice was low now. 'You spring a thing like that on me; your own child. Who is . . .? Where is your own child?'

He drew in a long breath and said, 'It isn't born yet; she must be seven months' pregnant.'

'Who, in the name of God! is seven months' pregnant?'

'Sh! woman. I've told you, keep your voice down. These walls have ears and you don't want to bring them down about my head, do you?'

'Well, Richard, all I can say is, the house'll come down about your head if what you're saying is true: that someone's seven months' pregnant and she's carrying

365

your child. Who is it?' She paused. 'Oh, my God!' She put a hand over her mouth. 'Not . . . not that girl up there, not that gypsy piece?'

'She's not a gypsy piece; but that's beside the point; it was a moment of madness.'

'A moment of madness,' she repeated. 'I can see now what drew you up those hills . . . that little slut. And after promising Mother and Father to be more circumspect!'

He sighed deeply and said, 'I'm listening to a woman's point of view, I know. Well, be she gypsy or whatever, at least to me she was a very beautiful and attractive girl; and don't forget that my wedding had been postponed again, so what with one thing or another I was frustrated.'

Her voice was loud again as she said, '*You* were frustrated! We all get frustrated. I am frustrated, but I don't go and give myself to some farm labourer as you stooped to the lowest possible grade of girl . . . woman. She wasn't even a decent servant!'

'*Will you, for God's sake, May, keep your voice down!*'

'Well, if you wish me to keep my voice down, you should've taken me out into the wilds to make this shocking revelation, because I cannot believe it; and if she's seven months' gone this must have happened just a month or so before you were married.'

'Yes. Yes, May, it did; and it was the outcome of . . . as I said, frustration.'

Of a sudden she sat down again and, placing her hands flat on the table, she looked at him; and more to herself than to him she said, 'The things that happen in this house, and are likely to go on happening if you carry out your plan. Now what do you propose to do?'

'She'll be having my child, and as its father I'll have a claim to it. I'll go up there and put it to her . . . to them, because the other two up there are acting like her jailers.'

'And if you get it, do you think Lillian will accept it?'

'Yes, after I've explained it to her, I'm sure she will. At the moment she wants a child, any child.'

'Well, you've got that cut and dried in your mind, but from a woman's point of view, I think you'll be in for a rough time. But then, myself, I'm not so concerned about Lillian's reaction – wives have to obey – but have you thought about the parents? This will break them. The Church and respectability is their lifeline.'

He walked towards the fireplace, shaking his head and saying, 'Don't I know it! Respectability and the Church. I have to ask myself, what have I done to deserve all this?'

She was on her feet again and, moving towards him she hissed, 'Oh, don't you come that, Richard Baxton-Powell. You sound just like Father. You know what you've done to deserve all this. It's all of your own making, because nobody was so well looked after and pampered, and given so many chances, as were you. As I've said before, and I'll say again, you've never earned a penny in your life. You haven't even sold a picture to provide for your paints. Everything has come from Father.' Her voice dropping now, she went on, 'At times he is not all I would desire as a parent, but he has stood by you and supported you. I tell you one thing, whatever happens up there in those hills must be kept absolutely secret, because were it to leak out it would kill them both. They couldn't live under that disgrace, that slut and you, their son.'

'Well, May' – his voice was flat now – 'when they do know, I don't think they could take a stronger attitude than you're taking now towards me. I want support at this time, not criticism, and nobody knows better than I do just what I owe them. But let me tell you, I've had to pay for what I owe them by being this dutiful son. That's on the surface, because underneath I don't feel anything like dutiful. And one more thing, and it is true, I am more suited to the life in Paris than I have been here, or ever will be, married or not, and if I get my way, and I will, Lillian is going back with me as soon as possible, once this other business is settled.'

'Settled, you say?' Her eyes were wide, her eyebrows arched. 'Do you think they're going to welcome your bastard child, no matter what, or how you will persuade Lillian to accept it? They'll both die if they know you've had anything to do with it. Adoption, yes, all right; but you must not let them know it is yours. Do you realise that?'

'Yes. Yes, perhaps. I had thought to clear the air and tell them everything. But you're right: it will be better to put it over merely as an adoption to pacify Lillian.' His face suddenly brightened. 'It could be the same with her: I needn't tell her the facts, need I?' He closed his eyes and took in a deep breath and said, 'Thank God.' Then he touched her face gently, saying, 'What would I do without you, May? You've always straightened things out for me.'

Her colour rose; and then she said softly, 'Oh, Richard. Richard. I care for you. I've only ever had you to worry about . . . or love.'

368

7

Jinnie had received the letter yesterday morning. Peter Locke had picked it up from the postman and delivered it to her at the door, and she had disappointed him by not opening it on the spot. Only once before had she seen her name written on an envelope, and this one plainly read 'Miss J. Howlett', with the address of the farm underneath.

After reading it she had called Bruce and Max into the kitchen and to them she said, 'I've received this letter from him.' There was no need to explain who 'him' was. 'He wants to come and see me on some special business. He has named the day as tomorrow at eleven o'clock in the morning. He says he wishes it to be private; but I'll see him only if both of you are present.'

'What d'you think he might want?'

None of them had any idea at that moment, but during the hours that followed their minds jumped from one thing to another, all seemingly impossible.

During the past week a number of events had occurred, all portending good. The main one had taken place yesterday when, for the last time, Bruce had been summoned to the solicitors' office. On his previous visit, weeks earlier, the suggestion was put to him that they sell the pieces of jewellery separately, that they had a London client interested in the bracelet, and that he had offered a realistic price. To this he had said, 'Yes, go ahead. Do what you think is best.' And yesterday

369

he had again sat at one side of the desk and looked from Mr Claire to Mr Fowler, who actually had his head up and a satisfied smile on his face as he said, 'It was proved once again in our business that it is never wise to rush things, because if you do you are likely to rush past the doors that fate and opportunity open for you.'

Mr Claire had nodded his agreement and, addressing Bruce, he had said, 'The rings and the necklace were also disposed of separately.' Then, tapping the butt end of his pen on a sheet of paper covered in figures, and his voice assuming its business-like tone, he said, 'You will be aware that because of the nature of these deals, there was a good deal of toing and froing in person, including two journeys to London made by Mr Fowler.'

He now lifted his head and, looking directly at Bruce, he said quietly, 'It is wiser to do this kind of business in person than through statements on paper. And so, although our expenses have been high, they do reflect how we managed to obtain realistic prices. I am sure, when you know the result, you will be as happy with it as we are.'

Mr Claire now lifted up the paper from his desk. 'I will put it like this,' he said, giving a tight little smile: 'Your share in the proceedings amounts to seven hundred and sixty-five pounds, ten shillings.'

When he stressed the ten shillings, Bruce had the strongest desire to burst out laughing. And when his eyes filled with water, he didn't know whether or not its cause was through laughter or tears.

Both men were now regarding Bruce with expressions most kindly, and it was Mr Fowler who uttered the one word: 'Satisfied?'

'Oh, sir, I don't know what to say, except that I am so grateful. This will set me up for life. I shall be able to build up a decent farm: get a good herd and buildings. Quite candidly, I cannot believe it has happened to me, and especially through my brother. And I must confess that, at times, my conscience has pricked me when I wondered just how he came across all that money and the jewels. In the ordinary way, he would have had to gamble a lot.'

'Oh—' Mr Fowler was again flapping his hand – 'don't let that worry you for a moment; it happens all the time. We've been in business a long time, and we know it's better not to ask too many questions, because rarely do you get a truthful answer. But your case has been quite an exception.' He looked towards his partner, who, in turn, nodded vigorously in agreement, before turning to Bruce and saying, 'You had nothing to hide, and that was unusual.'

Bruce's last memory of this event was of himself shaking, first, Mr Fowler's hand, and then Mr Claire's, and when he went to repeat the process, they both led him to the outer door, laughing as they ushered him out.

Yesterday had been a wonderful day, but what would today hold? they wondered.

So here they were seated in the long room and awaiting Richard's arrival.

Max was tidily dressed and Bruce looked more than tidy, as he was wearing his tweed suit and a collar and tie. Not, on this occasion, the string tie that he wore with his field clothes, but a proper one that went under the collar.

Jinnie wore a flowered print dress, which was waistless and hung, slack, down to the top of her house shoes made of soft leather. She was carrying the child high under her breasts, but the bulge did not seem to detract from her height: she appeared even taller than usual. Her hair was arranged up on the top of her head in a soft coil, rather than the usual plait. At this moment she appeared like a woman in her twenties, for there was a maturity about her, suggested not only by the bulk of her body, but more so by the expression on her face and by her carriage.

As Bruce looked at her admiringly he wished that he had kept some of the jewellery so that she could have worn the bangle or the necklace just to show him.

He glanced at the clock on the sitting-room mantel-piece. Ten minutes to eleven. He leant forward and, lifting a log from the wicker basket to the side of the fireplace, he threw it to the back of the blazing fire, sending wings of sparks up the broad chimney. It was as he straightened up that Max said quietly, 'There he is outside. W-w-will I go and take the horse?'

'No; no, sit where you are; let him tether it himself, he might need to leave quickly.' He had glanced at Jinnie as he said this, but she made no response. And when she was about to rise, he said, 'Sit where you are, I'll open the door to him.'

When the rap came Bruce remained seated until it was repeated; then he got up, walked slowly down the room, opened the door and stared at his one-time friend, who said stiffly, 'I have called to speak with Miss Howlett.'

'Yes, I'm aware of that. Come in.'

On entering the room, Richard looked to where Jinnie was sitting in a straight-backed chair and, seeing Max standing to her side, he addressed him pointedly: 'This was to be a private meeting between . . . well, Jinnie and me.'

Jinnie pulled herself round in the chair now, saying stiffly, 'Whatever you have to say to me can be said in front of my family.'

He now walked smartly up the room towards her, and confronting her, he said, 'This matter I wish to discuss has nothing to do with your so-called family; it concerns only you and me.'

'That is the way you may see it, Mr Baxton-Powell, but as I see it, anything you may wish to say to me must be said in front of them.'

He now turned and looked at Bruce, then from Bruce to the big fellow. It would be impossible, he told himself, to bring up the matter before them, and he voiced this: 'I can't discuss anything in front of them; it rests solely between us.'

Her voice changed as she cried now, 'Nothing rests solely between us. Get that into your head, Mr Baxton-Powell. Nothing, nothing.'

Her tone, her manner, the whole set-up angered him, and raising his voice, he cried, 'You are carrying my child! That concerns me. It is *my* child and I have some say in the matter, a great deal of say in the matter. I wish to give it a name and I can only do this if I adopt it.'

Following this statement, there was a dead silence in the room, although the exchange of glances between Bruce, Max and Jinnie spoke volumes for their feelings.

But it was Richard who spoke again, saying, 'You look surprised, but it is only right that I should do something in this matter; take on the responsibility.'

He was about to go on when he was interrupted by a laugh. It was a high, weird sound issuing from Jinnie's lips and the bulge of her body shook with it, and what she said, and to Bruce, was, 'The subtlety of it. That's the word, isn't it? It's a big word that, subtlety, isn't it, Bruce? Well, you've just heard somebody murdering that word: his wife's had a miscarriage and, as common gossip has it, she will not be able to bear another child; so I ask you, what does would-be papa do? He recalls a morning he had a bit of a romp with the slut up the hill; and she's carrying fine. And all he has to do is to tell her he is willing to relieve her of it.' And she returned her attention to Richard and in a mocking tone she said, 'Oh! Mr Baxton-Powell. Do you know what I'd do before I'd let you have my child? I'd drown it, and take the consequences!' And so vehement was her tone that it prompted Richard to come back to her with, 'I can take the matter to law and I shall do. You are carrying my child and I intend to lay claim to it whether you like it or not.' He now leaned towards her and emphasised, 'Do you hear me? I want that child, my child, and I'm determined to have it by fair means or foul, and a court will surely judge which house is preferable for the raising of my son . . . or daughter. And get it into your head: neither you nor anyone else will stop me.'

So much in earnest was he that the three of them suddenly realised that the law was always on the side of the gentry. What chance would she have of standing up against him in court? She had, after all, given herself freely to him.

He was saying, 'Now, there you have it. I'll give you a week to think it over before I take pro—' He hadn't finished saying the word before he felt himself being lifted bodily by an arm under his chin and then thrust against the wall, and hearing Jinnie crying, 'No! No! Max. Don't!'

When Bruce sprang forward, he was swiped viciously aside by Max's boot, and Max, his face almost touching Richard's, growled into it, 'L-l-listen carefully. I c-c-could k-k-kill you this minute. But I'll l-l-leave it; but sh-sh-should you t-t-take any steps to c-c-carry out your threat, I will d-d-do for you.'

Richard's face had blanched as he listened to the voice stammering at him. He realised the man meant what he said. He was almost choking now and instinctive reaction made him thrust his knee into Max's groin, causing the big man to stagger back, one hand holding himself; but the other, doubled into a fist, now went straight into Richard's face, and Jinnie screamed, 'Enough! Enough! Stop it! Max. Please. Please, for me, stop it!'

Max swung round and leaned over the back of the high winged chair, the sweat running down his face. Bruce now limped down the room and opened the door, crying, 'You'd better get going while the going's good.' But Jinnie's voice broke in, crying, 'Not for a minute, Bruce; I have something more to say.'

She was looking directly at Richard now, who was standing holding his face, and she said, 'You'd better know now before you take court proceedings, that it isn't your child I am carrying, Mr Baxton-Powell,' and the words were calmly spoken. 'You see, if I remember correctly, at that time you seemed to find me well-practised, aware that I made everything so easy for you – no crying or hysterics. It's a wonder you didn't twig.' And noticing the expression on his half-covered face, she added, 'You weren't the first, as you ought to have realised.'

There was a smothered gasp from Max and Bruce as they stared at her, although neither made any comment, for Richard was saying, 'I don't believe it, not a word of it. I *was* the first with you, and I know it.'

'You might think so. But there are many ways to deceive a man. I was never really the sweet, ignorant little girl you took me for. Anyway, there it is.'

'I still don't believe you.'

Now her voice rose and she said, 'Doesn't matter, but I'll swear every word of it in court, and as we're being married shortly—' she now turned and glanced at Bruce before looking back to Richard and continuing, 'so that his child can have a name, you carry out your threat

375

and take it to court and, I tell you, as I'm standing here looking at you and despising you for the weak creature you are, I will stand up in that court and describe the details of the events, believe me I will, just as they occurred on both occasions: I was taken by surprise in the first place with Bruce here, who had held back for so long, but I wasn't with you. Oh no, I meant to taste you, and I did.'

As if of one accord the three men cast their gaze downwards. Not one of them could believe he was listening to the Jinnie he thought he knew. This girl who was speaking did indeed sound like a town slut. Had they not known her since she came into this house a waif and expressing moral indignation at being handled?

They could have no idea of the turmoil that was raging inside her at this moment, and when the man she had loved, even adored, stared back at her with curled lip and said, 'I am the simple one. I see that now. And you are as you have been depicted for a long time: just a tinker's girl. You know now what I hope? I hope that you are speaking the truth and that you are carrying no part of me inside you, for I wouldn't want my breeding tinged with the creature I see before me now. Yes, indeed, I've been the foolish and blind one.' And with this, he bent and picked up his soft riding hat from where it had fallen to the floor. When he made his way towards the door, Bruce did not bar his way, nor was a glance exchanged between them.

The only sound in the room was the hissing and cracking of the logs on the fire; but Max was staring at Bruce and when he did speak he said the same word twice, though as a question, 'No? No?' and Bruce almost screamed back at him, 'No! No! You shouldn't have to be told that. She's lying.' Then rounding on Jinnie, he said, 'Why did you have to come out with that? And in that fashion.'

'For the simple reason I know him better than you, despite all your years of friendship,' she cried, her voice bitter now. 'He's desperate. His wife will never be able to give him a child, so I was his last chance. And whatever happened, he would have continued to think of it as his, as his own. Yes, Bruce, surprisingly, I know him better than you do. And in court, you know, everyone would have been on his side: there would be his poor wife who could not bear any more children, which would have brought him added support. In fact, everyone would have been on his side. I was the slut up in the hills and a product of the workhouse.'

When Bruce dropped into the armchair, she said to him, 'You needn't worry on one score: we'll hear no more from him. On the second, I don't think you need to let that worry you either.'

He passed no remark on this cryptic comment, but, bending down, pulled up his trouser leg and turned back the top of his stocking to reveal blood oozing from a number of grazes on his shin, then looked at Max, saying, 'You never do things by halves, do you?'

'Don't roll the black stocking back on that,' Jinnie said; 'it could be poisoned,' and to Max she said, 'Bring a dish of water, will you, and a soap and flannel.'

Without uttering a word, Max shambled down the room and into the scullery. On this, Jinnie dropped to her knees in front of Bruce and pushed his trouser leg further over his knee, saying, 'Keep it clear of the scratches.' Then, without pausing, she added, 'You never thought I had it in me, did you? Well, you're not the only one, I never thought I had it in me either. I think it must have come from my tinker's breeding, as he said, don't you?' She lifted her head and looked into his eyes. 'Anyway,

377

I'm glad that I've got that in me, because it's helping me to ask if you will marry me, Bruce.'

His injured leg jerked so quickly it almost hit her bulge, and he had to put out a hand to stop her from tumbling backwards.

'Oh! Jinnie. Jinnie.' He was on his feet now, his trouser leg dropping to his ankle again. 'You really mean that, don't you?'

'I really mean it.'

He drew his head back from her face now, saying, 'What about the brother bit?'

'Oh, I lost him some time ago.'

'You did?'

'Yes, Bruce; yes, I did. I wouldn't have been able to come out into the open and say what I've just said before this morning's events, for, at the time, I felt I was fighting for my life and for the life within me, and for the life lived with you and Max in this house. It seemed to me that these were all at stake.'

His arms were about her now and he said, 'Well, thank God for this morning,' and bending forward he gently put his lips on hers, just gently. She did not return the kiss but her gaze was soft on him.

When Max came back into the room, carrying the dish, Bruce greeted him loudly with, 'You know what the latest is? She's asked me to marry her.'

Max stopped, and the water jerked in the dish. Then, a wide smile lightening his face, he said, 'All by herself?'

'All by herself, Max, all by herself; but I don't know whether or not I'll go through with it.'

At this Max put the dish on the rug and said, 'No. You're r-r-right. It needs c-c-consideration.'

378

8

Where did the rumour start? With Eliza Fenwick? or Peter Locke?

During the course of enjoying some gossip, Peter had told Mrs Stevens that he had met young Mister Richard coming away from the farm up there. He was on his horse, but it was evident that he had been in a fight, for his face was scarlet and one eye was half-closed. He had passed him as if he weren't there. And he had said to Mrs Stevens, 'Now I ask you, why should anybody up there want to give him a black eye? And there's a funny tale going round; though of course you shouldn't believe all you hear. But it comes from the horse's mouth, so to speak: Eliza Fenwick. Second housemaid, she is, at the Baxton-Powells. Well, she is supposed to have told the cook what she heard in the dining-room through the let – bits and pieces of it – but you know what these lasses are. Cook warned her to keep her mouth shut but, you know, the cook is cousin to Mary Fitzsimmons up in The Hall, so you needn't ask how Mary Fitzsimmons got to know about that, and then the family rumpus that took place some time later in the drawing-room. But it's not up to me to repeat what's being said. It'll come to light soon enough.' And at that, the tantalising man had walked out of Mrs Stevens's kitchen.

9

Jinnie's child was born on the first day of May 1873, less than three months before her seventeenth birthday. Mrs Stevens weighed it on the kitchen scales and found it to be seven pounds ten ounces which, she said, was quite big for a girl, and she called up the room to Peg Carter, the midwife from Allendale, 'Not bad, seven pounds ten ounces, and it a girl.'

'That's the second time you've given me her weight. Are there twins, and I missed one?'

The large-breasted midwife laughed down on Jinnie and she, although weary from intermittent straining over the past ten hours, smiled back at her, saying, 'One was enough.'

'Yes, me dear. Yes, me dear; one's enough for any-body. Now, just rest there. I'll have you all fixed up in two shakes of a lamb's tail, and then I'll let them in. As I said to them a minute back, they're nearly as interested in you and it as they would be in a pig with a good litter. Now you just drop off and have a nap.'

'I don't feel sleepy, Mrs Carter; not that way sleepy, if you know what I mean.'

'Yes, I know what you mean, so let's get you all right for the presentation. Blow your nose, and I'll see there's no cabbage between your teeth. Have you ever noticed, me dear, that people always leave cabbage between their teeth? You can always tell what vegetable they've had for their meal; there's always a bit of green stuff sticking out.'

She was a very funny woman, was Mrs Carter, but so kind. They were all kind. Jinnie had been amazed at the kindness of everybody during these past two months. It had been as if she had suddenly turned into someone else. But then, perhaps she had, because she was no longer the little scullion up on the hill, or that tall young lass who could turn her hand to anything; she was Mrs Bruce Shaleman. But even before that, before they were married in that office in Newcastle, with Miss Caplin and her aunts and the two nice solicitor men, and Max acting as her father, and the lovely dinner they'd had after; and oh yes, the open carriage drives they'd all had to and from the station at Hexham, the whole day had been out of this world. At one time, she had almost cried when the two old solicitor men had kissed her hand. But before that day she had already changed. Was it from the time Richard scooted off to France with his wife? Yes, perhaps. How the truth had got around she didn't know, but it seemed that everyone was seeing her in a different light because she had kept her mouth shut about him. However, to her mind now, it was all a sad affair, for his people had also gone to France on what had been an extended holiday. Only three servants were left behind to look after the house. At times she felt very guilty, because the whole family seemed to have been broken up through her and that one glorious mistake. No matter what she thought or how she tried to forget it, that morning would live in her memory for ever. Yet she had managed to make him believe that he hadn't been the first. He *had* been the first, though, and here she was with his child.

And though she was married to Bruce, he was still the first; indeed, so far, the only one. But Bruce was good, more than good; in fact, he hadn't made any demands upon her at all. He had said he wouldn't do so until she was ready. He was good, and yes, she felt love for him, not with the ecstasy of that hot summer morning, but nevertheless she knew it *was* love she felt for him.

She heard Mrs Stevens crowing a tune to the baby. She had become a good friend, had Mrs Stevens, although she was gossipy. She had amazed her some time ago by telling her that Roy had known who the father was all the time; in fact, from the very morning when he had come up and found Mr Richard's horse in the stable. But he had kept his mouth shut. He was a nice boy, was Roy. There were a lot of nice people in the world, and a lot of nasty ones too, like Hal Shaleman. Oh, she was glad he was dead. And look what his death had brought them: a fortune. Life was very strange. Here she was, not yet seventeen, and the mother of a baby . . .

She wasn't aware of falling asleep. It must have been after she had held her daughter to her breast for the first time. She couldn't recall being visited either by Bruce or Max; she could only recall someone taking the baby away, before she dropped into oblivion.

But now she was awake, and there was a face hanging over her.

'Hello, there.'

'Hello.'

'How're you feeling?'

'Sleepy still, but fine. Have you seen her?' The question was tentative, and Bruce answered straightaway, 'Of course; and she's a bonny piece, and lusty with it.'

She looked up into his eyes, and softly she said, 'The next one will be yours, Bruce; and the next, and the

A SELECTION OF OTHER CATHERINE COOKSON TITLES AVAILABLE FROM CORGI BOOKS

THE PRICES SHOWN BELOW WERE CORRECT AT THE TIME OF GOING TO PRESS. HOWEVER TRANSWORLD PUBLISHERS RESERVE THE RIGHT TO SHOW NEW RETAIL PRICES ON COVERS WHICH MAY DIFFER FROM THOSE PREVIOUSLY ADVERTISED IN THE TEXT OR ELSEWHERE.

☐	13576 3	THE BLACK CANDLE	£5.99
☐	12473 7	THE BLACK VELVET GOWN	£5.99
☐	14063 5	COLOUR BLIND	£4.99
☐	12551 2	A DINNER OF HERBS	£5.99
☐	14066 X	THE DWELLING PLACE	£5.99
☐	14068 6	FEATHERS IN THE FIRE	£5.99
☐	14089 9	THE FEN TIGER	£4.99
☐	14069 4	FENWICK HOUSES	£4.99
☐	10450 7	THE GAMBLING MAN	£4.99
☐	13716 2	THE GARMENT	£4.99
☐	13621 2	THE GILLYVORS	£5.99
☐	10916 9	THE GIRL	£5.99
☐	14071 6	THE GLASS VIRGIN	£4.99
☐	13685 9	THE GOLDEN STRAW	£5.99
☐	13300 0	THE HARROGATE SECRET	£5.99
☐	14087 2	HERITAGE OF FOLLY	£4.99
☐	13303 5	THE HOUSE OF WOMEN	£4.99
☐	10780 8	THE IRON FAÇADE	£4.99
☐	13622 0	JUSTICE IS A WOMAN	£5.99
☐	14091 0	KATE HANNIGAN	£4.99
☐	14092 9	KATIE MULHOLLAND	£5.99
☐	14081 3	MAGGIE ROWAN	£4.99
☐	13684 0	THE MALTESE ANGEL	£5.99
☐	10321 7	MISS MARTHA MARY CRAWFORD	£5.99
☐	12524 5	THE MOTH	£5.99
☐	13302 7	MY BELOVED SON	£5.99
☐	13088 5	THE PARSON'S DAUGHTER	£5.99
☐	14073 2	PURE AS THE LILY	£5.99
☐	13683 2	THE RAG NYMPH	£5.99
☐	14075 9	THE ROUND TOWER	£5.99
☐	14039 2	A RUTHLESS NEED	£5.99
☐	13714 6	SLINKY JANE	£4.99
☐	10541 4	THE SLOW AWAKENING	£4.99
☐	10630 5	THE TIDE OF LIFE	£5.99
☐	12368 4	THE WHIP	£5.99
☐	13577 1	THE WINGLESS BIRD	£5.99
☐	13247 0	THE YEAR OF THE VIRGINS	£5.99

All Transworld titles are available by post from:

Book Service By Post, P.O. Box 29, Douglas, Isle of Man IM99 1BQ

Credit cards accepted. Please telephone 01624 675137, fax 01624 670923, Internet http://www.bookpost.co.uk or e-mail: bookshop@enterprise.net for details.

Free postage and packing in the UK. Overseas customers allow £1 per book (paperbacks) and £3 per book (hardbacks).